UNFAIR MATCH . . .

The two young Chickasaw hunters who had come upon Ena drinking at a stream had been on a combination long hunt and would-be coup-counting search.

The two Chickasaw widened the distance between them as they moved toward the woman. Her hand was on her tomahawk.

"If she tries to flee across the creek, I will catch her in the water," one of them said, thinking the Cherokee woman would not understand.

"You will catch this," the woman threatened, brandishing her tomahawk. "I am Ena, wife of the principal chief, Rusog, who has exchanged vows of peace with your chiefs."

"I see this Rusog not," said the larger of the two.

The smaller man lunged forward, swinging his tomahawk with the intention of knocking Ena's weapon away. Instead, his blade sliced empty air, and a yowl of surprise and pain came from his throat when Ena's tomahawk sliced open his deerskin tunic and left a four-inch gash in his arm.

"Look at the color of your blood, Chickasaw," Ena told him, "and consider your actions well."

"Thing of evil," the larger Chickasaw screamed in a shrill, angry voice as he slowly, cautiously advanced. . . .

The White Indian Series
Ask your bookseller for the books you have missed

The White Indian Series
Book XXII

SENECA PATRIOTS

Donald Clayton Porter

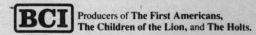

BCI Producers of **The First Americans,**
The Children of the Lion, and **The Holts.**

Book Creations Inc., Canaan, NY • Lyle Kenyon Engel, Founder

BANTAM BOOKS
NEW YORK • TORONTO • LONDON • SYDNEY • AUCKLAND

SENECA PATRIOTS

A Bantam Domain Book / published by arrangement with
Book Creations, Incorporated

Bantam edition / January 1992

Produced by Book Creations, Incorporated
Lyle Kenyon Engel, Founder

DOMAIN and the portrayal of a boxed "d" are trademarks of
Bantam Books, a division of
Bantam Doubleday Dell Publishing Group, Inc.

ISBN 0-553-29217-X

Published simultaneously in the United States and Canada

Bantam Books are published by Bantam Books, a division of Bantam Doubleday Dell Publishing Group, Inc. Its trademark, consisting of the words "Bantam Books" and the portrayal of a rooster,
is Registered in U.S. Patent and Trademark Office and in other
countries. Marca Registrada. Bantam Books, 666 Fifth Avenue,
New York, New York 10103.

PRINTED IN THE UNITED STATES OF AMERICA

OPM   0 9 8 7 6 5 4 3 2 1

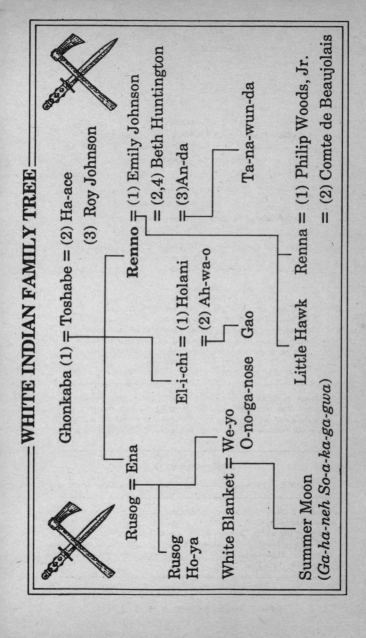

WHITE INDIAN FAMILY TREE

SENECA
PATRIOTS

Chapter One

The American brig *Dora E.*, laden with naval stores, had all sails set before a fair breeze for Naples. Taking the air on the *Dora E.*'s deck was William Eaton, a schoolmaster dressed in a drab suit just a bit too tight for his soft, slightly overweight body. Eaton was a Connecticut man who had made his permanent residence in Brimfield, Massachusetts, with a contentious woman almost old enough to be his mother. The citizens of Brimfield, he knew, wondered why, although he was often away from home, he remained within the bounds of wedlock with a nag whose shrillness of voice was in direct proportion to his proximity.

Slightly before midday the wind became less favorable, and the brig wallowed in the troughs as she held to her course. Eaton was not the best of sailors. The uncomfortable motion sent him to his cabin, where he loosened his collar and waistcoat, threw himself onto his bunk, and prayed earnestly to be allowed to live at least long enough to feel solid land under his feet.

1

He dozed and did not hear the commotion on deck that was caused by the sighting of a sail. Nor did the bellowed orders of the *Dora E.*'s captain awaken him as the brig was slowly overtaken by a swift, low, black ship of war. It was the change in the vessel's movement that revived him and sent him on deck to see that the *Dora E.* was lying dead in the water with a sinister-looking ship closing on her.

"I'd advise you to go below, sir," a seaman said as he hurried past.

Eaton stood stiffly as the dark ship flying the flag of the pasha of Tripoli grappled the *Dora E.* Swarms of swarthy, bearded Arab seamen dressed in dingy, one-piece robes and sweat-soaked head windings scrambled aboard the brig and began to scream orders that were incomprehensible to everyone but William Eaton. Two of the pirates leaped toward him, their scimitars at the ready. One of them said in the patois—a mixture of Italian, Turkish, and Egyptian-Arabic—that was the lingua franca of the North African pirate nations: "Your clothes. Take them off."

Eaton replied in the same language, "You fly the flag of the pasha Yusef Karamanli of Tripoli. Before you act further, consider what he will say upon learning that you have insulted the United States consul to the Barbary nations."

"Your clothing, infidel," the pirate demanded, jerking at Eaton's coat.

Eaton made the same decision that had obviously been made by the captain of the *Dora E.* The captain had known that for his unarmed ship to fight the man-of-war from Tripoli meant certain death for himself and his crew. Although surrender meant slavery for the ordinary seamen, at least there was hope of repatriation as long as the men were alive. Eaton, also, could see murder in the eyes of the two pirates who demanded his clothing. He had no doubt that he would be killed, in spite of his diplomatic credentials, if he resisted. After all, his captors were savages by ancient Greek definition. The Barbary Coast: coast of the barbarians, home to merciless pirates for centuries. And of the four Barbary states—Algiers, Morocco, Tunis, and Tripoli—the last was the most barbaric. Tripoli's ruler, Yusef Karamanli, had declared a unilateral war not only on American shipping in the Mediterranean but on the United States as a whole.

The captain of the Arab ship would have to account to the pasha for the captured ship and its cargo; but the pirate crew would be free to keep the personal possessions of the crew and passengers as loot. All clothing—shirts, vests, trousers, even smallclothes—were valuable commodities in the scruffy cities of the North African coast.

Eaton was willing to be shamed, stripped naked before the crew of the *Dora E.* and the scabrous Arabs, in order to remain alive to do the job to which he had been assigned by Thomas Jefferson. As the consul removed his clothing, being prodded more than once by the sharp tip of a Moorish scimitar, he vowed that he would not leave North Africa alive with his mission unfulfilled.

Within moments he stood naked on the deck. Taken along with his clothing were his watch, his purse, and a pair of gold-rimmed eyeglasses that he used for reading. His cabin, meanwhile, was being ransacked, and the crew of the *Dora E.* was being herded roughly onto the pirate vessel to be imprisoned below decks.

Arabs in their filthy, flapping robes leaped to the orders of an especially evil-looking brigand and set the captured brig sailing before the wind toward the African coast. To the surprise of Eaton and the *Dora E.*'s officers, they were set ashore not in Tripoli but in Tunis. The officers were put under light guard in a vermin-infested mud building.

Two days later Eaton was able to obtain an audience with the bey Ahmed Pasha, who was as much a pirate as his ally in Tripoli. The ruler of Tunis was, perhaps, a bit more aware of the affairs of the world outside North Africa than was his counterpart.

Eaton's anger did not move Ahmed, nor did a formal written protest receive an answer. "I have been appointed by President Thomas Jefferson as special consul to the Barbary nations," Eaton told the impassive pasha. "Moreover, I am attached to the United States Navy as a special adviser. You are going to find, sir, that the time is past when the Barbary nations can prey on unarmed American ships with impunity."

Ahmed Pasha made no immediate reply. He could respect the power of the Royal Navy and the navy of the French, although even those great nations chose to buy peace with the pirate states rather than assure it by force of naval arms. At one time, he knew that the obscure little nation across the Atlantic, the United States, had been under the wing of the Royal Navy. Now, however, with war looming between the two giants of Europe, Great Britain and France, the United States was impotent, left to her own devices in the Mediterranean.

Ahmed smiled benignly at the brash infidel. It was quite amusing to listen to his empty threats. "Safe passage can be arranged for your ships through Tunisian waters for modest sums," Ahmed said. "One hundred fifty thousand dollars—"

Eaton snorted.

"—and certain quantities of ship's stores," the bey continued.

"And what about safe passage through the waters of Tripoli, Morocco, and Algiers?" Eaton asked.

"You will have to discuss that question with my brothers in the aforesaid countries," Ahmed replied with a smile.

Ahmed, as had other men before him, misjudged William Eaton. On the surface the American looked weak, pudgy. In Ahmed's estimation the consul would not have been a match for the smallest man in the pasha's bodyguard. The ruler of Tunis did not bother to inquire into William Eaton's background, nor was he curious as to why Eaton had been selected to negotiate with the Barbary nations. Ahmed assumed that if President Thomas Jefferson had sent such a plump little dumpling of a man to do his work, then Jefferson, too, was weak.

The bey would have been surprised if he could have read the contents of William Eaton's letters to Jefferson, far away in Washington.

"I would use American arms to force these brigands to respect our flag. Only gunshot and powder will compel the deys and the beys of

Barbary to treat us in a civilized manner and to honor the lives and property of American citizens. These Arabs' attitude is insulting not only to every American but to every man who considers himself to be more than a savage barbarian. Pray consider my urgent request that a fleet of American warships, along with five thousand trained, armed, and well-equipped American infantrymen and cavalrymen, be sent to the Mediterranean. With these troops at my disposal I can guarantee that the rulers of the Barbary Coast will sing a new song that is more to our liking."

William Eaton was thirty-nine, and it was true that he had been enjoying a life of relative ease, which, since he was fond of good food, had left him soft and over-weight; but there was more to him than met the eye. He had been an underage enlistee in the Continental army and narrowly missed taking part in the climactic battle of the War for American Independence at Yorktown. Before leaving the army in 1783 at the age of nineteen, he had attained the rank of company sergeant major. Next he worked as a clerk in a store, and he discovered he possessed a natural flair for languages while studying Greek and Latin after the end of the business day. Inspired by his aptitude, Eaton saved enough money to attend college.

In 1792, after graduating with honors from Dartmouth, he accepted a commission from Secretary of War Henry Knox as a captain of infantry to fight with General Anthony Wayne and the American Legion in the Ohio Valley Indian wars, which culminated in the Battle of Fallen Timbers.

This was the man who appeared bland not only to the pirate ruler of Tunis but, years before, to Brigadier General James Wilkinson. Deputy commander of the American Legion and an active traitor to the United States for decades, Wilkinson disliked Eaton, saying, "We will never conquer the savages so long as men like Captain Eaton serve in the legion." Wilkinson's appraisal of Eaton was no doubt colored by jealousy, for Wayne and Eaton were kindred spirits—profane and jolly—who became firm friends.

"I will wager that his resolve will crumble when he is forced to sleep on the ground and eat meals less lavish than those prepared by Wayne's cook," Wilkinson had predicted. But when Eaton's time came, he proved Wilkinson not only wrong but very wrong. He spent a month scouting alone among the Indians, and when Fort Recovery was attacked by an overwhelming force and the major in command was killed, Eaton took charge. A young officer reported: "The captain was like a gale that blows in from the sea. He was everywhere, directing our operations, rallying the defenders, posting men to the weak places, and encouraging those who faltered."

Coincidentally, Eaton had taken an interest in Islam before joining the legion, and his reading while he was on the American frontier was the Koran and other volumes about the Mohammedan countries. At that time he wrote in his journal, "I wish to learn Arabic and to find out all I can about the Ottomans. Someday I shall visit that far-off part of the world and, if the Almighty wishes it for me, may even live there for a while."

Later, Eaton would call it kismet, the Arabic word for a predetermined fate willed by God, for there had been no evident reason for him to become interested in North Africa or in the Middle East. There was to be no mention of Algiers, Tunis, Morocco, or Tripoli in American newspapers until 1797.

By the time William Eaton joined the consular staff in the Barbary states, the United States had paid over one million dollars in blackmail to the dey of Algiers alone. When Eaton walked the streets, Arabs spat at him and cursed him, not knowing that he understood their language very well. He refrained, with effort, from defending himself. He also exerted self-control when he was presented to the dey of Algiers, Hussein, who, Eaton wrote, was "a great, shaggy beast, sitting on a low bench with his hind legs gathered up like a tailor or a bear."

He was compelled to kiss the dey's hand.

"The animal at that time seemed to be in a harmless

mood," he confided to his diary. "He grinned but made little noise."

Eaton astounded the dey and other diplomats by speaking in flawless Arabic. Later he wrote in his journal, "I believe it is my kismet to treat these thieves with the contempt they deserve."

Now he had only to bide his time and to convince Thomas Jefferson to send him men, ships, and guns.

Lieutenant Meriwether Lewis was greatly pleased to be chosen to deliver the decoded message from Paris to the new executive mansion in the city of Washington. The important missive stated that Napoleon was willing to cede all of the Louisiana Territory to the United States. Lewis, tall and slim, looking younger than his twenty-nine years, walked swiftly along dirt streets turned into quagmires by heavy April showers. Someone's hogs had gotten loose again, and a long-toothed boar looked up from his rootings in the struggling side garden of the mansion to grunt at Lewis as he hurried toward the entrance.

After cleaning most of the mud from his boots at the front door, he strode toward the president's office. The clicking of his iron-tipped heels echoed in the chamber.

Thomas Jefferson had been listening to the complaints of the bald, severe Speaker of the House, Nathaniel Macon of North Carolina. Macon was dressed formally for the occasion in a somber blue so dark as to appear black, a double row of brass buttons on his frock coat, pink linen at his throat.

"Mr. President," he was saying, "one after the other we have seen architects come and go. First it was the Frenchman Pierre L'Enfant, who was dismissed so wisely by President Washington when he began tearing down buildings instead of building them." Macon sighed emphatically to show his state of disgust. "We have endured the temperament of Dr. William Thornton and the squabbles between the good doctor and Mr. Stephen Hallet. We had hopes for a while for George Fadfield, but you know what happened there. He, too, was dismissed."

Jefferson sat with his back straight, his eyes locked on Macon's. His auburn hair was streaked with gray. He was tired. His face was pale. He had recently eaten tainted fish and was just recovering from the resulting illness.

"And now we have Mr. Benjamin Latrobe—"

"Who is," Jefferson interrupted, "very well qualified. He is, as you know, Mr. Speaker, academically trained."

"We can only pray," Macon said, "that his training will reveal to him some way of delivering the House of Representatives from our travail."

Jefferson leaned back in his chair. He knew what Macon was going to say. The representatives had been meeting in a temporary brick structure that had been hastily thrown up on the foundation of one wing of the unfinished Capitol Building.

"Summer is almost upon us again," Macon continued, "and soon we will be sweltering—something that we cannot avoid three seasons of the year."

Jefferson gave Macon a thin smile. "Mr. Speaker," he said, "I know. I have been in 'the oven' in July. I think you will be pleased to know that my first order to Mr. Latrobe was to demolish the oven and to begin to raise the walls of the House wing."

"And high time it is," Macon said. He rose, then bowed. "Thank you for your time."

"I am always free to see you, Mr. Speaker."

"When are you going to get the hogs out of the garden?" Macon asked, his lips twitching in what might have been the embryo of a smile.

"Perhaps the Congress can help me with that problem," Jefferson said as he stood to face the Speaker. "A law, perhaps, requiring local farmers to install stronger fences? A permanent swineherd assigned to executive-mansion duty?"

Macon's smile became more fully developed. He nodded and turned toward the door. "Perhaps I could muster bipartisan support for such measures."

The door burst open, and Meriwether Lewis thrust his head in. "I beg your pardon, sir."

"Come in," Jefferson invited. "Mr. Macon and I were just finishing our discussion."

Jefferson knew from his secretary's flushed face that something had occurred. Lewis, literally squirming with the need to share his news, glanced toward the Speaker, then back to the president.

"Either you have news for me or ants in your pants, Meriwether," Jefferson said. "Close the door, if you please."

"News from Paris, sir."

"Ah," Jefferson said. "Out with it, then. I can think of no more worthy man with whom to share our communication than Mr. Macon."

"He's going to give us all of it," Lewis said, smiling broadly. "New Orleans and *all* of it—all of the whole, blessed Louisiana Territory."

"By *thunder!*" Jefferson erupted. "Tell me exactly—"

"There are no details as yet, sir," Lewis said. "There is nothing more than the bare word that Napoleon is willing to cede all of the Louisiana Territory to the United States."

"Oh, by thunder!" Jefferson repeated. He came out from behind his desk and danced a little jig before shaking Lewis's hand, then Macon's. "Do you hear, Mr. Speaker? Do you realize what this means?"

Macon's face was glum. "We have not yet heard the price, Mr. President."

"By the Lord above, the price doesn't matter," Jefferson enthused. "With one treaty, with one purchase, gentlemen, we more than double the size of the United States. With the stroke of a pen we will catapult the United States into the ranks of the most powerful nations in the world." He sobered. "I will, of course, Mr. Speaker, consult the Congress. I pray that I have your support."

Macon cleared his throat. "And when have I not supported you, Mr. President?"

"Yes, yes," Jefferson said warmly. "And I am appreciative, Mr. Speaker."

"I am, however, concerned about the cost of this, uh, affair," Macon said.

"I will have you informed as soon as I myself learn Napoleon's terms," Jefferson said. He escorted the Speaker out of the office with one hand on his shoulder, closed the door, then turned, beaming, toward Lewis and let out a subdued war whoop. "Meriwether," he said, "we don't even know the extent of it, the size of it, or the diversity of it."

Lewis had seen a small part of the western frontier country. He had been with Mad Anthony Wayne at the Battle of Fallen Timbers. After the Ohio wars he served in the Southwest Territory under the command of General James Wilkinson. Jefferson, knowing Meriwether Lewis's background, had long since decided—even before he sent his special envoys to France to explore the possibility of buying New Orleans from the French—to put his fellow Virginian in command of an expedition into the uncharted West.

"Well, Meriwether," he said, "the time has come, I suppose."

Lewis straightened his shoulders. "Indeed it has, sir."

"I've had your orders drawn up," Jefferson continued. He walked to his desk, opened a drawer, and handed Lewis a sheaf of papers. "Read them, please, and let me know if you need any additions."

Lewis sat with his long legs spread wide. His lips moved as he read to himself: "—to explore the Missouri River and such headwaters as might connect with the Pacific; to take careful notes of your course, landmarks, and portages; to study the native Indian tribes, their customs, languages, the possibilities of trade, etc.; to report on soils, animals, minerals, and climate; and to keep a full journal of everything you do and see."

Lewis was jubilant. "One thing only, sir," he said. "I think it is no longer necessary to try to disguise the expedition as a scientific inquiry or a literary pursuit."

Jefferson nodded. Before the news from Paris he had been concerned lest the expedition disturb France or England. Now that only formalities separated the United States from owning the territory, such precautions could be abandoned.

"How I do envy you," Jefferson said.

Lewis hurried off to begin preparations for his expedition. Secretary of State James Madison, the president's friend and another fellow Virginian, was Jefferson's next caller.

"I have just been given the news," Madison said. "Congratulations, Thomas."

"Mr. Macon is concerned with the cost," Jefferson warned.

Madison negated that worry with a wave of his hand. "It is not Macon who will be in opposition," he predicted.

"Ah, the New Englanders . . ." Jefferson said.

"Exactly," Madison agreed. He grinned. "But it's your own fault, Thomas. It is your democratic theories that upset them."

"They're suspicious of all Virginians," Jefferson said.

"In this case, perhaps with good reason," Madison remarked with a chuckle as he settled himself comfortably in a chair. "It will happen exactly as they fear when we acquire Louisiana: settlers will move west; the population of the territories will grow; eventually new states will be formed and admitted to the Union, thus further diluting the influence of the New England states on the federal government."

"Talk to them, James," Jefferson urged. "Reason with them."

"I can possibly reason with some of them. George Cabot, perhaps."

"Yes, he's a responsible man."

Jefferson was popular with the people. Barring some catastrophe his reelection in 1804 seemed assured. George Cabot of Massachusetts had been asked by a cabal of Federalists to head a movement to establish an independent nation in New England. Cabot had refused, causing the disgruntled Federalists to turn to Vice President Aaron Burr, who had been defeated by Jefferson again for the presidency on the thirty-sixth ballot in the House of Representatives. Burr had agreed to run for governor of New York so as to be in a stronger political position to lead the secession movement or, as an alternative, to run against Jefferson for the presidency.

"James, don't we have enough problems without these antics by the New Englanders?" Jefferson complained.

"I could name a few," Madison said. "Barbary among them."

"By God, let's not get into *that* today," Jefferson said emphatically. He had sent a small squadron of ships to the Mediterranean, and to the surprise of the pirates—but not to Jefferson and Madison—the U.S. Navy was showing that it knew how to fight.

"Louisiana, James," Jefferson said, pounding his fist into his hand. "Louisiana is the priority. We have an opportunity, you and I, to do the greatest service to the United States since Valley Forge."

"I don't have to remind you that the Constitution makes no provision for purchasing land," Madison said.

"Well, since it was written in my hand, perhaps I can go back and forge a clause," Jefferson joked. "Think of the vastness of those lands west of the Mississippi. *Think* of it."

Madison smiled. "Half a dozen new states? All of them peopled by those who consider themselves to be the informed electorate?"

"Come now, James."

"I assure you, I share your enthusiasm," Madison said quickly. "Shall I handle the dialogue with the Congress?"

"I think I'll take care of that myself," Jefferson said.

Madison nodded in agreement. Jefferson's public speaking was not up to the quality of some; but one to one or in a small group, he was quite effective.

It happened quickly: the French-language treaty with Napoleon was signed, the price for the purchase of Louisiana stated; Jefferson submitted all the information to Congress even while Meriwether Lewis and his self-chosen co-commander, William Clark, traveled west; the Senate quickly ratified the treaty with France; the House passed the necessary acts of appropriation; a date for the formal ceremony of transfer, to be held in New Orleans, was set.

Jefferson wanted to attend, but he knew that his place was in Washington. Thus he named men to represent him. Almost as an afterthought, he remembered the advice given to him by George Washington: to maintain communications and friendship with those Indians who were allied with and were friendly to the United States. As a result, the president penned a personal letter to a man to whom he had written once before.

In certain cynical statements regarding native Americans, Thomas Jefferson had occasionally shown that his feelings were similar to the average United States citizen's. Generally Indians were looked upon as an inferior race. Jefferson had grown frustrated and impatient with the unabating Indian trouble in the Indiana Territory, where the Shawnee Tecumseh continued to urge war against the white man. But the president also remembered one man at the opposite end of the spectrum from Tecumseh—a tall, blue-eyed, well-spoken fellow who looked like a sun-bronzed frontiersman but claimed to be Seneca. And it was to that man, Renno, sachem of the Southern Seneca, that Jefferson addressed his personal request to represent the Indian nations at the ceremony of transfer of the Louisiana Territory in New Orleans on December 20, 1803.

Thomas Jefferson's letter reached Knoxville and was subsequently taken to the Seneca village in the Cherokee Nation by Renno's ex-father-by-marriage, Roy Johnson. Renno's youngest offspring, the ten-year-old boy Ta-na, greeted his "grandfather Roy." With his cousin Gao, son of the shaman El-i-chi, Ta-na generated enough enthusiasm and combined weight to cause Roy to stagger back and almost fall to the ground.

"By gum," Roy said, ruffling the thick, Indian-black hair of the two boys, "if you two aren't big enough to cut up and fry for breakfast."

"The hunting has been good, Grandfather," Ta-na said with an English accent that showed the influence of his stepmother, Beth Huntington. "But we can't get our fathers to take us out anymore."

"Well, we'll see about that," Roy said, "if you two rapscallions will turn me loose long enough to see if To-shabe's cook pot is full or empty."

"Horse-meat stew," Gao said, licking his lips with satisfaction at the memory of the meal.

"Horse meat?"

"A panther got one of my mother Beth's colts," Ta-na explained.

"Well, waste not want not," Roy said.

Toshabe, mother of Renno, El-i-chi, and Ena, having heard the rumpus, came out of her longhouse and smiled to see Roy approaching. The two wild young warriors leaped and cavorted on either side.

"Welcome," Toshabe said. Her almost six decades of age rested lightly on her. She was not as slim as a young maiden, but the fullness of her breasts and hips became her. Her French blood both lightened her skin and emphasized her Erie characteristics—high cheekbones, dark eyes, and thick, straight hair sprinkled with gray.

"I thank thee that thou art well," Roy said in perfect Seneca.

"Will you take food?"

"With the greatest dag-blamed pleasure," Roy said, grinning. He turned to the boys. "You two run off, find Renno, and tell him I've got a letter for him."

"Shall I take it to my father?" Ta-na asked.

"Nope." Roy winked at Toshabe. "We old ones get nosy, you see. I want him to open it here so Toshabe and I can find out what it says."

The boys went whooping off, and a pair of shaggy, yelping dogs nipped playfully at their heels.

Toshabe, meanwhile, ushered Roy into the longhouse that she had shared with two husbands, the great Ghonkaba, grandson of the original white Indian, and the Seneca senior warrior Ha-ace the Panther, both victims of murder. Within minutes Roy was seated cross-legged on a mat and eating horse-meat stew from a delicate bone china plate, which had been a gift to Toshabe from her daughter-in-law Beth.

"One of Beth's good colts?" Roy asked around a mouthful of savory, tender meat.

Toshabe nodded. "Beth was very upset. She herself demanded to be allowed to shoot the panther."

"And did she?"

Toshabe shrugged. "Of course. She is the chosen wife of Renno."

"Meaning she usually does whatever she wants?"

Toshabe nodded, resigned.

Roy laughed. "Might as well face it, Toshabe—she's quite a gal, that Beth."

"But she is not Seneca," Toshabe said.

Roy finished his serving, soaking up thick pot liquor with corn bread, and accepted seconds. After a comfortable silence he remarked, "I ain't exactly Seneca, either, Toshabe."

"That is true," she said, looking at him questioningly.

"That's why I've been a little reluctant to speak what's been on my mind for quite a while," Roy said.

"The grandfather of my grandchildren should feel free to speak."

"Well, that's just it," Roy said, grateful for the opening. "We have a lot in common, you and I. We both love our grandchildren, Little Hawk and Renna, and those other scamps out there. You know that I still look on Renno as a son and—"

Toshabe was silent. She looked straight ahead, her face giving no hint of her thoughts.

"And, dad-gum it, Toshabe, I'm sick and tired of living alone in Knoxville. I'm tired of playing part-time soldier in the Tennessee Militia with Andy Jackson. Most often when they talk about fightin' they want to fight the wrong people. They don't think of the British, who aren't ever going to be satisfied with staying up north of the lakes in Canada, as a constant threat. The militia didn't really want to fight the Spaniards, and even when they said they were ready to fight the Frenchies if they moved into New Orleans, they still talked about how they'd whupped a few Cherokee and Shawnee. It's the Indians, always the Indians they want to fight. I'm just sick and tired of it, that's all. I can't find anyone in Knoxville I want to talk to or be with. I spend my time remembering how Renno and I covered a lot of ground up north with Anthony Wayne. Or I daydream about being off and away over a ridge with El-i-chi or with Little Hawk—the way we used to hunt before he left to become an officer and a gentleman at West Point and—" He paused.

Toshabe looked straight ahead impassively.

"You're not making it any easier," he said accusingly.

"I have always known that in many ways you were like my sons and my grandsons," she said.

"Well, there are other things I'm tired of, too, Toshabe. I'm tired of not having anyone to help me warm my bed." He flushed. There was a long silence.

"There are widows," she suggested. "Young widows."

"I don't want any damned young widow," Roy said. "I want you."

She turned to face him, and her expression softened. "I am old, Roy. Much of the warmth has gone from me."

"Fiddlesticks," Roy scoffed. "You're more beautiful than most women half your age." He reached out and took her hand. "How about it, Toshabe? Think you could put up with an old codger like me? If you'll have me I want to live here, in the village."

"And leave me at a whim to go off on a hunt or a ramble with Renno and El-i-chi?"

He grinned. "Well, not for a while, Toshabe. Not for a while." He felt the need for her. He had been long without a woman. He pulled her into his arms and kissed her neck, her cheek.

"Old man," she said, "the boys will be back soon."

"Yep, and that's too bad," he said, for she was responding to him, pressing her body to his. "Can I interpret this unmaidenly behavior of yours as acceptance of my proposal?"

"If you can put up with me, I think I just might be able to put up with you," she said.

"Good girl," Roy said. He found that her kiss was warm and sincere and made him feel young. He grumbled in frustration when he heard the noisy approach of Gao and Ta-na.

Renno entered the longhouse immediately after the two boys burst in. He exchanged formal greetings with Roy—polite, ancient phrases in Seneca—then shared the warrior's handclasp. Finally the sachem sat down cross-legged and accepted the letter. He gave an un-Indianlike frown when he saw that it was from the president and hesitated before opening it.

Roy understood why: the last letter Renno had received from Jefferson had taken him south to New

Orleans, to encounters with an evil force the likes of which he had not experienced since his battles so long before with the shaman Hodano. Renno was content to stay home. He led his tribe with relaxed but steady discipline. He lived with a wife whom he loved deeply. Although Renna was far away in France and Little Hawk was in New York State, learning how to be an officer, the white Indian had the pleasure of watching Ta-na, his *Seneca* son, blood of the lovely young An-da, and Ta-na's cousin Gao. The hunting had been good. There had been no pressures against the Cherokee Nation, of which his Seneca had become a part.

"Well, are you going to open it or not?" Roy demanded.

Renno smiled and extended the letter toward Roy. "Here, you do it."

"Well, don't think I won't," Roy said, jerking the letter from Renno's hand and tearing it open.

"Might as well," Renno said. "Save me the time and trouble of telling you what it says."

"It's from President Thomas Jefferson," Roy said.

"That much I know," Renno said.

Roy wrinkled his brow with the effort of reading Jefferson's handwriting. "You hankering for a trip, Renno?"

"Please do me the favor of throwing the letter into the fire," Renno said in the way of an answer.

"No, wait. This one might be fun," Roy said. "No trouble this time. A pleasure trip. Mr. Jefferson wants us all to go down to New Orleans to represent Indian interests at a fancy shindig."

" 'All'?" Renno asked. "He mentions names other than mine?"

"Well, not exactly," Roy admitted. "But he says that you should take other representative members of the tribe."

"And of what tribe are you a member?" Renno teased.

"Well, if you want to be technical about it," Roy said, "Little Hawk made me a blood brother of the Seneca years ago." He chuckled. "Almost cut my finger off trying to draw blood."

"Well," Renno said, "since he wants us all to go to New Orleans, you can go in my stead."

"Now, Renno," Roy said, "it's you he really wants. But he says to take along any other representatives who would do credit to the Indian. I reckon I meet that definition if I brush my hair and shave. It'll be fun, Renno. We can take El-i-chi—"

"And me," Gao and Ta-na said as one.

"And Beth. I'll bet she's getting a little bit of cabin fever, too, even if she does live in a house big enough to hold three barns and a goat farm."

"So," Renno said, reaching for the letter to read the words for himself. He left the longhouse, followed by Gao and Ta-na.

"You forgot rather quickly," Toshabe said when she and Roy were alone.

"Nope, didn't forget. I thought you'd enjoy a trip down to New Orleans, too."

"I am too old and tired for such nonsense."

"Oh, come on, Toshabe. I'll buy you a French gown, and we'll show those youngsters how to dance."

"I have no need of a French gown," she said. "And I was never good at the white man's dancing." She put her hand atop his. "I have said yes to you, Roy Johnson, but that is no reason why you can't go with Renno." There was no doubt that Renno would go to New Orleans. He had never failed to obey a request from the leader of the United States, and letters had come to him from three presidents now. "I will be here when you return, the manitous willing. We have lived almost sixty years without being man and wife. Another few months won't matter."

"Well . . ." Roy said.

"Go," she urged. "Perhaps Beth Huntington will need to be persuaded."

"Then when we get back—"

"Yes," she agreed. "In the meantime, perhaps I can coax one of Ta-na's dogs into my bed to warm my feet at night."

"Aw, Toshabe—"

"Go," she repeated, laughing and pushing him out the door.

*   *   *

The trip began in a spirit of holiday. Beth had furnished horses for all. Ta-na and Gao insisted on serving as scouts, although the first part of the journey was through friendly Cherokee lands. The boys delighted in surveying the trail ahead, then galloping back toward the main group, consisting of Renno and Beth, Roy Johnson, and El-i-chi and his Rose, Ah-wa-o.

Many things had changed since the Seneca first came to the South. Lands that had been wilderness hunting grounds for the Cherokee, Choctaw, and Creek were now studded with the cleared fields of white settlers. Towns were growing with the white population. A well-traveled track led southwestward from Tennessee to Natchez, the outpost most southwest in the United States. Renno had traveled the Natchez Trace before, and as his little group rode at a comfortable pace through grand and gloomy forests and among the cultivated fields of the Choctaw, he allowed himself the luxury of memory, of the time spent with Little Hawk and Renna moving northward on the trace. Then he recalled still another journey, when he had gone to the vastness west of the Father of Waters, through Comanche lands, and to the waterless deserts of the Apache. The flame-haired one who was now his wife had been with him, as had El-i-chi; but the maiden at El-i-chi's side had been not Ah-wa-o but a willful Chickasaw girl named Holani.

Perhaps it was memories of Holani, for she had gone to the Place across the River, that gave him a feeling of unease. Thinking of the dead girl brought his beloved An-da to mind. An-da, his wife, a true Seneca woman, who had given him his son Ta-na. She, too, had passed over the river to await him.

A Seneca warrior was never alone. In times of peace—such as during the leisurely ride down the trace toward the bustling little river town in the southern Mississippi Territory—and in times of war and danger he was surrounded by the spirits of all those who had died before him. No one knew better than Renno how closely enmeshed life was with the spirit world. He did not usually set out on an undertaking without fasting to consult the manitous, but since the trip to New Orleans was, as Roy Johnson had said, a pleasure trip, Renno had merely chanted his prayers to the Master of Life before leaving the village. Now, as he found himself being more alert, as his eyes darted swiftly from one side of the track to the other, looking for any movement, an odd shadow, anything out of the ordinary, he felt a pressing need to remedy his oversight.

"I will go for fresh meat," he told the others.

"I'll go with you," Roy offered.

"If it pleases you, Roy, no," Renno said.

"It doesn't," Roy said grumpily. "But whatever you say, Sachem."

El-i-chi did not question Renno's decision. He had noted that his brother had ceased to be relaxed and knew why Renno wanted to be alone.

"Keep the pace," Renno told them. "I will join you."

"When?" Roy asked.

"When I join you," Renno said.

He left his horse to be led by Beth and took only his weapons. He looked back once at the edge of the forest and nodded reassuringly to his flame-haired wife. She lifted her hand, then let it drop. She, like El-i-chi, had recognized the growing restlessness in Renno, and like her brother-by-marriage, she knew why Renno needed to be alone in the forest.

As a Christian, however, she didn't understand. Her God did not materialize before her eyes and speak to her. Her ancestors did not come from beyond to give her counsel. In fact, there were times when she felt almost resentful toward Renno's manitous.

Chapter Two

As early as 1776 there had been talk of establishing a military academy to provide the United States with trained officers. Since there was a war of some importance going on at that time, nothing was done. In 1798, when Alexander Hamilton was named by President John Adams to be nominal head of the "new army," he began to think seriously about the need for a school for future officers; but as things often go with government, implementation of Hamilton's ideas was delayed. John Adams, who had the misfortune to follow George Washington as president—any man following the general as leader of the nation would have suffered by comparison—did little to build an officers' corps for the army, although he did get around to choosing a Revolutionary War fort on the Hudson River as a site for the academy. He chose West Point for two reasons: because facilities were already in existence and because artillery and engineer units were stationed there.

It was left to Thomas Jefferson, a man who wanted

nothing but peace, to take positive steps toward a training school for officers. Within a month of his election he named Jonathan Williams to head the academy at West Point and picked an Englishman, George Baron, to teach mathematics to the cadets.

Before Jefferson had been in office four months, he was naming cadets to report to West Point. One of the lads, tall, bronzed, and fair-haired, with eyes of piercing blue, was delayed by life-threatening adventures shared with his father along the Mississippi River.

As a result, he did not arrive at the old fort in New York until 1803.

He was nineteen years old and had no surname. For the academy he adopted Harper, the name of the family of his great-great-grandfather. Some of his fellow cadets would learn the hard way that the lad was exceedingly proud of his Seneca blood and had surprising strength. They called him "the Indian" behind his back and "Hawk" when speaking directly to him. Teachers and military cadre called him Harper or Cadet Harper. But in spite of these various monikers, he still thought of himself as Ossweh-ga-da-ga-ah Ne-wa-ah, the Little Hawk of the Bear Clan of the Seneca.

He had made the long journey from the Southwest Territory to New York State on one of Beth Huntington's finest horses. The animal was quartered along with government mounts in the post stables, for it was permissible for a cadet to provide his own horse. Other cadets had come from as far away as Georgia, but none had traveled alone through the sparsely settled frontier and the trackless wilderness. They professed to be unimpressed or dismissed the difficulty of the journey by saying, "Well, he's an Injun, after all."

Hawk Harper was not the first to conclude that something had gone amiss with regard to what the academy was supposed to accomplish. In Thomas Jefferson's words, West Point's scholastic goal was "to . . . eliminate the classics, add the sciences, and produce graduates who will use their knowledge for the benefit of society." But the cadets who reported to the academy in 1801 discovered that the Point functioned more as a secondary school . . .

and in some cases an elementary school. In 1803, with Little Hawk's class, things were much the same. A number of the cadets had never been taught to read and write. Only a few had any knowledge of arithmetic or grammar.

Little Hawk had expected to study such subjects as higher mathematics, astronomy, philosophy, and chemistry. Unfortunately, he found himself yawning through classes that merely rehashed concepts he had mastered long before under the tutelage of his father and his stepmother.

The military academy was a two-story building not much larger than a country schoolhouse. Green paint had been on hand, so when Mr. Jefferson gave orders to prepare a place for teaching cadets at West Point, the paint was used generously. The benches on which Little Hawk and other cadets sat echoed the theme of omnipresent green, the same green that covered the walls of the old Revolutionary War barracks that housed the cadets.

Classes began at nine in the morning and continued until two in the afternoon every day except Sunday. Field exercises were scheduled four afternoons a week. The work in the field taught Little Hawk how to measure heights and relative distances, how to build fortifications, and how to make maps. He very quickly absorbed the military sciences and, in the process, attracted the attention of Post Commander Major John Lillie.

When the youth was ordered to report to the commander's office, he spent a few minutes sprucing himself up. With boots shined and his best uniform spotless, Little Hawk stood in front of the major's desk, saluted smartly, and said, "Cadet Harper reporting as ordered, sir."

"Stand at ease, Cadet," Lillie said.

John Lillie loved the army. He had first donned the uniform of his country when he was in his teens. His greatest regret was that he had not been born soon enough to take part in the great war for freedom. Among his proudest memories was the sight of George Washington on a splendid white horse, reviewing the victorious troops after the Battle of Yorktown. Lillie had been a mere boy at the time, but he had decided then and there that he wanted to be a soldier like Washington.

Now, at thirty-three, he had been handed an assignment that did not please him. There were still Indians to
fight out on the frontier, and he was stuck in a moldering
old fort on the Hudson, playing nursemaid to a bunch of
youngsters who thought they had the character and the
courage to become officers. The fact that his sixteen-year-
old daughter, Mary Ann, loved West Point and was more
than content to stay there until life passed the ambitious
major by and left him to shrivel toward retirement age in
a backwater did not improve Lillie's opinion of the academy and its contingent of cadets.

The one consolation for him was to discover that now
and then a lad came along who just might have the stuff
to lead men in battle. Such a one stood before him.

"You're one-quarter Seneca," Lillie said.

"Yes, sir."

"Doesn't seem to hold you back."

"No, sir."

Little Hawk had made no attempt to hide his Indian
blood. In fact, he'd defended it more than once against
slurs from fellow cadets. There hadn't been any wrestling
matches of late, for the other students learned quickly that
it did not behoove them to tangle with Hawk in the one
form of man-to-man struggle that was allowed to the
cadets. Wrestling had long been a favored Seneca sport,
and Little Hawk had done his share of it from the time
he was a small child. His skill in throwing larger oppo-
nents was, for a time, the talk of the small corps.

Little Hawk indulged in some mild, Indianlike brag-
ging in order to pull the white man's leg. He confided to
a cadet who was known to be a talker that back in the
wilderness of the Cherokee Nation, he had trained himself
by wrestling bears. After that story made the rounds, chal-
lenges to the Indian ceased.

"I have heard, Harper, that there's been a spot of
trouble between you and some of the other cadets," Major
Lillie said.

"Nothing serious, sir."

"You know, Harper, that this academy will not toler-
ate the harassment of any cadet by members of the Cadet
Corps."

"Yes, sir."

Lillie was getting a bit impatient. "Damn it, Harper, I've giving you a chance to put it on record that you've been harassed because of your Injun—uh, Indian blood."

"There has been no harassment, sir."

"Oh?" Lillie raised one eyebrow.

"None, that is, sir, that I can't handle."

"I see," Lillie said. "I wonder, then, if you think you might be able to handle the position of cadet officer?"

"Yes, sir, I think I can," Little Hawk said, snapping to attention.

"Stand at ease," Lillie said, waving a hand. "You've earned it."

"Thank you, sir."

"That's all."

"Yes, sir."

He was halfway out the door when he performed a snappy about-face because Lillie called him back. "If there's any trouble, Harper, I want to hear about it—from *you*. Do you understand?"

"Yes, sir."

The trouble began immediately after Little Hawk donned the insignia of a cadet officer. The revolt was led by a cadet who, up until that point, had been content to keep his mouth shut and do his duty. His name was Sidney Forrest. He was from the Georgia frontier, where raiding Creek warriors made life both exciting and uncertain. On the Forrest plantation there were graves of relatives who had been mutilated and killed by the Creek.

"I will have my soul damned in hell before I will salute to a savage," Forrest declared. The cadets had just returned from a field exercise during which Little Hawk had wielded his authority for the first time. Forrest spoke loudly enough to make certain that the new cadet officer heard as he entered the barracks.

Little Hawk's impulse was to take up the challenge immediately, but he remembered Major Lillie's orders. The major had said, "If there's any trouble, I want to hear about it from *you*."

He let the matter drop for the time being. After

morning formation, however, Cadet Captain Harper requested permission to speak with the post commander and was admitted to Lillie's office.

"I didn't expect you back quite so soon," Lillie said.

"I am here, sir, only because you ordered me to report any trouble to you. If it is the major's wish, I will handle the problem myself."

"Speak," Lillie ordered.

"I have come to you for another reason as well," Little Hawk said. It seemed inevitable that he would be pushed into violence by the prejudice of cadets such as Sidney Forrest. His intention was to explain in advance that he was not one to start trouble but that when trouble came, he believed in swift and decisive action. Thus it would be necessary to tell the commander about the incident in Philadelphia when two of his fellow Senate pages tried to kill him by pushing him in front of a racing coal wagon. "When I was in Philadelphia there were certain problems—"

"I know about all that," Lillie interrupted. When Little Hawk raised his eyebrows in question, Lillie went on, "Oh, it's not in your file, Harper. I had a separate communication about you from President Jefferson. He spoke specifically of the affair in Philadelphia and held you blameless."

Little Hawk nodded.

"Same problem occurring here?" Lillie asked.

"Right now, sir, the problem can be solved by a private discussion between one cadet and me if the commander would see fit to grant me a bit of latitude in the academy rules."

"Harper, we can't have fighting in the Cadet Corps. You know that is an offense that leads to expulsion of the man who strikes the first blow."

"Sir."

"On the other hand, I will not have some snotty kid questioning my judgment in the selection of cadet officers," Lillie continued. "I want the names of all those who don't obey any legitimate order you give, Harper; and I want the name of any cadet who harasses you because of your Indian blood."

Little Hawk stood rigidly at attention and maintained silence.

"I see," Lillie said after a moment. "Well, I guess it is good for cadet morale to have a code of honor, although I think you're making a mistake by not telling me."

"I'm sorry, sir," Little Hawk said.

"I won't stand for anyone bending the rules," Lillie continued. "There will be no fighting among cadets." He paused. "Not on this *post* there won't be."

Little Hawk refrained from grinning, for there had been a sparkle and the answer in Lillie's eyes. He saluted, then turned smartly.

He found his section of the Cadet Corps between classes. The men were grouped around Sidney Forrest. The big Georgian stopped talking when he saw Little Hawk and glared at him. Forrest had never challenged Little Hawk to a wrestling match, so his strength could be judged only by appearances; but the size of the Georgian was impressive. Little Hawk pushed through the group of young men around Forrest and faced the larger lad. "I have a detail for you, Cadet Forrest," he said.

"That so?" Forrest asked with a sneer.

"I think, Forrest, that it's one you've been asking for," Little Hawk said. "Come with me." He turned and walked away. Forrest made no effort to follow. At ten paces Little Hawk stopped and faced the group. "The rest of you get on to your next class, or I'll assign demerits to every man."

"Go on," Forrest taunted, "if you're all afraid of a demerit or two."

"You don't care about demerits?" Little Hawk asked.

"Lay 'em on, big Chief Red Bottom," Forrest said, "and see who cares."

"Not just yet," Little Hawk said. "First I want you to come with me."

"Say please." Forrest tried unsuccessfully to imitate Little Hawk's classic English accent.

"Cadet Forrest, will you please come with me?"

"Now that's more like it." The Georgian swaggered toward Little Hawk. "I guess it's up to us Southerners to teach you savages some manners."

Little Hawk waited until Forrest was beside him, then he started walking briskly toward the sally port of the fort.

"Where are we going?"

"Outside," Little Hawk replied.

"Off post?"

"Off post."

Forrest's eyes narrowed in thought. He stood two inches taller than the slim, long-muscled boy who called himself a Seneca, and he weighed perhaps thirty pounds more. He grinned at the thought that the Indian was going to face him man-to-man. Then he frowned because it seemed too good to be true.

"Why are we going off post?" he asked as they neared the portal.

"A private training session," Little Hawk answered. "Just the two of us."

"Well, I'll be damned," Forrest said.

There was no more talk as they made their way to the rocky point where, on the bank of the river, they were hidden from the sight of anyone inside the fort. Little Hawk led the way onto a small, sandy beach.

Forrest said, "You're really going to fight me?"

"No," Little Hawk replied, spinning to plant first one fist and then the other in Forrest's midsection. The force of the first blow caused the cadet's breath to explode from his lungs; the second sent him to the ground, where he sat holding his stomach and looking up in aggrieved surprise at Little Hawk.

"That wasn't fair," Forrest protested, his voice sounding like a young boy's.

"I didn't intend for it to be," Little Hawk said. "I've seen you in action, Forrest, wrestling with some of the cadets. You're bigger and heavier than I, and maybe even as strong." He smiled, held out his hand. "I hate being hurt, you see."

Forrest continued to gaze up at him with a puzzled expression, but he knocked the extended hand away.

"Come on, let me help you up," Little Hawk urged.

"All right," the Georgian agreed, taking the hand

and letting himself be pulled to his feet. "But when I get up—"

He was unable to finish because two rock-hard fists buried themselves in his stomach again, and he found himself sitting on the ground, gasping for breath, tears in his eyes.

"Damn you," he managed. "Fight like a man."

"If that's your pleasure," Little Hawk said.

Forrest struggled to his feet. He was wobbly, and his face was red. When he struck out, his blows were easily avoided. As he regained his breath his efforts became a bit more serious. Little Hawk had to use all of his agility to avoid the mighty swings of his adversary's big arms and meaty fists.

"You gonna fight or dance around like the wild Indian you are?" Forrest demanded.

"Well, now, there you go again," Little Hawk said disapprovingly. He danced in and laced two quick blows to Forrest's stomach, and as he moved back he delivered a very painful clout to the bigger man's left kidney. The cadet cried out.

"I'm being very careful not to mark you, Forrest," Little Hawk said. "Because, as you know, fighting within the Cadet Corps is punishable by expulsion from the academy, and I happen to think that once you get the fog cleared out of your thick head, you'll make a halfway decent officer."

"Stand still, damn you!" Forrest yelled, lumbering forward.

Little Hawk leaped in and drove his right fist into Forrest's midsection. He heard the big fellow gasp and felt as if a mule had kicked him in the face as the Georgian landed a right to his left cheek. Little Hawk moved back, shaking his head to dispel the white spots in front of his eyes.

"Well," he conceded, "maybe I will have to mark you. Just a little."

He landed a left to the belly and, as Forrest reacted, another left to the chin, then a hard, swinging right that took Forrest on the hinge of the jaw. The big cadet sank slowly to the ground, his eyes dazed. He tried to get up, but Little Hawk sent him onto his back with a precisely aimed right that brought blackness.

Little Hawk squatted beside the fallen cadet and raised one eyelid. Forrest's eye was rolled back whitely. Several minutes passed before he moaned and opened his eyes. After he had recovered enough to sit up, Little Hawk put his hand in Forrest's long hair and jerked the bloodied face upward.

"You may be thinking that this won't be the last of it, Forrest," he said. "You're not the kind to take a beating and not try to avenge it. That's your choice. But it will be you who must strike the first blow, and if it happens on the post, it will be you who is expelled from the academy."

"Unnnnnn," Forrest moaned.

"One more thing," Little Hawk said. "I will allow you to strike the first blow, but I will strike the last one." He knelt beside Forrest and put his nose only a few inches from the Georgian's. "You might get the idea to bring in some help. If you do, if you best me by sheer numbers, then you had better kill me, because if you don't, I will come for you. I will cut your heart out and feed it to you bit by bit."

"If you'd fight fair—"

"If standing toe-to-toe with a lout like you and letting myself get hit in the face means fighting fair, that I will never do," Little Hawk vowed, rubbing his cheek where Forrest's blow had connected. "I'm going to look like a chipmunk as it is."

"And you said you weren't going to mark me," Forrest complained, touching his face, which was already turning purple from just below his right eye to his chin.

"I think you and I were playing Indian stickball," Little Hawk suggested, "and we had a collision. What do you think?"

Forrest thought about it. Finally he grinned. "Well, I still think I could take you in a fair fight, but that Indian stickball is one rough game, isn't it?"

"Very rough," Little Hawk confirmed. "Look, I didn't ask to be made a cadet officer. I just did my work and kept my record clean. But now that the major has given

me the honor I intend to see that the job is done right.
I think you know me well enough to believe that I won't
give any unnecessary orders; but when I do give an order,
I expect it to be obeyed. Understand?"

Forrest nodded.

"Answer me, if you please," Little Hawk said.

"I understand, Captain." Forrest climbed to his feet
and shook his head. "I need to lie down for a little while."

"You go ahead. I'll be along shortly."

He sat on a boulder at the water's edge. A fish broke
the surface, creating a large swirl. Overhead a hawk cried
out its defiance to the world. Little Hawk was wondering
if Forrest and his friends would let the matter drop now,
so that they all could get on with the business of being
educated, when he heard a noise at his back. He jumped
to his feet, turning in midair, poised to defend himself.
But it was Mary Ann Lillie, daughter of the post commander, making her way gingerly down the rocky incline.
He had never seen her up close. He waited until she
had reached the sandy little cove and looked at her with
curiosity.

She had pale, porcelain skin much like his stepmother's. Her hair was a rich chestnut brown mass piled atop
her head to show a graceful length of neck. There was a
hint of delicate elegance in her posture.

"I saw you two boys down here playing," she said as
she drew near. Her eyes were the color of her hair, shin-
ing with speckles of stardust. Her full lips parted in a
smile, showing even, white teeth. "And then I asked
myself, was it play? And so I came down to see if you
were hurt."

"I'm not hurt," Little Hawk said. There was something about Mary Ann Lillie's poise, the way she held her
little pink parasol to protect her face from the sun, the
way she was smiling at him teasingly, that made him feel
awkward. He brushed at his uniform, which hadn't been
mussed by the quick set-to with Sidney Forrest, then
looked down at his boots.

"But you are hurt," she said with concern. She
stepped forward and touched his bruised jaw.

"No. It doesn't hurt," he said, taking a step back.

"From up there it didn't look as if he laid a hand on you," she said with a silvery little laugh.

"You saw it all?" he asked nervously.

"I'm afraid so."

"And now you'll tell your father."

"Will I?"

He looked into her eyes. "I hope not."

"It's a serious matter, cadets fighting." She tilted her head, reminding him of a curious little brown wren. "Very serious."

"Miss Lillie—"

"Oh, do call me Mary Ann."

"Ah, Mary Ann, if you could see fit to refrain from telling your father about my, uh, little discussion with Cadet Forrest, I would be forever in your debt."

"I can be bribed," she said.

He spread his hands.

"Not money," she said. "Your horse. He's so beautiful. I want your permission to ride him occasionally."

"Gladly," he agreed. "He's quite gentle, having been trained by a woman."

"An Indian woman?" she asked.

"No, by my stepmother, the lady Beth Huntington."

"I want to hear about her," Mary Ann said. "My father said that your father was married to a member of the English nobility. I find that very interesting. You may walk me back to the fort while you tell me about her."

Little Hawk, captivated as surely as if the pink tassels of her parasol were chains binding him to her, obeyed. He told Mary Ann about Beth and her house in the Cherokee land, and of his father and sister.

Mary Ann was enthralled to learn that Renna was married to a French nobleman. "My my," she said with a wink, "you do come from quite an unusual family. I suppose, then, that you're actually a prince as well."

"In a way," Little Hawk replied. "I will be a sachem of the Seneca someday."

"A mere chief?" she teased. "That's not nearly as grand as being an English lord or a French count."

"That depends on one's perspective," Little Hawk said. "For myself, I would not trade my heritage for that of any king."

"Well, bless me," Mary Ann said. She looked at him closely. "By the way, my father will skin you and throw you out of the academy if he knows that you've been flirting with me."

Little Hawk stopped in his tracks. "I? Flirting with you? Who climbed down the bluff? I? Who ordered me to walk her back to the fort?"

"Oh, come along," she said lightly. "We'll just have to be very careful, that's all."

"Miss Lillie," Little Hawk said, "I intend to do nothing that would raise the ire of your father. In fact, I shall tell him that I encountered you by the river and escorted you back to the fort because it was unseemly for a young lady to be walking forth alone."

"You're kind of backward after all, aren't you?" she asked, and with a swish of her skirts, she was running toward the sally port.

With a mixture of emotions he watched her go. His common sense told him to stay far away from the commander's daughter. She was beautiful, yes, but her behavior seemed a bit odd. His heart went after her nonetheless, swimming in stardust-flecked eyes, delighting in her silvery laugh. And there was another awareness as well, for he had been initiated into manhood by the witch Melisande in New Orleans. Now, having known the delights of woman, he ached to feel his lips on the full, sweet mouth of Miss Mary Ann Lillie.

Major Lillie halted in front of Cadet Sidney Forrest. Forrest's face was livid from temple to jaw. Lillie had already noted during his inspection that the left side of Cadet Captain Hawk Harper's face was bruised and swollen.

"Have an accident, Cadet Forrest?" the major asked.

"Yes, sir!" Forrest shouted.

"And the nature of that accident?"

"We were at sport, sir. We were playing a game with a ball and sticks, Injun style."

"Ah, I see," Lillie said. "And by chance did you happen to run into Cadet Captain Harper during your sport?"

"Yes, sir," Forrest said.

"Rough game, that Indian stickball," Lillie remarked.

"Yes, sir!" Forrest thundered.

Lillie completed his inspection, having handed out only a few demerits for lapses in personal hygiene and care of uniform. He stood before the Cadet Corps, his hands clasped behind his back. "All right, men," he said, his voice carrying and reverberating from the walls of the old fort, "hear this and hear it well. I'm only going to say it once. When I make a decision, as far as you're concerned, that decision is carved in stone, just like the Ten Commandments. When I hand out an honor or a reprimand, it is final. There is no appeal, for that's the way it is in this man's army. Moreover, my authority extends through the other members of the West Point cadre—the instructors and the cadet officers whom I have appointed. To defy one of them is to defy me. Do you get my point?"

"Yes, sir!" shouted the corps in unison.

"I don't care about excuses or personal feelings. I don't care if you hate the guts of some teacher, some member of the staff, or some cadet officer. You salute. You say 'yes, sir,' and you honor the uniform and the insignia of rank of that man. It's as simple as that. Do I make myself clear?"

"Yes, sir!" came the roar of reply.

Autumn had always been Renno's favorite time of the year. South of the Cherokee Nation the Great Bear in the sky had not yet spilled out his carnival of color into the leaves of the trees, but there was a smell of fall in the air as Renno ran parallel to the Natchez Trace. He ran for the joy of it, for the feeling of completeness that came to him after his labored breathing reached a crescendo and suddenly eased off, after the pain in his muscles turned into that good, loose feeling of the runner's euphoria. And he ran because of a feeling of dread that was incongruous to the cloudless autumn day.

Once, he halted and drank from a spring-fed rill, lying on his stomach to suck the cool water. Around him squirrels were preparing for winter and in the process providing for new growth by burying acorns. The white Indian rose and continued his journey, but at a slower pace, looking for a place to make his camp for the night. He selected a clearing formed by the fall of a forest giant, a mighty water oak. Dry, cool air had moved in from the north so that there would be no dew.

The sachem sat with his back to the fallen bole of the old tree. As night came and the stars filled the portion of sky that was visible to him, he leaned against the tree trunk and let his mind go blank.

Never had he gone out of himself so quickly. Usually he needed to fast for long hours before attaining the state where he could separate himself from his body and roam the realm of the manitous; but on that autumn night they were waiting for him in the heavily wooded lands of the Choctaw Nation—a host of spirit warriors wearing the distinctive markings of all five member tribes of the League of the Ho-de-no-sau-nee.

Something else was different, too. Instead of appearing before him, the manitous brought him up, up. As Renno ascended to join the lights in the sky, he saw the legendary Dekanawidah, the prophet who was the author of the Great Peace of the Iroquois. Hiawatha the statesman, who had transformed Dekanawidah's dream of peace among the five tribes into the long-lasting League of the Iroquois, nodded to the white Indian. Other faces and forms swam among the stars. He saw his own ancestors: the stern-faced Seneca sachem old Ghonka, with his mighty arms crossed; his great-grandfather Renno; his grandfather Ja-gonh; and his father, Ghonkaba. A solemnity about them was, in itself, both warning and something akin to a welcome.

A twig snapped, at once both far away and nearby. Renno's ears registered the sound and identified it as the scurrying of a little nocturnal animal—a raccoon, possum, or skunk. The spell was broken. The sachem's eyes, suddenly dazzled by the brightness of the lights in the sky, closed, and he fell from the realm of the spirits. He experienced a bittersweet sadness, for he had felt himself to be a part of the gathering.

Now the night deepened, and a half-moon dimmed the stars. He chanted to the manitous and the Master of Life, then fed his small fire with dead twigs from the fallen oak. Morbid thoughts came unbidden. Death was in the darkness around him. He saw the body of his father, Ghonkaba, who had been slain by a treacherous white man. Ha-ace the Panther, stepfather, husband of Toshabe, was dead, murdered by another white man. An-da's mutilated body appeared to Renno, and he wept bitterly.

"Manitous, what are you saying?" he cried, his voice rising, only to be lost in the surrounding forest. "Is death to be your only message to me?"

Next to appear was the pale-haired Emily, his first love, wife, mother of Little Hawk and Renna. She knelt, sobbing, beside a stream half-filled with flowering lilies. Her face was hidden behind her hands, and her shoulders shook with grief; but then, as Renno stood and approached her, Emily looked up, and her face became utterly radiant. She lifted her arms to gather him in. He felt a peace so total, so rhapsodic that when Emily began to fade, he shouted out in protest of his penetrating feeling of loss.

"Speak to me," he begged. "Speak to me, for I am sad, and the burden of it weighs upon me."

A gift of vision overtook him. Suddenly he was a hawk soaring on a wind, covering vast distances with the beating of his wings. Below him he saw rank after rank of cleared farmlands, white men's fields, extending into the distance as far as he could see. Although he flew as fast as he could toward the horizon, a long, long time passed before he was soaring over uncut forestlands. This was the result of the white man's land hunger in action. The cleared lands were advancing, mile after mile, and devouring Indian hunting ground.

Renno ached with a sense of betrayal as the sensation of flight ebbed and he returned to earth. In his mind he saw the face of the Tennessee politician William Blount and heard him say, as the man had said once in Renno's presence, "When we want more land, we just renegotiate the treaties with the Indians."

The image melted and changed. Now Ghonka, in full war regalia, pounded the deadly head of a huge war club into his hand, and his message was clear. The manitou spoke in the language of the Seneca: "It is too late, too late. If things had been different, all of us who are of one blood would have met them on the beaches and driven them back into the sea."

Renno heard wails of grief and realized that the keening was coming from his throat. He shook himself and added more twigs to the fire. The moon was falling down the sky, and the fresh smell of morning was growing.

"What is this great sadness?" he asked. "Speak to me. Counsel me."

They came in the gray light of predawn, a pride of warriors—his great-grandfather, his grandfather, and his father. They walked side by side, weapons in hand. Facing them, waiting, was a sea of long-knife soldiers, some in the red coats of the British, some in the buckskins of the frontier, some in the ornate uniforms of the United States Army. The first white Indian, for whom Renno was named, led the charge into a hopeless battle. Ja-gonh and Ghonkaba, shrilling war cries, soon caught up with Renno, and the three Seneca were quickly swallowed up by the hosts of white faces. Only an agitation among the mixed uniforms showed that the battle went on.

Beside the campfire, Renno was straining at his body, his spirit intent upon joining the uneven fight. For a moment he was free and running toward the churning battle that surrounded his ancestors. And then, abruptly, he was back beside the fallen water oak, his fire burning low.

His emotions roiled. How was he to interpret the visions? What message had been intended? True, he rarely set off on a journey without fasting and praying to the manitous. But when he had begun this so-called pleasure trip to New Orleans, he had felt secure in the belief that no danger would threaten and that it was unnecessary to seek spiritual advice. Were the horrific visions nothing more than a reprimand from the manitous? Were they telling him, "Man, your sight—even that of your brother, El-i-chi, the shaman—is limited to that which is immediately before you. Do not tempt the manitou by pretending to see the unseeable"?

As dawn broke and he covered the embers of his fire, the sachem decided that the spirits must have had more in mind than a scolding. When he sought them, the manitous did not always give information pertaining to the immediate future; many of their prophecies were for the long run. Once, he had been told that his son Little Hawk, then a boy, would be a great sachem. That had been a prediction for the future, for Little Hawk was now a man of nineteen and his father was, thank the spirits, still alive. Was the message of the night also for the future? He had been reminded of the white man's attitude toward Indian lands and been shown the futility of fighting against the vast armies that could be put into the field by the white man. Was that all? Was it all just a reassurance that his policy of gradual integration into the white man's world was the correct course of action?

Puzzled still, Renno began his run to catch up with the others. He had considered taking another day and night for fasting, but there had been a feeling of finality in the last spirit scene that had been shown to him. He ran to the trace, found the tracks of his party, and set off toward the southwest at a pace just short of a sprint. After a few miles, when his body had adjusted, he slowed slightly. His moccasins made little noise as his churning legs ate miles of distance.

He smelled the camp before he saw it. Fresh meat was roasting. To warn El-i-chi and Roy, Renno slowed to a walk and gave the greeting cry of a nesting hawk. El-i-chi answered. Soon the sachem was seated on the ground near a roaring fire and was nibbling from a very hot and very juicy hunk of fresh venison. With his wife at his side and his son Ta-na near him, Renno had no difficulty dispelling all thoughts of death.

Roy tossed the tough remnants of a chunk of meat into the bushes and wiped his mouth on his sleeve. "I've been thinkin', Renno," he said. "We were going to keep it a secret till we all got back from the big city, but I reckon maybe El-i-chi and you ought to have some time to get used to the idea."

"Sounds ominous," El-i-chi remarked, winking at Renno.

"Depends upon how you look at it," Roy said.

"Perhaps you'd better tell us so we might determine for ourselves," Beth suggested.

"Well, I'd been thinking that it was silly for me to live in Knoxville all by my lonesome. I said to myself, Roy, you spend most of your time out in the backwoods or at Renno's place anyway."

"That's what he said," Renno told El-i-chi, nodding wisely.

"Rather astounding, what?" El-i-chi asked in an aristocratic English accent.

The frontiersman was undeterred. "And I said, Roy, there's a fine woman all by her lonesome, and maybe—just maybe—she'll let an old boar bear like you spread your blankets alongside hers."

"By the manitous," El-i-chi said, grinning. "He's in love!"

"You hush," Roy said. "I'm just gettin' to the good part."

"Speak on," El-i-chi said.

"So I asked her, and by gum she said yes." He leaned back against a tree, pulled his hat down over his eyes, and without another word crossed his arms.

"Roy . . ." Beth protested.

El-i-chi, determined not to be the one to ask for further enlightenment, looked at Renno and waited.

Renno sighed. "Roy, not that it really matters, but there are some curious ones among us. You know how it is with women and children. You give them a hint, and they want to know everything. So perhaps you could tell us who said yes."

"Could . . ." Roy said, pulling his hat lower.

Renno looked grimly at El-i-chi and nodded. The brothers rose as one, and before Roy knew what was happening they had seized his legs, upending him, holding him by the feet, and dangling his head toward the ground.

"Now look here!" Roy protested.

"As I have noted," Renno intoned softly, "there are those who are curious."

"Well," Roy squealed, "if you really wanted to know, why didn't you just ask?"

"With you as my witness, Brother," Renno said, "did I not ask this old boar bear nicely to tell us what foolish woman agreed to live with him?"

"With my own ears I heard," El-i-chi agreed. He grunted. "This one is getting heavy. Let's warm his hair over the fire so that he will talk faster."

"You two cut it out!" Roy shouted. "All the blood is running to my head."

"Be careful not to burn the hair, Brother," Renno said as they moved toward the fire, dangling Roy between them. "I hate the smell of burning human hair."

"Renno, dag-blast it!" Roy yelped as he felt the warmth of the fire on his face.

"I believe my father-by-marriage is ready to converse with us," Renno said.

El-i-chi and Renno carefully moved back and lowered Roy to the ground. He sat up, brushed off his tunic, and looked around with a grin. "Only the women and kids are curious, huh?"

"Yes," El-i-chi said. "It is a matter of little concern for a warrior, this goatish passion of an old man."

"Ha," Roy said.

"You asked, and she told you yes," Beth said. "What did you ask, and whom did you ask, Roy?"

"Now you see there?" Roy asked, spreading his hands. "Beth knows how to treat a fellow. Knows how to be polite." He stood and brushed off the back of his pants. "Happens that I and a certain Seneca matron you all might know are going to share blankets when we get back from down south."

"Which Seneca matron, Grandfather?" Ta-na asked.

"Well, young fellow, who else but your grandmother?" Roy asked, casting a quick look in Renno's direction.

El-i-chi drew his tomahawk threateningly and asked, "Brother, can you believe that our mother would make such a choice?"

"Oh, I don't know," Renno allowed. "Bathe him, get him a shave and a clean shirt, and he's not all bad."

"As for myself," El-i-chi said, "I'm trying to decide whether to scalp this white man or give him a bear hug."

"Don't know if I'd relish either one," Roy said, his eyes twinkling. "Besides, since I'm gonna be your pa, you'd best watch your step, sprout."

Renno gave a great whoop and began a little dance. El-i-chi joined in, followed by Ah-wa-o and the two boys. Soon Beth was dancing with them, with just a little more inhibition. They circled Roy. Beth and Ah-wa-o gave him hugs and kisses on the cheek. El-i-chi and Renno exchanged the warriors' clasp with him.

"That'll make you our real grandfather, won't it?" Ta-na asked.

"I reckon it will," Roy said, stepping into the dance, lifting his feet high and stomping them down onto the ground with great enthusiasm.

Chapter Three

Natchez had grown since Renno was last there. Wide-eyed and awed, Gao and Ta-na were silent as they took in the sights and sounds of the white man's town. Ah-wa-o stayed close by El-i-chi.

The sachem and his party rode on deeply rutted dirt streets toward the center of town. As they passed a heavily laden cargo wagon that was mired, they saw two mule skinners indulging in torrents of vile language and urging the six-mule team to greater efforts. Nearby, a small group of solemn-faced Choctaw men stood watching. On the boardwalk in front of a general store a bearded, bushy-haired hunter in buckskins yelled out ribald suggestions to the muleteers and laughed heartily at his own wit.

The tallest structure in town was the hotel, two stories of whitewashed clapboard and logs. A neatly dressed young man with a thin mustache came to the counter when Renno rang the hand bell. The clerk looked curiously at the bronzed warrior, then let his eyes rest momentarily on the two Indian boys and Ah-wa-o.

"What can I do for you?" the young man asked.

"Three rooms," Renno answered.

The clerk glanced again at Gao, Ta-na, and Ah-wa-o. "And whom will these rooms be for?"

"For me and mine," Renno said.

Beth, who had become accustomed to the comfort of her own home, was looking forward to a bath in a tub. Standing beside Renno, she said, "My husband and I will occupy one room." She indicated El-i-chi and Ah-wa-o. "This couple will have a room. The boys will sleep with Mr. Johnson."

The clerk cleared his throat. "Lady," he said, "you and the white men are welcome. As for the Injuns—"

El-i-chi's hand flew to the handle of his tomahawk. Renno moved with the swiftness of a striking snake to seize the clerk by the shirtfront and lift him over the counter. "We will have three rooms," he said, holding the clerk's feet off the floor without seeming to exert any effort.

"Listen, mister," the clerk said, "it's not my policy. I just work here."

"Please, Renno," Beth said, putting her hand on Renno's arm.

He set the clerk on his feet.

"It would mean my job, mister, if I gave a room to Injuns," the clerk explained.

Renno's expression was dangerous.

"Renno, let's go," Beth urged, putting gentle pressure on his arm.

"Friend," Roy said in a soft voice, "might there be another hotel where we Indians might be allowed to pay good money for a sleeping bed and a bathtub?"

"I'm sorry," the clerk said, glancing nervously at El-i-chi. "Really I am."

"I think that means no, Roy," Beth said. She smiled up at Renno. "So we'll simply make camp somewhere outside town." She was disappointed, but she wanted desperately to get Renno and El-i-chi out of the hotel before they made someone pay dearly for the insult to Ah-wa-o and the boys.

"So," Renno grunted. He picked the clerk up, using

both hands this time, and set him down on the other side of the counter. "Good day to you, sir," he said.

Outside, Roy said, "There was a pretty place back up the trace about a mile. Good water, some graze for the horses . . ."

"So," Renno said again, still seething. He made a concerted effort to calm down, then waved his hand dismissively. "All right, Roy, all right. You take them there. Beth and I will stock up on provisions and get some grain for the horses, then join you before nightfall."

"I will go with you, Father," Ta-na offered.

"No, you go with El-i-chi," Renno said, patting his son on the head.

At the general store Beth began to gather the items needed to replenish their larder. Renno stood in the open door and stared moodily toward the hotel. Many times, in private conversations and in council, he had said that the future of all Indians lay with the United States, that sooner or later the Indian must adapt his life-style to that of the white man. But how could a man tell his son to become a member of the white man's society when the white man would not allow the Indian into his facilities? He had seen puzzled looks on the faces of his son and his nephew when they were turned away from the hotel, and it had pained him.

He could hear Beth chatting cheerfully with the storekeeper. Renno turned. The consumptive-looking fellow was obviously quite taken with Beth's green eyes and flame-colored hair. He asked a question or two, and Beth told him who she was and why she and the others were in Natchez.

After arranging for the storekeeper to send the purchases to the camp, Beth wanted to explore the town. She bought silken scarves for herself and Ah-wa-o, then a few pieces of hard-sugar candy for the boys. Renno's one purchase was for his father-by-marriage, a bottle of whiskey.

Without difficulty they located camp north of town. El-i-chi had left a marker of broken branches at the spot where he had left the trace. Roy accepted the whiskey with gratitude, offered the bottle around, and when no one accepted, he tilted it, drank deeply, said "Ah," and slapped the cork back in place with the palm of his hand.

Ah-wa-o had the evening meal preparation under way. Beth wrinkled her nose at the smell of roasting venison. Trail rations had a certain sameness. When she heard the rumble of wagon wheels on the trace coming toward Natchez, she brightened, for among the things she'd bought at the store were dried peaches. When boiled in water, they would make a welcome change from the diet of meat and nuts. Gao and Ta-na ran to the trace to guide the wagon to the camp. When two uniformed soldiers emerged into the clearing ahead of the wagon, Renno came to his feet slowly.

Both the soldiers were young. One had the stripes of a sergeant on his sleeve. "Sir," he said, "the storekeeper says that you're from the Cherokee Nation. Would you by any chance be the sachem Renno, of the Seneca?"

"I am," Renno said, nodding.

"Then I bring you greetings from General James Wilkinson, commander of this military district," the sergeant responded. "The general invites the sachem and his party to put up at headquarters and to have dinner with him."

Roy caught Renno's eye, and Renno knew what his father-by-marriage was thinking. Renno and Roy had exposed Wilkinson's treachery during Mad Anthony Wayne's Northwest Territory campaign. Wilkinson had been illegally selling supplies and munitions down the river to the Spanish in New Orleans instead of sending them north to Wayne and the American Legion.

Renno remained silent. Beth, filling the void, said, "Renno, I think it quite gracious of General Wilkinson to extend the invitation."

Renno looked at Roy, who shrugged. Both of them were thinking the same thing: James Wilkinson might or might not be aware of their role in stopping the shipment of American Legion supplies and arms to New Orleans.

"Might be a chance to get something into our bellies besides deer meat," Roy commented.

"I am instructed to guide you to your quarters," the sergeant said. "I'll have the wagon driver follow us and deliver your store supplies there."

"So," Renno said.

Gao and Ta-na, always ready for a new adventure, were quickly at work saddling the horses.

As the group set out, the two soldiers riding in the fore, Renno drew close to Roy. "I think we should exercise some caution in the good general's company."

"My thoughts exactly," Roy agreed.

After the two soldiers took the horses to the stables, Renno's group was given three rooms inside the stockade. The buildings had log walls chinked on the inside with plaster. The accommodations were not luxurious, but there were real beds and a washtub in each room.

Beth began to undress immediately and was soon sitting in the zinc tub, her knees up to her chin, trying to find room to lather herself with soap that she'd brought from home. Renno laughed at her contortions and squatted beside her to wash her back. When she stood in the tub to allow him to pour cold water over her body to rinse away the soap, the sheer wonder of her mature, shapely body made his throat constrict.

"Absolutely not, sir," she said, as his hands sought soft, cushiony curves. "You will not spoil the first real bath I've had since leaving home."

"Oh?"

"Now, Renno, you stop that."

He said nothing while pursuing his explorations.

She said in a soft, yielding voice, "Darn you. . . ."

After a bit of a delay she was just putting the finishing touches on her hair when Roy pounded on the door and yelled, "Victuals, folks. Come and get 'em."

General James Wilkinson, at forty-six, had become heavy and bald with age. Dressed in a regulation uniform, he greeted his guests politely, shaking the hands of the men, bending over Beth's and Ah-wa-o's hands with a courtly bow.

"Welcome to what will be, until December, the southernmost outpost of the United States," Wilkinson said.

"You honor us, General," Renno said.

"On the contrary," Wilkinson stated. "I am well aware of your contributions during our campaign in the Ohio country, Sachem, and of yours, Mr. Johnson. General Wayne speaks highly of you both. And, needless to say, any man acting as an emissary of President Jefferson is welcome here."

"Thank you, sir," Roy said. "You'll be going south, too, I imagine?"

"Indeed," Wilkinson confirmed. "Well, shall we go in?"

The table was of rough-hewn planks, but it was sturdy and laden with edibles. Wilkinson said grace before the meal, and Renno wondered if Wilkinson ever explained to his God why he committed treason against the United States.

Renno ate with a hearty appetite and listened to polite small talk carried on mainly by Beth and Wilkinson. The general was having difficulty keeping his eyes off the beautiful Englishwoman.

Wine was served. Everyone lifted a glass when Wilkinson offered an after-dinner toast to Mr. Jefferson and the new territory that was to become part of the United States. But only Beth and Roy drank.

Since no hostess was present to attend the ladies, the traditional separation of the sexes after dinner was not observed. Wilkinson asked Beth and Ah-wa-o if they minded if the men lit up at the table. Roy accepted a cigar. Swirls of smoke drifted upward in the lamplight.

Wilkinson's face, Renno concluded, was decadent and feminine. His lips were full, and he kept them pursed as if readying a kiss. He had thick lashes under dark, neatly pruned eyebrows.

"Well, Sachem, Roy," Wilkinson, said, "I'd be pleased if you and your party traveled with me down to New Orleans."

"Thank you for the offer, General," Roy replied.

"I'll be leaving in about two weeks," Wilkinson told them. "I daresay we can find ways to entertain you during that period."

Beth had clearly had enough of Wilkinson's eyes on her. He was the kind of man who made a woman feel unclean by the obvious lust in his expression. Not wanting to spend weeks in his company, she leaned forward before Renno responded to the general's invitation and said, "I know it would be very pleasant to travel with you, sir, and ever so safe with a military escort, but my husband promised me two weeks in New Orleans to see the sights and to shop. You wouldn't want to deprive me of that, would you, General?"

"I would not, lovely lady," Wilkinson said, "although I was looking forward to having your company during the journey." He puffed on his cigar. "You'll be leaving for New Orleans soon, then?"

"As soon as we can find a vessel going south," Renno said. He had visibly relaxed after Beth's intervention.

"That won't be hard," Wilkinson said. "There are a couple of flatboats overnighting here, as a matter of fact."

"General, I wonder if we could induce you to have our horses cared for here on the post," Beth requested sweetly.

"Of course," Wilkinson said.

Renno rose. Roy followed suit, saying, "Yep, it's been a long day, General, and we backwoods types like to be in bed with the chickens."

"Then I wish you all a pleasant good night," Wilkinson said, and escorted them to the door.

The general stood watching as his guests walked toward their quarters. He threw his cigar stub in a glowing arc, turned, and closed the door, then walked hurriedly down a hallway. He felt fevered. He was thinking of the creamy skin of Beth Huntington and deplored the waste of such womanhood on a savage. He went through his sitting room to a door that opened at the north end to yet another room, with a large, soft bed. Filled with desire, he opened the door but found the room empty.

"Damn you," he whispered.

He poured brandy and threw himself into a leather chair that he had brought down from the north. His thoughts wandered over the memories of the flame-haired woman until the bedroom door opened. He looked up.

"Where have you been?" he demanded.

The woman standing in the doorway was younger than Wilkinson. She had Gypsy-dark hair and odd, flashing eyes, which bored into Wilkinson's and made him forget his impatience. He looked at her hungrily. Since becoming Wilkinson's paramour she had fleshed out a bit, having been nothing much more than skin and bones upon her arrival in Natchez in the company of her silent, pockmarked brother, who soon became recognized as a loony one.

"I have been waiting for you," whispered Melisande, the witch who had come from the Pyrenean forests across the ocean. She opened her arms, exposing full, firm breasts. No man who looked into her eyes could resist her. With James Wilkinson, she had used her powers only briefly, for her natural sensuosity was enough to keep the general under control.

Of all the prominent rascals who had paraded across the brief pages of the history of the young United States, James Wilkinson was, perhaps, the most enigmatic. He had first become a man of authority and power in 1776, having entered the Continental army at the outbreak of the war. While serving under General Benedict Arnold in the Quebec campaign he met and became friends with another young officer, named Aaron Burr. Later in the war he was adjutant general under General Horatio Gates.

Wilkinson settled in Kentucky upon the arrival of peace and helped in the fight for Kentucky statehood. But in 1787 he took an oath of allegiance to Spain. He promised the Spanish governor in New Orleans to work with other frontiersmen to detach the western settlements from the United States and align them with Spanish Louisiana. During Anthony Wayne's Ohio campaign, "Number Thirteen," as Wilkinson was known to the Spanish, diverted badly needed arms and provisions from Wayne's army and actively tried to sabotage Wayne's war with the Ohio tribes both on the battlefield and in the political arenas of the east.

The federal government knew that Wilkinson received regular payments in gold and silver from Spain but oddly enough took no action against him. Renno, who discussed Wilkinson's perfidy with President George Washington, had been incredulous to learn that Wilkinson had been awarded his commission in the army in the hope that it would keep him out of mischief.

So it was that a traitor became a general and commanded the American troops who marched into Natchez when it was evacuated by the Spaniards. Now, in 1803, he was to be one of the commissioners to receive Louisiana from France in the ceremonies on December 20. On this October night, however, his mind was far from his duties as the senior military commander in the Southwest Territory. He had eyes only for the feminine charms of an odd woman whose teeth, when she was unaware of his scrutiny, seemed to be gleaming black jewels.

Melisande, the Witch of the Woods, performed her duty to Wilkinson in a leisurely manner, teasing and touching until the overweight general was gasping for breath. After he was sated and snoring loudly, she eased out of his quarters and ran lightly across the dark compound. She climbed wooden stairs to a room over the stables to join the man whom Wilkinson believed was her brother.

Inside, Othon Hugues, murderer, sadist, devil worshiper, and a deadly enemy of the white Indian, was lying on his bed. When he saw Melisande he leaped to his feet and knelt before her, his hands clutching her buttocks, his face pressed to the softness of her stomach.

"There, there," Melisande soothed, running her fingers through his hair.

Soon she was nude and abed with him. She willed her breasts to become fecund, and Othon drank from them greedily.

"He is here," Melisande told Othon when he had drunk his fill.

A low, feral growl rumbled from his throat.

"I saw him," she said. "The boy is not with him, but there are others." She cupped Othon's face in her hands and beamed at him, her black teeth gleaming. "And there are two tasty tidbits for you, my little love. One is tall and regal."

Othon moaned in need.

"With hair the color of an autumn sunset," Melisande went on. "The other is Indian but shapely."

"They will wait until after I have killed the yellow-haired sachem," Othon said. "Slowly."

"Yes," she agreed.

He sat up. "He is here," he said. "I'll do it tonight."

"Fool," she said, holding his arm. "You can't murder a man in the midst of almost a hundred soldiers."

Othon's pockmarked face twisted with frustration. He had not been the same man since he had been bested by Renno and drowned in the muddy waters of the Mississippi. The sensation of dying was never far from his mind. His lungs would feel engaged and heavy, as they had been as he sank slowly into the depths of the river.

"Soldiers," he said, dismissing them with a wave of his hand.

"My little love," she whispered, "I did not rescue you from the river and empty the water from your lungs to have you commit suicide. Go after him now, and you will be the one to die, either by his weapons or by those of the garrison. There is time. We have no need to hurry. They will travel to New Orleans, and then, after the ceremony, they will come back here. At some point during their journey we will give them an unexpected surprise."

"I cannot wait," Othon said, jerking away from her.

She moved to face him, then turned his eyes to hers. "You will come back to bed with me," she intoned.

He relaxed, for he, too, was susceptible to her powers.

"Come, make love to me, hold me, hurt me. You cannot truly damage me, little love. Come."

He lost himself in lust for her. She accepted him with her eyes open. As she studied the contortions of his pock-scarred face, she wondering if saving him had been worthwhile. She herself had almost died that day, for she had drained all her reserves of power first to locate him in the dark muddy waters of the Mississippi and then to drag him to shore. He had not been breathing when she put her mouth over his and forced her breath into him, and emptied him of water while chanting silently to her master, the sovereign of darkness.

But Othon and she had come a long, long way together, and he was amusing at times. The master had inspired him—she could not have invented the ingenious ways Othon had of giving pain. His talents, she promised herself, would be given full freedom when she delivered into his hands the bronzed man who called himself Renno.

Now Othon lay at her side, breathing softly. When she was sure that he was asleep she rose and bathed. Yes, they had come a long way together, and because he was still physically strong, he would be of use in spite of his near madness. Her powers and his strength would be a potent combination as she assisted James Wilkinson in the latest of his perennial plans to seize some portion of the American wilderness for his own. There, in a new country where she and Othon could never be punished for the murders and human sacrifices they had committed in New Orleans, she would build her empire, for Wilkinson was pleasingly helpless before her powers.

And there, in the wilderness, Othon could roam the forests, appeasing his strange passions with impunity. She had been keeping Othon on a close leash of late, for he was already infamous in the Choctaw and Creek villages along the river. Mothers frightened their children into obedience with threats of the unearthly beast of the forests, the spirit thing that mutilated before killing.

Melisande, like Othon, was offended by the very thought of Renno's being so near and alive. But she, more so than Othon, remembered not only Renno's skill with weapons but the fact that he had the aid of the powers of good. He alone had withstood the force of her witchcraft. He had fought and won against all the imps of evil that she could bring up from the regions ruled by the master. The white Indian had entered her home in New Orleans and had lived to escape from the very citadel of evil. And on the bank of the Mississippi he had fought legions of demons and had almost killed Othon. This time she would be more careful. This time she would not allow Othon to battle him face-to-face.

The next day she watched from concealment as Renno and his party boarded a flatboat and floated downriver.

On that day she began a campaign to get Wilkinson's help in killing the white Indian and all those who traveled with him. To get Wilkinson's agreement was easy, but to plant the idea firmly in his mind so that he would not waver required more effort.

"I have no objection to seeing the Seneca dead," Wilkinson told her. "Once, he and the white man with him, Roy Johnson, interfered in a certain enterprise of mine and caused me no small problem. But, my dear, we must not let our desire for vengeance cloud our purpose, which is to accomplish the peaceful transfer of Louisiana to the United States. At the moment it is more important to weaken Spain than to kill this Seneca, for the basis for Spanish lands will become our empire."

"I know the importance of what you say," she told him while stroking him tenderly. "But my blood boils when I think of Renno."

"Do with him as you please after the ceremony, but not before," Wilkinson warned.

"Would you help me in this?" Melisande asked, her lips brushing his skin.

"It can be arranged for him to meet a small detachment of carefully selected soldiers from my command. We will say later that my men mistook him for the renegades who have been spreading terror in the Indian villages."

"Thank you, James," Melisande whispered. Later she would arrange to have the white Indian and those with him captured and turned over to her and Othon, rather than shot down by soldiers.

Winter had come to the Hudson Valley. The cadets' uniforms were no match for the frigid air that swept down from the wastes of Canada to send their winds howling around the old fort at West Point. Little Hawk found himself wishing for the bearskin cloak that hung in his father's longhouse or even for a good, woolen blanket.

The young man was feeling restless. Since his riverside discussion with the big cadet from Georgia, Sidney Forrest, no one had questioned his authority as a cadet officer. The inclement weather limited fieldwork, and classwork gave him little challenge. He had received one letter, in Beth's hand, from home. She informed him that his father and she would be going to New Orleans for a short stay. By the time the letter got to West Point, he calculated that his stepmother and Renno were already in the city at the mouth of the Father of Waters. He envied them; it would be far less cold there in the South. He wished he could join them, not so much to visit New Orleans but for the enjoyment of the trip home, for the days on the trail and evenings with a campfire burning and meat roasting. He had a good case of homesickness when he was informed that he was invited to have dinner with the commanding officer and his family.

Major John Lillie's family consisted of his daughter, Mary Ann, and a lively little dog named Bedford. Dinner was generous: chicken, beans, potatoes, and corn bread. Dessert, Little Hawk found with mixed emotions—sheer terror and undeniable need—was Mary Ann Lillie.

The opportunity presented itself quite by accident. The family had finished dinner and Mary Ann was clearing the table when the officer of the guard arrived at the commander's house with the news that one of the men had fallen and broken his leg nastily.

"Harper, if you'll excuse me—?" Lillie said.

"Perhaps I could be of some help, sir," Little Hawk offered.

"No. I won't be long. You stay with Mary Ann, if you don't mind."

He was gone before Little Hawk could say that he did, in fact, mind being left alone with Mary Ann. Since the day he'd had his discussion with Forrest on the rocky point, it seemed to him that Mary Ann made it a point to run into him. At such times he had been polite but cool. She had warned that her father would skin any cadet that he caught "messing around" with his daughter. Little Hawk had no desire to be skinned, and he wanted very badly to graduate from West Point and to take up his duty, whatever it might be.

"I think that it was very considerate of that soldier to break his leg," Mary Ann said as her father slammed the door on his way out. "Perfect timing, don't you agree?"

Little Hawk rose and walked to the front window.

She came up beside him and closed the curtains. "I know why you've been avoiding me," she said.

He looked down at her.

She smiled. She smelled good, and her skin seemed to glow with health. He decided that her hair had the clean, fresh fragrance of vanilla.

"You're afraid of my father," she said.

"That I readily admit," he said with a laugh.

"But he isn't here now." She stood on tiptoe, and her lips were almost even with his.

He felt himself trembling with the need to kiss her.

"He can be back any minute," he said, but his voice was low, weak, as weak as his resolve.

Her kiss was slow fire and honey. Her slim body molded to him perfectly. He could feel the hardness of her thighs as she pressed against him, the softness of her stomach, and, most wonderfully, her sweet breasts.

He pushed her away, gasping for breath. She came back and put her mouth on his. He moved again. "Mary Ann—"

"Oh, shut up," she said fiercely.

He sank into her kiss, and the rest of the world didn't matter. She made no protest when his hands explored her. Instead, she took his arm and led him out of the dining room and into the parlor, where she guided him to a large couch. He didn't know exactly how it happened, but he found himself atop her, her dress and petticoats bunched at her waist, his trousers around his ankles.

"Don't worry," she whispered as he found that little bit of heaven on earth that only a girl can provide for a lusty boy turning into a man. "We can hear him as he comes onto the porch."

There were no more words, only her long, pleased sighings, a little moan as she clung to him. His own release was simultaneous with hers. After a few minutes of happy recovery, he raised himself off the couch and struggled with his clothing.

"You don't have to be in such a hurry to leave," she said accusingly.

"I thought I heard—"

"You did not," she said, standing and straightening her clothes.

"Look, Mary Ann—"

"There's a drainpipe that comes directly to my bedroom window," she told him. "You'll have no trouble at all climbing it, and my father sleeps like a log."

"To be caught away from the barracks after lights out is serious."

She frowned. "So now that you've had your way with me I mean nothing to you."

"Don't say that," he protested. "It's just that I have certain responsibilities. As cadet officer, I must set an example for the other men. I can't just—"

But she was pressing against him, looking up into his face, her mouth red from his kissing.

He kissed her and sighed, then asked, "What time does your father go to sleep?"

"He's snoring by nine o'clock."

"Oh, manitous," he whispered to himself as he kissed her again just as they both heard the heavy tread of boots on the front porch. They were sitting demurely in chairs facing each other when Lillie came in. Little Hawk rose to his feet.

"Sorry," the major said. "The surgeon needed my help in setting the man's leg." He yawned and looked at the big grandfather clock standing against one wall. As if on cue the clock gonged the half hour, eight-thirty.

"Sir, I enjoyed the dinner very much, and I thank you for inviting me."

"Like to keep in contact with my cadet officers," Lillie said. "Keep up the good work, Harper."

Little Hawk's cheeks burned with guilt as he left the commander's home.

The weather had been mild in the eastern portion of the Cherokee hunting grounds where Rusog, husband of Ena, brother-by-marriage of Renno and El-i-chi, was principal chief. Perhaps as a result of the good weather, there had been more than the usual number of visitors, both white and Indian. Many came to see the big, rambling house that Roy Johnson had christened Huntington Castle. But in December the delegation of white men from Nashville who requested a meeting with Chief Rusog were not sightseers. They had come with purpose, a purpose with which Rusog was overly familiar.

At the request of the officials from the state of Tennessee, Rusog called a council of senior warriors and village chiefs. They met in the men's house in Rusog's village. A few of the Pine Trees of the Seneca, senior warriors experienced both in war and in dealing with the white man, were asked to attend. Ena asked Toshabe to sit beside her in her place at Rusog's side, for Toshabe was the senior matron of her tribe. Ena's daughter, We-yo, sat on her other side.

For the first time in formal council Rusog's son, the male half of twins, sat proudly to his right. Ho-ya was fourteen. He combined the powerful build of his father with the graceful litheness of his mother. Unlike his sister, We-yo, his skin showed only a hint of his one-quarter of white blood. He was half-Cherokee, with one-quarter Seneca from his mother's side. The boy was willing to fight anyone who mentioned that he had the blood of the white Indian flowing in him, for the word *white* overpowered, in his mind, the word *Indian*. He took his turn with the pipe when it was passed, then folded his arms and glanced sideways at his father to see that Rusog's face was impassive. He let his eyes linger on the three white men who had come from the capital of the state of Tennessee.

The spokesman for the envoys was impatient and began talking before the pipe had made its rounds. Rusog held up one hand for silence, but the spokesman didn't understand until an older man, at his side, tugged on his sleeve and put one finger to his lips.

Ho-ya was laughing inside in derision, although his face showed nothing. His father lifted both hands and in a sonorous voice began speaking in Cherokee. Rusog was deliberately being very formal, and Ho-ya realized that his father intended to deliver a long oration before giving the visitors an opportunity to speak. He glanced at his mother. Ena was sitting stiffly, her eyes unblinkingly focused on the men from Nashville. Ho-ya followed her example, and although his eyeballs began to tickle with the need to blink, he refrained.

The white men shifted uneasily. The older man beside the spokesman was whispering a translation as Rusog spoke of the ancient friendship between the Cherokee and the great men of Tennessee. He mentioned Colonel Roy Johnson of the Tennessee Militia and spoke at length of General Andrew Jackson. And all the while the spokesman was squirming, waiting for Rusog to get to the point.

The sun had moved in a two hours' arc in the sky before Rusog finished recounting the history of the Cherokee Nation and its relationship with the white man. He threw in colorful Indian phrases such as "as many as the lights in the sky" and "as long as rivers run and grass grows." But he never mentioned the one fact that most colored his own feelings toward the white man: that once he had been accused of murder and had almost been hanged before his innocence could be established.

When at last he finished, the white men sighed in relief and sat up straighter, only to slump again when Rusog called upon the village chiefs one by one. The chiefs spoke in powerful voices, used extravagant hand motions, and repeated many of the things that Rusog had said about the history of the tribe and its relationship with its white neighbors. By the time each chief had spoken, the sun had traveled another two-hour arc. At last there was silence in the men's house.

The official from Nashville said, "Chief Rusog, we salute the great Cherokee Nation and hail all Cherokee as friends and allies." He halted, and the translator spoke Cherokee so poorly that the warriors on either side of Rusog's family leaned forward trying to catch the meaning. Rusog let it go on that way for a couple of minutes, then raised his hand. In perfect English, with an accent influenced by his long association with the family of the white Indian, he said, "Gentlemen, I don't want you to feel bad, but I'm afraid your Cherokee isn't very good."

The face of the spokesman went beet red, and he whispered to the translator, but so loudly that Ho-ya heard, "Why that old son of a bitch."

Ho-ya stiffened at the insult. Rusog's face showed no change of expression as he said, "It is understandable that you have difficulty with the language of the Cherokee. You see, it is a living language, not yet set in its final form by being imprisoned by the written word, although"—he winked at Se-quo-i—"there is one among us who is trying, even now, to do just that. This one tells me that Cherokee is actually simpler than English, in that it uses fewer sounds. Perhaps it is this simplicity that makes it so difficult for most white men." He gave them a little smile. "We will converse in English, for your convenience. Most of the people here will understand, not having limited themselves to knowing only one language."

The spokesman was sputtering when he realized that he had been given the floor. Because of his anger he got to the point even more quickly than he had intended.

After the guest had finished, Rusog nodded knowingly, then looked all around, into the face of each member of his family, the Seneca senior warriors, the Cherokee chiefs and warriors. "It is as I told you," he said in English. "The white officials from our neighbor the state of Tennessee visit us only when they think that it is time to take more of our land."

"Chief Rusog—" the spokesman protested, then went silent when Rusog held up both hands and gave him the same look he might have accorded an enemy over the blade of a tomahawk.

"Do you deny that you are here to ask for what you call a renegotiation of our last treaty with you?" Rusog asked.

"No, I don't deny that," the spokesman said. "But it is not as simple as that."

"In Cherokee, which is, as I have told you, a simple language, we could state your purpose in only one way. That would be, 'Give me more of your lands, Cherokee.'"

Grunts of approval came from the warriors. Ena allowed herself one very Caucasian smile.

"This is my son," Rusog said, putting his hand on Ho-ya's arm. "And there is my daughter. What will they say to my ghost when I negotiate away their heritage? What will their children say to my ghost if, by the time they are born, the white man has cleared their forests and made plowed fields of their hunting grounds?" He held up his hand to prevent any reply, then turned to Ho-ya.

"Speak, my son, for the first time in the council of men."

When Ho-ya spoke up, he clipped his words as he'd heard his aunt Beth and his uncle Renno do, for he had just learned a lesson from his father: it was no shame to be able to speak the white man's language. In fact, it could be a great advantage. It had pleased him and amused him to hear his father have his joke at the white man's expense.

"My father, my voice is still small, for I am not yet a warrior, but I will gladly use it to cry out loudly and tell the men from Tennessee: no more. Come to us no more with your demands for the lands of our ancestors. If you call us friends and allies, then you must act accordingly. Friends do not try to drive friends from their traditional hunting grounds and from their homes!"

When the white men were gone, Rusog, Ena, Ho-ya, and We-yo escorted Toshabe back to her longhouse in the Seneca village, which adjoined Rusog's.

"You spoke well, Rusog," Toshabe said.

"Coming from you, Mother, who have heard the great orators of both our tribes, that fills my heart," Rusog said.

"And you, Grandson," Toshabe said. "You spoke with the wisdom of a man."

Ho-ya bowed his head in acknowledgment.

"And we will hold them back . . . for a while longer," Toshabe predicted.

"Forever," Ho-ya said with fire in the word.

"No," Toshabe said. "And I pray, Grandson, that you will not make the mistake of fighting the inevitable."

"I *will* fight," Ho-ya said. "And there are others who will fight."

"In all probability that is true," Toshabe agreed sadly. "There are always more men willing to fight than men willing to do what is necessary for peace."

"You speak thus, Grandmother, because my uncle

the sachem advises us to become a part of the white man's world," Ho-ya said.

"And Renno has seen much more of this world than you have," Ena reminded.

"So," Ho-ya said. He knew that it was not advisable to continue the discussion. His mother seemed to agree with his uncle Renno. As for his father? Ho-ya believed that in the end Rusog would fight to keep his lands and dignity. And Ho-ya himself hungered for the feel of a blade in his hand, for the pale skin of the. enemy under the blade.

Chapter Four

At least one Frenchman was aghast when he learned that Napoleon had sold a major portion of the North American continent to the United States for the sum of fifteen million dollars. The comte de Beaujolais, younger brother of Louis, duc d'Orleans, was at sea when the world was informed that an upstart nation on the far side of the Atlantic had doubled its geographical size with a few sweeps of the nib of a pen. Beau, as he was called by the slim, tanned, fair-haired young lady who was his wife, was going home to France after adventures that had carried him from the now lost French colony in Haiti to New Orleans, then up the Natchez Trace to the home of the Seneca sachem and the English milady who were his new in-laws. From the lands to the west of the Great Smoky Mountains, Beau and his wife, Renna, had traveled by foot, horse, and coach to Wilmington, North Carolina. There they boarded a ship owned by the Huntington Shipping Company.

The family of the white Indian became more widely

separated with each watery league as Beth Huntington's newest transoceanic trader sailed eastward. Renna, who would observe her seventeenth birthday just off Land's End, did not know that her father and stepmother were en route to New Orleans, putting the length of the United States between father and son. She knew only the almost unimaginable distance that separated her from the beloved faces and familiar places of her childhood.

Not one of the ship's company would have guessed that the pale-haired and beautiful countess was so young, for she carried herself with the poise of the true sophisticate, spoke English with an elegant, aristocratic accent and a French that was touched by the often charming colorations acquired by generations of French explorers, trappers, and hunters in the great American wilderness.

Ever since the days when Renna could be found rolling on the ground after violent collisions with her cousins in games of Cherokee stickball, she had matured past girlish thinness. Womanly hips curved admirably outward from a small waist. Her bust was pert, youthful, and noticeable. Her fair hair, corn-silk pale, radiated delicate yellow-gold highlights. It had the thickness of the hair of her paternal grandmother, Toshabe, which made it easy for her to wear it in becoming, upswept styles. Her eyes, with lashes and eyebrows darker than her pale hair, gleamed with a striking exuberance. Her eyes smiled for the most part, even when her full lips did not; but, like the eyes of her father, Renna's could become as cold as the blue ice of the southern oceans.

When the ship fought her way into the English Channel and out of raging storm winds into safe harbor, the uneasy peace that existed between France and England was intact. Beau had agreed to spend some time in England so that Renna could visit with her uncle-by-marriage, William, Lord Beaumont, and his wife, Estrela. Since Renna was eager to see the man who was her stepmother's brother, Beau immediately hired a coach to take them to the family manor Suffolk, in the southeast of London.

Although she had not seen Lord Beaumont since she was a babe in arms, which hardly counted, Renna felt that she knew her uncle-by-marriage, having heard so much about him from Beth and Renno.

After Renna and Beau were admitted to the old manor house by a stiff, formal butler, the young woman hurried forward and surprised William mightily by giving him a quick embrace, which was delightful, William found, but a bit too familiar when compared with the behavior he was used to. But then the striking Renna introduced herself, and William laughed and returned the hug.

Then Estrela, dark and still magnificently beautiful, welcomed Renna with a warm kiss on the cheek. Beau and William bowed stiffly. Beau brushed his lips close to Estrela's hand.

Formalities over, William was so full of questions that Renna still held the floor during dinner, telling William and Estrela all about Beth's great house in the Cherokee Nation and bringing William up-to-date on El-i-chi and the others whom he remembered with such fondness. She told Estrela all that she knew about Adan, Estrela's brother, who now managed Beth's maritime business in Wilmington.

After she and Beau described their experiences in the ill-fated French colony in the Caribbean, Beau talked about the vastness of the American West. Not once did he mention Renna's encounter with Othon Hugues, and for that she was grateful. As brave as she—the daughter of the white Indian—was, she wanted only to forget the horror of twice being in the power of the evil Frenchman.

"Now that France has taken Spain's American possessions," Beau said, "there will be a third power in North America."

William looked at Estrela with raised eyebrows before saying, "But haven't you heard, Comte, that Napoleon has sold all of the French possessions in North America to the United States?"

"Ah, well." Beau sighed. Renna reached for his hand to ease his obvious distress. "But it was Frenchmen who found those lands," he protested. "Frenchmen were the first on the Mississippi. No one knew Louisiana like the coureurs de bois, the ragged men of the woods.

They claimed it, and they fought for it." He sighed again. "True, it was all lost on the plains before Quebec, but—" His brow knitted in puzzlement. "Napoleon took it all back from Spain." He pounded his fist on the table. "To give it away? To sell it?"

"Perhaps you can blame it on the comte de Buffo and others like Voltaire and the abbé Reynal," William said. "Buffo said—"

"Who is this Buffo?" Estrela asked.

"Sorry, dear," William said. "The comte de Buffo was possibly the greatest naturalist of the eighteenth century. He said that the two American continents were, quite literally, a New World, having been the last landmasses to emerge from the waters of the Noachian flood."

"What on earth has that to do with anything?" Estrela asked.

"Then he said that since the waters had only recently receded, America was nothing more than a swamp with cold and miasmal air. Thus, the natives were cold, the animals runty."

"Then he never saw a black bear in a fighting stance," Renna said, laughing.

"Voltaire and the abbé Reynal went even further," William said. "Voltaire said that because the American Indian had no facial hair, he lacked the . . . uh, shall we say amative powers of the European. The lions of America, he said, have no manes and are thus cowardly." He fell silent, then smiled. "I was just remembering the time that Renno was forced to kill two mountain lions that were attacking an Apache boy."

Beau was fuming. "This is madness, basing the transfer of lands on erroneous information."

"I agree," William sympathized. "Reynal was even more damning in his appraisals of the New World and its peoples." He grinned at Estrela and said, "For a man of God, he had a rather extraordinary interest in erotic matters. He said that the beardless men, meaning the Indians, showed indifference to women because of some organic imperfection."

Renna laughed. Estrela, blushing, hid her face behind a black, lacy fan.

"It's quite clear why France lost America," William said. "She failed to populate the lands discovered and claimed by the coureurs de bois. The government and the people of France listened to men like Reynal and Voltaire instead of to the explorers. North America might well be French or French-Indian if the people in the home country had read more of the writings of men such as Radisson, Delisle, and Champlain."

"If you will pardon my saying so," Beau commented, "that might have been to the benefit of the Indian. You see, we French never looked down on the original population. Our men became friends with the Indian and intermarried freely."

"We have a perfect example of that here," Renna said, laughing.

"But my dear," Beau told her, "I do have so much difficulty thinking of you as an Indian."

"I am Seneca," Renna said.

"The most beautiful Seneca in the world," Beau agreed.

William laughed. "With your complexion, Renna, and your hair, if you tell the people of France that you are Indian, they'll begin to wonder if Baron Lohontan wasn't right."

"You'll have to excuse my husband," Estrela said. "He's showing off for you, proving that he's well read on the subject of America."

"Better read than I," Renna admitted. "Who was this baron, Uncle William?"

"Somewhat of a rascal and most definitely a prevaricator," William answered. "Early in the eighteenth century, he wrote that he had discovered a tribe of American Indians who spoke Welsh. They were, he claimed, descendants of Prince Madoc, who, in Welsh legend, sailed to lands far to the west. The Welsh Indians lived on the River Longue. Lohontan even included a map in his *New Voyages to North America*, showing that the Longue flowed all the way to the west coast and the Pacific."

"I once had the ambition to travel to the Pacific," Beau said. "When my brothers and I were traveling in the Southwest Territory—on the trip that led me to see Renna for the first time—we often talked about making our home in America. We had nothing left in France. The Revolution had taken all. Our father, who had supported the Revolution, had been beheaded as a reward. Napoleon was just another general in the Army of the Republic."

"And what changed your mind?" William inquired.

"Hunger," Beau admitted with a wide smile. "We were often without food or money. We depended upon the hospitality of the Americans. They were quite nice to us, but they were not always handy at mealtime." He laughed.

The talk turned to the friction that was growing again between France and England. Napoleon, master of the Continent, was not satisfied, and he knew that he could not claim total victory without first defeating England. He was massing ships on the Channel coast, for the only way to beat England once and for all was by invasion.

"I'm sure that all of this makes the government quite nervous," William said. "I'll admit that it is disquieting to know that Napoleon controls the entire continental coast-line from Genoa to Antwerp."

"Will there be war, Uncle William?" Renna asked.

"At the moment the diplomats are busy trying to form new European alliances," William replied.

"I will not hear this talk of war," Estrela said vigorously.

"Well, you may be forced to hear it, my dear," William said sadly.

"I fear so," Beau agreed. "He is an ambitious man, our Napoleon."

"Men of good sense can prevent war," Estrela said, "but I will light a candle in the chapel tonight and pray for peace. And I will pray that my husband and our new friend, the comte de Beaujolais, will never have to face each other in battle."

"Hear, hear!" William said as Beau nodded vigorously.

Thanks to a swift passage by flatboat down the Missis-sippi, Beth was to have more than two weeks in New

Orleans before the ceremony of transfer on December 20. They found accommodations in a hotel that had no objections to renting rooms to Indians.

It took Beth only a few days to come to love the city. She led the way in scouting out little restaurants where the specialty was French cuisine. She stormed shops and stores under full sail, hauling Ah-wa-o along with her.

Ah-wa-o enjoyed the rich, savory foods, but she steadfastly refused to allow Beth to dress her in European clothing. She wore a bleached white buckskin skirt and tunic with the usual Seneca accessories. So it was, by circulation, by being seen in the best places, that the red-haired Beth and the dark-haired Seneca beauty became the sensation of New Orleans. Dinner invitations from New Orleans's elite flooded into the hotel.

El-i-chi, who appreciated the occasional joke on the white man, joined Renno in wearing morning clothes, dapper street suits, and formal evening wear. Ta-na and Gao, given their freedom, spent time exploring the city, then usually came back to their room at mealtime, to talk excitedly about the odd and peculiar ways of the white man.

Roy Johnson, after eating at two or three of the French restaurants chosen by Beth, went off in search of "some real food."

"The Frenchies," he complained, "use all that rich sauce to cover up the taint of spoiled meat."

Renno's weapons, except for the Toledo steel Spanish stiletto that never left him, remained in his room, although he could remember clearly having encountered danger in the so-called civilized city. There he had fought Othon Hugues and the Witch of the Woods for the first time and had left the field of battle with the outcome undecided—a most rare occurrence.

Renno learned that General James Wilkinson had arrived in New Orleans with an army escort and set up his headquarters in a Spanish municipal building. He sent out invitations to a wide range of people, the Seneca contingent among them, to attend a preceremony ball. El-i-chi expressed the opinion that he'd about as soon watch a boar hog urinate as go to a formal ball.

Ah-wa-o, however, rebelled. "These things you and Renno have done during your travels," the little Rose said, "but I have not. I would like to attend the ball."

"You have done some traveling," El-i-chi said. "As a matter of fact, I danced with you, more than once, in Beth's house in Wilmington when you were but a girl."

"That is true," the Rose admitted, "but it was not a formal ball. And, Husband, you look so handsome in the white man's fancy clothes."

Roy remarked that since he didn't have a wife to tease him into going, he'd send his regrets to the general. Beth promptly accepted that challenge and by dint of sheer flattery and coaxing had Roy in a store trying on evening clothes before the day was out.

Some eyebrows were raised when El-i-chi, who could have been a sun-bronzed white man, came into the hall with a beautiful woman on his arm. Her flowing, white formal gown was European, but she obviously was not. New Orleans, however, was a cosmopolitan town. As noted by Beau far away in England, the French in the old city had intermarried with Indians and had cohabited with black slaves to produce a class of Creoles, many of whom had worked their way into New Orleans society. In general, the citizens of New Orleans, having lived under several flags, were more tolerant of the native Americans than were the people of the United States. Unlike many who lived on the turbulent western frontiers of the nation, most of the people in New Orleans had not seen the results of a savage Indian raid . . . had not lost a friend or a relative to the cruel and bloody struggles over land that dated back to the time of the first white settlements in North America.

James Wilkinson had fought Indians. He had seen what remained of a white prisoner of the Shawnee after the squaws and children finished with him. There was no doubt in his mind that the Indian, regardless of tribe, was a lesser human being, a throwback to the age of savagery. Watching Beth whirl around the floor in the arms of a man who, in spite of his white blood, professed to be an Indian, made Wilkinson angry. It was, he felt, a crime to waste that beauty on a savage who, for the night, was playing at being a white man.

At the first opportunity the general asked Beth for a dance. He led her onto the floor after signaling the orchestra to play a waltz, a dance that was still considered by many to be vulgar. Wilkinson's arm went around Beth, and they whirled away. He was a good dancer in spite of being overweight. When the music ended he offered Beth refreshments. She walked with him into a room where tables were laden with punch bowls and trays filled with the finest delicacies that New Orleans could provide. Beth chose a nonalcoholic punch. She nibbled at the hors d'oeuvres.

Wilkinson stood quite close. "I have never seen a more beautiful woman," he said, blowing his hot breath onto the back of her neck.

She moved away and turned to face him.

"I know New Orleans well," he continued. "It would be my pleasure to lay the city at your feet." He knew she was no ingenuous girl who had never been flattered, and he felt encouraged when she smiled.

"I feel, General, that I've already had the city at my feet, having walked over a good portion of its streets."

"I can open many doors for you, my dear," he offered, leering knowingly.

"Yes, I imagine you could," Beth said.

"If, by some chance, the sachem should be too busy to escort you to see the finer things that New Orleans has to offer—"

"The sachem, my husband, has been very kind," she said. "He, too, knows the city quite well."

"Well, yes," Wilkinson replied, beginning to know doubt. "But—"

"But you know it better?" Beth asked sweetly.

"Perhaps," he said. "I imagine I can go places that an, uh, a man of the frontier cannot go."

"Such as?" Beth asked.

"Well, for example," he explained, edging closer, "there are certain forms of, uh, entertainment, um, performances, that are not open to just anyone who might walk past the door. I would think that a woman of your sophistication would like to sample *everything* the city has to offer."

"Would that entertainment feature both male and female performers?" Beth asked with a tight little smile.

"Exactly," Wilkinson replied, beaming. "I think you'll find it quite stimulating, my dear."

Beth was still smiling. "General," she said, "your suggestion is as abhorrent to me as your continued presence."

"I beg your pardon?"

"I was under the impression that I was speaking quite clearly," she said. "Will you understand if I say that I find you contemptible?"

Wilkinson's face flushed bright red. He opened his mouth, but only a sputter came out. He turned and walked away to fill his glass from a punch bowl that was definitely alcoholic. When he turned around, the red-haired bitch was gone.

There were, he consoled himself, many more women in New Orleans, many of whom would be thrilled to be in the company of the senior military commander of the Southwest Territory and a commissioner of the Louisiana Territory. He encountered what he thought was one of them almost immediately.

During his time on the frontier he had occasionally accepted the favors of Indian girls. Some of them he had found to be a bit odoriferous, for they used some rather strange unguents for their skin and hair. This woman, however, seemed to have been cleaned up nicely.

Ah-wa-o had allowed Beth to purchase a ball gown and all the accessories for her. She was having some difficulty adjusting to the footwear, since she was accustomed to wearing soft, yielding moccasins. But, she decided, a little discomfort was a small price to pay, for it was grand to see all the city's finest ladies in a rainbow of colors and the stiffly dressed, elegant gentlemen. She had left El-i-chi standing near a window to get some fresh air and was on her way to the refreshment room when she encountered General Wilkinson.

She could not predict what Wilkinson's attitude toward her might be. She knew that Renno and Roy had little regard for the general, but he had been polite enough to her in Natchez. When he asked her to dance she told him, with genuine regret, that she had never learned the white man's dances.

"That is no great loss," Wilkinson said.

"I was on my way to find something to drink," she said.

"Come," Wilkinson invited. He took Ah-wa-o's arm and led her to the bowl with the potent punch, poured a cup, and handed it to her.

She sniffed it and said, "I don't take alcohol, General."

"One must learn to experience new things," Wilkinson encouraged. "Try it."

"No," she said. "I don't share your sense of adventure."

He shrugged and led her to the other table. She drank a mixture of fruit juices, put down the cup, and said, "Thank you."

"It's getting quite stuffy in here," Wilkinson remarked.

"Yes," she agreed.

He took her arm. "Come, then. We'll walk in the gardens and have some air."

"Thank you, no," Ah-wa-o said, resisting.

He jerked her arm. "Oh, come on," he said. "You'll enjoy it."

She walked a few paces with him, his hand on her arm.

"As a matter of fact," he said, "this affair has become quite dull. I don't think they'll miss us. I just happen to know a place quite near here where a very handsome couple of Creoles put on a show of dancing—and other things—that I think you'll find quite amusing."

Ah-wa-o jerked her arm away. "I don't care to walk, General Wilkinson," she said, coming to a stop.

"Fine, fine," he soothed. "I'll have them bring my carriage around."

"I do not care to go to see this dancing," she told him.

"My dear, you don't know what you're missing." He took her hand. "Take my word for it. Trust me. You will enjoy it immensely."

Once again he was forcing her along, lifting her so

that she had to tiptoe. She jerked away, and in her hand there appeared a short, thin knife. "I have said that I do not care to go with you either to walk or to ride," she said, her face expressionless, her eyes unblinking. "If you put your hand on my arm again, you will risk losing one or more fingers."

"You dare threaten me, squaw?" Wilkinson asked, moving closer. He danced back as Ah-wa-o sliced the air dangerously close to the protruding front of his waistcoat.

"You savage," he squealed, lifting his hand.

Ah-wa-o turned away, not running but moving swiftly.

Wilkinson, his face burning, let her go. She was replacing the small, deadly dagger in the hiding place at her waist.

On the morning of December 20 a gathering of dignitaries including General Wilkinson, Renno and El-i-chi, and representatives of the Spanish, French, and United States governments stood in the square before the old Spanish headquarters building to watch the flag of the United States being run up over New Orleans. There were, of course, speeches.

Wilkinson introduced the guests, naming Renno and El-i-chi as Seneca allies and friends of the United States. The small force of U.S. troops passed in review. A twenty-one-gun salute was fired. The flag of France was folded with care and presented to the French representative. And then the ceremony was over.

Renno and El-i-chi closed in on Wilkinson as he shook hands with other dignitaries and well-wishers from the crowd. They waited until the crowd around Wilkinson thinned. Renno stood to the general's right, El-i-chi on the left.

"You spoke to my wife last night," El-i-chi said.

"Why, yes," Wilkinson said. "She was alone. I got her some refreshments."

"And offered to escort her to see one of the performances for which the city is well-known in some circles?" El-i-chi asked.

"Ah, I may have, er, invited her to—"

"Don't ever speak to her again," El-i-chi ordered.

"Don't ever lay a hand on her, even politely, or you will go through the rest of your life without that hand."

"Now you listen—" Wilkinson began. He felt Renno's hand on his shoulder and suddenly experienced intense pain as Renno's fingers dug deeply to find a nerve.

"It is beyond my understanding why the United States has not hanged you," Renno whispered into Wilkinson's ear. "Be that as it may, insult my wife again, and I will take it upon myself to rid the world of your presence."

Wilkinson gasped and slumped as Renno released his grip. The two warriors strolled away nonchalantly. Wilkinson, rubbing his shoulder, reviewed what Renno had said. The remark confirmed the general's guess that two of Anthony Wayne's scouts, Renno and Roy Johnson, had exposed and quashed his profitable business of selling U.S. Army property to the Spanish before the Battle of Fallen Timbers. He had not been sure until now. He had underestimated them, discounting Johnson as a Tennessee rustic and Renno as just another Indian. He knew at this moment that he'd been wrong. He had not been keen on doing as Melisande asked. But now, with his shoulder sending lances of fiery pain throughout his body, he wanted more than anything to see Renno dead. He would grant with pleasure Melisande's desire.

Following the ceremony a fine surprise awaited Renno and the others. Adan Bartolome, manager of Beth's maritime business, had come to New Orleans to get a head start on making commercial contacts. Because the new American city was at the mouth of the Mississippi, it would be, he believed, the country's busiest port.

First Adan had encountered an old friend of his youth, Julio Ronda de Alda, who, he learned, had settled in the New Spain Territory north of the Rio Grande. De Alda had become the hidalgo of a ranch as big as Connecticut and Rhode Island put together.

Then, to his surprise, Adan spotted Renno and El-i-chi on the reviewing stand. He caught up with them as they re-joined the women and the boys. After greetings of genuine fondness, Adan introduced de Alda and told Renno the location of the Spaniard's holdings.

"I think that my brother and I once traveled quite near your ranch on our way to Corpus Christi," Renno remarked.

"From inland?" de Alda asked incredulously.

Renno nodded.

"You came from Apache country?"

"From the desert," El-i-chi said, "where the men of old built cities of dried mud atop mesas."

"Dios," de Alda breathed. "Fantastic. But you would have been to the south of my ranch, I think."

"Interesting country," Renno said.

The reunion adjourned to the decks of the *Seneca Cloud*. The ship's cook, having availed himself of the plenty of the New Orleans shops, served up a side of roasted beef. Adan handed out an extra ration of rum to the crew.

Beth and Adan disappeared into the captain's cabin to go over ledger books and to talk business. Meanwhile, Julio de Alda asked the brothers questions about the lands to the west of his ranch in the arid territory of the Apache.

"I'm sorry I missed that trip," Roy said after hearing Renno's and El-i-chi's descriptions. "I always had a hankering to see some of that country." He chuckled. "Of course I wouldn't expect to find a mountain of gold, the way Renno and El-i-chi did, but it would have been mighty fine just to see that desert, and the plains where you can see tomorrow coming."

"Not to brag," Julio said, "but I can step out my door and ride hard in a straight line all day long and still be on de Alda land."

"Big country," Roy mused.

"It would be my great pleasure to show it to you," de Alda offered.

"Ho! Don't tempt me," Roy said with a chuckle.

"In fact," de Alda said, "I am talking with Adan about the possibility of his coming there with his ship. He seeks trade. I, on the other hand, have items to sell and no transportation to get them to New Orleans."

"Renno, are you all in any big hurry to get back home?" Roy asked.

"You are the one getting married upon our return," Renno pointed out.

"Well, yes," Roy said. He let the subject drop.

Beth and Adan re-joined the party. Roy, Adan, and Julio drank toasts to the United States and to Spain.

"To eternal friendship," Adan said, lifting his glass once more.

"I'll drink to that," Julio said. "And hope that the sentiment spreads to those who would cause strife between our two countries by coveting Spanish lands."

"Who's that?" Roy asked before he drank.

"They are many," Julio replied. "A few of them have come to talk to me. They claim to represent a high-ranking military officer of the United States who has the men and the power to protect us if we will break away from the authorities of New Spain and form a new and independent nation."

"By gum, I think you got Renno's attention," Roy said. He winked at Renno. "Wilkinson, do you suppose?"

"Wilkinson," Renno responded.

"At it again," Roy said, shaking his head. "Wonder who's in on it with him this time."

The idea of forming a new and independent nation on the western frontier of the United States was not a new one. George Rogers Clark had espoused it. At various times crusty old John Sevier, Indian fighter and governor of the territory and then the state of Tennessee, had been ready to take an army of Kentucky and Tennessee men down the Mississippi to seize Spanish North America.

"Well, he's going to be in a fine position to do some damage," Roy remarked, "what with being military commander of the whole dad-gummed area."

"What are the names of these men who ask you to break away from Spain?" Renno asked.

Julio shrugged. "I don't remember. They come and go. Gringos, mostly. They promise much, but so far they have delivered nothing. Their numbers are increasing, however. They come into what they are calling Texas and squat on Spanish lands. I myself have evicted them from my ranges."

"Do you think there is a serious threat, or is it just idle talk among a few?" Renno asked.

"This time it may be serious," Julio predicted. "My

country has been humiliated by this Louisiana affair. First that fool of a king in Spain trades a good portion of this continent to France for a principality in Europe. We are further betrayed by the sale of what was ours to the United States. If ever there was a threat, it is now, for those men who would have an empire of their own view Spain and our forces in New Spain as being weak."

"Adan, you will go to Corpus Christi?" Renno asked.

"Julio has dried beef, leather, and corn to sell," Adan said, nodding. "I plan to buy it, then resell it here in New Orleans."

"I will go with you," Renno said.

"How 'bout that?" Roy whooped.

"El-i-chi, you will stay in New Orleans with—"

The shaman shook his head emphatically.

"He will not stay in New Orleans with me because I'm going, too," Beth said.

Renno's face became stern. Beth moved to his side. "Don't act the steadfast sachem with me," she said teasingly. "After all, this is my ship." She squeezed his arm. "We'll all go. The boys will have their chance to live the life of a sailor. We will have a pleasant, short voyage, get all sorts of sun and healthful sea air."

"So," Renno said. He could envision no danger while they were aboard the *Seneca Cloud*. He turned to Roy. "When I deliver you late to my mother, I will make amends."

They moved their belongings that evening from the hotel to the *Cloud*. Renno wrote a letter to his mother and Rusog, informing them of his plans . . . although who would deliver the missive from Knoxville to the villages, he could not guess. Roy always served that function.

Before the moon had risen Ta-na and Gao had climbed the ship's mainmast, found that cook kept a secret hoard of sweets in his galley, and had decided that they would sleep on the open deck under the stars.

On the western bank of the Mississippi south of Natchez a young warrior of the Natchitoches was so intent on stalking a yearling buck, he did not realize that he himself was being stalked. Suddenly the manifest spirit of all evil leaped upon him. Its feral growling and foaming at the mouth froze the young man's blood even as his weapons were knocked from his hands. He was rendered helpless by a strong blow to the back of his neck.

When he was next aware, he was sitting on the cold ground, and he could not move his hands. His arms had been drawn behind him around the bole of a tree.

The spirit beast watched him from the form of a man, a man with a shaggy, unkempt beard and long matted hair, which hung to his shoulders.

The young warrior tried to clear his head by shaking it.

The beast laughed dementedly and leaned to kiss the young warrior on the forehead. It spoke in Choctaw, a dialect that the young Natchitoches warrior understood: "You will come to love me as I love you, for we will share the ultimate experience together, you and I."

For the young warrior the "experience" began with pain that he could withstand. He spat in the eye of the beast, for, upon closer inspection, the Indian saw that his tormentor was but a white man. As the tortures increased in severity, the captive shouted his defiance, for he was a warrior and brave. Just before the end he was thankful that he and the white man were alone, that there were none of his people to hear his screams of agony, to feel ashamed as he begged the white man to kill him.

After James Wilkinson had left for New Orleans, Melisande had crossed the river from Natchez with Othon Hugues. She had long ago taken to calling him "my little love," because she had first begun to give him strength and guidance when he was only a boy in France. She and Othon were forced to relocate frequently, and she had known from the start that it would be madness to stay in Natchez for long, since the blood lust of her little love could not be held in check. Thus she had taken Othon back to the encampment where they had once lived and gathered renegade followers of Spanish, Indian, Negro, and American blood.

Now, when Othon entered her hut and sat down quietly, she knew that he had once again satisfied the strange yearnings that frequently sent him into the forests. Fresh blood stained his filthy buckskins.

"You saw?" he asked.

"No, tell me about it."

Smiling, he told her. He put his face against her stomach and laughed as he spoke of his triumph. When he had finished recounting the affair, he strengthened himself with the rich milk from her breasts. She patted him tenderly and told him that he had done well, that the master had been pleased. Then she said, "I did not have the pleasure of watching you because I was involved with other things, which will have a bearing on our future."

Othon growled, for the rapport he had with his Melisande told him that she had been using her supernatural gift of seeing at a distance to check on the whereabouts of the man they had sworn to kill, Renno, the Seneca.

"He is meddling in matters that concern us," Melisande said.

Renno had interfered with their pleasures before, when he and his son had come to steal the captive Renna away from Othon and rescue the comte de Beaujolais from torture. The renegades who had not been killed by the white Indian had scattered. Now the place was deserted. Only the witch and her little love heard the lonely hoot of an owl from a cottonwood beside the river.

"I can see you are angry," Othon said. "Tell me what Renno has done."

"No, my anger is for Wilkinson," she said. "The fool risks all by making advances to the women in the white Indian's family."

Othon's face blackened. "Are you jealous of the white general's affections?"

"Don't be stupid," she reprimanded. "We need him. He is lucky that the white Indian did not kill him."

Melisande had only contempt for Wilkinson, but he represented her base of power. Wilkinson had promised that he would settle a huge land grant on Othon in the vicinity of the Red River in that new nation to be formed around the northern areas of New Spain. She would become ruler of many through him and his plans to seize lands from the weakened New Spain colonies and establish an independent nation west of the Mississippi.

That Wilkinson would be the figurehead didn't bother her. It didn't matter if anyone else knew that she was the power behind the throne as long as she knew it, and as long as she was free to wield it.

"We must go to New Orleans," she said, "to keep an eye on Wilkinson and to keep our plans intact."

Othon's eyes rolled in fright.

"It's all right, my little love," she said. "I will change your appearance. I will blind the eyes of those who look upon us so that we will not be recognized."

She cut Othon's hair, trimmed his wild, black beard, and fitted him with clean clothing. A passing flatboat picked them up, and they were in New Orleans within days.

James Wilkinson was preparing to go back up the river, for he was to be given a new command as governor of a large portion of the Louisiana Territory and commanding officer of the Army in the West. He felt a surge of swift need when he saw Melisande enter his room.

"Melisande," he said. "Why are you here?"

She had made contact with his eyes. By her will her beauty was multiplied. By her suggestion Wilkinson's need grew to near bursting. He moved toward her.

"Wait," she said. "You made me a promise."

"Yes, I know," he said, reaching for her.

She avoided him. "You have not kept that promise yet."

"I told you that I would help when he began his way back toward Natchez," he said.

"But he is not going to Natchez. He sails west, to New Spain."

"What? Why would he do that?"

"That doesn't matter," she said. "He sails. The ship is called the *Seneca Cloud*."

"Come to me," he whispered. "I need you."

"No."

"I will send a ship after him."

"Good." She turned and called out softly. Othon Hugues entered the room.

Wilkinson looked nervously at the Frenchman. The man had been cleaned up, but his pockmarked face, his frantically searching eyes, made Wilkinson very uneasy.

"Give Othon money," Melisande said. "He will find a ship and hire men to do the job." She sent a new surge of suggestion into Wilkinson's already fevered passion. He sat down and quickly wrote out a letter.

"This will authorize your brother to draw on army funds," he said.

Othon took the letter, read it, nodded in satisfaction, and folded it.

"Go then," Melisande told him.

She waited until Othon was gone, then she slowly removed her clothing. She teased Wilkinson until she feared that she would lose him to apoplexy, and then gave him his reward.

Chapter V

The sloop *Julien*, a stiff, new flag flying at her stern, worked her way down the river from New Orleans. The *Julien*'s captain, twenty-three-year-old Jean Laffite, had decided that for this voyage—a charter to the coast of New Spain north of the Rio Grande—the colors that the United States had recently raised over New Orleans served the purpose better than would the flag of the republic of Cartagena, sponsor of his privateer's commission.

As the sloop sailed grandly past his growing settlement on the Baratarian coast south of New Orleans, Laffite was having second thoughts about the voyage. He had accepted the assignment and payment from an odd, confusing woman and a Frenchman with a severely pockmarked face. Whatever could have possessed him to agree to take Othon Hugues and as scruffy a band of cutthroats as he'd ever seen, even in the privateer settlements on the Baratarian Gulf, to Corpus Christi?

Laffite had not even asked the pockmarked Frenchman the purpose of his desire to go to Corpus Christi.

Payment had been made in advance, in good French and Spanish gold and silver.

When Othon Hugues showed up on the dock with his mixed group of scoundrels, Laffite had called his officers together and whispered warnings for the crew to be on the alert and remain armed at all times.

As he passed the settlement from which he often ranged outward into the Gulf of Mexico to prey on ships of all nations, Laffite was tempted to turn the *Julien* with the southeast wind and seek the security of his own private cove, where there would be enough friendly force to overwhelm Hugues's suspicious group. Laffite was just about to give the order when the peculiar woman who called herself Melisande approached. He saw her out of the corner of his eye. She was a bit too gaunt, her hair was unkempt, and there were wrinkles at the corners of her mouth and eyes. She was smiling, and her teeth gleamed with a sheen of darkness.

"Captain?" Melisande said.

Laffite turned his head. Her eyes caught his. Her white teeth showed in a full-lipped smile. Her curvaceous body pleased him. Her face was glowing with the smoothness and color of youth. Her dark hair was thick and shone with rich highlights. He no longer thought it necessary to put into his cove.

"Ah, mademoiselle," he said, bowing, "we are making good time in spite of a less-than-favorable wind."

"Captain," Melisande responded, "we have the utmost confidence in you."

There was no trouble on board as the *Julien* entered the gulf and turned westward. Laffite's nights were made interesting by a visitor who came padding in on bare feet with nothing but a thin chemise covering her lush body.

Laffite used Spanish charts drawn by Don José de Evia. He kept the *Julien* close to the coast. When the need for fresh water became acute, he took the sloop into a wide, beautiful bay that de Evia had named Galveston. As Hugues's men joined the crew in filling the ship's water casks, Laffite made notations on his chart. The bay of Galveston was protected from the sea by a long island, and the lands thereabout were unpopulated. In his business it was good to know about a place such as Galveston Bay, just in case things got too crowded or too dangerous at the mouth of the Mississippi.

As the *Julien* approached Corpus Christi, the masts and furled sails of the *Seneca Cloud* were visible. When Laffite moored the sloop near the larger vessel, two seamen could be seen on the deck of the *Cloud*.

Using the ship's longboats, Laffite had Othon Hugues and his men put ashore. Melisande made another generous payment in gold in exchange for Laffite's agreement to wait in the harbor for thirty days, in order to transport Hugues and his men back to New Orleans. The woman whose appearance changed so drastically stayed aboard to keep the young captain's bed warm. Laffite was content . . . until, without an explanation or word of goodbye, Melisande vanished.

Renno found it good to be on solid land again. Upon the arrival of the *Seneca Cloud* in Corpus Christi, the party guided by Julio de Alda was mounted on horses with bloodlines going directly back to the steeds of the conquistadores. The way was northward. As usual, Ta-na and Gao rode ahead of the others and acted as scouts. Once, Ta-na was thrown from his horse when the animal was spooked by an evil-looking, fat-bodied rattlesnake. He flipped and landed with a thud on the dry sand about five feet from the reptile. The force of his impact caused white spots to dance before his field of vision. The snake was coiled and sending out its dry, rattling, warning buzz.

Renno, riding beside Beth a hundred feet behind Ta-na and Gao, saw the danger and instantly kicked his mount into a gallop and closed on the fallen boy.

Ta-na looked directly into the cold eyes of the rattlesnake. He did not stop to calculate the peril, for he had seen copperheads and the cottonmouth water moccasin in his native land. This snake had the same evil-looking head. He remembered his aunt Ena saying, "All snakes may *look* harmful, but when you see a snake that is truly poisonous, there will be no doubt in your mind."

There was no doubt in the boy's mind that the reptile buzzing at him was dangerous. Ordinarily he would have merely detoured around the snake on the theory that the reptile was doing nothing more than it had been intended to do by the Master of Life when it was created. But Ta-na's horse was galloping away with Gao in hot pursuit, and it seemed as if the snake was not going to leave that option open.

"We will talk, you and I," he said to the snake, moving closer. The snake followed the movement of his hand with its wedge-shaped head, then struck. With the reflexes of youth Ta-na's hand moved, his razor-sharp knife flashed, and the head of the snake fell to the sand.

Renno hurled himself from his horse and ran to Ta-na's side. Ta-na was holding the headless snake up by its tail. The bloody stub at the other end dragged the ground.

"Had he been peaceful, Father, I would not have killed him," Ta-na said.

Renno said, "So." He hid a smile, for he had seen the lightning speed of Ta-na's action and was extremely pleased. "You are Seneca and will be a fine warrior."

Ta-na grinned at the praise, then quickly assumed the impassive warrior's expression.

"It is said that the rattles are strong medicine," Renno said.

Ta-na took that in, then cut the rattles away from the snake's body.

Gao, having led Ta-na's horse back to his cousin, had to get down to examine the dead reptile and shake the severed rattles with wonder.

As the journey resumed, Ta-na reflected upon the experience, not out of conceit but to think about how he had reacted and what he had learned. One of his most pleasing pastimes was the sharpening of his knife. He had his own whetstone, a small, rectangular one given to him by his "grandfather" Roy. Whenever time began to hang heavy, Ta-na would spit on the whetstone and rub the blade of his knife in a circle on the wet stone. He and Gao kept their knives sharp enough to shave the hair off the nape of their necks. Now he realized how important it was to keep his weapons in top form always, and he vowed to do so.

*   *   *

The de Alda hacienda was a rambling, stucco structure of Spanish frontier style. There were shady, hidden courtyards and balconies designed to catch the evening breeze. A few trees were grouped around the house, but beyond, the surrounding plains extended off to the distance except on one side where there was a tree-lined creek. The richness of the fertile soil was evidenced by fields of corn and grasslands on which grazed wild, long-horned Mexican cattle.

Adan and Julio began to talk business immediately after the party's arrival and left the house to examine stacks of hides and cribs of corn. The boys, meanwhile, explored the house and outbuildings and began to discover that Beth's attempts to teach them Spanish had been valuable, after all.

It did not take long for Renno to hear direct confirmation of de Alda's statements regarding political machinations originating from the Southwest Territory of the United States. On the first evening after their arrival, an hour before sunset, an unexpected visitor arrived. De Alda introduced him as Marcus Bergman.

Bergman had the stiff back and stern look of a certain type of army officer. He was a tall man with a weathered face and a shock of white hair. He accepted de Alda's invitation to dinner.

Before making conversation de Alda waited until each of his guests had been served. Bergman inquired about the events in New Orleans.

"The ceremonies were quite impressive," de Alda said. Then, to confirm Renno's guess that Bergman was an ex-officer, he added, "I met your former commander, General Wilkinson."

"And how was the general?" Bergman inquired.

"He looked well," de Alda said.

Bergman seemed thoughtful. "Interesting man, the general. Did you have the opportunity to talk at length with him?"

"No," de Alda answered.

"Too bad," Bergman said. "I think you would have discovered a common interest."

"Perhaps," de Alda allowed.

"I will tell you this," Bergman said. "General Wilkinson would never betray you, as your own country did, and as Spain's great ally, Napoleon, did."

"How interesting," Beth said. "Why do you say, Mr. Bergman, that Señor de Alda was betrayed by Spain and France?"

"I think the señor could explain that better than I," Bergman said.

De Alda shrugged. "There is this," he said. "My poor old country lives in the shadow of the great conqueror of Europe. Since Spain cannot resist Napoleon militarily, she is his reluctant ally. When Napoleon ordered it, Spain had no choice but to retrocede Louisiana to France." He lifted one finger. "The forced action was made more acceptable, however, by the knowledge that a strong France would be better able than a weak Spain had been to hold the territory against the expansion of the United States. In effect we expected France to become a buffer between the United States and Spain's possessions in New Spain and in Central and South America."

"I see," Beth said, nodding.

"I must admit that there are many of my countrymen who view the events in New Orleans with both horror and fear," de Alda confided. "It didn't matter to Napoleon that Spain had not formally given sovereignty of the lands in question to France, nor that the retrocession treaty specifically prohibited any sale or, for that matter, any form of alienation of Louisiana."

"You were betrayed," Bergman said forcefully. "Now the Americans are squarely on the borders of Mexico and California. I would say, my friend, that the entire colonial system of Spain has been placed in peril."

De Alda said nothing.

"The United States even claims that the Floridas were included in the purchase," Bergman said.

"Never," de Alda said heatedly. Then he smiled and spread his hands. "My friends," he said, looking at his guests in turn, "please take no offense. I confess I am bitter about the whole affair."

"Understandably so," Beth sympathized.

"I have told Señor de Alda that there is a remedy to the problem," Bergman said.

"I'd be interested in hearing your solution," Renno said.

"Señor de Alda spoke of France being a buffer," Bergman said. "I have been advising him—and all the other hidalgos in the lands north of the Rio Grande—that they create their own buffer state."

"And what form would this buffer state take?" Roy asked, casting a quick look at Renno.

"An independent nation composed of the Spanish landholders already in place and settlers from the Southwest Territory of the United States," Bergman explained. "There are plans already in existence to seize the area south of the Red River before the United States gets used to the idea of owning it as part of the purchase."

"And the lands to the Rio Grande?" de Alda asked.

"Not *seize*, in that case," Bergman said. "We would ally ourselves with the Spanish areas."

"And the government, of course, would be run by your friends from the Southwest Territory of the United States?" de Alda asked.

"We envision a republic," Bergman said, "giving everyone a voice in the affairs of the new nation."

" 'We'?" Renno asked.

Bergman smiled. "At this moment I am not at liberty to put forward the names of my principals. But I assure you that you would recognize the names and that I am referring to men of great ability, men who have made a name for themselves in the United States."

"James Wilkinson, for example?" Roy asked benignly.

"I can neither confirm nor deny your guess," Bergman said.

"Well, whoever it is," Roy said, trying to draw Bergman out, "he's not the first to have the idea. At one time I was about ready to go off with old George Rogers Clark and John Sevier to take the Southwest away from New Spain. I reckon I could have been head general of the republic of Clark-Sevier if the idea had hatched." He rubbed his chin. "I felt then, and I feel it more now, that things were getting too all-fired crowded back in Tennessee. I had a hankering for owning a place like Señor de Alda's here."

"There will be land grants for those who participate," Bergman said. "A man of your military experience, Colonel Johnson, would be welcome."

"Know me, huh?" Roy asked.

"I know *of* you," Bergman said.

"One thing I learned listening to Clark and Sevier," Roy added. "There's a mite of difference between talk and action. Now, you convince me that these men you represent have a force both large enough and strong enough to take a pretty big piece of land and hold it against any action by the United States and New Spain, and I just might be your man."

"I can only give you my assurances—" Bergman began.

"Yep, that's what Clark and Sevier did. They gave me their assurances. And if I'd listened to them and sold out and got ready to go west, I'd have been one disappointed fellow." He rubbed his chin again. "Maybe you have something in writing? A list of men who are definitely committed? A list of available ordnance and arms?"

"If you're really serious, Colonel, that might be arranged," Bergman said. "I'm sure that it would be very well received if you could bring with you a good number of your friends in Tennessee, and perhaps some of the men who have served under you in the Tennessee Militia."

"I suppose I could." Roy shrugged. "But before I even begin to consider it, I'll have to have names, Bergman. Names."

"You have already spoken one of the names."

"Wilkinson?"

"Yes," Bergman confirmed. "You will have to admit that he is in an excellent position to move. He is senior military commander. He will be named governor of at least a portion of Louisiana."

"But can he bring his army with him?" Renno asked.

"At least a part of it," Bergman replied. Then he turned back to Roy. "You mentioned George Rogers Clark and John Sevier. At the moment they are not fully committed. But they will become so after General Wilkinson makes his move. And there is one other name that I will give you. Our movement has the covert support of the vice president of the United States."

"Aaron Burr?" Roy asked.

"And soon his covert support will become overt," Bergman said.

"I thought he was running for governor of New York," Beth remarked.

"A position that will make him even more capable of giving support to the new nation," Bergman said.

"He gave us the information too easily," Renno told Beth when they were alone in their bedchamber.

"He is a fatuous, foolish man," Beth said, unpinning her hair and brushing it out. "If he is indicative of the type of man involved in this scheme, I don't think Señor de Alda needs to worry."

"We know that Wilkinson is a traitor to the United States," Renno said. "Thus he would just as willingly betray the Spaniards who have been paying him."

"Could he, acting alone, gather enough support to challenge both the United States and Spain?"

Renno thought for a moment. "Spain has been weakened. She is old and tired. And, unfortunately, in President Jefferson's desire for peace and government economy, he has reduced the United States Army to a force that would be hard-pressed to fight a battle on the western bank of the Mississippi."

"You're concerned, then?" she asked as she joined him in bed.

"I think that our purpose here has been accomplished," he told her. "I think that we must return and report what we have heard to Mr. Jefferson."

"Oh, drat," Beth said. "Can't we at least stay until we go on the buffalo hunt that Julio has promised us?"

He smiled as she snuggled into his arms. "I find it difficult to refuse you any reasonable request," he whispered.

*　　*　　*

A visitor from the northwest came to the village, then the home, of the principal chief Rusog. The newcomer was young and strong, and he wore the paint of a Seneca warrior. His name was White Blanket, and he called himself a Mingo.

"And yet you speak Seneca," Rusog said as Ena listened.

"Yes. My people were Seneca," White Blanket explained. "We grew sick with being crowded into one small part of the vast hunting grounds that had once been the lands of the Ho-de-no-sau-nee. Just as your Seneca cousins followed the great sachem Ghonkaba southward, so we followed our leaders to the west."

"To lose your identity?" Ena asked.

"When one leaves his homeland," White Blanket said, "he grows different."

"And yet we have not changed *our* name," Ena pointed out. "We are Seneca."

White Blanket nodded and was silent before speaking, but his eyes penetrated Ena's gaze and met her challenge. "And does your husband, a Cherokee, think of you and the children he has fathered on you as being Seneca?"

"Enough," Rusog said quickly. "We are all brothers. We are all of the same blood. Mingo or Seneca, you are welcome. Cherokee or Seneca, Ena is my wife."

"And the son of Rusog is Cherokee," said Ho-ya.

"As you so wisely point out, Chief, we are all of one blood," White Blanket said. "So preaches the Prophet. So states the Chief of the Beautiful River."

"You know Tecumseh?" Ho-ya asked, excited.

"I have shared a fire with him," White Blanket replied. "I have exchanged the warrior's clasp and the warrior's oath with him. When Tenskwatawa the Prophet speaks with the Master of Life he sometimes mentions my name."

"One man came before, bearing the tidings of the Chief of the Beautiful River," Ena said. "We do not welcome messages of hate and war for our young ones."

"Are the messages of the white men who come from Nashville seeking Cherokee lands more welcome to the ears of women?" White Blanket asked.

Ena's hand closed on the haft of a tomahawk hanging on the wall near her. The weapon flew swiftly, narrowly missing White Blanket's left ear, to bury its blade in the log wall of Rusog's lodge.

White Blanket let out a yell of surprise and bounded to his feet, his own weapon springing to his hand. He faced an arrow pointed at his heart. Ena's drawn bow was the weapon of a man, and her strong arm did not tremble in the drawing of it.

"Mingo," she warned in a low voice, "have a care. Much can be forgiven you, since you are a guest. But think about your words before they leave your mouth, lest your careless tongue's contempt for women bring about the loss of your hair."

White Blanket lowered his tomahawk. "I stand corrected, matron," he said. As he sat down slowly on his crossed legs, a smile came to his lips. "This, then, is the warrior-woman, Ena, daughter of the white Indian," he said. "Your fame is not unknown among the Mingo. I regret any insult to you, matron, and scold my careless tongue."

"So," Ena said, sounding much like Renno.

"I admit that I am a zealous disciple of the Shawnee chief—"

"Who is not a chief," Ena interrupted.

"—the great Tecumseh. I have taken on a mission to support Tecumseh and his brother the Prophet in spreading the word that a new Indian alliance is being formed to push the white man back beyond the mountains, back across the Ohio."

"As my wife points out," Rusog said, "another came to us to apprise us of Tecumseh's dream."

"Would you deny me the opportunity to speak with your chiefs, your warriors, your young men?"

"Speak if you must, White Blanket," Rusog invited. "But here you will find no warriors willing to travel the path that leads to destruction. Since the treaty of Hopewell we, the Cherokee, have allied ourselves with the United States."

"Eight years have passed since the Cherokee signed away their freedom at Hopewell," White Blanket said.

"Has your careless tongue not yet learned its lesson?" Rusog asked.

"Have the Cherokee not agreed that all of their tribes and towns were under the protection of the United States and of no other sovereign whosoever?" White Blanket asked.

"That is so," Rusog confirmed.

"And have you not agreed that the Congress of the United States has the sole and exclusive right to regulate trade and to manage the affairs of the Cherokee in such manner as they think proper?"

"I do not remember the exact words," Rusog said.

"I remember them well," White Blanket said. "You speak proudly of the Cherokee Nation. But, in fact, as far as the United States government is concerned, when you signed that treaty, when you admitted that the Congress was your lord, all Indian territory became a part of the United States."

"Not so!" Ena protested.

"No?" White Blanket laughed without mirth. "Have you looked at a new map of the United States? If not, I suggest that you do so. You will see, my friends, that all the hunting grounds of the Cherokee are shown as being a part of the United States proper. You have accepted the protection of the United States. Your treaty means that if a foreign power, such as Spain or France, invaded your lands, the United States would send long-knife soldiers to repel the invaders. So, Spain and France and all other nations look upon the so-called Cherokee Nation as being a part of the United States."

"And yet we are not governed by our white neighbors in Tennessee," Ena pointed out.

"Not at this moment," White Blanket said.

Agree or not, Rusog and Ena enjoyed the exchange, for along with story telling and oration, the Indian enjoyed a good discussion. There was no doubt that the young Mingo was very intelligent, and the strength of his beliefs added extraordinary life to his words.

White Blanket was invited to live in Renno's empty longhouse in the Seneca village and was the centerpiece of several meetings of Cherokee and Seneca warriors and matrons. Toshabe firmly told White Blanket that war against the United States would be folly, that the sachem, her son Renno, had embarked long before on a policy of alliance with the United States, and that her son was, at that very moment, traveling on a mission assigned to him by the president of the United States.

White Blanket did find sympathetic ears among the young men of the Cherokee village, however. To a group of Ho-ya's age he said, "The white man's learned ones invent terms to mask their greed. They talk of Manifest Destiny. This rhetoric speaks of the United States as a young and growing country. This is, of course, true. But the United States is growing through swallowing the lands of the Indian. Just as a bear cub eats to grow, so does the United States gobble up our forests, our streams, our meadows. In the land of the Choctaw, I am told, there is hunger."

"How can a man allow his family to go hungry when there is game?" Ho-ya asked.

"Hear me," White Blanket said. "Before the white flood poured across the southern lands, the Choctaw hunted game, and the women cultivated the gardens. They hunted, as did we, to eat. The women used the skin of the deer to make clothing. They killed no more than was needed, and game was plentiful. Then the white man came to the land of the Choctaw. He offered guns and liquor in exchange for the skins of animals. The white man had steel knives and copper kettles. He had cotton cloth and woolen blankets. The Choctaw saw that these things were good. Even as the Choctaw's hunger for whiskey and gunpowder emptied the forests of game, the white man pushed himself among the Indian, marrying his women, starting cotton plantations, and promising wealth and plenty. But the wealth was solely for the white man. For the Choctaw, the emptying of the forests to feed the white man's hunger for pelts and meat meant that there was no game to feed their families."

"But that is the Choctaw," Ho-ya said with disdain. "He who never fought the white man."

"Ah, but he did," White Blanket corrected. "He was among the first to die before the muskets of the Europeans. Ask a Choctaw shaman to tell you about Mobila, where thousands died under the hooves of Spanish war-horses. No, the Choctaw is only the first to become dependent upon the doubtful generosity of the white man. Who will be next? The Cherokee?"

"No, no," came the chorus in reply.

"I have been told that the sachem of the Seneca advocates living in the manner of the white man," White Blanket went on. "His fundamental advice to you is to transform yourself to fit into the white man's culture, to strive to be equal to your white neighbors. How is this possible when the white man looks upon us as children?"

"So," Ho-ya said, nodding, for he had heard Christian missionaries talk of the duty of the white man to take parental responsibility for the Indian "children."

"Our chief tells us," a young warrior said, "that to throw ourselves against the antlike hordes of white soldiers would result in our total destruction."

"Not if we are all united," White Blanket responded.

"There was union at the fallen timbers," said We-yo.

White Blanket smiled at Ho-ya's twin sister. "It is pleasing for me to see that the fair women of the Cherokee are given leave to speak in council."

We-yo blushed. At fourteen, she had recently celebrated the rites of womanhood, although she had not yet allowed any young man to speak for her. It was obvious from the light in her eyes that the Mingo was the most beautiful man she'd seen.

"Not all Cherokee maidens are allowed in council," a young man said. "Only We-yo."

"And why is the fair one allowed such a privilege?" White Blanket asked.

"Because she has wrestled with her twin brother so frequently, her fighting skills are like a warrior's. If we tried to exclude her, she would fight each one of us at times when she caught us alone," the same young warrior explained to general laughter.

"And best most of you," Ho-ya put in.

We-yo lowered her head. When she looked up White Blanket was staring directly at her, and his dark eyes caused her bones to melt.

*   *   *

So it was that We-yo, daughter of Ena and Rusog, came to the attention of the visiting Mingo warrior. When next he saw We-yo after that night, she was walking alone outside the village and wearing a white dress purchased for her by her aunt Beth. White Blanket, who had sought the solitude of the forest to pray to the Master of Life, saw her and ran to catch her.

"You look more white than Cherokee," White Blanket said. "It does not become you."

She tossed her black hair angrily and stared at him coldly.

"Your beauty is Cherokee," he said. "Indian. It is a gift of the Master of Life to one of His own. To play at being a white woman is—"

"I am one-quarter white," she said, quickening her pace a bit.

"Through choice?"

She laughed in spite of herself. "Did you choose your mother?"

"She was beautiful, as you are," he said. He chuckled. "No. I stand corrected."

She was almost of a height to him, tall and regal, slim and radiant. Blossoming womanhood mounded the bodice of her garment.

"I can understand your confusion," he said. "You speak English?"

"Yes," she answered. "I was taught by my mother and by my aunt Beth."

"The Englishwoman with the red hair," he said, nodding. "You strive to be like her?"

"Yes," she said. Then, quickly, "No." She sighed. "Even if I wanted to be like Beth—"

"What were you going to say?" he asked after she fell silent.

"I don't know."

"You were thinking that even if you wanted to be like the Englishwoman, even if your accent matched hers and you could speak in large words of the white man's politics and philosophy, you would still be Cherokee. You would still be looked upon by the white man as a child."

"Must you always be so serious?" she asked.

He halted and pulled her to a stop. He held both her hands in his. Her heart pounded. They had walked to a point where they were out of sight of the village. The trail had led them among great trees into shadows.

"There is one thing about which I will always be serious," he said, "and that is my desire to make you my mate."

"Oh." She gasped, going so weak that he put his arm around her to support her.

He pulled her toward him, and his hand began the first appreciation of her body even as she leaned against his chest. Wave after wave of . . . something—weakness? love?—left her helpless to move away. He led her off the pathway and into a secluded bower beside the swimming creek. He placed her on a blanket of soft, resilient moss and bent over her to put his weight on her. His hands explored her, for in the code of the Cherokee, such youthful experiments were permitted. The merging of mouths was a white man's custom. White Blanket tasted the smooth skin of her neck and, after pulling her white dress down, the warmth of her breasts. His hands found her, and to her shame and surprise his fingers were wetted. To his honor, although he was sorely tempted, he observed the code of courtship and made no attempt to penetrate that flowing softness. After a few more minutes, he climbed to his feet and loosed a muffled utterance of frustration.

During the next few days, after White Blanket spoke of Tecumseh's dream to the young warriors, We-yo and he found occasion for steamy bouts of youthful but unfulfilled passion. White Blanket asked the beautiful Cherokee girl to be his mate. She agreed.

"Now that you are promised to me," he said, "you will act the Cherokee, abandoning the clothing of the whites."

"Yes," she said.

"When it is time for me to return to the north, to be with Tecumseh, you will be at my side."

"Oh, yes."

"Tonight I will speak with your father about us," he said.

"Ask for me wisely," she warned. "It would be a good idea if you could moderate your talk of certain war with the whitefaces."

"Would you change my face, my bearing?"

"No, for yours are a beautiful face and a proud bearing."

"Then don't try to change my heart," he told her.

Although Ena was not a parent who tried to bind her children to her, she was a good mother, and she had known for days that something had happened to change her daughter. Because of her trust in We-yo she made no inquiry, but she was not surprised—only disappointed— in We-yo's choice. When her daughter and the young Mingo appeared hand in hand before the chief, White Blanket's speech asking Rusog for We-yo was a model of Indian formality. After the young man was finished, he searched Rusog's stoic face, trying to find some hint of reaction.

It was Ena who spoke. "I would prefer, Mingo, that you were Cherokee or Seneca."

"Some Mingo are Mohawk, some Oneida, some Cayuga, some Onondaga. I am Seneca."

"And yet you are not of us," Ena said. "True, you are worthy, White Blanket. You are a warrior who would be prized in any family. I am utterly opposed, however, to the course of action advocated by the man you follow. I will not send my only daughter into the Indiana wilderness to see you die on the bayonet of an American soldier."

"Does Ena speak for the chief?" White Blanket asked.

Rusog brooded for a long moment before he spoke. His naturally gruff voice was pitched lower than usual. "Stay with us, Mingo," he invited. "Hunt our lands. Let your wife make her garden alongside that of her mother, and you will have my blessings."

"That I cannot do," White Blanket said.

"Then I, too, must forbid this match," Rusog said.

"Oh, Father—" We-yo begged.

Rusog looked at her sadly. "Now, my daughter, your heart will burn with pain, and your eyes will redden with tears. My own heart will be heavy, even as I harden it against your sorrow. But you must accept the will of your mother and of your father."

"Yes," We-yo whispered. "Yes, Father."

In the night, when the full moon filled the smoke hole in the roof of the lodge, We-yo, sleepless, rose, pulled on her clothing, and crept from the house, leaving her mother and Rusog sleeping soundly. She had no intention of disobeying. As Rusog had predicted, her burning heart was filled with pain. But We-yo knew her duty. She was Cherokee, the daughter of a great chief, granddaughter of a great sachem of the Seneca. She left the lodge only to be alone where she could allow the sobs to come, the tears to slide down her cheeks.

She walked toward the outskirts of the village. Dogs investigated her, sniffed, then went back to their favorite pastime of barking at the moon. At one time, she knew, a barking dog would soon have been in the cook pot, lest his yelps guide an enemy to the village. Now the village would have been lonely without the sound of the dogs in the night.

When We-yo found the spot where White Blanket and she had first experimented with touch and feel, she sat on the moss and wept. After her emotions had been spent and a feeling of exhaustion enveloped her, she saw that the moon was low in the western sky. She started back toward the village. She moved silently, by long habit, and was able to hear the sound of an approaching runner. The girl hid behind a tree. White Blanket's face was easily recognizable in the moonlight. Behind him was her twin, Ho-ya. Both warriors were laden with weapons and travel packs. She stepped out after they had passed and gave the coo of a mourning dove. The warriors halted and whirled, hands at their weapons.

"You would leave, both of you, without telling me good-bye?" she asked, moving into the moonlight.

"What are you doing out here alone?" Ho-ya demanded.

"My question is for you, Brother," she said. "Do you travel to become a part of Tecumseh's confederation?"

"Yes. Now go home, We-yo," Ho-ya said. "We must be far away before daybreak."

"You defy our parents?"

"To my sorrow," he admitted. "But I must follow where my heart leads me."

She wiped tears from her face. "If my brother can defy them to follow his heart, then so will I."

White Blanket came forward and took her hands. "What you are offering to do, dear one, will cut all contact with your parents forever. To defy them will cause them to say that they no longer have a daughter."

"I know," she whispered.

"Come then," White Blanket said happily.

With Ho-ya as their only witness, We-yo and White Blanket exchanged the vows of marriage first in Seneca and then, with We-yo's guidance, in Cherokee. The ceremony was performed at the end of a long day of travel during which We-yo proved that she could match the warriors' pace. The union was consummated in a leafy bower beside a gurgling stream. The next morning, before light, the bride was awake, stirring the fire to warm meat left over from the evening meal.

A woman now, she ran beside her husband toward the far river to the north. There was sadness in her, for she loved her parents very much and was genuinely sorry to give them pain. But her reasoning was colored by her love and by a strong urge that nature engenders in the human body. Whatever the future would bring to her in the lands of the north, she would accept as the wife, the willing mate, of the Mingo warrior White Blanket.

Chapter VI

Thomas Jefferson and his secretary of state were at tea. Madison sat with his well-shaped, tightly trousered legs crossed as he stared moodily out the window of Jefferson's office. The president was reading a lengthy letter from William Eaton, his consul to the Barbary nations. Eaton's mission was to establish peace with Tripoli, although the events of the past few months made that goal seem impossible. Jefferson, a self-professed man of peace, was troubled daily with the knowledge that good Americans were being used as slaves by the bashaw of Tripoli. The three hundred men and officers of the frigate *Philadelphia* had been captured when the ship went aground at the entrance to Tripoli Harbor while chasing a Tripolitanian warship. According to Eaton, among the officers who were confined in an old stone fortress overlooking the sea were Captain William Bainbridge and a young first lieutenant named David Porter.

Jefferson's mood darkened as he read Eaton's letter. It described the treatment of the ship's men, who were forced to toil on harbor fortifications. The best that Eaton could say was that none of the Americans had been beaten to death or starved, since they were worth more alive to the bashaw than dead. Their treatment, however, was barbaric. Those who objected to working were whipped, and their already meager rations were reduced. Attempts at escape resulted in solitary confinement.

The *Philadelphia* tragedy had produced indignation in the United States as the year 1804 entered its second month. Congress had increased taxes on imports to raise money to strengthen the navy. "Bash the bashaw!" one newspaper headline urged.

Meanwhile, Eaton reported that the bashaw of Tripoli was demanding five hundred thousand dollars now and an equal amount paid annually as a price for the release of Americans held in slavery.

Jefferson finished the letter, placed it on the table in front of him, then pinched and rubbed the bridge of his nose. He sighed heavily.

"The public mood is ugly, Thomas," Madison said. "The average American has a frontier mentality and a code that says when you're hit, you hit back twice as hard."

"Eaton continues to ask for troops," Jefferson said.

Madison compressed his lips thoughtfully. "Not necessary. I think that naval power alone can accomplish our purpose."

"I agree," Jefferson said. "But where are the men to use that naval power effectively? By God, what kind of a ship's captain would run a new and powerful frigate aground and then turn it over to the enemy?"

"In all fairness, sir, Captain Bainbridge is a fine officer, as courageous and able as any man in the navy. He was in unfamiliar waters, without proper charts, and he was in hot pursuit of the enemy. We can only believe that he surrendered his ship and his crew to keep his men from being killed. Aground on the reef, the ship was defenseless against the Tripolitanian gunboats."

"And now the *Philadelphia* has been refloated and repaired and will sally forth soon to destroy American ships," Jefferson said. "Perhaps we should send Eaton a thousand men."

"I believe, Mr. President, that to do so would court disaster. Eaton, in spite of his army experience with the American Legion, is an unknown factor as far as military knowledge and leadership are concerned. The deserts of North Africa would swallow up any American ground force, be it composed of a thousand or ten thousand men."

"By God, James, I'm so frustrated!" Jefferson grated. "We must do something."

Alone in his office Jefferson turned his attentions to domestic matters. The chill of February invaded the room. He shivered, got up to put more wood in the fireplace, then stood with his hands clasped behind his back before the fire. Later in the year he would face an election campaign. The Federalists in New England were threatening to withdraw from the Union. Continuing Indian trouble plagued William Henry Harrison's Indiana Territory. Having just spent millions to buy the Louisiana Territory, Jefferson faced the problem of asking Congress to come up with funds to strengthen the navy and the army. Many people believed that during his first years in office he had gutted the armed services in the name of peace and economy, so the idea of begging Congress for money to reverse his own policy toward the military establishment did not sit well with him.

And piled on top of those weighty concerns were the day-to-day, mundane duties that had to be performed. He went back to his desk and took pen in hand. General Henry Dearborn had just made a new agreement with the Choctaw Indians, who had agreed to sell certain of their lands along the Mississippi.

"Don't pay high prices," he wrote to Dearborn. "They are poor and will probably sell for just enough to pay their debts so as to be entitled to an annual pension from the federal government. This is one of the best holds we have on them."

It was true that the "Indian Problem" was less severe in 1804 than it had been in the past, but it was still a problem. Jefferson prided himself on being a man of science. At times it seemed that he took more sheer pleasure in being president of the American Philosophical Society than in being president of the United States. He could not agree with the theory of polygenesis that was being advanced by some men of science. Such people believed that God had created *Homo sapiens Europaeus* first, saving lesser efforts for the black, yellow, and red races. Jefferson had, in fact, gone on record as saying, "I believe the Indian to be in body and mind equal to the white man."

His true opinion, however, was that the Indian was inferior to so-called civilized Americans. Jefferson also had a strong attachment to the land. He considered himself to be an agrarian. To have a goal of turning the Indian hunters into yeoman farmers seemed logical to him. He had told a delegation of Ohio Indians in 1802, "We shall with great pleasure see your people become disposed to cultivate the earth, to raise herds of useful animals, and to spin and weave. . . . These resources are certain, they will never disappoint you, while those of hunting may fail and expose your women and children to the miseries of hunger and cold."

To Congress he had said, "In leading the Indians to agriculture and civilization, I trust and believe we are acting for their greatest good."

That Indians such as Tecumseh did not care to have any whiteface "acting for their greatest good" in a self-appointed paternalism seemed irrelevant and bothersome to Jefferson. He felt, and so stated, that because of the evident strength of the United States and the obvious weakness of the Indian nations, even the Indian must realize that the United States had only to shut its hand to crush them.

All in all, in 1804, with the Barbary thorn in his side, he was impatient with the Indian Problem. He turned his attentions back to William Eaton's request that troops be sent to serve under his command. Just as the president had decided that he needed more information about Eaton and the situation in Tripoli, the door burst open without a knock. James Madison rushed in, waving a letter.

"Mr. President, a fresh communiqué from the fleet," Madison said.

"Give me its contents in brief, please, James."

"With great pleasure," Madison said, standing squarely with his feet spread. "On the sixteenth of February Lieutenant Stephen Decatur of the United States Navy sailed into Tripoli Harbor aboard the ketch *Intrepid* with a crew of seventy-five men and twelve guns. He boarded the *Philadelphia*, set fire to her, and withdrew to the *Intrepid* without losing a single man."

"God be praised," Jefferson breathed.

"By the Almighty, Thomas," Madison said, "our men *can* fight. The *Philadelphia* burned to the waterline. She won't come out to fight against us."

"Remind me of our strength in North African waters now," Jefferson requested.

Madison rubbed his chin. "There's just the one frigate, the *Constitution*."

"Ah, yes, the good commodore Edward Preble has complained to me that he has only one forty-four-gun ship."

"He has two sloops, the *Argus* and the *Syren,* each with sixteen guns; the schooners *Vixen* and *Nautilus;* and two converted prize ships, *Intrepid* and *Scourge*."

"Decatur used a captured enemy vessel to burn our own captured *Philadelphia?* There's some grim irony there." Jefferson became thoughtful. "So, James, we're sending more ships, but it will take time. Meanwhile, this fellow Eaton intrigues me. I would like to know more about him. Can I send in someone to spy on him?"

"No. He's quite an intelligent fellow," Madison said. "I believe he would resent someone looking over his shoulder."

"As a consul of the United States, does he not have a marine guard?"

"I would think so. A small one, perhaps."

"Might it be useful to speak with the officer in charge of the marine unit?"

"Probably, but it would waste time and prove awkward, especially if the man has developed loyalty to Eaton." "How about a man sent from home, then?" Jefferson suggested. "He'd have to be a junior officer, but someone in whom we could have confidence." He mulled this over for a moment, then brightened and snapped his fingers. "James, we established West Point as a school to produce officers. The graduates of the first class must have been assigned to duties by now, but perhaps we can take a look at the current class and find a worthy young man for our purpose."

"Shall I contact the commandant and ask him to send recommendations?"

"Yes, good idea, James." He paused. "No," he said suddenly, holding up his hand. "There's a young man there whom I appointed myself. His father fought with George Washington and has been a good friend to the United States. Send a letter to the commandant and ask him if the cadet Hawk Harper could be released from his class immediately to be given a commission as a second lieutenant in the marines."

Cadet Officer Hawk Harper moaned softly as his passion exploded inside the lovely warmth of the daughter of his commanding officer. She clung to him, sighing her pleasure. He stiffened, slowly moved away, and began pulling on his clothing.

"Where are you going?" she asked.

"I heard something."

"Damn you, you heard your imagination."

It was the same each time he climbed the drainpipe and crept into Mary Ann Lillie's bedroom window. Always he found her nude and waiting. With the power of youthful need surging inside him, the risk seemed acceptable. He knew from experience that Major John Lillie slept soundly. And yet, once his pent-up desire had been expended, sheer terror chilled him and sent him scampering away from the girl he had come to love with a fire that threatened, at times, to consume him.

"Mary Ann, we can't do this anymore," he whispered as she came to him and pressed her naked body to his. "I'm going to ask your father to allow us to be married as soon as I graduate."

"Not yet," she said. "There's time. When will you come again?"

"Oh, blast," he said. Already the feel of her was beginning to course through his blood.

"Soon? Tomorrow night?"

"No. My common sense tells me not to."

She pouted. "If you truly loved me, you'd come to me every night."

"After we're married—"

"If you won't, I know men who will," she threatened.

"I know men who will die if they try," he warned fiercely.

"Sunday night, then," she said. "Come early. He's asleep before nine o'clock."

Her kiss was the only persuasion required. "Yes," he said.

As Little Hawk climbed down the drainpipe he had the fright of his life. His foot slipped, and he slid out of control down the pipe to land with a crash. Hearing sounds from inside the house, he lay quite still, hidden by the darkness. John Lillie, in nightdress and cap, opened the sitting-room window, stuck his head out, and looked around. He was holding a wedge of bread and cheese. Little Hawk's heart pounded. All that time, while he was making love to Mary Ann, her father had been walking around the house, having a midnight snack.

"Humph," Lillie grunted as he closed the window.

Little Hawk lay motionless for long minutes, then crawled away on his belly as if he were stalking a deer. When he was at a safe distance from the commander's house, he ran to the barracks, entered by an unlocked window, and sought his bed. He lay awake, reliving the terror he had felt when John Lillie opened the window. The young man did not sleep until he had made a firm resolution to speak to the major as soon as possible in request of his daughter's hand in marriage.

Since Ho-ya slept with other fledgling warriors in the men's lodge, it was the absence of We-yo that alerted Ena. When neither of her twins appeared for any meal that day, she merely thought that Ho-ya was off and away on a hunt or a ramble and that We-yo was, most probably, mooning in the company of her beloved.

Ena and Rusog talked of the events of the day while partaking of the evening meal. They walked side by side to the top of a small hill outside the village to watch the sun set into the forests. Then, in comfortable silence, the couple strolled back to the lodge to share a quiet pipe of tobacco between them and to speculate on the present whereabouts of Renno and the other travelers. Rusog said that he expected to see them all riding into the village in the first warm days. Ena nodded. It would be pleasant to see them.

Rusog went to sleep while Ena, bending close to her work in the glow of the fire and an oil lamp that had been a present from her sister-in-law Beth, worked on a new deerskin shirt for We-yo. When her eyes became heavy she put the work aside and leaned back. She awoke to see that the fire had burned to embers. She banked it with ashes so that she would not have to start it afresh in the morning, then moved sleepily toward her place among the warm skins beside Rusog. A glance toward We-yo's empty bed brought her to instant wakefulness.

There was a certain latitude in Cherokee customs governing the courtship of the young, but the permissiveness did not extend either to consummating the sexual relationship of young lovers or to a girl's staying out after midnight.

Ena noted that everything was in its place in that portion of the lodge that was We-yo's personal area. She turned, took a step toward the sleeping Rusog, then decided against waking him. Instead she draped a blanket over her shoulders and hurried out into the cool night. At the entrance to the young warriors' house she heard a chorus of snoring, grunts, coughs. She opened the door, stepped in, and made her way to Ho-ya's bed. The dim light coming in the smoke hole showed her that her son's bed was empty. Moreover, his weapons and his blankets were gone.

She knew that Ho-ya had been swayed by White Blanket's fiery appeals. It would be like him, for he was young and impulsive, to follow the Mingo to Tecumseh. It was We-yo's absence that puzzled her. The girl was too commonsensical to pursue such a course. She knocked over a pot on the way to the door but slipped out before a sleepy voice asked, "Who's there?"

Again she decided to let Rusog sleep. It would be day soon, and there would be time enough to go to the Seneca village, where White Blanket was allowed the use of Renno's longhouse, to confirm her strong suspicion that the Mingo had something to do with the disappearance of her son and daughter.

As the seconds passed, however, Ena felt the edge of anger build. She woke Rusog immediately, told him the situation, then gave him warmed-over food for breakfast.

As he ate, Ena readied herself for the trail. All of her weapons were at hand. Rusog grimly prepared himself as well, then they walked together to Renno's longhouse. It was empty. The Mingo's possessions were gone.

"They will be traveling north," Ena said, "unless they try to set us a false trail."

Rusog did not question Ena's intention to accompany him. He had seen her in action against an enemy, and although neither he nor his wife had the swift reactions of youth, the Cherokee chief knew that she was still as capable as any man in either his tribe or hers. That she would be at his side as he set out to reclaim son and daughter was taken for granted.

"I will tell my mother," Ena said, for Toshabe's long-house was just across the commons from Renno's. She ran across the open space and entered. It was dark inside, and cold. The fire had been allowed to burn down. She called out her mother's name. She could see the shape of Toshabe under a warm bearskin in her bed, but her mother gave no answer. She stood beside the bed and spoke softly, and then she leaned close. Toshabe's face was beaded with sweat, and perspiration. Ena put a hand to her mother's forehead. It burned with fever.

Ena went to the fire, found a few glowing embers, and used fine shavings to start a blaze. Rusog, a questioning look on his face, appeared in the doorway. She nodded toward Toshabe's bed. Rusog examined Toshabe and felt her heated forehead.

"The winter fever," he said.

"The fire was almost out," she told him. "Poor thing must have been like this all night."

For a woman of Toshabe's age, the winter fever was

a serious matter. Rusog stood silently as Ena spooned water into her mother's mouth.

"You go," Ena said. "And may the manitous go with you."

"Yes," Rusog agreed. He put his hand on Ena's shoulder, squeezed, and then was gone. Ena warmed more water over the fire and bathed the stale perspiration from her mother's face and neck. Once Toshabe mumbled in delirium, "Ah, Ghonkaba, Ghonkaba, my husband."

"No, Mother," Ena said with great intensity. "It is not time. There is still need for you here. You must postpone your reunion with my father."

Toshabe's eyes fluttered open. "Ena?"

"I am here."

The eyes closed, and once again Toshabe spoke with the spirits. Ena went to the door, hailed a pair of young boys who were racing past toward the woods. One of them greeted Ena by name and with a formal Seneca phrase.

"I need help," she said. "The senior matron is ill. Go to the Se-quo-i and tell him to come to me. Tell him that Toshabe has the fever and that he must bring his medicines."

"Our shaman should be here to tend his mother," said the older boy.

"It is not for you to question the actions of El-i-chi," Ena said flatly. "Go now."

Soon Se-quo-i came limping hurriedly across the commons. Since his accident while experimenting with the white man's method of deep plowing, one of his legs was shorter than the other. He cursorily greeted Ena in English and felt Toshabe's brow.

"You must sponge away the heat," he said.

"Yes. I have been doing that."

He opened a carefully constructed wooden box slung by a leather thong around his neck. He poured a powder into a cup, added water, then mixed it well. "Help me."

Ena lifted Toshabe's head and held it while Se-quo-i spooned the medicinal mixture into her mouth.

"Sweet flag for the fever," he explained. "The white man's botanists call it calamus."

Ena knew the plant. It grew in marshy places and had a pungent root.

"When she regains consciousness," he said, feeding Toshabe the herbal mixture, "we will burn cedar twigs to help clear the congestion."

"She is old."

"Don't worry," he said. "This one is enamored of life. She will not leave us." He finished giving her the potion, then straightened. "If you want to rest, I will stay with her."

"Thank you, but I am not tired."

"Well then, the boy sent me here before I had indulged that terrible white man's habit," he said.

She laughed, for she knew how much Se-quo-i prized his morning tea. "Sit and be patient," she said teasingly.

Soon water was boiling, and then the savory aroma of tea filled the longhouse. Ena made him a cup with honey, and Se-quo-i sighed with satisfaction as he took a sip that almost burned his lips.

Through a long day and a longer night the Cherokee stayed with Ena, patiently and tenderly dosing Toshabe with his herbal brews.

Rusog, forty-three years old, considered himself to be in his prime. His endurance could match that of men half his age. He began to realize quite soon after striking the trail of the three travelers, however, that he was a bit out of condition. He excused it as a result of his administrative duties as principal chief, but that didn't keep him from being angry with himself when he had to stop the warrior's pace and walk.

There were times during the next three days when he lost the trail. Fortunately, the Mingo was arrogantly moving directly toward the north, apparently to pass through middle Tennessee toward Kentucky and the Ohio country. Each time, by casting around, Rusog found the trail again.

For the first four days he ate little. The resulting loss of girth allowed him to breathe easier. He pushed his sore muscles to the limit and now could keep up a warrior's pace for most of the day. On a morning when he found that the ashes of White Blanket's campfire were still warm, Rusog grunted in satisfaction and set off down the trail at a pace that would have done credit to Renno.

By late afternoon he had the feeling that he would see his son and daughter as he crested the next rise or as he broke from a wooded copse into a flowering meadow. At worst, he felt, he would be able to smell or see the campfire when White Blanket called a halt.

At last Rusog encountered the Mingo. White Blanket was alone, having left an early camp to circle back in pursuit of a deer. Rusog was moving swiftly down a deer track in dense woods when he saw a hint of movement ahead. He slowed and crept cautiously forward, to see White Blanket stalking the animal through dense underbrush.

Rusog, always the practical man, waited until the Mingo had killed the deer with an accurate shot from his musket; he and his son and daughter would need food for the trip home. It was just as well to let the Mingo provide it, since he had caused all of the trouble.

"You shoot well," he remarked, from a point not more than five yards behind White Blanket.

The Mingo leaped and turned in midair. His tomahawk was in his hand.

"There is no need for the blade," Rusog said mildly, stepping into the open. "Unless, of course, that is your choice." He hoped fervently that it would not be, for he was tired and sore, and he was concerned about Toshabe, for whom he had the greatest respect, and wanted to get back to the village.

"Great Chief," White Blanket said, "she is of age. We performed the ceremony of marriage with your son as witness."

Rusog felt pain knife into him. White Blanket, seeing the look on Rusog's face, leaned his musket against a tree, hefted his tomahawk.

"And Ho-ya is a man, Rusog. He chose to come with me of his own free will."

"So casually you rob me of my only son, my only daughter," Rusog said, nodding grimly. "I will speak with them."

"No," White Blanket said. "Go home, old man. Leave life to the young and to those who are willing to fight for it."

Rusog's musket jerked upward to point at the Mingo's belly.

"You can kill me, old man, but by doing so you will only compound your loss, for neither your son nor your daughter will forgive you."

Rusog leaned his own musket against a tree, drew his tomahawk. "Perhaps I will just damage you slightly, then."

"I ask you, old man, not to do this," White Blanket said. "Go home. I assure you that your daughter is loved and that she will be safe with me."

"Until you lose your life on a long-knife soldier's bayonet?" Rusog asked. "Leaving her alone in a strange country?"

"You ignore my pleas?"

"I think, Mingo, that we must settle this thing thusly," Rusog said, leaping forward to try to disable White Blanket with a blow to the lower leg. White Blanket jumped back, avoiding the stroke, and then steel rang on steel as he countered Rusog's powerful blows.

To Rusog's shame it was a brief battle. In the end it was he, not Mingo, who was disabled. White Blanket had deliberately kept his blows low. To kill the father of his beloved was obviously not his desire, but he had no intention of risking a tender reunion between father and daughter lest parental loyalty overcome We-yo's love for her husband. His blade sliced through buckskin and left a long, open gash in Rusog's thigh. Blood ran. Rusog roared in anger and pain, then went back to the battle, his heavy blows causing White Blanket great concern until, with a groan of agony, Rusog fell, his leg having given way.

"I will bind your wound," White Blanket offered.

"Go your way, Mingo," Rusog seethed. "But keep looking over your shoulder."

"Unless your bleeding is stopped, you will die," White Blanket said.

Rusog used his knife to slice away the leg of his trousers. He cut the buckskin into a thong, which he tied above the wound to stanch the flow of blood. The wound was deep and debilitating, making the thigh muscle useless; fortunately, no major carrier of blood had been severed. He pressed the rest of the buckskin against the wound, and soon the bleeding stopped.

"A day's march ago we passed within a mile of a village," White Blanket said. "Do you think you can make it there?"

"That is not your concern," Rusog said.

"I leave you with my wish that the manitous will care for you," White Blanket said. He picked up the fallen deer, slung it across his shoulders, and disappeared into the trees.

Rusog leaned back against a tree. He felt dizzy, but he knew that he could not surrender to the need to close his eyes and sleep. He took needle and catgut from his travel pack. He lifted his face to the sky and prayed to the spirits. Then, lips compressed, face impassive in spite of the pain, he sewed the bloody edges of the gash, making the stitches close, for he planned to move again to the north before the morning.

When he loosened the thong, blood oozed through the stitches and the pain came in a wave of torment that enveloped the chief in blackness. He awoke in the chill of morning. His leg was stiff. When he stood on it, the pain made his vision dim. He knew then that there would be no immediate reunion with his son and daughter. By midmorning he had cut a forked limb and padded the fork with a blanket, for use as a crutch. He turned toward the southeast, a defeated man.

It had taken him five days to reach the spot where he met White Blanket. It would be ten days before he struggled across the swimming creek, burning with fever from a wound gone septic. By sheer dint of willpower and the need to revenge himself on the Mingo who had stolen his children, he made it to the edge of his own village, where he fell on his face in the dirt. Children at play saw him and ran screaming for help.

Toshabe had survived the fever. She was still weak, although she insisted on tottering around the longhouse to help Ena prepare the evening meal. Both women looked up when an excited boy burst into the house shouting for them to come quickly.

"Rusog?" Ena asked, dropping a pot of stew to splash across the floor.

Four Seneca warriors carried Rusog to Toshabe's longhouse, since it was near. Again the Cherokee Se-quo-i was summoned. When he saw the swollen, discolored wound, he shook his head. "There is but one thing to do."

Ena helped him remove the catgut stitchings. Once cut, they slid easily out of the infected flesh. The wound gaped open. Rusog remained blessedly unconscious while Ena cleansed the wound, scrubbing and cutting away putrid flesh. Se-quo-i, meanwhile, was heating a broad-bladed knife in the fire.

"He is ready," Ena said after she had cleansed the wound as best she could.

Rusog had not moved, but when Se-quo-i pressed the white-hot knife blade to the raw wound, the chief's muscles spasmed, and he roared like a wounded bear. The stench of burning flesh filled the house. It was all Ena could do to hold him down.

"Now we can do nothing but wait," Se-quo-i said.

Ena was awakened just before dawn. For a moment she didn't know why as she tried to remember the sound that had disturbed her sleep.

"Ena . . ."

She jumped to her feet and lit a lamp. Rusog's feverish eyes were open.

"Ah, Ena," he moaned sadly.

"I will get water," she said.

He drank greedily, then pushed the cup away. "I failed," he told her.

"You are alive. That is all that matters."

"I should have tried to kill him." He had suffered ten torturous days, with his mind wandering in and out of delirium, to find a way to lessen his shame. He was certain that if he had been fighting to kill and not merely to disable, he would have bested the Mingo. He tried to explain, but tiredness overcame him and he slept. He awoke later to continue this explanation.

"You did right," Ena consoled. "To have killed him, since our little fool loves him, would have alienated her forever." She spoke more reassuring words. She gave him water and tea and food. The wound had a clean scab. For Ena's convenience and to give Toshabe her privacy, Rusog was carried to his own home, where Se-quo-i continued to treat the healing wound with herbal ointment. When, on the morning of her husband's second day at home, Ena began to prepare to travel, he nodded.

"It is just," he approved, "for you to avenge my shame."

"The great chief Rusog knows no shame," she said angrily.

"His route would have taken him into Tennessee. It seems that he plans to cross Kentucky to the Ohio."

"Odd that he would choose to travel an area so well settled," Ena mused.

"You will travel far," he said. "Perhaps you should take someone with you."

"I prefer to travel alone."

"So," he said.

By following Rusog's directions, in three days she reached the spot where her husband had battled the Mingo. She had made such good time because it had not been necessary for her to track or waste hours casting around to pick up a lost trail. Rain had fallen in the meantime, but she found the traces of a campfire not far from the spot. She continued in a northerly direction to a Cherokee village not far from the Tennessee border, where she was told, yes, two young warriors and a pretty girl had passed through.

"To the north?" she asked.

"Toward the sunset," she was told.

She was not surprised. It would have been odd indeed for a declared enemy of the white man to travel, dressed in the trappings of a Mingo, through well-settled Tennessee and Kentucky. She ran westward, and at the next village it was confirmed that White Blanket and her twins were now headed toward the Tennessee River. They had rested for a night and a day in the village, and the

Mingo had inquired about canoes to take them down the Tennessee to and across the Ohio.

Ena spent a night as a guest of the village chief of the westernmost Cherokee settlement. Those whom she followed had been there before her, traveling in a leisurely manner, stopping to feast and exchange tales with the villagers.

The woman was warned that she would be traveling in Chickasaw hunting grounds after one day's march to the west. There had been no serious trouble between Chickasaw and Cherokee since the Spanish had coaxed the Chickasaw into the small war that had ended Spanish ambitions to move into the lands of the Cherokee; but the wilderness was wide, and she was alone. The Cherokee chief urged to to allow him to send two warriors with her. She thanked him but refused.

"This is a private matter," she explained. "I prefer to act alone in all ways."

Feeling great optimism she left the village. By staying to visit and feast in the Cherokee villages, White Blanket had allowed her to close the gap of days that separated them.

The travel had made her lean, and she kept the warrior's pace without effort. Her body felt as if it were a precision machine, all the parts humming and clicking in perfect order. Toward evening she killed a rabbit, feasted on it with the coming of darkness, slept soundly rolled in her one blanket, and with the dawn she was moving west again.

Around her the trees grew thick and tall. Their overhanging branches cut off the sunlight and left the forest floor relatively free of growth. She felt as if she had run into a different world—a world of quiet, peaceful woodlands, little glades, and clear, sparkling streams. At such a stream she sank to her knees and drank deeply. A sound at her back brought her to her feet, her hand going to her tomahawk. At a distance of perhaps ten paces, two Chickasaw warriors were studying her with great interest.

Chapter VII

On a Sunday morning Cadet Captain Hawk Harper was awake with first light. He heated a flatiron and pressed his dress uniform, shined his boots and polished them to mirrorlike perfection, and was generally more meticulous than usual in his personal grooming.

He attended services conducted by a visiting minister in the rude post chapel. The Cadet Corps sat at attention, backs straight, eyes front. The preacher's topic was the sin of lust and fornication, and for his texts he went back to the Book of Genesis.

To Little Hawk it seemed that the stern, bearded man of God was looking into his head, which was filled with sweet thoughts of Mary Ann and a dread of facing Major Lillie.

"And when," the preacher intoned, "in your mortal weakness, you fall prey to the mighty lusts placed in your breast by the devil, you become like the serpent, whom God cursed, saying: thou art cursed above all cattle and above every beast of the field, and dust shalt thou eat all the days of thy life."

Little Hawk, shifting in his seat, cleared his throat. As the preacher's rumbling bass voice soared to new heights, assuring each and every cadet—for they were young, and their juices flowed hotly—of burning in the lake of fire, Little Hawk turned his mind from the biblical phrases and the eternal damnation and to composing his speech to Major Lillie.

When the preacher moved on from the sin of lust to the gamut of evil of which man is capable, dwelling on the tale of Cain and Abel, Little Hawk once again paid attention. Having been reared as a Seneca, he never tired of hearing a rousing tale, sad though this one was, about brother killing brother.

"And the sin of Cain continues to be committed right here in our own country!" the preacher shouted. "And by the descendants of Cain, those who were created apart from God's chosen people who dwelt in the fragrant, idyllic Garden of Eden. For such lesser people were there, even in the days of Adam. Did not Cain go out from the presence of the Lord and dwell in the land of Nod, east of Eden, where he *knew* his wife?"

The preacher paused and looked meaningfully at the cadets. "If any of you doubt the fact of polygenesis, you have only to consult the Good Book, Genesis chapter four, verses sixteen through seventeen. God's chosen people, from whom you and I are descended down through the countless generations, originated in the garden and nowhere else. But there were others, created, perhaps, in one of God's weaker moments, created in imitation of His image but lacking the God-given qualities that make us civilized men."

The preacher paused again, to wipe his sweat-drenched face and take a quick swig of water from a glass at his fingertips. He swept his fiery eyes over the corps of cadets. "It is up to you, young gentlemen, officers-to-be in the army of this United States—a land blessed by God, conceived under God, and dedicated to God's principles—to stand as a bulwark between our civilized endeavors and the savagery of the redskinned devils who lurk in the dark forests of our frontier. But I warn you, men: as you perform your God-given duties against the heathen, have a care. I say that God will damn any white man who *knows,* as Cain did, the heathen women of this lesser race. And I call upon you, the elite of our youth, to condemn such men and to drive them from the fold to perish in the fires of hell with the barbaric seeds of Cain."

The sermon ended with a prayer taken from several psalms. Then the preacher, garrison members, and their families filed from the chapel. Upon a muted order from Cadet Captain Harper, the corps rose as one, pivoted smartly on their heel, and marched in perfect step and single file past the preacher and Major Lillie, who were standing side by side outside the chapel door. Captain Harper was last. He halted in front of the preacher and post commander, did a snappy right-face turn, and saluted.

"Sir," he said, "permission to comment on the sermon."

Lillie smiled and nodded, obviously expecting his student leader to do the right thing, to compliment the reverend on a rousing effort.

"Reverend," Little Hawk said, "I just wanted you to have a good look at me."

Both the preacher and the commander were puzzled.

"I am one of those whom you call upon to be a bulwark against the descendants of Cain."

"Yes indeed," the preacher said, beaming.

"I am pleased to learn from you that I am endowed with all the faculties of human nature and made in the image of God, in the likeness of the Creator. But I must apologize to you for finding a fault in your reasoning."

"Oh?" the preacher asked, frowning.

"There are two facts that refute your thesis," Little Hawk said. "One, a man cannot be judged by the uniform he happens to be wearing at the moment. Two, I, personally, cannot be both a member of the European race—God's chosen people in your estimation—and be the Seneca that I am. I assure you, however, that as a member of that red race that you call the seed of Cain, I feel no indication of being damned."

The preacher's mouth fell open. Major Lillie's face darkened.

"Good day to you, Reverend," Little Hawk said pleasantly. He saluted Lillie. "Thank you, sir."

As he walked back home, had lunch, and relaxed, Major Lillie didn't know whether to be angry or proud of his cadet officer. He had to admit that he agreed, at least in part, with the preacher. Surely there was plenty of overt evidence to prove that the black, yellow, and red races, plus the dark-skinned races of such far-off places as East India where, it was said, men worshiped cows and rats, were inherently inferior. In the case of Cadet Harper, the inferior blood was mitigated certainly by the vigorous blood of European man; Harper was three-quarters white and, for all practical purposes, a member of the chosen race.

Lillie decided that he rather admired Harper for calling the preacher's attention to his Indian blood. It had taken spunk, and the reprimand had been delivered in a diplomatic manner, which was a credit to the training received by members of the corps.

When Little Hawk presented himself at the commander's house for their all-important discussion, the cadet was much encouraged when Lillie met him at the door with a smile, returned his salute, and shook his hand.

"Glad you stopped by, Harper," Lillie said, escorting him into a small, smoke-filled study. "I've been thinking about what you said to the preacher."

Little Hawk came to attention, ready for the reprimand.

"At ease. Sit down."

He sat stiffly on the edge of a chair.

"I understand how you feel," Lillie said. "A man can't choose his ancestors. I will tell you this: you are to be congratulated for lifting yourself above your background, Harper. I have every confidence that you're going to make a fine officer."

"Thank you, sir."

"All the same," Lillie continued, "even though you handled it well and didn't exactly call the preacher a fool, was it really necessary to offer even so mild an insult to a visitor to this post? After all, what did you gain by pointing out that there might be an exception to the preacher's theory?"

"Perhaps, sir, a bit of personal satisfaction."

"Harper, that will not be the last time you hear someone express contempt for or disapproval of the Indian."

"Yes, sir."

"Wouldn't it be best, since you have decided to make the army your career, if you were to go easy on telling everyone that you are Seneca? You're just causing yourself needless trouble."

Little Hawk felt a quick dizziness, and in his mind he could see a line of stern faces in the war paint of the Seneca, his father among them. "I will never deny my ancestors," he said, leaving off the "sir."

"Well," Lillie said, "perhaps with time you might come to agree with me." He reached for his pipe. "You wanted to speak with me?"

"Yes, sir, on a matter of some importance."

"Speak, then," Lillie said.

Little Hawk stood and came to attention. After a pause during which his heart rate increased alarmingly, he blurted, "Sir, Cadet Captain Hawk Harper requests permission to speak to the major regarding his daughter."

Lillie put down the pipe and frowned. "What about my daughter?"

"Sir, I have the honor of asking the major's consent to allow me to make Mary Ann my wife upon graduation from the academy." There, it was out. He took a deep breath. He had been staring at the wall above Lillie's head. He let his eyes drop, and what he saw in the major's face stopped the racing of his heart and caused a coldness to creep upward from his stomach.

Lillie's face had gone florid. His eyes squinted at Little Hawk with what could only have been anger or hatred. "What in Hades makes you think that my daughter would want to marry you?" Lillie asked, making an obvious effort to control his voice.

"Sir, she has expressed her willingness to do so."

Lillie leaped to his feet. "What in hell have you been doing with my daughter?" he roared. He lifted his hand as he moved close.

Little Hawk's muscles tensed. He was Seneca. He had never been struck by his father, his mother, or by anyone else other than by peers in spirited play or by an enemy. It was not in his nature to turn the other cheek. The son of Renno, the grandson of Ghonkaba, would not suffer that ultimate insult, not even from his commanding officer.

Fortunately for his physical safety, Lillie decided against striking the blow that he threatened. "If you have laid a hand on my daughter, you savage," Lillie threatened from between clenched jaws, "I will personally take a horsewhip to your red back."

Fury boiled up in Little Hawk. The man's words of praise had meant nothing. His own record of achievement at the academy was rendered instantly meaningless. The honor that the major had bestowed upon him by making him cadet captain was an empty vessel. His face became stoic. His right arm and hand ached for the feel of a weapon. And then he smiled, although it held no warmth.

"I take it, sir, that your reaction indicates that your answer to my request is negative," he said, his smile widening, his eyes not joining his mouth in the expression.

"You—" Lillie sputtered. "I ask you again. What have you done to make my daughter agree—"

"Sir," Little Hawk said. "I think I will leave it to your daughter to answer that question."

"You heathen bastard," Lillie said, his anger almost out of control. "Get out of here before—"

Little Hawk clicked his heels and saluted. "Sir, permission to leave."

"Get—get—" Lillie could not speak. And yet, so ingrained was the habit that he returned Little Hawk's salute.

The cadet captain strode from the room. Mary Ann was cowering near the front door, having heard her father's raised voice from the study. Little Hawk paused. "Will you come away with me?" he asked.

Mary Ann gasped. "Are you crazy? Get out of here before my father kills you, you idiot."

"I have asked your father for your hand, and he has refused. Will you be my wife in defiance of his wishes?"

"No, you fool, no," she said. "Get out of here, now."

He did not move.

She glared at him. "Do you think for one minute that I would run away with you to live like a savage?"

"So," he said. "I bid you good day, Miss Lillie."

Humiliated, bereft, he walked down to the river. The wind was harsh, from the northeast. He let his mind drift and merge with the wind, to travel over the hills, streams, farms, and woodlands until in his mind he saw the forests of his homeland. For a few minutes his need to be with his own was so great, he considered desertion, but he quickly decided that such a course of action would be not only defeat but cowardice. He was due to finish his schooling and training within a very few months. He had made a choice to be an officer of the United States Army, and he would not allow a girl to deprive him of his goal. Although she quite obviously found him to be more than adequate as a lover, she just as clearly felt that he was not up to her standards for a lifelong mate.

And yet the boy was in pain; in the young, sexual infatuation is the beginning of love. He would gladly have given up his commission for her if she had agreed to leave with him; but since she had made her choice, he made his. He would finish his term at the academy and hope for assignment at a post far away from West Point and Mary Ann Lillie.

The results of his frustrated attempt to become a part of the Lillie family were several. First, on Monday, Major Lillie stood before the corps and announced, "It is my policy to honor cadets who have performed well, and I feel that it is highly desirable to spread the honors around. Therefore, since Cadet Hawk Harper has had the privilege of being cadet captain for more than half of this school year, I hereby appoint Cadet Sidney Forrest to finish out this year in the position previously occupied by Cadet Harper."

Demotion was not the end of Lillie's intentions for Cadet Harper. On a field exercise the next day, as Little Hawk's squad wheeled a cannon into position and prepared it for firing, Forrest ordered the men to change the direction of fire by almost ninety degrees. The object of the exercise was to direct accurate fire onto a target that was not directly visible because of an intervening ridge. Forrest, Little Hawk saw, had become disoriented.

"Captain," Little Hawk said as Forrest ordered the men to load, "you're going to fire off range."

"Harper," Forrest said, "I am in command here."

"You'll be lucky if you don't drop the ball on the barn of that farm near the post if you fire that gun in the direction you've got it pointed."

"Harper," Forrest said angrily, "when I need your advice, I'll ask for it. At ease."

"Yes, sir," Little Hawk said with his cold little smile.

"Since you doubt my ability to sight in a target," Forrest said, "I'm going to give you the honor of firing the round."

"With all due respect, sir, I must refuse that order," Little Hawk said. "I will not be the man to kill some farmer's chickens, or worse."

"You refuse a direct order?" Forrest asked, his face dark with anger.

"With respect, sir," Little Hawk said.

"Noted," Forrest said. He turned to the men and yelled, "Fire!" To prove his efficiency he had the men reload quickly and send a second ball soaring over the ridge. Both landed squarely on the roof of a barn. The farmer was spared another round when a sergeant came galloping down from the artillery observation post, shouting orders to cease firing.

Cadet Hawk Harper stood at attention before Major John Lillie.

"So," Lillie said, "you admit refusing a direct order from your cadet captain?"

"I do, sir, for I knew that Captain Forrest was confused and that the fire would endanger the civilian community," Little Hawk said.

"I didn't ask for excuses, Harper," Lillie said sternly. "You do know that refusing an order from a superior officer is a serious matter."

"Sir," Little Hawk barked.

"Even when you think you're right, Harper, you must obey orders. Now I will admit that in this case there are mitigating circumstances." He winced inwardly, thinking of the problems that had been created when two cannonballs smashed through the barn roof, one of them destroying a corn crib and spreading its contents over the muddy yard. "I will not dismiss you from the academy. You will, for the next ninety days, do four hours of fatigue duty daily. To begin your punishment you will, before reveille tomorrow morning, dig a hole in the parade ground that measures six feet in width, length, and depth. When you have completed digging this hole, you will awaken Cadet Captain Forrest, who will inspect your work and confirm the dimensions. Upon his approval, you will then fill in the hole, smooth it down, and transport any surplus soil off the parade ground. Is that clear?"

"Sir!" Little Hawk shouted.

He went to the barracks and changed into fatigue dress. The digging was difficult at first, for there was a hardened crust on the soil of the parade ground. Then he hit a layer of softer loam before digging into a gravel-filled clay. By sunset he had reached a depth of two feet. He worked by lantern light into the coolness of midnight. Blisters formed and burst on his hands. His back and shoulders ached like fire. He was at a depth of four feet when he heard movement behind. Groaning, Little Hawk straightened his back and saw two of his fellow cadets in fatigue clothing.

"Since Forrest was wrong, he shouldn't have reported you to the commander, Hawk," one of the young men said.

Little Hawk shrugged.

"He's an ass," said the other fellow as he stepped down into the pit. "Take a rest, Hawk." He pulled the shovel out of Little Hawk's hand and began digging.

"I can't allow this," Little Hawk said. "I don't want to get you into trouble."

"What trouble?" the cadet asked.

Little Hawk, filled with gratitude, climbed out of the hole and rested for a few minutes before he began to push the dirt back from the edge so that it was easier for the diggers—his two friends were taking turns at the shovel—to toss up the excavated earth. Another pair of cadets joined the effort. They brought another shovel along. And soon Little Hawk's entire section of the corps was grouped around the hole. Two men at a time dug. Others began to sing. More lanterns were lit. Little Hawk tried to quiet the singers, but the rest joined in.

Cadet Captain Sidney Forrest, awakened by the singing, came out of the barracks half-dressed and began shouting orders. Four of the larger cadets closed on Forrest. Two of them picked him up under his arms.

"Captain," said one of the boys, as they held Forrest's feet over the edge of the pit, which was six feet deep. "It's time for you to make your inspection."

Forrest dropped six feet and went to his knees.

"Ah'd say it's about deep enough, wouldn't you, Captain?" drawled a Virginia cadet. "Ah'd say that Cadet Harper has done a fahn job of work, wouldn't you?"

"I'll report you all to the major," Forrest threatened. "Harper was supposed to do this punishment detail by himself. You're all going to be—"

"We're all going to be just a little bit unhappy with you, Captain," someone said. "And that unhappiness just might turn slightly violent when we're all out in the field alone, with no cadre around."

"You're talking mutiny," Forrest accused.

"What are you going to do, Captain?" the Virginian asked. "Request that the major kick the whole class out of the academy?"

"Look around you, Forrest," a cadet said.

In the moonlight their faces were stern. They grouped themselves on the edge of the hole and looked down at him.

"Want to take the chance that we don't intend to break your leg if you go to the major?" one of the larger boys asked.

"Isn't that a nice six-by-six hole?" another asked.

Forrest swallowed. "Harper, good job. I approve. You may now fill the hole."

"Thank you, sir," Little Hawk said.

The cadets began to kick and shovel soil into the hole before Forrest could scramble out. When he finally emerged, he was covered with dirt. He started to walk away, but he was seized by the same two large cadets who had dropped him into the hole. "Now, Captain," one of them said, "a good officer always stays at the side of his men. You wouldn't want to be sleeping comfortably while your men were out here filling in this hole, would you?"

Forrest was handed a shovel.

At morning muster Major Lillie noticed that the men in the graduating section of the Cadet Corps seemed less alert than usual. Some of them had dark circles under their eyes. Harper himself looked fresh as he stood at attention for roll call.

On the parade ground a fresh plot of earth marked the spot where Harper had dug his hole. Lillie couldn't help but think that the man had turned in one hell of a night's work. That near admiration turned to spite quickly as he recalled his conversation with Mary Ann from the night before. His daughter had denied encouraging Harper.

"I don't know whatever gave him the idea that I wanted to marry him," she had said. "Why, I've hardly spoken to the boy. Never have I done anything more than return his greetings politely."

Yes, Lillie was thinking, Cadet Harper would find himself in more difficulties as the days passed. The major had no intention of allowing an impudent savage to rise above his station in life and become an officer in the United States Army.

The two young Chickasaw hunters who had come upon Ena drinking at a stream had been on a combination long hunt and would-be coup-counting search. True, they hadn't looked too hard for enemies. They had not, for example, traveled far enough south to encounter any Creek or Choctaw hunting parties, and they had carefully avoided entering Cherokee lands. Admittedly, it had been a pleasant enough outing. They had found plenty of game, they had walked trails that they'd never traveled, and now, as they were pointing their way back toward their village, a very interesting opportunity had presented itself.

The woman's dress indicated that she was Cherokee. True, there was peace between the two tribes, but peace, in the wilderness, was always a relative thing. Now and again a warrior had to prove his manhood, so little clashes between individuals or small parties were not defined as war. Both tribes recognized the facts that boys will be boys and that the warrior's code demanded some exhibition of courage.

So, too, was it accepted that the occasional use of a woman of another tribe was not punishable in tribal council. It was the right of the strong to sample the spoils of his victory. It did not matter to the two Chickasaw that they had done nothing to earn the reward that faced them. They had merely stumbled across her in the wilderness. But they had been gone from the company of women for over three weeks. Moreover, neither of them had yet taken a wife, so even when they were with the tribe their youthful appetites were seldom satisfied.

The two Chickasaw widened the distance between them as they moved toward the woman. Her hand was on her tomahawk.

"If she tries to flee across the creek I will catch her in the water," one of them said, thinking that the Cherokee woman would not understand.

"You will catch this," the woman threatened, brandishing her tomahawk.

The young men halted and looked uneasily at each other. "She speaks our language."

"Yet she dresses as a Cherokee."

"I am Cherokee," she said. "I am Ena, wife of the principal chief, Rusog, who has exchanged vows of peace with your chiefs."

"I see this Rusog not," said the larger of the two.

"You see me," Ena said as the two intruders began once more to move to block her flight. "I have no time to cajole you, for I am on the trail of one who has stolen my children from me."

The large Chickasaw laughed. "We will keep you from your quest only for a little while." He rubbed his bulging loincloth.

"If you value that which you caress so shamelessly," Ena said, "then leave me."

"In a little while," snickered the smaller warrior.

To the surprise of the Chickasaw, Ena made no effort to flee. She braced herself, tomahawk at the ready, legs parted. "I ask you to go on your way," she said calmly. "Hear me."

"Put away the blade, Ena."

"I ask you to let me go my way in peace," she said.

"In a little while."

As if to prove his worth, it was the smaller man who decided to disarm the Cherokee woman. He lunged forward, swinging his tomahawk with the intention of knocking Ena's weapon away. Instead, his blade sliced empty air, and a yowl of surprise and pain came from his throat when Ena's tomahawk sliced open his deerskin tunic and left a four-inch gash in his arm. He backed away, looking in disbelief at his own blood.

"The Cherokee has cut me!" he sputtered in amazement. He threw back his head and let out a howl like a wildcat and, murder in his eyes, pranced toward her. "We would have let you go in a short time, Cherokee bitch," he said. "Now my blade will make an orifice more painful to you than would have been the one we intended to use."

"Look again at the color of your blood, Chickasaw," Ena told him, "and consider your actions well."

She leaped to one side and avoided the Chickasaw's rush, and as he tried to recover, she left another welling slash, this one on his right shoulder.

"Is that not enough?" she asked as he screamed again and rushed at her, all caution forgotten. She aimed for his throat, and his momentum carried him past her even as his great, severed arteries pumped out his life. Gargling his own blood, he fell to the ground to try to crawl away.

"Observe that this action, which I did not want, was forced upon me," she told the remaining warrior, who stood in amazement as his companion's legs twitched feebly and then were still. "I am older than you—old enough to have learned the value of life. Do not force me to kill you, too."

"Thing of evil," the Chickasaw screamed in a shrill, angry voice.

He was not going to make the same mistake that had caused the swift death of his friend. He approached cautiously, feinting this way, then that way, lunging forward and dancing back, making the air whistle with the speed of his weapon's swipes.

The woman Ena backed away slowly, obviously saving her energy. The Chickasaw smiled at that; her need to reserve her strength made him feel all the more powerful. He launched a serious attack, but she sank down and fell to one side under a swinging blow that would have decapitated her.

Slashing at his lower leg as she rolled away, she bounced to her feet. He yelled in pain and anger. Her blade had sliced through his calf muscle, and blood poured over his moccasin.

This time he limped forward with even more bluster, screaming a war cry, aiming a blow at her middle. She skipped quickly to one side, narrowly avoiding the backswing of his weapon. The force of his effort combined with the weakness of his leg to throw him off balance. She hit him in the back of the head with the flat of her tomahawk. He fell heavily, rolled to his knees, and shook his head.

"I have no wish to kill you," she said again.

His scream of outrage was the cry of a wounded panther. He, a warrior of the Chickasaw, a tribe of warriors, had seen his best friend die, and his own life's blood was seeping from a deep cut in his calf muscle. And it had been done by a woman. He chanted a prayer to the spirits, for he was sure that the Cherokee woman was indeed a manifestation of evil, a thing of the unseen world, and thus unbeatable by ordinary man. But his pride would not permit him to accept her offer to end the fight. He came to his feet and moved toward her, chanting his death song, asking his ancestors who had gone before him to prepare a place for him.

"Come then, Chickasaw," Ena said grimly. "If death is all you desire, you force me to give it to you as a pleasant surprise."

She ended it quickly, stepping under a powerful blow aimed at her right shoulder and causing his blade to glance harmlessly away as she parried. Immediately she sank her own blade into the side of his neck to cut the tendon there. He fell, his head hanging lopsidedly. She ended his pain with one blow to the bridge of his nose.

She stood breathing hard in the little glade, and a shudder of revulsion rippled through her. "May the manitous be with you, Chickasaw," she said sadly.

She put the scene of battle behind her on the run. As she vaulted over the little creek, she saw that the blood of the first man she'd killed had run into the clear water to discolor it.

Pedro Valdez, vaquero on the ranch of Señor Julio de Alda, had a little cabin of his own at a distance of some miles from the hacienda. There he lived with his wife, Red Flower, who was Comanche. Valdez had three children, all girls. When he realized that he had not seen his oldest, who was thirteen, for several hours, he immediately asked her sisters where she had gone. The girls said that when they last saw her, she had gone bathing in the creek. Valdez's concern increased as time passed, and finally he saddled his horse and rode off toward the distant creek, where his daughters swam and caught crayfish.

Valdez saw fire on the south side of the creek and made his way across a spot with a sandy bottom over which flowed the clear, clean water. He began to feel very uneasy when he saw that there were several men gathered around the campfire. He had not brought a weapon other than his long knife. Nonetheless he felt it necessary to approach the fire, for his daughter was beginning to show the curves of womanhood, and he suspected that the men might have something to do with her absence . . . although he prayed that were not so.

"Hello, the campfire," he called out in Spanish.

"Who's there?" a voice asked in English.

"*No hablo inglés,*" Valdez said. "*Hablo español.*"

"What is it you want?" a voice asked in heavily accented Spanish.

"I search for my daughter," Valdez said. "Have you seen a girl with long, black hair?"

"Come forward," the voice invited.

He rode close, dismounted, and let the reins of his well-trained horse trail on the ground. He walked to stand near the fire. "She is thirteen, my daughter. I thought perhaps you had seen her, since she was last known to be coming to the creek to bathe."

"There is no thirteen-year-old girl here," said a pock-marked man.

"I thought perhaps you might have seen her," Valdez said weakly. The gringo who had spoken had a face of true ugliness, and the way the others looked at him made Valdez nervous. He turned to go back to his horse.

"Perhaps we can help you look for her," the ugly man offered.

"You are very kind."

"Are you from the de Alda ranch?"

"*Sí, señor.*"

"Some friends of mine are visiting there," the man said.

"Ah, yes, the gringos and the pretty women," Valdez said. In his nervousness he babbled. "They have gone with Señor de Alda to hunt the buffalo."

"Too bad," the man said. "I had hoped to see them."

"You do not stay here?"

"No, no," the stranger answered. "We travel to the south, to Corpus Christi."

"Too bad," Valdez agreed. "If you traveled to the northwest for, oh, two days' ride, you would hear their guns as they kill the buffalo."

"That so?" the man asked. "I've always had a desire to kill a buffalo. It is possible, then, that we would find them if we ride to the northwest?"

"For a certainty," Valdez said. "You have merely to cross the large stream that you will reach in two days' ride. Look then for a distant ridge shaped on the eastern end like the hump and head of a buffalo. The group will be on the plain to one side or the other of the buffalo ridge."

"I wish you success in finding your daughter," the pockmarked man said. "Do you have other daughters?"

"Two who are younger," Valdez answered.

"Guard them well," the stranger advised.

Valdez rode away.

"Tomorrow," Othon Hugues said, "we will ride to the northwest."

The Frenchman laughed. He had spoken truthfully to the father about his daughter; she was not at the camp-site. He had left her ravaged and mutilated body in an erosion ditch several miles away.

"We did not agree to go with you into the lands of the Comanche," one of his men said.

"Would de Alda take women into danger?" Hugues asked. "Are you not brave enough to go where an Indian squaw and an Englishwoman ride?"

He nearly regretted his vow to kill the white Indian's party, for the Spanish thirteen-year-old had been so deli-cious, so inspiringly frightened, that he wished he could stay to make the acquaintance of the other daughters of Valdez. On the return trip, perhaps, he decided.

The tracks of the hunting party were quite easy to follow, for the group traveled with a cook's wagon, plus other wagons to transport wet, heavy buffalo hides and meat. The sun of the southwestern plains was hot, and Othon's men complained about their discomfort until Othon told them that if they were successful in killing everyone who was on the hunt, then nothing could stop them from looting the de Alda hacienda on the way back to Corpus Christi.

"You have seen the richness of the country, the cat-tle, the vast expanse of de Alda's holdings," he reminded them. "Think of the valuables that await you in his house. Think of the warm Spanish women who will open them-selves for you once you have killed the few men who will be at the hacienda."

"We will go with you," declared the same man who had questioned Othon's judgment.

De Alda's party, they found, had camped just below the slope of the buffalo ridge. Othon rode close enough to see the tents and the wagons, and his blood quickened when he saw the red-haired woman come out of a tent and walk to drink from a water barrel.

"When they hunt," he told his men, "they will become separated. We will take them one by one or in small groups. We will kill the vaqueros first. I don't care who kills the old white man, the two Indian boys, or de Alda. It might be best if some of you concentrate on the younger brother of this Renno. But as for Renno and the two women, they are mine."

"Both women?" someone protested. "Just because you pay us does not mean that you have the right to all the benefits of our work."

"You have a point," Othon agreed. "All right, you may share the Indian squaw, but I will kill any man who touches the red-haired woman or the white Indian."

Othon made his own camp on the other side of the ridge in heavy brush and cautioned all of his men to await his order to ride. He posted a lookout atop the ridge. As expected, the vaqueros from de Alda's camp rode out toward the north just after sunup. De Alda and his special guests followed in a leisurely fashion.

A scout sent out by Othon rode hard and reported back before midday that there were buffalo not far away.

"Now we are ready," Hugues announced. He divided his men into two forces and repeated his orders to kill the vaqueros singly or in small groups.

Chapter Eight

The second fatigue duty assigned to Cadet Hawk Harper consisted of marching up and down the length of the parade ground. He put in two hours of the duty in predawn darkness, before the other cadets were out of bed. Alone on the parade ground he would shoulder his musket and march stiffly to the far end, do a smart about-face, and march back. He did not stint on his time on the parade or compromise his rigid posture. After the evening meal he would return to the parade and march back and forth for another two hours. He was getting about five hours of sleep each night.

Major John Lillie searched Little Hawk's face each day at the morning formation in an effort to find telltale signs of exhaustion or resentment. He found none. Moreover, Lillie gave Harper's uniform, personal appearance, and his bunk and locker areas inspections so strict and detailed that the other cadets rolled their eyes in sympathy. For days the commander was unable to find the slightest fault with Cadet Harper.

On a dismal morning after a nightlong rain Lillie, after inspecting Harper's bunk and locker, walked to the window that was centered between Little Hawk's bed and the bed of the cadet on Little Hawk's left. The major opened it and ran his white glove over that part of the sill that was exposed to the elements. His gloved fingers came away blackened. "Harper," he said, "you have just added a week to your punishment."

"Sir!" Little Hawk barked. "Yes, sir."

A moan of protest came involuntarily from several young male throats. Lillie stomped into the aisle. "Who made that sound?" he yelled, his anger flaring. He was fully aware that because of Harper's stoic acceptance of punishment and of the way he was completing it without showing strain, the cadet was becoming a hero to the corps. "Who made that noise? The guilty cadet will step forward."

Almost as one the senior class of cadets, with the sole exception of the new cadet captain, Sidney Forrest, stepped forward.

Lillie's face went red. "So that's the way it is," he seethed. "We have here a corps of heroic martyrs." He walked up and down the aisle, pausing to stare into the faces of all those who had stepped forward. "All right," he roared. "If that's your game, I'll show you that I can play. Cadet Harper's punishment tour will be shared by all of you heroes. At four tomorrow morning this entire section, with the exception of Cadet Captain Forrest, will be on the parade. We'll see how much you admire your hero when you join him for four hours a day."

So it was that long before dawn a jauntily defiant group of senior cadets marched in perfect formation, with Cadet Hawk Harper calling out orders. After an hour someone began to sing in cadence with the step:

> *Yankee Doodle went to town*
> *Upon a spotted pony—*

The others took up the singing. It was a joyous, defiant sound, the young, strong voices raised in unity.

Cadet Captain Forrest, who had gone back to sleep

after being awakened as the senior section got out of bed and dressed for fatigue duty, sat up in surprise. A wave of hatred swept through him. He had the insignia, he had the title of cadet captain. But the action of the corps in support of the Indian had shown him that he did not have the loyalty of his fellow cadets. And now this—singing as they marched! He went to the window and in the pale light of dawn saw that they'd put Hawk in front and to the side, in the position of the cadet captain, and they were following his orders as if he still wore the insignia.

Another man was awakened by the singing. John Lillie pulled on a robe and walked onto his porch. In the dim light he could see the perfect formation and could hear the barked orders of the drill officer, Harper, as the cadets wheeled to march back the other way. They had sung before while marching, but never with so much enthusiasm. The strength of their voices made the singing a direct challenge to the major.

"Damn you, Harper," he whispered.

Later, at inspection, he walked to the window near Harper's bed and opened it. A groan of protest came from the stiffly standing seniors. "All right," he thundered, "let's have a look at your windows."

He opened window after window to find the sills freshly scrubbed and dried. He walked past the bunk of Cadet Captain Sidney Forrest.

"You forgot to check the cadet captain's window," someone said.

Lillie whirled. "Who broke silence in ranks?" he bellowed. "The guilty cadet will step forward."

As if by order the entire corps took a forward step.

Lillie was incapable of speech for a moment. When he recovered his voice he said, "You act as if you think that I can't dismiss an entire senior class. Do you think I can't?"

"No, sir!" the cadets bellowed.

"Do you think I won't?"

"Yes, sir!" the cadets said as one.

For another moment Lillie was rendered speechless, for, if the truth be known, he could not wipe out the

entire graduating group. Too many questions would have
to be answered when it became known in Washington
that something had gone badly awry with President Jefferson's pet project.

"Perhaps the thing to do, then, is to cite every third
or fourth man for insubordination," Lillie said. He started
at one end and counted, "One, two, three, you. One,
two, three, you."

"You skipped over Forrest," someone called out from
the other end of the large room.

"You have not inspected Forrest's window," another
voice said.

Lillie threw open Forrest's window and ran his gloved
hand over the outside sill. His fingers came away gummy
and sticky. He looked. He smelled. Someone had smeared
horse manure on the sill.

"Sir," Forrest breathed, his face going white. "Sir, I
washed that sill just before—"

"All right, Forrest," Lillie said. "I'm sure you did."
He walked to the center of the aisle, took off his glove,
and threw it to the floor. "I suppose that you're all going
to claim that you soiled the cadet captain's windowsill?"

There was silence.

"You are right," Lillie said. "I won't dismiss the
entire senior class from the academy. I won't even dismiss
every fourth man. I will, however, see to it that the army
career of the man who is responsible for this mutiny—
because that's what it is, mutiny—does not stay around to
foment more trouble. I will see to it that he is out of the
uniform of the United States Army within the hour."

"Good-bye, Forrest," came a voice, and the remark
was met by snickers.

"Laugh as you will, gentlemen," Lillie said. "Your
last months here will be a personal hell for each of you.
And those who complain, who break under the pressure,
will follow Harper in dishonorable dismissal from this
institution."

He turned and, heels thumping hard on the wooden
floor, marched to the door. "Harper," he said, "report to
me in my office."

*   *   *

Lillie was waiting, standing in front of a window, his white-knuckled hands behind his back, his fingers twitching, when Little Hawk knocked and entered the office.

"Cadet Harper reporting as ordered, sir," he said.

"You are no longer a cadet," Lillie said, turning. "Do not act in the manner of a cadet. Do not call me sir. In all of my years in the army and in all of my time here I have never seen a more disruptive influence in any unit. Your evil power over the men in your section is at an end, Harper. I don't even want you to go back to the barracks to clean out your locker. I will have that done, and I will have your things delivered to you at the front gate."

"Major Lillie," Little Hawk said, "you know and I know that this is not about my influence in the corps."

"Watch your tongue," Lillie warned.

"Since I am no longer a cadet," Little Hawk said, letting his arms relax, "and since I am no longer in the army, I am free to say to you, Lillie, that it would be my pleasure to meet you off post with the weapons of your choice."

For a moment the major welcomed the idea, then he considered what would be said in the executive mansion and at the Department of War if the commander of West Point killed one of his ex-cadets in a duel. "You do tempt me," he said.

"Face me, then," Little Hawk challenged. "Face me now or at our next meeting."

Lillie's face showed that he was fighting an inner battle. In the end he bellowed, "Guards!" Two regular army enlisted men entered the room and saluted. "Corporal, you will escort this man to the gate and hold him there until his personal belongings have been delivered to him. Send a man to Harper's bunk to gather his possessions. Do not, I repeat, do not include any item of government property."

The corporal reached for Little Hawk's arm. Little Hawk brushed the hand aside. "I know the way to the gate, Corporal Jagger," he said. "Thank you, though, for your offer of assistance."

"Yes, sir," the corporal said.

Once they were outside, walking across the parade, the corporal asked, "What in the name of blazes did you do to the old man?"

"It's a story too long and complicated for the telling," Little Hawk replied. His hand ached to hold a tomahawk, a knife, a gun, any weapon, as long as he could direct it toward Major John Lillie, for he was not the only one being dishonored. He was being kicked out of West Point because he had one-quarter Seneca blood in his veins. He knew a bitterness that soured his mouth as he walked toward the gate with Corporal Jagger at his side. Being forced to give up his commission in the United States Army was a blow, but that was not nearly as painful as the knowledge that he would have to go home to tell of his failure. He would tell his father that he was wrong in advising the tribe to adapt to the ways of the white man. He would say, "Father, Sachem, no matter how hard we try, even if we do a better job than the white man at being white, he will not give us a place at his side. He will never, never allow us to be on an equal footing with him."

Corporal Jagger paused just inside the gate. "If it means anything to you, Hawk," he said, "we fellows in the garrison think you've been getting a raw deal from the major."

"Thank you, Corporal."

"That Georgia-boy Forrest is a manurehead."

Little Hawk was silent. Across the parade the private soldier emerged from the barracks carrying a carpetbag.

"Guess you'll be going home now," Jagger said.

"Soon as I get my horse from the stables," Little Hawk answered.

"I envy you. I wish I were going off with you. I haven't seen the country west of the mountains." He scratched his chin. "I might, one day, if things keep going the way they're going. Might go out to Illinois Territory and fight Tecumseh with William Henry Harrison."

Little Hawk nodded.

"You being an Indian and all, I was wondering if maybe you knew Tecumseh."

"Not personally. Tecumseh is Shawnee," Little Hawk

said. "I am Seneca, of that portion of the Seneca Nation that followed the sachem Ghonkaba to the south. I did hear Tecumseh speak once, though."

"What did he say?"

"He wanted all Indians to form a confederation and kick you whites back across the mountains."

"By gum. Just like they say, eh? But you didn't join up with him."

"No," Little Hawk said. He'd been watching the private walk toward them, carrying the carpetbag.

"What's this, then?" the corporal asked.

Little Hawk turned to watch a small group of mounted men and a closed carriage coming up the road toward the gate.

"Good Gawd," the corporal said, eyes wide. "Look at all the medals."

The four mounted men were officers, and they ranged in rank from captain to general. Outside the gate the guards snapped to attention. The newcomers halted and went through the formalities of identification.

"Halt, sirs. Who goes there?"

"Friends."

"Advance, sir, and be recognized."

"I am Lieutenant Colonel Freeman. Inform the commandant of this post that I am escorting the military agent for the northern district and Secretary of War Henry Dearborn."

"My Gawd," Corporal Jagger uttered.

"Yes, sir," said the guard. "Please enter at your pleasure, sir."

"Hold it, Freeman," said a large, deep voice from the coach. A barrel-chested man with a long, straight nose creased at the top by knitted brows stepped down and stretched. He walked toward the guards, who were standing at attention. "Let's not inform the garrison of our arrival just yet," he decided.

"Yes, sir," said Colonel Freeman.

"You, guard, what kind of a post is this?" asked the secretary of war.

"It's a fine post, sir."

"Feed you well?"

"Pretty well, sir, 'specially when one of the boys goes out and gets us a deer or two."

"Any friction between you members of the regular army and the cadets?"

"No, sir. They's mostly a bunch of good lads, eager to learn."

"And in your opinion is the military academy turning out good officers for the army?"

"Sir, I ain't qualified to say."

"Your opinion. You will not be quoted."

"Well, sir, some of the boys is pert nigh smart. The others might have a little trouble pouring piss outen a boot."

Henry Dearborn chuckled. "I suppose it might seem that way at times." He turned, saw Little Hawk's cadet uniform, and beckoned him forward. Little Hawk and the corporal approached and came to attention. The corporal saluted.

"Is it not the habit of members of the cadet corps to salute a superior?" Colonel Freeman bellowed out.

"I am no longer a cadet," Little Hawk responded.

Dearborn's heavy brows lifted in question. "And why is that?"

Little Hawk was stiffly silent.

"May I speak, sir?" Corporal Jagger asked.

"Speak, Corporal," the colonel said.

"Cadet Harper, uh, ex-Cadet Harper, here, refused to fire a cannon that the cadet captain had aimed directly at a farmer's barn."

"Explain that, please," the secretary of war said.

"The cadet captain was confused. Mr. Harper, here, told him that he was going to kill the farmer's chickens or something, but the cadet captain wouldn't listen, and Mr. Harper said he wasn't going to be the one to turn the cannon on the civilian community."

"And for this you have been dismissed from the Cadet Corps?" asked Dearborn.

"That is the simple explanation," Little Hawk answered.

The private soldier arrived with Little Hawk's personal possessions. When he recognized the importance of the gathering he came to a halt and stood at rigid attention.

"I think it might be interesting to hear more than just the bare facts. Your name?" Dearborn asked Little Hawk.

"I am known here as Hawk Harper."

"Bedamned," Colonel Freeman muttered.

"Also called Little Hawk?" Dearborn asked.

"Yes, sir."

"Stay on the post," Dearborn said. "I will want a word with you later."

"Sir, I have been ordered to leave by the post commander."

"And you are ordered to stay by the secretary of war, who is the direct representative of the president, who is the commander in chief of the army," Dearborn said.

"Sir, I believe that's good enough to countermand the order of a major," Little Hawk said solemnly.

Dearborn's solemn, stern face relaxed. "You can bet your commission on that, *Cadet* Harper."

A flustered Major John Lillie received word from a sergeant that there was a passel of personages at the gate, getting ready to move across the parade ground.

"Turn out the garrison," Lillie ordered. "Parade dress."

But there was no time. He stepped onto the porch of the post's headquarters building and snapped to attention and gave a salute. He recognized the northern area military agent and Colonel Freeman. He did not know the face of the general, but having seen pictures of the secretary of war, he recognized Dearborn when the portly man dismounted from the coach.

"At ease, Major," said Colonel Freeman, continuing to act as group spokesman.

"If I had only had advance notice, sir," Lillie said, "I could have—"

"But that's the idea, isn't it, Major?" Dearborn asked. "Since Mr. Jefferson takes a special interest in the academy, I thought that it might behoove me if I had a look to see how things are being run here."

"Yes, sir," Lillie said. "I'll arrange a review of—"

"Major, relax," Freeman said. "The secretary wants to take a quiet look around without causing any upset to the routine of the academy."

Lillie felt panic, then reassured himself. After all, he was a good officer. Things were in order, and the garrison was smartly uniformed and well trained. The cadets? Well, they'd been kept at a point of ultrasmartness by his forced inspections. He believed that he had nothing to worry about. He felt grateful that he'd gotten rid of Hawk Harper that morning.

"Before I ask one of your sergeants to conduct me on a tour of the post and academy," Dearborn said, "there is a little matter. . . . I have orders here from the president himself concerning one of your cadets." He handed Lillie a paper and watched the man's expression closely as the major read. Lillie felt the blood drain from his face. "Sir," he said, "the cadet Hawk Harper has been a severe discipline problem. This very morning I dismissed him from the corps. As far as I know he's on his way back to his Injun—Indian teepee or whatever."

The military agent for the northern district spoke in a quiet voice. "It has been my experience, Major, that a good commanding officer has few discipline problems. A good officer heads off problems before they arise."

Lillie flushed. He knew that he'd have to change his plans regarding the seniors in the corps who had defied him in support of Harper. He didn't know why President Jefferson wanted Cadet Harper in Washington, but the major did know that he was on thin ice.

Henry Dearborn felt he had heard just enough from the corporal and a member of the garrison to whet his curiosity. Having been told the story of the Seneca lad's difficulties in Philadelphia when Hawk had been a Senate page, the secretary had been eager to meet the boy who had attracted the personal interest of the Virginian who sat in the executive mansion. He knew that Jefferson planned to send Harper to join the tiny contingent of marines in North Africa.

As he considered the situation he'd encountered at West Point, with Harper's having been dismissed from the corps, the secretary came to two conclusions. First, Lillie had been appointed commander of the post by Jefferson himself. The major's record was a good one, and the cadets who had graduated from the Point already showed signs of being good officers. True, the corporal had indicated that Harper had been dismissed unfairly, but it was Dearborn's experience that in the army the more you stirred garbage the worse it smelled.

Secondly, since Harper was to be called upon to report back to Thomas Jefferson on the situation in the Barbary nations and on William Eaton himself, it didn't matter whether or not Harper had a commission from West Point. In fact, Dearborn knew, if he insisted on investigating the reasons for Harper's dismissal, it would call unwanted attention to the boy. Although Hawk was not going to be infiltrating hostile territory to spy on the enemy, he would be in a position where notoriety would serve as a handicap.

Thus the secretary took Colonel Freeman aside and gave him a copy of Harper's orders. "Take these to the boy. Tell him to make his way to Washington City as quickly as possible. He'll need funds, so advance him enough for board and room during his journey."

Then Dearborn made his tour, seeing the Cadet Corps at study, on the drill field, and in a field exercise during which Cadet Captain Forrest sighted in the cannon accurately and the cadets performed well. Dearborn said nothing more about the cadet Hawk Harper.

It was a puzzled young man who mounted his horse for the long ride south to Washington. His orders had been signed by the secretary of war himself, and they had been written before Little Hawk presented himself to Major Lillie to ask for Mary Ann's hand in marriage. Colonel Freeman, in delivering the orders to him, had not been helpful in easing Little Hawk's curiosity as to why

the president was ordering him to Washington before
graduation.

When Little Hawk asked Freeman why, the colonel
had said, "Son, if you intend to be a career officer, one
of the first things you must learn is not to ask why." He
laughed. "And that's one way of admitting that I have no
idea why Mr. Jefferson wants you in Washington. Perhaps
the secretary knows; but he didn't tell me, and I didn't
ask."

Because of Little Hawk's renewed status, he was permitted to return to the barracks and bid farewell to the
cadets who had been so loyal in their friendship.

Now the Seneca traveled alone down the Hudson to
bustling New York City. He rode through peaceful, fruit-
ful farm country that had once been a part of the territory
ruled by the League of the Iroquois. He used the money
given him by Colonel Freeman to buy feed for his horse
and shelter and food for himself. South of New York City
the roads were muddy. More than once he had to detour
around freight wagons mired to their axles.

Long stretches of the road to Philadelphia were
lonely, and during those solitary times, as he let the horse
pick its own pace, he reviewed his life.

It was not unmanly for him to feel his eyes sting and
become wet when he thought of Mary Ann Lillie, for she
had made the fires burn brightly inside him, and in his
limited experience the passion she had engendered in him
was love. He regretted the loss with an intensity that, at
its worst, caused him to bend over the pommel of his
saddle and yell out his pain to the deserted countryside.

Before reaching Philadelphia he had come to accept
as a truth the fact that Mary Ann had not truly loved
him. If she had loved him she would not have spoken so
quickly—more quickly than Peter the Fisherman had
acted in denying his Christ—to disaffirm any affection for
him.

As Little Hawk rode down the street in front of the
house that had been the presidential mansion before the
capital of the United States was moved to Washington, he
remembered walking the street years before with his

father. It was bittersweet to recall Renna as a young girl all goggle-eyed at the big city, and that brought memories of Philip, the boy who had become his sister's husband, only to die on the banks of the Mississippi River far away from his home. Although recent events caused Little Hawk's mind to take a somber path, he wasted little time thinking about his battles with the jealous Senate pages from New York or of his near death under the wheels of a racing coal wagon on that same street.

He treated himself to a good, hot meal and bath, then spent the night in an inn on the southern outskirts of the city. With the morning he was riding south once more.

The journey through the most densely populated area of the United States took him through towns and villages and past prosperous farms. How different it was from his journey north from Tennessee, when he would travel for days without seeing a sign of human habitation, white or Indian. These white men did indeed multiply like field mice, and their numbers equaled the lights in the sky. Because he was determined to do so, he would tell his father that the white man would never accept the Indian as a peer. But that would not change the inescapable fact that the teeming millions of whites in the United States were capable, if given the proper provocation—such as a full-scale uprising led by Tecumseh—of putting hundreds of thousands of troops in the field.

He didn't like dwelling on such thoughts. He dreamed idly of leading his tribe—this he put in the distant future, for he had no desire to wish his father to the Place across the River before his full time—into the vast reaches of the continent. He would take them so far from any white man that it would be generations before the insatiable hunger for land led to confrontation again.

But even as he dreamed he knew that steps were being taken to stamp the claim of the United States on all that vast territory west of the Mississippi. The Lewis and Clark expedition would, if successful, give knowledge of the land all the way to the far Pacific. Soon—quite soon, judging from the expansion of the United States in the relatively few years since his father and grandfather had fought to help establish the nation—there would be no place to hide from the exploding white population.

One stray thought made the idea of following his father's advice and becoming like the white man more palatable. His memory went back, back, to a time when he was going home from Philadelphia, to a time when he was given hospitality in the farmhouse of a white settler named Frank Burns.

Naomi . . . The name of Burns's daughter still engendered sweet longing and pleasant memories of a taffy-haired, freckled girl who smelled cleanly of lye soap and youth and whose lips were soft, tentative, and sweet as they gave him his first kiss. By now she would be . . . in her early twenties. On the frontier a girl, white or Indian, became a woman when nature said that she had come of age. She would be married, he thought with a tinge of regret, perhaps with a cabin running over with taffy-haired, exuberant little girls and boys who looked like her.

By the time Little Hawk saw the unfinished outline of the Capitol Building and rode the rutted dirt streets of Washington, his eyes no longer burned with loss when he thought of Mary Ann. He no longer felt sorry for himself, although he was justifiably lonely, with his family so widely scattered. Renna was in France. His father and stepmother, he presumed, were probably back in the Cherokee Nation by now.

As he rode up to the executive mansion and tied his horse to a hitching rail, he was beginning to feel a jolt of excited anticipation. He'd spent long, long hours on the trail wondering why he had been asked to report directly to President Jefferson. Why, since he had been reinstated, had he not been allowed to graduate from the academy?

Unlike Corporal Jagger, who wanted to see the wild frontier, Little Hawk had no desire to join the command of William Henry Harrison in the Illinois Territory, the current battle line in the drawn-out war between white settlers and the Indian. He could not endorse Tecumseh's clarion call to all tribes to join in fighting against the United States, but neither did he want to kill men whose blood and his had come from common ancestors.

Although the Illinois Territory was the current area

of crisis, there were other possibilities for army service. Posts would have to be set up in the newly acquired Louisiana Territory. Perhaps the president wanted him, because he was Seneca, to take an assignment in the new territory to serve as a liaison with various Indian tribes.

Actually, short of his informed guesses, he had no idea of what was coming, but he had the feeling that his audience with the president would change his life dramatically. In that expectation he was not wrong.

White Blanket the Mingo was a zealot in preaching Tecumseh's dream of an Indian confederation. As a result, his progress down the Tennessee River was as easy to follow as if he'd left physical markers. Wherever he found an Indian village, he halted long enough to deliver his message of war. With each day of travel Ena drew closer to catching White Blanket and her twins, although she had to waste considerable time searching out areas of Indian population to inquire about the threesome.

Her approach to the juncture of the Tennessee and Ohio rivers was not without distraction. It was unusual for a woman to travel alone. More than once she was forced to be firm in rejecting the advances of men, both white and Indian, although it had not been necessary to kill since her encounter with the two Chickasaw warriors.

At Fort Henry, where the Cumberland joined the Tennessee, she replaced her worn moccasins, paying with a silver coin from among those that she had saved from Rusog's share of the Spanish treasure intended for General James Wilkinson. She left the fort as quickly as possible, for she was aware of the curious stares from soldiers of the United States and a motley variety of frontier types. Before leaving she spoke with a family of Shawnee and learned that before crossing into the state of Kentucky, White Blanket had passed through with two young ones, male and female, and had paused to talk of Tecumseh's dream.

She traveled carefully across the southwestern tip of Kentucky to the Ohio River. Caution was necessary because for a long time the Kentuckians had teetered at the confrontation point between the United States and the

Indian nations. They remembered Little Turtle's war and were very much aware that the savage struggle between white and Indian was still being waged across the river in Illinois Territory. In the opinion of men who had used their long rifles against Cherokee, Shawnee, and Miami war parties, the only good Indian was a dead Indian—be that Indian male or female.

Ena was given a ride across the Ohio on a raft transporting a party of trappers and long hunters. These men had spent much of their lives among the Indians. Their attitude toward her was more friendly than that of the residents of the Kentucky and Tennessee towns and farmlands. She was an attractive, shapely woman, and before the raft drifted with the current to the northern side of the Ohio, she firmly but politely turned down three invitations to share blankets.

Now the wilderness closed in around her. White Blanket, We-yo, and Ho-ya had crossed the river only two days before. She picked up their trail soon after striking out from the river. The party of trappers who had given her a ride across the Ohio headed northwest; White Blanket was traveling slightly northeast, a direction that would, if continued, take him to Fort Harrison on the Wabash.

When she found hot ashes where White Blanket and her twins had spent the night, she was, she predicted, a mere four hours behind. The terrain was heavily wooded. The Mingo was following a game trail that wandered but went mainly northerly. She had traveled far and fast. The effort had honed her down to what she had weighed when she first married Rusog. Her long, lithe legs effortlessly covered the distance, and in her heart she knew that before the owls came out to hunt in the darkness she would find her children.

To her left and rear the sun was hiding behind the trees, and in the bowers and glens of the forests dark shadows foretold of nightfall. She caught the scent of wood smoke and slowed her pace. She could smell water, too. Not familiar with the country, she was not aware that White Blanket had set his path toward the mouth of the Wabash River. When the strong smell of smoke told her that she was near a camp, she could see the broad Ohio to her right. She crept closer and, from a little wooded knoll, looked down upon her daughter at work cooking a leg of venison. Her son stood on the bank of the river, a fishing line in hand. Even as she watched, his line jerked, and he hauled in a fat, slithery catfish.

"We-yo," he called, "here is a change from venison. Catfish."

"Then you will prepare it for the fire," We-yo called back. "I don't care to risk its barbs."

Ena smiled, for her first thought had been to reprimand the two for being so confidently loud in their speech in an unknown land. She looked around for the Mingo. His travel pack was lying beside We-yo's, but there was no sign of him.

Ena waited until Ho-ya had gutted the large catfish and skewered it on a green branch. "May I approach the camp?" she called out in Seneca.

Ho-ya's quick reaction pleased her. His weapons were in his hands in one split second, and tense and alert, he was facing the direction of her voice.

"Who calls?" he demanded.

Ena stepped out from among the trees.

We-yo gasped. "Mother!"

Ho-ya lowered his musket. Ena made her way down the knoll. We-yo greeted her with a clasp of arms, then pulled away.

"You have traveled far, Mother," Ho-ya said.

"So," Ena agreed.

Ho-ya was on the alert, listening for sounds from the forest, fully expecting his father to come into the glen beside the river at any time.

"If you have come to convince me to return with you—" We-yo began, but was silenced by her mother's uplifted hand.

"We will talk of those things after we have eaten," she said, moving to the fire to slice a piece of venison from the sizzling, roasting haunch.

"I will not leave the man I love," We-yo said.

"And you, my son?" Ena inquired. "What will you do?"

"Mother, I am old enough to choose my own destiny," Ho-ya replied: "It is not my wish to become a lap-dog of the white man."

"And who exactly are these lapdogs?" Ena asked, her eyes narrowing dangerously.

"I would so call my uncles Renno and El-i-chi."

"Not if you were face-to-face with them," she guessed. "But you do not include your father with your uncles?"

"No, for I believe that in his heart he hates the white man as much as I do."

"And what reason do you have to hate the white man?" she asked. "Have you crossed blades with him? Have you faced his long knives in battle?"

Ho-ya made an angry gesture of denial.

"As for me, Mother," We-yo said, "the witness of my marriage to White Blanket is my brother. He will tell you that we vowed eternal commitment by the customs of the Seneca and the Cherokee."

"So," Ena said. So the Mingo had informed Rusog.

During the long days of the chase she had resigned herself to the loss of her daughter, for custom called for a woman to leave her family and go to the lodge of the man who became her husband unless that man chose to join his wife's clan. She had only to look at We-yo to see that she was no longer a maiden. She had filled out, apparently thriving on the travel. She carried herself with the confidence of a young matron. Ena realized with sadness that it was too late for her to keep her daughter as a part of her life. Perhaps, however, she could convince Ho-ya to give up his desire to fight with Tecumseh and return with her.

"I wish you great happiness," Ena told We-yo, and this statement of acceptance sent the young girl flying into her mother's arms.

Ena rubbed her daughter's glossy, black hair, then kissed her on the cheek.

"I love him so much, Mother," We-yo said. "I am very happy."

"Then we must offer thanks to the manitous, for happiness is a gift not given to all," Ena said.

"You did not come alone," Ho-ya said incredulously,

although he heard nothing, saw nothing to indicate otherwise.

"I did," Ena said.

"That was foolish," Ho-ya said.

"I have traveled as far, and in more danger."

"But—"

"Your father would have come for you, had not the Mingo wounded him so severely—"

We-yo gasped in alarm. Ho-ya cried out, "What are you saying? We did not see my father."

"The Mingo saw him and took advantage of the fact that Rusog chose not to kill the husband of his only daughter."

"Oh, please, no," We-yo whispered.

"I don't believe you!" Ho-ya said. "White Blanket would have told us."

"You may believe you are old enough to fight with the Shawnee who is not even a chief," Ena said coldly. "But you are not, nor will you ever be, old enough to call your mother a liar."

"Forgive me," Ho-ya said, his eyes downcast.

"Mother, what are you going to do?" We-yo asked.

"When your father reached home with his wound septic and his life force so weak that we despaired for him, I wanted to kill the Mingo," she said. "And I would have killed you, my son, had you tried to prevent my vengeance." She held up her hand when the twins started to protest. "Rusog was well, if weak, when I left him. He did not cry out for revenge, nor do I now. I came here in the hopes of taking both of you home with me."

"I have told you—" We-yo began.

"Yes, yes, you have told me. And I respect the traditions of marriage, even while I bewail your lack of respect for your parents in taking the Mingo to mate without our consent. No, I will not—"

She did not finish. It was dusk, and the Mingo had approached unseen in the growing darkness. He loomed up on the opposite side of the fire from her, his musket pointed at her heart.

"I expected to be followed," White Blanket snarled, "but not by a woman."

"So," Ena said. She was tense, for in the light of the fire she could see that White Blanket's finger was on the trigger. "Are you going to shoot, Mingo?" she asked evenly, readying herself for swift movement, even if in vain, if she saw his finger twitch.

"Perhaps I should," White Blanket replied.

"Lower your weapon, White Blanket," said Ho-ya.

The Mingo glanced to his side to see the young Cherokee's musket directed at his midsection.

"She is not here to annul our marriage," We-yo told him.

"Then why *is* she here?" White Blanket asked, lowering his musket and squatting on his heels.

"Rusog lives," Ena said.

The Mingo showed no expression. "I had no desire to wound him. He gave me no choice."

"So," Ena said.

"The meat is ready," We-yo said into the tense silence. "Will you eat?"

"Gladly," White Blanket answered. "But there is a yearling deer by the river. I must clean him before the denizens of the forest find an easy meal."

"I'll do that," We-yo offered. "If you'll help me carry him, Ho-ya. Mother, you and White Blanket can talk and, I hope, overcome your differences." She gave an imploring look to her husband before leaving the campsite.

Ho-ya followed close on her heels, obviously relieved to have an excuse to get away from the penetrating, questioning gaze of his mother.

Left alone with the Mingo, Ena remained silent. Nonchalantly he sliced off meat and chewed for a time before saying, "She will not go with you, woman."

"No," Ena said.

"Nor will the boy."

"About that we will see," Ena said.

"You have traveled far for nothing."

"So," she said. She rose. His hand reached out for his musket.

"If you were going to kill me," she said, "you missed your chance, for if you touch the rifle now, I will cut off your hand before you can reach it."

When he saw the glint of steel, the blade of her tomahawk in her hand, he laughed harshly. "Not even the
great Rusog bragged so much."

"Nor did he need to," Ena said. "Thank the spirits
that you were married to his daughter, Mingo, or the
denizens of the forest would have had you for a meal long
since."

"My desire is to be on friendly terms with the mother
of my wife."

"Between us there can never be friendship," Ena
said, "for you came into my home as a guest and left as
a thief. There can be a lack of violence, if that is your
choice."

He glared at her, his eyes reflecting the fire redly.
She rose and, seeking water to wash her face, walked to
the river. She could hear her twins talking from a point
just to the south, but she was separated from them by
riverside brush. She was leaning over the water when the
Mingo, not at all certain that she had been sincere in
indicating that she would not try to steal away his wife,
attacked her, swinging his tomahawk with all his strength.

Ena, having caught a hint of movement out of the
corner of her eye and having heard the grunt of effort as
the Mingo launched his blow, threw herself aside just in
time to avoid the weapon's cutting edge. But the flat of
the heavy blade smashed against the side of her head and
glanced away. She fell limply into the water.

White Blanket was satisfied. Before he had crept up
behind Ena at the river, he checked to make certain Ho-
ya was working diligently beside We-yo. Both of them
were bloody up to the elbows, dressing out the deer that
he had brought to camp. So it was that the Mingo confidently stepped into the mud, dragged Ena out of the shal-
lows, and released her to the current. She turned onto
her stomach, her face down in the water, and floated for
a moment before being lost to his view in the darkness.

Chapter Nine

Ho-ya had known from an early age that having a twin made one's life different in many ways. He could remember a time when his sister could match him in almost every physical endeavor. It was often difficult for others to tell them apart at a distance, for before We-yo had become a woman she had worn the breeches of a boy, kept her hair cut as short as her brother's, and was equally slim and straight. Then, when she reached thirteen, her maturing body reacted to the juices generated by nature and began to show curves she could not hide underneath a breechclout and a deerskin shirt.

Then, within a period that seemed to be mere days, she began to braid her hair, wear fringed buckskin skirts, curve outward from the waist and the chest, and stop playing stickball with Ho-ya and his friends. He was understandably aggrieved to have lost one of his team's most ardent and fearless players.

"When the boys try to prevent me from making a

play," she told Ho-ya in explanation, "they select carefully
the places where they put their hands."

At first Ho-ya didn't understand what she meant.
Then he started observing closely and saw a Seneca opponent close both his hands over We-yo's budding breasts,
being more interested in the resulting sensation than in
preventing her from scoring a goal. Ho-ya made it a point
to throw a very hard block into the offender at the next
opportunity and agreed with We-yo that perhaps it was
time for her to concentrate more on woman's activities.

But having a twin sister made other differences in
Ho-ya's life. He was so accustomed to doing things in her
company that he often found himself sharing woman's
work with her. A few times, when he was younger, his
peers jeered at what they considered to be a weakness,
but no one mocked him more than once.

And so it was that he worked now in comfortable
harmony at her side, cleaning the deer that White Blanket
had killed. In order not to attract night creatures, We-yo
and he were throwing the offal from the deer into the
river. While We-yo did the fine trimming with her knife,
Ho-ya, the stronger, hacked off the head and legs and
tossed them with a *kerplunk* into the river. The hide followed. He regretted the waste of a fine deerskin, but it
would have been impractical to try to carry an uncured
hide with them. He tossed it as far out as he could and
watched it float off into the darkness. He was about to
turn back to his work, but something dark floating there
caught his eye. He was about to dismiss it as a log or
some other piece of drift until he caught just a hint of
movement.

Ho-ya couldn't be sure that he had seen a human
hand, but he did not hesitate. He plunged into the river
and swam hard to catch the drifting form of blackness. He
realized with horror that it was the back of his mother's
head. He seized her by her shirt, treaded water as he
rolled her over and lifted her face, and cried out in shock
to We-yo. He put his hand under Ena's chin and swam
to the shore a full hundred feet below his point of entry
and dragged her up onto the mud. We-yo had followed

his progress as the current carried him downriver and was waiting on the bank to help.

They turned Ena onto her stomach. Ho-ya put both of his hands under his mother's stomach and began to lift in rhythmic jerks. After what seemed to be forever Ena vomited river water and gasped harshly for breath.

Ho-ya had been chanting a plea to the manitous. He knew that Ena survived because even as she floated face-down, unconscious, her lungs filling with water, there was in her a desire to live that caused her to flail out with one pale hand just as he started to turn back to the work of cutting the deer into quarters.

His prayer changed to a chant of thanksgiving as Ena spat more water, coughed, and began to breathe regularly. She tried to sit up, but We-yo held her shoulders and eased her mother's head down.

"Rest a moment," We-yo said, moving to cradle Ena's head in her lap.

"The Mingo," Ena rasped.

"Ho-ya, feel this," We-yo quavered.

Ho-ya put his hand on his mother's head and felt a huge bump. His fingers came away bloody.

"Tell me," he said urgently, his face close to Ena's.

"The Mingo," Ena whispered. "From behind."

"So," Ho-ya said. He rose.

"No, please," We-yo begged. "Mother, what are you saying?"

Ho-ya was already stalking up the bank toward the campsite.

"Ho-ya, please," We-yo implored. "There must be some explanation."

"He will have his opportunity to give it to me," Ho-ya said.

Again Ena tried to rise, but she fell back weakly. We-yo, her heart breaking, wanted to run after her brother, but Ena was retching. We-yo held her mother's head and prayed to the manitous.

When Ho-ya entered the circle of firelight, White Blanket was seated, legs crossed, hands on his knees. He noted that the boy had his tomahawk in his hand. His own blade was at his side within easy reach.

Ho-ya stood directly across the fire and looked down at the Mingo. "I heard your words and knew them to be true," he said in a low voice. "You spoke of the sacred mission of every man of Indian blood, and I agreed. I have followed you, White Blanket, and I have listened to your orations regarding the honor and the greatness of your leader and those who spread his message. I have come far with you, and I have witnessed your marriage to my sister. And so it is with a heavy heart that I ask this of you: you will tell me what occurred between you and my mother."

"Only what you saw and heard," White Blanket said innocently.

"If you lie to me about this, then are all your words lies? Is Tecumseh truly the great leader that the Indian nations cry out for? Are you and the others like you interested in the welfare of all Indians, or are you interested only in personal gain?"

"Have a care, boy," White Blanket warned, rising. "You have the stature of a man, and no man calls me a liar."

"Speak then," Ho-ya demanded.

"I have said."

"And yet my mother, when I pulled her half-drowned from the river with a great knot on her head, said that you struck her from behind."

White Blanket was silent for a moment, obviously digesting the news that Ena was alive. "I do not strike from behind, not even if the target of my blade is a whiteface."

Ho-ya took a deep, ragged breath. The arm holding his tomahawk was hanging at his side. "I have never known my mother to lie."

The Mingo moved carefully around the campfire to face Ho-ya. "I have warned you, boy."

With a swiftness that made Ho-ya blink, a blade appeared in White Blanket's hand. Only the quick reflexes of youth prevented a killing blow on the Mingo's first effort. Ho-ya stumbled backward even as he caught the sharp edge of White Blanket's tomahawk with the flat side of his blade. Steel rang on steel, and sparks flew into the darkness.

With a roar the Mingo pressed the attack. Ho-ya, forgetting grace and pride, scrambled rapidly in retreat. At last he began to perceive the rhythm of White Blanket's attack, and then he, in his turn, came close to ending it. His blade slashed past White Blanket's throat, missing by a tiny margin.

The Mingo ceased his pressing attack, for the nearness of his escape had chilled his blood. "You have been taught well," White Blanket said after the exchange of several more feints and blows that were parried by each with equal skill.

"You have only to explain," Ho-ya said.

"No one takes away from White Blanket what is his."

"If you speak of my sister—"

"My wife." White Blanket lashed out, and his blade was halted in midair by a powerful counterblow from Ho-ya.

"—my mother had resigned herself to that," Ho-ya continued. "You fight well, Mingo. But at heart are you a coward who found it necessary to strike a woman from behind?"

The insult sent White Blanket surging forward recklessly. After another narrow escape, when the flat of Ho-ya's tomahawk grazed the top of his head as he ducked, the Mingo became methodical once again, intent now on wearing his younger opponent down.

We-yo heard the clash of steel, and hot tears burned her eyes. Two of the men she loved most in the world, her husband and her brother, were engaged in a combat that would leave only one standing, perhaps only one alive.

"Mother, I must leave you," she said. "I must stop them."

"Help me," Ena said.

Ena felt better when she was on her feet. Her tomahawk was still in its loop at her waist. She braced herself, fought off waves of nausea, and, with her vigor returning, rapidly accompanied We-yo up the bank and into the clearing where the two men faced each other, lunging, feinting, parrying, or avoiding blows that would have killed.

We-yo ran forward and, when the combatants stepped away from each other, thrust herself between them. "Stop it!" she cried. "You must stop."

"We-yo, get out of the way," Ho-ya commanded.

"No! If you must strike, then strike me."

"Perhaps it is time to talk," White Blanket said.

"I would hear what you have to say," Ena agreed.

White Blanket whirled to face her. "This is your doing, woman."

"I am listening," Ena said.

"I saw you on the riverbank," White Blanket explained. "I saw you walk into a limb hanging low. Now you say that it was I, that I struck you from behind."

"My brother Renno has said that he has never known an Indian who was a good liar unless he was speaking to a whiteface," Ena declared. "If you saw as much, why, then, did you let me fall into the water where I would have drowned? Why did you not take me from the water or call my children for help?"

"It was dark," White Blanket said, moving slowly to flank We-yo and give himself a clear blow at Ho-ya. He lunged suddenly. Ho-ya saw the blow coming, and he fell away, but not in time to avoid the blade entirely. Blood sprang up on his chest as he hit the ground and rolled to avoid White Blanket's follow-up stroke.

Ena drew back her arm and with all her strength sent her tomahawk flying. It struck White Blanket's back at the base of his neck, burying itself between two vertebrae, cutting the spinal cord. The weapon dropped from the Mingo's hand. He collapsed limply, all muscle control gone from his lower body. He lay very, very still. Only his eyes moved.

We-yo screamed and screamed as if she had been mortally wounded. She fell to her knees. Her husband's blood was flowing freely. She could not bring herself to touch him. His eyes rolled toward her, and his mouth opened. But before White Blanket could speak, Ho-ya's tomahawk smashed into his temple.

We-yo's screaming stopped abruptly. In a strangely calm voice she stated, "You did not have to do that. He no longer threatened you or my mother."

"It is my scalp," Ho-ya claimed, although he had seen Ena's blade buried in the back of the Mingo's neck and knew that the wound was fatal. But he felt that his sister would need her mother more than she would need him to help to ease her grief, and thus was he willing to accept the bulk of responsibility.

"Touch him to take his scalp and I will kill you," We-yo said. Her dry eyes held an unnatural light.

"When it is day we will give him a warrior's burial," Ena said.

"You will not touch him, either," We-yo said, her voice low and strained. She took a blanket and covered the Mingo. She knelt beside him, bobbing her head, singing the death song of a Seneca widow.

Ena motioned Ho-ya to her.

"Are you well?" Ho-ya whispered.

"Yes."

"You did not have to intercede, Mother."

"I know. I have every confidence that the son of Rusog would have triumphed," Ena said. "But, like you, I did not want you to bear the burden of your sister's blame."

"I chose to share it."

For the first time in a long time Ena embraced her tall son. "And I do thank you," she said earnestly. "Now we will see to your wound."

"It is nothing," Ho-ya said. "A scratch."

"Sit," Ena ordered.

The wound was shallow and did not require stitching. Ena cleaned it with river water and put pressure on it until it had stopped bleeding. Then Ho-ya slept.

When the young man awoke, he saw that his sister was already at work. She was using White Blanket's tomahawk and a cooking pan to dig a shallow grave. Ho-ya offered to help, but she refused with a shake of her head.

When Ena tried to help her carry the Mingo's body, We-yo shook her head again. Not a word did she utter. Ena respected her daughter's wishes and watched as she dragged the blanket-wrapped body to the grave.

It took several hours for We-yo to dig the grave, place the Mingo in it, cover him with a blanket, and then arrange over the top long strips of bark cut from the riverside trees. With the cooking utensil she shoveled dirt onto the bark covering and packed it carefully, then covered all with the detritus of the forest floor, until only an expert woodsman could have detected the fresh grave. When all was finished, she knelt and again keened the songs of mourning.

Ena cooked a haunch of the deer. Ho-ya and she ate and rested while We-yo paid her last respects to her dead husband. Ena told her son about Toshabe's fever and more details of Rusog's ordeal.

"I have been a fool," Ho-ya said.

"Not so," she disagreed.

"Not in thinking that Tecumseh is right," Ho-ya clarified. "I will see We-yo and you home, and then, when the time is right, I will go to join Tecumseh's alliance. My stupidity was in not recognizing the Mingo as a man of dishonor."

"A man's true character is not written on his face to be read like the white man's books."

"I thought that the Mingo was my friend."

Ena nodded sympathetically. No words were necessary.

"I fear that We-yo will blame you for his death," he said. "She will say that had our father, then you, not come after us, the Mingo would be alive. This reasoning may have merit. We can only conclude, We-yo and I, that you and our father view us as children, lacking the ability and intelligence to make our own decisions. And yet, were you not as young as We-yo when you chose Rusog? Was not my uncle Renno a sachem of the Seneca when he was only slightly older than I?"

"No, we were quite a bit older. I chose Rusog when I was twenty. Renno was nineteen when Ghonkaba was killed. But if you think that your father and I came after you because we wished you ill, then it *is* time for you to go your own way."

"Soon," he said. "But let us have no rancor between us, Mother."

"I will never feel ill will for you, Ho-ya. Only concern."

He grimaced and shook his head. "All right," he said at last. "I will accept that. You came for us because you were concerned." He shook his head again and grinned ruefully. "When I am long in the tooth and shaky of limb, will you still be following me to protect me from my own folly?"

Ena laughed. "By the manitous, I hope not."

It was decided that Ena would trade the last of her coins for two canoes so the threesome might float down the Ohio to the Mississippi, past New Madrid to Chickasaw Bluffs. The cross-country journey would take them through Chickasaw lands to the Tennessee River, across which would be the Cherokee Nation and home.

For long days We-yo maintained a stony silence as she did her share of the paddling and helped with the preparation of food and the camp work. In the night, however, Ena could hear the young woman sobbing. Often, while Ho-ya slept and Ena pretended not to see, We-yo left camp to seek solitude to wail out her songs of mourning.

The Father of Waters accepted them onto his broad breast and sped their canoes southward on rising floodwaters. They had to be very careful to avoid floating logs and even whole trees that were washed into the mighty stream by the rains to the north.

"It is odd to think that all the lands we see on either side of this great river are claimed by the whitefaces," Ho-ya said. "President Jefferson and the Congress give the Frenchmen something that can neither be worn, nor eaten, nor used for shelter. Lands that have been the hunting grounds of the Indian since the time of the beginning are suddenly the property of the United States. How can that be?"

"Because the white man says it is so with his musket, bayonet, and cannon," Ena said grimly.

Little Hawk sought out an inn upon his arrival in Washington. The funds that had been given him by Colonel Freeman were depleted almost totally after he had paid for a room and a meal. He had just enough money left to pay a servant girl to wash and press his uniform. He shined his boots. His thick blond hair had grown quite long during his journey from the Point. Having no money left for a barber, he pulled his hair behind his head, tied it with a leather thong, and let it hang down his back.

Laborers' hammers rang out in the morning air as the young man walked up muddy Pennsylvania Avenue toward the executive mansion. It was a brilliant day of mild temperatures. He could see the unfinished Capitol Building, where construction was progressing at an industrious pace. Green grass was beginning to spot the executive mansion lawn. A black servant emerged from the executive mansion to shoo away a goat that was nibbling on a piece of struggling shrub near the front entrance.

Little Hawk presented himself to a member of the executive mansion staff and was invited to take a chair and wait. He sat with his back straight, his eyes examining a portrait of George Washington that hung on the opposite wall. At last a bespectacled man with a decided widow's peak and a large, red nose escorted him down a hallway, opened a door, and said, speaking through his nose, "Mr. President, Cadet Hawk Harper of West Point."

Jefferson had been standing before a window, arms crossed over his chest. He examined the tall, blond, blue-eyed lad who came to attention in front of his desk.

"Cadet Hawk Harper, reporting as ordered, sir."

Jefferson came around the desk and extended his hand. He bested Little Hawk's six-foot height by two inches. His large-boned but slim body made him seem to be somewhat undignified, but then one noticed that there was grace in his movements. He smiled at Little Hawk. His sandy hair showed some gray. His hazel-flecked gray eyes were friendly. "You've grown some since Philadelphia."

"Yes, sir."

"How was your trip?"

"Quite pleasant, sir."

"Good, good." Jefferson glanced longingly out the window. "Come," he decided. "Let's walk."

Jefferson led the way to the back entrance, waving off two aides, papers in hand, who tried to intercept him. He squinted into the sun, drew a very deep breath, then started to walk. "Hawk," he said, after a while, "I understand you were in trouble again."

"I'm afraid so, sir," Little Hawk said ruefully.

Jefferson shook his head. "Over a girl?"

Little Hawk looked at the president. He had not tarried on the trip from West Point to Washington. How, he wondered, could the president have had word from the old fort on the Hudson?

"Sir, must I answer that question?"

"No, I think I have the gist of it." He turned his head, studied Little Hawk's face. "I considered firing Major Lillie, for I will not abide such prejudice as he exhibited." He smiled crookedly. "However, considering your youth, perhaps the good major did you a favor by refusing permission for you to marry his daughter."

"Perhaps, sir," Little Hawk allowed.

"Will your injured heart, pride, or whatever interfere with your doing a job for me?"

"No, sir," Little Hawk assured him.

"Are you aware that we are having trouble in North Africa?"

"I've read about the demands for tribute from the Barbary states," Little Hawk replied. "And that you, sir, have strengthened our navy in that area."

"Your father is always eager to see faraway places," Jefferson said. "I hope this is a case of like father like son."

Little Hawk laughed. "Yes, sir, my father does like to see what's on the other side of the hill, and I confess that I share some of that curiosity."

"I want you to go to Tunis," Jefferson said abruptly. "You will be commissioned as a midshipman in the Marine Corps."

"The marines, sir?"

"Yes, because a handful of marines is already in place as guards at the American consulate in Tunis. As an army officer you'd be too conspicuous there."

"Yes, sir."

"Your mission will be to observe. I'm not asking you to be a spy, for the man you will be observing is a loyal American. I just want to have an observer on the scene, a man I can rely upon to tell me just what sort of fellow Mr. William Eaton is. I'll want you to assess whether or not Mr. Eaton is being overly optimistic when he claims that with no more than five thousand fighting men he will be able to stop the piracy of the four Barbary nations."

Little Hawk nodded, although he was filled with doubt. Jefferson's assignment seemed to call for more judgment, for more experience, than he possessed. "I would, of course, do as you say, sir, and do my best. But am I qualified for this?"

Jefferson halted to face Little Hawk. He studied the cadet closely. "Hmm . . . two eyes, a nose, a mouth, hands and fingers so that you can write. I assume you have a brain. You were in the top five at West Point. Yes, I think you're qualified."

"I know nothing of North Africa, sir."

"Nor did Mr. Eaton until I made him consul," Jefferson responded. "Also, there is some urgency, my boy. I hope that you have no objections to being on your way immediately."

Little Hawk mused momentarily about the distance. He had felt far removed from his home and his family when he had been at West Point; now he was being asked to put an ocean between himself and all that was familiar to him. He hesitated for only a moment, however, before saying, "I'm ready, sir."

Mr. Jefferson had ordered an aide to provide the new marine midshipman with funds, so Little Hawk was comfortably bedded in the inn and eating well while he waited for a ship. A tailor fitted him for the rather flashy marine uniforms. He arranged to sell his horse, and with a part of the proceeds he purchased a brace of pistols, a pocket watch, and some toilet articles that would not be provided him.

He became well acquainted with the new city. Once, he spent an hour listening to a debate in the House of Representatives and left shaking his head, wondering why the elected leaders of the United States argued so vehemently over issues that would have been decided almost instantly by his father or any sachem worthy of the name.

When word came to him that the frigate *John Adams* was due to leave for North African waters in a matter of days, he spent an afternoon writing letters to his family. That same day a messenger came bidding him to dine with Thomas Jefferson.

Jefferson was alone when Little Hawk was shown into a room in the living area of the executive mansion. He had been working at some papers as he sat at a dining table.

"I wanted to have a chance to speak with you before your sailing," he said.

"My pleasure, sir," Little Hawk said.

"Just let me finish an irksome little chore," he said, seating himself. He wrote hurriedly, then laid down his pen. "Hawk, wouldn't it seem to you that the president of the United States should not be constantly needled by financial problems?"

"I would think so, sir."

"And so it seems to everyone else," Jefferson said. "And yet, in the fiscal year ending March fourth, my expenses totaled twenty-seven thousand seven hundred twenty dollars and ninety-two cents. My income was twenty-six thousand four hundred forty-six dollars and ninety-nine cents."

Little Hawk could think of nothing to say. Twenty-six thousand dollars seemed like a lot of money to him, but then there had been little need for money in a Seneca longhouse.

Jefferson laughed. "And last year was one of my better years." He waved Little Hawk toward a chair across the table from him, pushed the papers aside, and rang a bell.

"Some people might say that I could balance my books merely by cutting down on the four hundred fifteen to five hundred bottles of champagne that are consumed here at my table"—he lifted one hand, palm out, and smiled. "Not all quaffed by me alone, mind you." He looked up as a servant entered and began to lay table settings in front of him and his guest. "Given a choice I would prefer to spend my money on my own extravagances, such as books and scientific instruments. Unfortunately certain things are expected of me, as the leader of a great nation." He waved his hand. "But I didn't ask you here to tell you my troubles, Hawk. You're ready to board the *John Adams*, are you?"

"Yes, sir."

"Do you have everything you need? I'm told that nights in the North African desert are surprisingly cold. Odd, that. One associates a desert with a burning sun and white-hot sands, but it seems that the arid environment, devoid of significant vegetation, does not hold heat well. In fact, it radiates the heat away into space soon after sundown, and thus, the nighttime temperatures can fall below freezing."

"Well, I don't have any especially warm clothing," Little Hawk admitted.

"I'd imagine that Mr. Eaton can see to that once you're in Tunis, if it becomes necessary," Jefferson said. He mused in silence as food was served. He sampled the dishes, then nodded. "Quite good," he remarked. "Hawk, you know that there are over three hundred Americans in slavery in the Barbary states?"

"I did not know the exact number."

"I accept most of the blame for this situation," Jefferson said.

Little Hawk was gratified that the president was finding it so easy to talk to him. Perhaps it was because Jefferson knew that his words would not come back to haunt him as they inevitably must when he was too frank with even his most intimate political associates. Perhaps, Little Hawk mused, it was only because Thomas Jefferson was lonely. He had never remarried after the death of his wife, whom he had loved dearly. His daughter and his grandchildren, on whom he doted, were in Virginia.

"In the interest of governmental economy, I reduced the power of the navy during my first years in office. I have paid dearly for that mistake, and only recently that lack of foresight came back again to punish me. Mr. Robert R. Livingston, our representative in France, is greatly concerned about the Americans who are prisoners of the pirates. He, along with our man in Russia, joined efforts to ask France and Russia to interpose their good offices on behalf of the captives."

He put down his fork and knife, his face flushing with the memory of his fury and his mortification upon learning that the United States had been forced to go humbly, hat in hand, to beg intervention from European nations. His hazel eyes narrowed; his expression was fierce. "I only pray that the Europeans drag their feet in this effort, for I want nothing more than to see American ships and American men restore our prostrated honor." He tapped his fingertips on the table. "In time, in time."

Little Hawk waited in silence.

"I envy you, Hawk, for it just might be your good fortune to participate in removing this stain from our national character. The navy will take responsibility for this effort. The *John Adams* is to be a part of a fleet that will avenge us. I want the squadron that I am sending to reach Tripoli before Russia or France arranges for our countrymen's release. I want it to be American muscle, American men of war that bring that bedamned town down about the bashaw's ears."

"I am honored, sir, that you think I am worthy to be a part of that effort."

"You will remain on shore, Hawk, with Eaton and his marine guards. I want to hear from you as quickly as possible after your arrival, after you've had a chance to take a look around. We taught you military tactics at West Point. Put that knowledge to use. Eaton seems to be a good man, and he served under General Anthony Wayne; but to me he's an unknown quantity. I'm not sure how wise he is in military matters. I want you to send me information that will help me decide whether or not to send ground forces to be led by William Eaton. I hope we can break the power of the Barbary pirates with sea power alone, though, without committing an American ground force to the desert sands. Observe, ask questions, report to me."

"Yes, sir."

Jefferson ate in silence. Little Hawk tasted a bit of champagne and frowned, for the beverage seemed to him to be nothing more than a form of vinegar.

"And, Hawk, although your military duties must come first, if by any chance you get an opportunity to travel in the deserts of North Africa, I would appreciate your taking advantage of it. Note the climate, the vegetation, the animal life. Do you draw, by the way?"

"No, sir."

"Too bad." Jefferson smiled. "Well, I wish you Godspeed. Your communications to me will be handled directly by the navy, and you will be given the name of the officer to whom you can deliver any messages you might have for me. You do not like the champagne?"

"No, sir."

"Pass it to me, then. Since my enemies say that extravagance is the reason for my continual personal financial problems, I will prove them wrong by being frugal and drinking your portion of this bottle myself."

Although Tunis had not followed Tripoli in declaring war on the United States, the bey Ahmed Pasha was openly sympathetic with the bashaw of Tripoli. Having seen no harm come to his brother pirate, the bey called William Eaton to an audience and demanded, in exchange for passage of American ships through his waters, $50,000 worth of grain each year and $100,000 worth of good, American timber cut into planking. Half the wood had to be oak for shipbuilding.

"It's an odd thing," William Eaton said, "but our American farmers and lumbermen really expect to be paid for their produce."

"So let your government pay them," the bey said. "It

is Mr. Jefferson's concern how he raises the money, not mine."

"And what, sir, would Tunis offer in trade for American grain and lumber?" Eaton asked.

"Peace," the bey intoned, using the same inflections that both warmongers and pacifists have used since the beginning of human speech to make a perfectly honorable word, *peace*, sound like profanity. "I will not join my brothers in Tripoli in jihad against you. Instead of a holy war, you will get my hand extended to you in eternal friendship."

William Eaton said, "I'm not certain whether we can afford your friendship, be it eternal or temporary. I fail to see the difference between what you define as friendship and what civilized nations call enmity."

"Are you insulting me, infidel?" the bey asked, bristling.

Eaton bowed slightly. "Sir, since you think of yourself as the most intelligent of men, I'm certain that you can solve that conundrum for yourself."

That night Eaton wrote to his president: "I beg that I be given a corps of one thousand marines between eighteen and thirty-eight years of age, native Americans all, properly officered. Let them be sent to me under cover of a single forty-four-gun frigate. I pledge myself to surprise Porto Farina, the principal defense bastion of Tunis, and destroy the bey's arsenal. This will compel him to seek an honorable peace."

But he had sent such urgent requests to Washington before, and thus he had little hope that this one would bring results any more than had the others. After sealing the letter he leaned back, lit an Arab water pipe, and let the harsh, fragrant smoke ease him. He allowed himself the luxury of dreaming, something he'd been doing a lot of late. In his mind he created a force of men. If the president of the United States would not send him an army, then he would form his own.

The plan, really nothing more than a pleasant reverie, centered around one Hamet Karamanli, who had been deposed as bey of Tripoli by his younger brother, the bloodthirsty Yusef. With a relatively small land force, supported by the American navy, Eaton was sure that he could restore the throne of Tripoli to Hamet. Hamet, grateful, would sign a treaty with the United States based on mutual regard for national honor.

Seeing the simplicity of it all angered Eaton. He rose to pace the room, then seized an Arab scimitar and whirled it expertly above his head. "Lord God," he prayed, "send me a few good men. Only a few!"

Aboard the *John Adams*, Midshipman Hawk Harper was an object of curiosity. He observed careful military courtesy for the officers and men of the ship's force and ate at the captain's table, but the young blond officer was not a part of the frigate's own contingent of marines.

It was rumored that he was not actually a junior marine officer but some sort of secret agent representing the powers in Washington. When asked about his reasons for going to North Africa, Little Hawk answered with nothing more than a smile.

He exercised daily on the frigate's deck, often taking saber practice with the marines. First Lieutenant Frank Jones, in charge of the shipboard contingent, found the young lad to be a worthy opponent whose skills increased with each mock encounter.

At that stage in its history, the United States Marine Corps was a small force that traced its origin to November 10, 1775, when the Continental Congress authorized the formation of two battalions to be used as landing forces with the fleet. Actually, the Continental Marines were deactivated after the war, but Congress reestablished the corps on July 11, 1798. Marines fought bravely in the undeclared naval war with France from 1798 to 1801.

The corps of which Little Hawk was not a part was controlled from marine headquarters in Washington. Since the corps was small in number and beginning to build a morale that made for pride of belonging and comradeship, most officers knew one another. Frank Jones, the lieutenant with whom Little Hawk was practicing saber techniques, raised his brows when he learned that Harper was going to join the marine contingent in Tunis.

"Do you know O'Bannon?" Jones asked.

"I'm afraid not," Harper said.

"That's right," the lieutenant said. "You're fresh out of Quantico, aren't you?"

Little Hawk nodded. He didn't care to have to explain that he had not attended the marine training school, that he owed his commission to having attended West Point.

"You'll find First Lieutenant P. N. O'Bannon to be a good officer," Jones said. "A fair one. Play straight with him, and he'll play straight with you. Get my meaning?"

"Yes, sir," Little Hawk said.

"I'm not sure you do," Jones said, his eyes holding Little Hawk's. "Don't give O'Bannon any of this shit about being a marine."

"I don't follow you," Little Hawk said.

"Harper, you're obviously not a marine. You're either army or you're nothing."

Little Hawk's blue eyes went cold for a moment, then he smiled. "All right, sir," he allowed, "but let's keep that information between ourselves, shall we?"

"I don't know what you're up to," Jones said, "but O'Bannon will see through you quicker than I did." He answered Little Hawk's grin. "I have a feeling, Midshipman, that you're going to have one hell of a lot of fun in Tunis, and, by God, I'd like to go with you."

"I'd love to have you, sir," Little Hawk said. "But I don't write the orders." He parried a blow from Jones's saber, then moved in close. "How did I give myself away?"

"First of all, the way you walk a deck. Any marine officer has spent enough time on board ship, even if he's just out of training, to have sea legs. You were obviously a landsman when you first came aboard, even if you didn't get seasick. And there were other ways—how you wear the uniform, how you attach your saber, your lack of familiarity with it when we first started working out together."

"Think I could learn to be a marine before we reach Tunis?"

"Not well enough to fool O'Bannon. He's still a young man, but he's as seasoned as officers twice his age. I'd advise you to level with him. If you're army sent to spy on us, then give your heart to God, because O'Bannon will have your ass."

"And if I'm not going to Tunis to spy on the marines?"

"You can trust P. N. O'Bannon."

"*En garde*," Little Hawk said. "At least you can polish up my saber handling so that I'll look like a marine in that respect."

Chapter Ten

Othon Hugues stood atop a grassy ridge and looked down on the camp where his band of ruffians slept near dying fires. Then he gazed upward into an ocean of stars, his thoughts directed toward Natchez and Melisande.

The Frenchman was burdened with a melancholy that had paralyzed him for days. Soon after seeing the unexpectedly large number of riders that de Alda had with him for the buffalo hunt, Othon had sent a messenger back to Corpus Christi. He had offered Laffite double the amount of gold to bring his crew northward and join the fight.

Othon knew that there was grumbling among his men. They wanted to get the attack under way, kill all the people who were involved in the buffalo hunt, and go quickly to the de Alda ranch to enjoy the spoils of victory. He knew that he should move, but something—some dread, some lack of resolve that he could not overcome—kept him poised on the brink of a decision.

From the time that he was a mere boy, Othon had

rarely been far away from Melisande. In the past when they had been separated, he could still feel her presence and be guided by her wisdom. Here, however, in the wide spaces of New Spain's northern province, he felt very much alone. He would not have admitted fear or doubt, but what else was it that kept him from going after the sun-bronzed Indian who had almost killed him, who had humiliated him twice and robbed him of one of the most tantalizing little girls he'd ever seen?

"Melisande," he whispered. "Ah, Melisande, speak to me. Send me your thoughts, for confusion haunts me and makes me weak."

He knew that Melisande would stay on Laffite's ship in Corpus Christi for only as long as the young pirate amused her. After that? Hugues did not know, although he had hoped she would appear at his side, to help him dispose of their enemies.

From far away a coyote serenaded the vault of white-lighted sky. Below, in the camp, a dying fire collapsed in on itself, creating a feeble shower of sparks.

Othon spoke to the source of his inspiration, the evil one, his master, pleading for a sign, for the assurance that his endeavor would be successful. A feeling of power came to him. Inspired hatred straightened his shoulders. He lifted his fist and shook it at the heedless night sky. With the day he would move, whether or not Melisande had come.

And yet, when dawn broke and a scout returned to say that the hunters were riding northward toward the buffalo herds, moving in separate groups that could be ambushed at will, Othon hesitated. "We wait one more day for Laffite and his crew," he told his followers.

"We don't need them," a bearded Spaniard protested. "We are enough."

Othon's eyes caused the Spaniard to turn away. "We will wait one more day."

That his judgment had been correct was proven when, just before sunset, the smiling Frenchman and his ship's crew rode into camp. Laffite looked around, then took Hugues aside and spoke in French. "The woman you left behind on my ship . . . she left. She is not here?"

Othon felt a pain in his heart. "No, but she comes and she goes." He laughed and tried to sound unperturbed. "You know how women are."

Laffite nodded sagely. "And what is it that you propose for me and my men?" he asked.

"That you handle a few Spanish vaqueros, that's all."

"Only a few?" Laffite asked.

"They hunt in groups of four or five."

"Then there should have been no problem for you," Laffite said.

"My men and I will kill the most dangerous ones— de Alda, the old one, and the white Indian brothers." He sneered. "Is it too much to ask a fellow Frenchman to kill a few cowherds?"

Laffite smiled, but it was a dangerous smile that held a warning. "I am not sure, Hugues, that I want to be considered your peer." Othon surged forward, his pocked face blackening at the insult, but Laffite's hand had already gone to a pistol at his belt. He laughed as Hugues was brought up short, his eyes riveted to Laffite's hand on the butt of the weapon. "But for your gold we will do your killing for you. Take care that I do not have to include you among those who die."

Othon had no choice but to control himself. There would be time to give Laffite his due. Once they were back aboard ship it would be a simple matter to find the captain and his men relaxed and unprepared for a swift attack. Then the gold he had paid Laffite would be his own again, and he would have a ship that should bring a good price in New Orleans.

"We will attack late in the day," Hugues said, "after they have tired themselves with the hunting and skinning."

Roy Johnson's only day of shooting buffalo was exciting at first. Ta-na and Gao, armed with small bows, had attached themselves to him. Several Spanish ranch hands were assigned to hide in the brush on either side of a little valley, down which the others would drive a portion of the buffalo herd. The ranch hands were playfully solicitous of the two boys as they rode to take up their places.

"You must shoot only very small calves," a musta-chioed rider teased, eyeing the little bows.

"Our grandfather will shoot enough for all of us," Ta-na declared. Roy would be using two rifles, and the boys would reload for him.

They dismounted to lie in the tall grass on the sides of the valley. It narrowed to fewer than a hundred yards before opening out onto a grassy plain. Buffalo had grazed all around, leaving fresh chips to attract flies. The insects seemed content to divide their attentions among the animal droppings and the eyes, noses, and mouths of the hunters. The sun burned down with an intensity heretofore unknown to an old Tennesseean like Roy.

"I wonder why we didn't stay back in camp," he said disgustedly after they'd waited for two hours with no indication that the herd was being moved in their direction. "Right now I'd be willing to fall, clothes and all, into the creek."

"But then, Grandfather, we'd have to wait days for the stream to cleanse itself before we could drink from it," Gao said.

"Nothin' like a smart-assed Injun kid," Roy muttered, hiding a grin.

"And we'd have to work hard to keep the horses away from the creek lest they be poisoned," Ta-na said.

"That's right," Roy said, nodding. "Go on. Make fun of your poor old grandfather. Enjoy it while you can, because I might just head out for the mountains to find me a cool stream running over rocks into a sweet little pool—"

"Grandfather," Gao whispered, pointing.

A cloud of dust was billowing beyond a rise topped by waving grass. And then the hunters heard the low, distant thunder of the herd. Roy looked across to the other slope. "Well, I just hope that those fellows over there keep their muskets pointed down into the gulch."

"Look!" Ta-na cried.

A dark wave had crested the rise. The herd poured in a roiling mass over the grassy knoll. Dust swirled up from their pounding hooves. Gao pointed in excitement as a yearling galloped ahead of the leaders. Its neck was outthrust, its tongue lolling.

"Well, boys," Roy said, "are you ready?"

"Yes!" they cried together.

Roy waited until the leaders of the herd were almost even with him. The men on either side and across the gully began firing. A big bull went down limply. A panicked cow tripped over him and somersaulted through the air to land with a terrible thud and lie still, her neck broken by the fall. Roy saw the fleet yearling, which had led the stampede, go down. He sighted and fired, and another buffalo dropped, then skidded on the dirt. Gao thrust the other rifle into Roy's hands, and yet another animal went down.

It seemed that an endless wave of frightened, bellowing, panting animals was passing through the funnel of death below the spot where the hunters sat in the grass. Ta-na, apparently stunned by the sheer numbers of the buffalo, awed by the relentless hail of death that came from the muzzles of a dozen rifles, was letting Gao do the reloading for Roy.

Within seconds, dead animals littered the ground, and there was no indication of thinning in the continuing flood of animals pounding down the slope into the gully. The fleeing herd trampled bodies or swerved around them. Now and then a bull would pause to paw the ground and bellow at the scent of blood, only to join the dead himself as the sharp reports of the guns made themselves heard over the steady rumble of the herd.

Roy fired and saw a charging buffalo's legs go rubbery. The heavy body hit the ground and slid for several feet with the beast's momentum. Then the Tennesseean took the loaded rifle from Gao, lifted it, sighted, lowered it.

"Grandfather?" Gao asked, having loaded the last weapon fired.

"I reckon we've done our share," Roy said grimly.

Ta-na's eyes were swimming with tears. He himself had killed. With his bow he had bagged turkey, rabbit, and squirrel. He had seen the blood flow out of the

arteries of a newly slain deer hanging by its hind legs.
It was the nature of things that one killed in order to
eat. Man was a hunting animal like the wolf, the bear,
the panther. Each time he killed, he spoke to the spirit
of the animal in the time-honored tradition of the Seneca hunter, thanking it for its life, for its flesh that would
fill his belly.

This slaughter, however, was not the work of men
but of butchers. They were not killing to eat but to profit
in money. The spirits of the animals would mourn. Ta-na
wiped the tears of unhappiness from his cheeks.

The gesture did not go unnoticed. Roy caught the
boy's attention and nodded in understanding. "Yep," he
said sadly, "I think we've done our share."

Still the river of life flowed through the bottleneck to
leave its dead behind before spreading out onto the grassy
plain and rumbling off into the distance. Mounted men,
loading and firing, burst over the crest of the rise, pacing
the stragglers of the herd. The hunters left the prairie
behind them studded with dark, dead mounds. Already
buzzards were circling.

At last the muted roar of the herd faded into the
distance. Vaqueros and their women, whooping in triumph, ran down from the slopes and began the job of
skinning the kill. By the time they would finish—hundreds of dead animals littered the earth—the carcasses
would have begun to swell and stink.

Roy and the boys walked among the dead animals as
the skinners began their work. The smell of fresh blood
was enforced by the stench of warm entrails.

"Hah, *chico*."

The call came from a skinner who had made it his
duty to choose good horses for the two young boys. He
had been drawn to them because he shared Indian blood,
being half-Comanche, half-Spanish. He was called Chirlo
because of a terrible scar that distorted the corner of his
left eye, made a pale canyon in his cheek, and lifted the
corner of his mouth into a permanent sneer.

"Gao, Ta-na, come. I will share with you." He had
cut into the belly of a young buffalo to extract the steaming

liver. "Come, let me give you a treat that was taught to me by my Comanche mother."

The vaquero cut off a slice of the hot liver, squeezed sprinkles of green fluid from the gallbladder onto it, and popped it into his mouth. "Ah," he said appreciatively, rolling his eyes. He cut a small piece, seasoned it with fluid, and thrust it toward Gao.

"You try first," Gao urged Ta-na.

"He has offered the treat to you," Ta-na said politely.

"Good," Chirlo said, extending the piece of liver.

Ta-na took the meat into his hand, swallowed hard, then thrust it into his mouth. There was a bitter taste and then the feral, sweetly rich pungency of the liver.

"To a Comanche," the skinner declared, "this is the best part of the hunt." He was talking around a mouthful of the raw liver. "My mother told me that she learned it from a Sioux slave woman from the northern plains." He cut another large piece, squeezed the gall over it, and offered it to Roy.

"I think I'll pass," Roy said. "Save my appetite for a good portion of roasted tongue when we get back to camp."

Gao, not to be outdone, ate a larger piece than Ta-na had taken. Both refused seconds, however, leaving the skinner to his feast.

Blood stained Gao's chin. Roy shook his head at the sight. He'd seen all the blood he wanted to see that day. "I been thinking about that cool water in the creek," he told the boys. "And no smart remarks."

"I think my grandfather is the wisest of men," Gao said. "We will come along."

Soon the threesome were headed toward cool waters. Ta-na halted his horse at the top of the ridge and looked back. As far as he could see, dead buffalo made dark, pathetic lumps, some of them almost hidden by the rich, tall grass. He kicked his horse into a gallop to catch up with Roy and Gao.

Roy pointed upward to the circling buzzards. "They'll celebrate this day. It'll go down in buzzard history. Years from now when some old mama buzzard comes home to the nest and disgorges choice bits of carrion for her babies, she'll be telling them the story of the day when there was so much food that all the buzzards in the world couldn't eat it."

"Well," Gao said, "it is bad that the meat will be wasted, but Señor de Alda and his men will cure the hides. Adan's ship will carry them to New Orleans to be sold, and with the money, things that are needed here on the ranch will be purchased."

Neither Ta-na nor Roy made comment.

"What do you say, fellers, to riding up past that buffalo ridge and seeing what the creek looks like from up there?" Roy asked.

The ridge shaped like the hump of a buffalo was near, to the north. East of its grassed slope they could see the line of trees that indicated the course of the creek, which curved south and west to the de Alda camp.

"It'll be a little more private, if we can find a hole deep enough to swim in," Roy said. "With Beth, Ah-wa-o, and the women from the ranch in and around the camp, a man can't strip off buck naked and have a good wash."

A rattlesnake spooked Ta-na's horse, but he had become a skillful rider. He controlled the animal, guided it around the buzzing snake, and left the reptile to its territory. Prairie dogs barked from their mounds, and to avoid riding through the prairie-dog town, Roy led the way on a sweep to the north toward the brushy side of the buffalo ridge. As they rode, Roy explained to the boys that a horse could break a leg stepping into a prairie-dog hole.

They came even with the end of the ridge and could see the creek a half mile ahead. Sunlight burst into millions of diamonds on the surface of a broad pool. Roy grinned happily and guided his horse down a beaten buffalo track into a brush-filled depression that lay at the foot of the ridge. At the unexpected smell of wood smoke he pulled his horse to a halt just in time to foil the aim of an ambusher. The musket ball made a whistling sound that chilled him as it passed within an inch of the tip of his nose.

"Hieee!" he yelled, jerking the horse around. "Go, go, go!"

More shots rang out. Ta-na and Gao were bending low over their horses' necks as they kicked their mounts into a gallop. Roy was shouting encouragement. The three horses surged up the slope of the depression and gained the grassy plain. Because bullets zipped past, making loud *thunks* as they hit the ground on either side, the animals did not have to be urged to their utmost speed by the riders. After it was clear that they were out of their attackers' range, Roy looked back and saw only the grassy ridge, the brush at the edge of the depression. He slowed the pace slightly but kept a close watch over his shoulder as he and the boys rode quickly to re-join the others.

Like Roy, Renno, El-i-chi, and Adan had decided to leave the skinning of the kill to de Alda's men and their women. They had returned to the camp with Beth and Ah-wa-o. De Alda rode in just before Roy and the boys came on lathered horses into camp to tell an excited tale of having been ambushed by wild Indians.

De Alda listened with his head cocked, his expression serious. "It's unusual for the Comanche to venture so far south," he said. "But I've never seen so many buffalo in this area, so they may have been forced to follow the herd here. I don't think we have to concern ourselves too much. If indeed they have come south, there will be only small hunting parties. If we stay in strong groupings they will not attack."

"Comanche have rifles?" Roy asked.

"Some of them do. They take them in raids, and there are those men among us who will trade guns for furs and hides," de Alda said.

"There wasn't one arrow fired," Roy pointed out.

Renno glanced at El-i-chi. The shaman drew close to his brother. "Perhaps I will take a ride and look around before sunset," he said.

Renno thought for a moment, then nodded.

"There is no need to alarm them," El-i-chi said, indicating Beth and Ah-wa-o.

El-i-chi was not surprised when he heard his name called as he walked to the brush enclosure where the horses were kept. He turned and waited for Ah-wa-o to catch up. She walked at his side, then helped him saddle and cinch his horse.

"The manitous will be with you," she said as her husband mounted.

"I will not return until after dark," he told her, and squeezed her hand.

"I will warm food for you then."

He crossed the low, western end of the long buffalo ridge and rode on its north side as the sun sank toward the horizon. When he was nearing the higher, eastern end of the ridge he tethered his horse and climbed the slope. In the twilight he could see the trees that lined the creek.

El-i-chi made his way silently through the tall grasses to the highest end of the ridge. In the brushy depression below he saw the glow of fires and smelled smoke and the aroma of roasting meat. Like a snake he slithered on his belly down the ridge. Only an occasional movement of the grass betrayed his presence. On the lip of the depression he found cover in the brush and could move more easily, musket at the ready, until he heard voices speaking not in the language of the Comanche but in French. Flat on his belly he moved closer, closer, and observed about a dozen men, dressed as mariners, grouped near and around a fire. There were other fires nearby.

The shaman moved silently through the brush and heard voices talking softly in Spanish. At one fire he saw Indians, Choctaw and Creek. He estimated that there were about thirty men altogether, the Frenchmen and a motley mixture of white, Spanish, and Indian ruffians. He retreated, made his way back up the slope, found his horse, and rode back to camp.

Upon his arrival, El-i-chi sought out Renno, and then both of them went to talk to de Alda.

"I can only guess why such men—French, Spanish, Indian, and American—are on my property," de Alda said. "Perhaps the talk of wresting the northern provinces away from New Spain is not merely talk. Perhaps these men make up an advance party of an army from the north."

"They are careless," El-i-chi said, eager for a confrontation. "They could be easily surprised."

"My men are peaceful vaqueros," de Alda said, frowning. "And we have women and children with us."

El-i-chi growled in frustration, but Renno lifted his hand and said, "Señor de Alda is right."

"Then I will take Roy and ten men," El-i-chi said. "That will be enough to do the job."

"And if they are nothing more than peaceful hunters or trappers?" de Alda asked.

"They fired at Roy and the boys without warning," El-i-chi said. "Does that make them peaceful?"

"What you say is true," de Alda agreed. "And they have invaded my land. All right. But let me suggest this course of action: we will take our hides and return to the ranch. Once the women and children are safely delivered there, we will organize a force and ride back to see just what these men are doing here."

"By then they could be a hundred miles away," El-i-chi protested.

"So," Renno said, and El-i-chi knew that the discussion was closed.

With the morning the skinners continued their work, and by nightfall the job was done. Wagons were loaded with the stinking, wet hides. De Alda led the hunting expedition toward the hacienda. The wagons and women and children were protected by an encircling formation of armed men. Meanwhile, Renno, El-i-chi, Roy, and Adan rode to the buffalo ridge and with great caution approached the brushy depression and the creek. They found dead campfires and the signs of many men. The trail of what Renno estimated to be at least thirty horses skirted the ridge on the north side and then angled off toward the northwest.

"Looks like they're heading for Comanche country," Roy said.

The men returned to the rest of their group and reported to de Alda. The hidalgo nodded in disgust when he heard the information. "Comancheros," he said. "The worst kind of scum—men who live among the savages and trade weapons and whiskey for the Comanche's furs.

That's why they opened fire on Roy and the boys; they feared being discovered and reported to the authorities. Any self-respecting man would shoot on sight a man who supplies a Comanche with a rifle."

De Alda rode off to the front of the column.

"Nevertheless," Renno said to Roy and El-i-chi, "we three will keep a close watch to the rear."

Othon had been furious when he heard the rifle fire and had run through the brush to discover that his men had been stupid enough to open fire on intruders before they were close enough to make killing them a certainty. He raged at them. They claimed that the man and the boys could not have seen any of them, but Othon was not sure that the men were telling the truth.

"They'll just think it was Indians," Jean Laffite assured him.

Laffite wondered if he'd been wise in agreeing to join the mad, pockmarked Hugues in his murderous design. Something was disturbing about the way Hugues's eyes sometimes seemed to blaze with fire, and the man's bizarre manner was unsettling. When Hugues ordered the men to break camp, Laffite gathered his crewmen and rode with them, apart from the main party, on the pretext of being a protective force on the flank.

Hugues took his force to the northeast, past the end of the buffalo ridge. Then, finding an area of sparse growth where the semiarid soil was pocked with buffalo wallows and the disturbed earth would disguise signs of the passing of some thirty horsemen, he turned back toward the south.

He cursed mightily when he saw that the de Alda party had already broken camp and was heading toward the ranch.

"We have lost our opportunity to take them in small groups," he fumed. "We will hit them in force tonight while they sleep."

Ta-na and Gao left Beth and Ah-wa-o, riding near the cook's wagon, and galloped ahead to join the riders at the front of the column. De Alda was there. He winked at the boys and said, "Ah, two more scouts, eh?"

The half-Comanche Chirlo said, "Señor, they are good boys. True Indians as well, for they like fresh liver with bile."

De Alda raised an eyebrow. Ta-na shrugged and turned down the corners of his mouth, causing de Alda to laugh. "Chirlo, I can't believe that even you like raw liver with the excretions of the gallbladder spread on it."

"Señor, you know not what you miss."

When Chirlo separated himself from de Alda, Gao guided his horse to ride beside the scar-faced man. "You mentioned a tribe of Indians called the Sioux," Gao said. "Once before I heard that name, from a man who came from the valley of the Ohio River. Have you been to the lands of the Sioux?"

"Not I," Chirlo said. "Great warriors, the Sioux. They guard well the lands on which they live and hunt."

"The tribes of the Iroquois were also great warriors who guarded their lands well," Gao said. "Then the white-faces came."

Chirlo spat to show his contempt. "Like the Spanish, the English whitefaces are fools, thinking that a mere man can own the land." He spread his hands, indicating the endless plains that surrounded them. Far-off trees were dwarfed by distance. A band of dark clouds lay to the northwest, low on the horizon.

Gao nodded in agreement. "How can man own what the Master of Life has made for all things?"

From the crest of a gentle rise Gao looked westward to enjoy the peaceful landscape. Green grasses waved in the wind, distant trees marked a watercourse, a small bunch of buffalo grazed peacefully not more than a mile away. He pointed. Chirlo nodded, and his perpetual sneer became a contorted smile. "So, young one, do you want more raw liver?"

"Haven't we killed enough of them?" Gao asked.

Chirlo laughed. "They outnumber the blades of grass," he said. "It is a service to kill some of them, lest, in their millions, they leave the prairie a barren desert of sand."

"Chirlo," de Alda called, riding toward them, "take a pack animal and go get us fresh meat for tonight."

"You see?" Chirlo asked Gao. "I knew that I would have one more meal of fresh liver. Want to come with me?"

"Yes," Gao said.

"Wait for me here while I get a packhorse," Chirlo said.

Gao gave the whistle of a hawk. Proof that Ta-na had heard came minutes later, when he rode slowly toward Gao. Gao pointed to the buffalo a mile away. "Chirlo has been told to kill one for meat."

The threesome rode slowly down from the gradual rise and circled to approach the buffalo from downwind. After tethering the horses, the hunters crept the last hundred yards through high grass. Chirlo sighted his rifle, and the roar of its fire sent the buffalo rumbling away, tails flicking, save for a yearling cow who lay on her side as her legs jerked for only a little while before she was still.

Chirlo, his unloaded rifle slung over his shoulder, walked toward the dead animal. Gao and Ta-na lagged behind, not at all interested in the process of skinning and gutting the buffalo and wondering how they could gracefully get out of eating any more raw liver.

Ta-na spotted a puff of smoke from behind a bush. Chirlo's legs went limp, and he started a melting, slow-motion fall before Ta-na heard the report of the rifle that had killed the vaquero. The boy leaped forward, seized Chirlo's weapon, and jerked the powder horn and ball pouch from the dead man's belt.

Gao was yelling, "Run, run!" for two men had emerged from the brush and were running toward them from a distance of perhaps a hundred yards.

Ta-na did not have to be urged. He ran as fast as he could without losing the rifle. Gao got to the horses first. The two men had been gaining on them. Gao, shouting for Ta-na to hurry, hurled himself into the saddle. The horses began to prance nervously.

Ta-na glanced over his shoulder and judged that he had time to load Chirlo's musket. Standing near the horses, ignoring Gao's urgings, he poured powder, tamped the ball, lifted the weapon, sighted down the long barrel at the larger of the two men, and fired. The kick of the muzzle-loader sat him down forcefully, but the big man, now only a hundred feet away, threw up his arms, sending his rifle flying, and fell facedown. The other man halted and lifted his weapon.

Ta-na bounded to his saddle just as the rifle ball penetrated his horse's neck with a sound like that made by the cook's cleaver cutting meat. The horse reared and collapsed. Ta-na threw himself clear.

Gao caught the reins of Chirlo's horse and led it on the run to meet Ta-na. And then they were both mounted and fleeing even as the man who had killed Ta-na's horse finished reloading, lifted his rifle, and sent a ball screaming past Gao's head.

Renno and El-i-chi were trailing the de Alda party to watch their rear. When they heard the sound of galloping horses they turned and saw their sons burst up over a low rise. Renno noted the musket in his son's hand. The boys were bent low over their horses, fanning the animals with their heels to get maximum speed. Renno called out. Ta-na heard and turned his horse toward the sachem.

"Don't worry," Gao yelled as they drew near, "Ta-na killed one of them."

"But they killed Chirlo," Ta-na yelled.

"Easy," El-i-chi said, soothing his horse as the animal reacted to the boys' rapid approach.

Ta-na and Gao reined in, and both talked at once. Their horses were breathing hard.

El-i-chi said, "Hold. One at a time, if you please."

Renno was searching the horizon to the west, whence the boys had come, as he listened. "There were only two men?" he asked when Gao had finished describing the death of Chirlo and Ta-na's shooting of one of the killers.

"We saw only two," Ta-na answered.

"And they were afoot?" El-i-chi asked.

"We did not stay long enough to find out if they had horses," Gao replied.

"Take us to the place," Renno requested.

"First let me reload," Ta-na said.

Renno made no objections as his son expertly reloaded the long rifle. The boys pointed the way and found the spot by noting the trampled grass where the buffalo had stampeded. Ta-na's dead horse showed up as a roan-colored mound in the grass. The man Ta-na had shot had not died immediately. He had tried to crawl away, leaving a trail of blood until his final collapse. He wore the tight trousers and wide-brimmed hat of a Spanish vaquero.

Chirlo had been shot through the right eye and had died instantly. In the brush to the north were horse tracks.

"Here they dismounted," El-i-chi said as he read the sign. "They, like Chirlo, must have been after the buffalo."

"They found other game," Renno said. He directed Ta-na to double up with Gao, for there was no sign of the packhorse. Soon Chirlo's body was lashed across the saddle of his own horse. Then Gao and Ta-na, who considered themselves to be the dead man's friends, led the horse carrying the body as they rode to catch up with the main party.

Julio de Alda's face showed both anger and sorrow as he looked at Chirlo's corpse. "We must increase our pace," he said, "so that we can get the women to the ranch and safety. Then we will find these renegades. It is bad enough that they invade my ranch. Now they kill my men."

Roy pulled Renno to one side. "What do you think?" he asked.

"I wonder why a man who is on his way to trade with the Comanche would kill for no reason."

"Does seem a little odd. You'd expect them to want to escape notice, wouldn't you?"

"So," Renno said.

"You figure to do a little backtracking this evening?" Roy asked.

Renno nodded.

"Reckon I'll go along."

Renno nodded again.

El-i-chi and Adan joined them.

"I believe I will do a bit of scouting," El-i-chi announced.

Roy laughed. "Thought you might have that idea, Shaman."

"But should we not listen to de Alda, who advises us

to get the women to safety before we go after these men?" Adan asked.

"For myself," El-i-chi said mildly, "I am merely going on an evening ride to enjoy some of the countryside."

"My brother will not object to having company?" Renno asked in Seneca.

"I will be honored by my brother's presence," El-i-chi said formally.

"I don't care whether or not you'd be honored by my presence," Roy said. "Just shut up the fancy talk so we can get going."

"Well," Adan said with resignation, "if you think this is really necessary, Renno . . ."

"Has the comfort of your master's cabin aboard ship caused you to forget how to fight, Adan?" El-i-chi taunted.

"It's simply that I like to do my fighting from a distance," Adan said. "Preferably by sighting down the barrel of a cannon. At worst on a clean, solid deck with a good saber in my hand."

Renno, who knew from past experience not to question Adan's bravery, grinned. "If the prairie grass is not clean enough or solid enough for you, Captain, you can go and guard the ladies."

"It isn't the grass so much," Adan explained, "as those infernal buffalo chips."

"If we dismount, you can walk with your head down and eyes open," Roy suggested.

"You're all very helpful," Adan said. "Before this conversation gets so witty that I won't be able to stand it, shall we go?"

"Good idea," El-i-chi said. "Isn't that a good idea, Renno?"

"Excellent idea," Renno agreed. "Don't you think so, Roy?"

"Indubitably," Roy replied. "What about you, Adan? Think it's a good idea?"

"*Dios mio*," Adan groaned, spurring his horse.

Chapter XI

At Beaumont Manor, William, Lord Beaumont, eagerly opened a small packet of letters. The poor condition of the finely crafted paper envelopes was testimony to the difficulty of getting communications from Paris to England. Some of the sweeping, feminine letters spelling out William's name had become blurred, as if from being exposed to water. The wonder was that the letters from Renna had managed to reach England at all.

Napoleon had declared a new French empire with himself as emperor, and now he was raging on the Continent, making threats and trying, through intimidation, to compensate for France's sad state of affairs on the seas. Horatio Nelson and his "band of brothers" were enjoying success in hounding French ships across the Atlantic and back.

William saw that only one letter was intended for Estrela and him. Others were to be forwarded to Renno and Beth in the Cherokee Nation and to Little Hawk at West Point. Renna announced in her letter to the Beaumonts that she was with child, the birth expected in midsummer. Two months had passed since the letter was written, meaning that the baby was almost due.

"How wonderful and how terrible it is," Estrela said. "I know that Renno will be so pleased. And yet she is so far away. Will Beth and he ever see the child?"

"It's an uncertain world," William replied obliquely.

He did not discuss the international situation with Estrela, for she preferred to leave wars and the rumors thereof to the men while she devoted her energies to chasing after the growing Beaumont brood. William decided against burdening her with his own certainty that sooner or later Englishmen would be fighting on the Continent again in spite of the fact that the Royal Navy and Admiral Nelson controlled the seas.

For the moment Napoleon was reduced to crude and unprofessional schemes to secure mastery of the English Channel so that, in his words, he could conquer "perfidious Albion" once and forever. The emperor had demonstrated his mastery of land warfare, but his scheme to make invasion possible by drawing the British fleet away from home waters was a dismal failure. By staging an elaborate rendezvous of the Brest and Toulon fleets in the West Indies, the emperor accomplished nothing more than exposing his ships to the rapacious Nelson.

Napoleon had over 100,000 men gathered along the channel. He had given the title *Armfie d'Angleterre,* the Army of England, to the elite forces he had massed around Boulogne. And only the Royal Navy stood between England and a desperate battle on her own soil.

No, William would not discuss his concern with Estrela, and to his pleasure Renna mentioned nothing of the war save to state that Beau was attached to the French Foreign Office as a military liaison officer.

"One cannot tell by the actions of Paris society that there is a war," she wrote. "I have had made several gowns to hide my expanding condition, for my comte is in constant demand, and I enjoy the dancing, the music, and the opportunity to talk with people from odd and interesting places such as Württemberg and Franconia, from Italy and Austria and Spain. Hardly anyone can

detect that I am not a native Frenchwoman, for I have
worked diligently on my accent. I have found that my
grandmother and Beth, who taught me French, did an
excellent job, although some of Grandmother Toshabe's
pronunciations had a definite Seneca inflection to them."

"Oh, I will pray for her," Estrela said fervently, "for
I know that she is lonely being so far away from family
and home."

William took his dark and pretty wife into his arms.
"I carried you far from home, far from your family," he
reminded, nuzzling her neck. "And I do not see you
weeping."

"Well," she said with a sly smile, "being Lady Beaumont is *marginally* better than being the squaw of an
Apache warrior in the southwestern desert, isn't it?" She
was referring to her rescue from Apache captivity by
William.

"I am pleased that you appreciate your status," William said, tweaking her playfully on the rump. He
laughed, for in spite of the fact that she had borne five
children to him, such familiarity always made her blush.

"I suppose it will have to do," she said.

William, not knowing that Little Hawk was no longer
at West Point, forwarded Renna's letters. He added a letter of his own to Beth, telling his sister that he was
pleased to see that her marine enterprise out of Wilmington, North Carolina, under the management of Adan Bar-
toleme, was booming. With France and England involved
in a fierce naval war, American maritime interests were
enjoying juicy commercial pickings.

William had a warm feeling for the United States, for
in his opinion the country was made up principally of
good Englishmen who just happened to have separated
themselves from the home country. It was only proper
that the young nation flex her muscles a bit against the
Barbary nations. It was high time someone did something
about the brigands of the Mediterranean. It would be interesting to see what was going to happen in North African
waters as the American squadron there built its strength.

In his long letter he also told Beth that Estrela and

he had seen Adan within the last year on one of Adan's voyages to England and that it would be splendid if, when things settled down, Renno and she came to England for a long visit. He sent the letters off, knowing that months would go by before they were read, if ever.

He thought of the route that the packet would travel: by coach to a port, by American or British ship to the Eastern Seaboard of the United States, by coach, rider, or by accident across the width of North Carolina to Knoxville, and then by messenger or by Roy Johnson to Huntington Castle. Although the world had shrunk since Columbus set out into the unknown in three frail, tiny ships, it was still a vastness that separated one with unheeding tyranny from those whom he loved.

Beth Huntington Harper was not thinking of her brother at the moment when William was writing to her. She was wishing that she had brought her own English longbow with her to New Spain. No doubt remained that the mixed-race force that El-i-chi had scouted harbored evil intentions toward the de Alda party. First shots had been fired at Roy and the boys. Next there had been the attack that killed the vaquero, Chirlo. At about the same time a group of four vaqueros had been ambushed and killed. All four had been scalped but not, Renno observed, by an Indian. An Indian familiar with the technique would have done the job neatly, not taking all of the hair but just a token topknot.

The four men had been killed late in the day. Renno, El-i-chi, Roy, and a somewhat reluctant Adan left camp, only to be forced to return as a dark band of clouds low on the horizon reared up. The front rushed across the skies with swollen, purple-black clouds. Winds turned grains of sand into painful projectiles, and then a deluge of rain obliterated the tracks of the attackers.

The tumultuous storm passed as quickly as it had arisen. The crashings of thunder and flashes of lightning moved to the east, leaving behind a clean, sweet scent as if the prairie had been bathed and perfumed. In the growing darkness Renno directed the formation of a defensive

ring around the camp, with the hide-laden wagons to be
used as shields. "If they were just comancheros," he told
El-i-chi, "they would have moved on."

"And yet Señor de Alda says that he has no enemies
who would go to this extent," Adan said.

"I can't swallow the idea that this is the start of an
uprising designed to steal land from New Spain," Roy
remarked. "Those fellows out there are acting more like
brigands than an organized army."

"Soon we will know," El-i-chi predicted, honing the
blade of his tomahawk.

The attack took place after midnight. Othon Hugues
had hoped for complete surprise, but his men kept disobeying his orders. True, they had killed five of the
vaqueros, four in the latest batch. But they had stupidly
let the old man and two boys escape to carry warning.
Now, as he and his men stole across the dark, level ground
toward the de Alda camp, he cursed those who had been
so careless.

"You see the result of your ignoring my orders?" he
raged. "Now they have formed a defensive circle with the
wagons. If, however, we can infiltrate their encampment
before they are aware, we might be able to overcome this
disadvantage. Once we start toward the camp, we must
not falter. If we are lucky we will be inside the wagons
before anyone awakens. If not, move swiftly, for we can
still benefit from their confusion and fear."

Much to Othon's chagrin, Jean Laffite had not committed himself fully to the plan. Othon wanted Laffite and
his crew to flank the camp and, if de Alda's expedition
was alerted before Othon's men were inside, to lay down
a covering fire.

"Remember," Othon told his men, "the white Indian
must be taken alive. And the red-haired woman is mine."

Just before midnight Renno had come to relieve Roy
Johnson from guard duty. Roy was sitting atop a wagon-
load of buffalo hides. His perch insulted his nose but gave
him a field of vision all around the camp. He had decided
that if any attack would come, it would be from the west,

where the level land dipped a bit. From that direction an attacking force could remain undetected until it topped the little rise at a distance of about a hundred yards from the camp.

Renno climbed up by stepping on the hub of a wheel. He wrinkled his nose. "You picked a great spot," he joked.

"I've been in worse places," Roy said, keeping his voice low. "Gives a good view. Saw two coyotes awhile ago. Highlight of my night."

"If it's all the same to you," Renno said, "I'll find another post."

"Help yourself," Roy said. "But if you're planning to tromp around all night, just remember to be quiet. These educated ears of mine can hear a mouse rubbing two grass seeds together at a thousand feet."

"Yes, sir," Renno said with a grin.

"Well," Roy said, stretching hugely, "reckon those blankets are going to feel good."

The sachem went to stand outside the circle of wagons facing the west. Far to the east he could hear the steady rumble of thunder from the storm that had passed. Overhead the sky had cleared. A crescent moon rode high, adding its feeble light to that of a brilliant canopy of stars. A coyote called and was answered from another ridge. Behind Renno in the camp a horse blew wetly through its lips.

The white Indian walked away from the wagons until he could get an overall view and, after checking carefully for sleeping rattlesnakes, sat down on a prairie-dog mound. He was so motionless, so quiet, that a field mouse scurried across the barren ground near his feet.

The moon had changed its position. Renno shifted his weight and swiveled his head to check. An hour had passed. He rose and moved silently in a large circle around the camp. He was turning back toward the west and the point where the land fell away in a gentle, rolling slope. A sound, a clank of metal, froze him. First one head and then another became visible.

Renno sank down in a crouch and waited. If there were only two of them, he could handle them without waking the camp. But then, quite quickly, he could count fifteen men, then twenty, moving silently toward the camp. He ran to a gap between wagons, found the spot where El-i-chi slept beside his little Rose, and woke the shaman with a touch.

Roy Johnson sat up and reached for his rifle as the sachem moved rapidly from man to man, waking them softly and warning them to be silent.

When Renno returned to the west side of the circle, the intruders were moving slowly toward the camp. Beside him El-i-chi whispered, "I count twenty-one."

"We have fourteen in our force," Renno said. "We must make our shots count, Brother."

"Fifteen," Beth corrected as she moved beside him, a musket in her hand.

"So," Renno said. She had fought at his side before. While he could not vouch for the skill of de Alda's vaqueros with a rifle, he knew that Beth's aim was deadly.

"I would say about now," Roy Johnson said.

"Not yet," Renno whispered.

But two wagons away a nervous vaquero could not wait. The blast of his musket shattered the night. The oncoming men halted.

"Fire!" Renno called out, and weapons blazed up and down the line of wagons facing the west.

Othon Hugues, at the fore of his men, saw the flash of a rifle. No one was hit, but his men halted.

"Keep going," he ordered, but then the entire line of wagons blazed with fire, and to his left a man went down.

"Now! Now!" he yelled. "Now, while they are reloading."

But even as he broke into a run, another fusillade of balls burst from the wagons. He realized that the vaqueros had been on a buffalo hunt, and each of them would be equipped with two or more rifles. Around him men began to flee.

"Damn you," he screamed. "Come back here."

He stood alone. Two musket balls zipped past him. He lifted his fist and screamed out his hatred as yet another ball tugged at his loose tunic. Then he, too, retreated. Jean Laffite's crew had not fired a shot. Othon found his men waiting in the gully where they had left their horses.

"Cowards," he called them.

"There are easier ways to vanquish an enemy," a man snarled, "than walking into the muzzles of men who know you're coming."

When Renno saw the attackers turn and run, he tapped El-i-chi on the shoulder. The shaman followed him through a gap between wagons. Each man carried only a bow and arrows and hand weapons—tomahawk and knife. Although the brothers ran swiftly after the retreating attackers, they slowed as they went over the crest of the rise. Ahead they could hear men running. When Renno saw movement in the darkness, he jerked to a halt, his English longbow in his hand. He sent an arrow buzzing through the darkness; then after he heard a strangled cry of pain, El-i-chi and he were on the run again.

The man Renno had shot lay on his face, the arrow deep in his back. While El-i-chi went on ahead, Renno silenced his victim's groans with a blow from the tomahawk. El-i-chi waited for Renno on the rim of a gully. Below them men were mounting their horses. Someone was cursing in French. The voice sounded familiar to Renno.

"Let us give them our greetings," Renno whispered, notching an arrow.

El-i-chi followed suit. Their aim was questionable in the darkness. Renno shot at movement, reached for another arrow, then shot again. A shout of fear erupted from below. In the confusion horses bumped one another, and then the group was fleeing, dust blossoming up to make visibility even less certain.

El-i-chi led the way into the gully. Two men were down. One of them lifted a pistol as El-i-chi approached. The shaman's tomahawk flashed. The other was dead, Renno's arrow deep in his chest.

"So," El-i-chi said. "I counted twenty-one. Now there are seventeen." He wiped the blade of his tomahawk on a clump of grass. "Who are they, Brother?"

Renno was haunted by the voice he'd heard cursing in French. If he was right, he had last heard that voice on the banks of the Mississippi River long months before as Little Hawk and he rescued Renna and the comte de Beaujolais from Othon Hugues and his witch.

"I hesitate to share my suspicions just now," Renno said. "Let me say only that I will make a sincere effort to find out."

El-i-chi grunted, his teeth showing in a grin, for he recognized the steely tone of his brother's voice. There was in Renno's words an unyielding determination that boded ill for the attackers, whoever they were.

"I will stay with you," Beth offered the next morning when de Alda gave the order to move.

"Humor me," Renno said, smiling. "Go with the others."

"You have never sent me away before," she protested.

"Ah-wa-o needs you," he said.

"Nonsense. She would stay, too, if El-i-chi would let her."

"We will be moving fast," El-i-chi pointed out.

"Oh, curse both of you," Beth said in exasperation. She seized her rifle and mounted her horse. She, like Ah-wa-o, who had listened in silence to the exchange, was wearing the buckskins of a Seneca woman.

"Stay by de Alda's side," El-i-chi requested.

"Keep an eye on the boys," Roy Johnson added.

"*You're* going to keep an eye on the boys," Renno told him.

"Not likely," Roy responded.

"It would mean much to know that our sons were in your hands," El-i-chi said.

"Well, then, as Beth said, curse both of you." Roy grinned. "But look after your hair. I've gotten used to having both of you around."

Renno nodded, put his heels to his horse, and rode off without looking back. El-i-chi turned in the saddle to wave to Ah-wa-o. The wagons were rumbling toward the south, vaqueros riding guard on each flank and at the rear.

The brothers picked up their attackers' trail at the gully. The original pack, seventeen as El-i-chi counted, was, to their surprise, joined by more men, at least another ten.

"At least twenty-seven guns," El-i-chi said.

Renno nodded grimly.

The trail paralleled the route of the hide wagons. Within an hour the Seneca could see the dust of a large group of horsemen. Renno crawled to the top of a grassy ridge and looked down at several men and horses on the edge of a small creek. He counted nine of them. He did not find the pock-riddled face to match the voice he'd heard in the darkness of the night. He motioned El-i-chi to his side.

"Now," he said, arming his bow. He waited until El-i-chi was likewise ready, then two arrows flew as one, and two men went down. After one splashed heavily into the shallow waters of the sandy creek, shouts of alarm went up from the others. Men fired without finding a target.

"Here I am!" Renno shouted, leaping to his feet to send another arrow. All the force of his arm was behind the power of his English longbow. The number of his enemies was reduced by one.

El-i-chi's arrow fell short, for his Seneca bow did not have the reach of Renno's weapon. Shots rang out but did not come close to the brothers. Men were mounting their horses. Three brave ones, yelling war cries and profanity, charged up the slope. Two were tumbled from their mounts by arrows. The third wheeled his horse and joined the other survivors in fleeing.

"I don't think they will have further interest in attacking the main group," El-i-chi predicted.

They mounted and rode down the creek. Five men lay dead on the slope, on the banks of the little stream, and in the water. Renno and El-i-chi salvaged two of the better muskets with powder and shot before setting out on the trail of the survivors.

"Comanche! Comanche!" a man was yelling as he spurred his horse to catch up with Othon Hugues. "They got five of us."

Othon's face contorted in anger. "You fool," he grated. "How many attacked you?"

"I don't know. Dozens."

Othon's heart went cold, for he knew the man was lying or, at best, frightened out of his wits. In his dark mind he knew exactly who had killed five of his men. His hatred was acid.

"Perhaps, Hugues," Jean Laffite remarked lightly, "you have taken on more than you can handle?"

"Had you followed orders and supported our attack," Hugues said, "it would be over."

"You have lost nine men," Laffite said, "while killing five. For how much longer do you think you can sustain such astounding success?"

Othon growled and reached for his knife, but Laffite smiled arrogantly and put his hand on the butt of a pistol at his belt. "Take out your frustration on the men who are making a fool of you, Hugues, not on an ally."

"Yes, you are right," Othon growled. "Tomorrow I will set things right."

He pushed the group hard during the day, so by nightfall they were far ahead of the slow-moving wagons. He made camp at the mouth of a shallow defile where the road to the de Alda ranch passed close between two brush-covered ridges. "Here we will finish the job," he told his men.

With the morning he positioned his remaining men in good cover on the slopes of the ridges. "Let all of the wagons enter the defile before you open fire," he instructed. "Aim first for the drivers of the wagons. The mules will run. In the confusion you can pick off the vaqueros." He grinned. "Of course, if you do not shoot the women, you will not have to wait until we get to the ranch to begin to enjoy your rewards."

Jean Laffite, still unwilling to put himself totally in Hugues's hands, refused to position his men in the cover of the brush on the sides of the defile. "We will be grouped at the far end of the canyon," he said, "to provide greater firepower and pick off any man you have not killed."

"If you fail me this time," Othon warned, "I will seek you out."

"I'm always easy to find," Laffite said with a cynical smile.

During the night it was possible for Renno and El-i-chi to ascertain the exact number of the enemy. In the light of the fires the brothers counted twenty-four men. A dozen of them, the men dressed as mariners, kept themselves apart from the mixed batch of Spaniards, Indians, and bearded frontier types who clustered around a man well-known to Renno. With a chill of recognition, Renno identified Othon Hugues. Taking precautions not to disturb the guards, the sachem crawled through the grass and was close enough to hear Hugues giving his orders to his men. After he had overheard Hugues's entire plan for the coming day, Renno crept back to join El-i-chi.

"I can take two of the guards quickly," El-i-chi offered. He grinned wolfishly. "Do you remember how once before, to the west of this place, the hunters became the hunted?"

Renno nodded, remembering how they had stalked the Spanish soldiers retreating from the Mountain of Gold in the dry lands of the pueblo builders.

"While they sleep we can reduce twenty-four to perhaps twenty before the dawn," El-i-chi continued.

"Our work begins tomorrow, Brother," Renno said. "We will let them feel secure this night."

El-i-chi growled in disagreement.

"While it is true that we could reduce their numbers during the night," Renno said, "this might serve to deter them from a plan that will ultimately work to our advantage." He repeated what he'd heard.

"Yes," El-i-chi agreed. "When the day comes they will not be alone in the brush that covers the ridges."

"Watch them while I'm gone," Renno said, gathering his weapons. The de Alda party had to be warned.

El-i-chi nodded. "It will be best if it appears that the wagons are going to stick to the road," he suggested.

"So," Renno agreed.

"You know the big man who struts, the one who swears at the others and has the pockmarked face," El-i-chi said. It was not a question. "He is the same man who killed the husband of my niece?"

"Othon Hugues," Renno confirmed.

"This time," El-i-chi said, "we will not entrust his death to the river."

Renno's eyes narrowed and glittered with a dangerous light. Yes, this time he would be sure. The very intensity of the Frenchman's hatred for him gave him pause. It chilled his blood to realize that Hugues wanted him dead so badly that he would follow him all the way from New Orleans and into the plains of New Spain.

The white Indian ran with the night breeze in his face, legs pumping smoothly, lungs expanding with the clean, sweet air. In startled surprise a coyote bounded into his path before veering off and away. Renno reached the de Alda camp to see that the fires had been allowed to burn low. He signaled his approach with the hooting of an owl. A guard was sitting atop one of the wagons. He waited for an answer but got none. He started forward, and a shot rang out. A ball clipped through his hair at the top of his head. Never had he been nearer death.

"Hold your fire!" he shouted in Spanish.

The shot had awakened the camp. De Alda was profusely apologetic. The vaquero who had fired at Renno was crestfallen.

"Since you missed," Renno forgave him, "it no longer matters."

He pulled de Alda, Adan, and Roy off to one side and told them of the planned ambush.

"Well," de Alda said, "that is no problem. We will simply skirt around the ridges and make a dash for the ranch."

"They will follow," Renno said.

"Who are these sons of *putas*?" Adan asked.

"I fear, my friend, that I have brought this trouble down upon you," Renno said. "The leader of the men who attack us is my enemy."

"He who attacks my guest is also my enemy," de Alda responded.

Roy was curious; some explaining was required to satisfy him. He nodded grimly as Renno told him that he had definitely recognized the Frenchman who had killed Renna's first husband, Philip Woods, and had held Renna and the comte de Beaujolais captive.

"What we need to do," Roy said, "is take care of this feller once and for all."

Renno nodded. "Hear me, señor," he said. He outlined his plan.

De Alda rubbed his chin in doubt, then nodded.

"There is one thing we must remember," Renno said. "We must not under any circumstances allow any woman or any child to fall into the hands of this man."

"From what you've said of him," Roy remarked, grimacing, "I wouldn't want him to get his hands on me, either."

Just before dawn El-i-chi answered a softly hooting owl with the coo of a dove. Renno was upon him before he heard any movement. He himself was not a clumsy man by any means, but he had never known anyone to move as silently as his brother.

"It is arranged," Renno reported.

"Then it is time for us to take our places before the light."

"So."

"I go to the east."

Renno nodded and gave his brother the warrior's arm clasp. "Do not fall into the hands of this man," he said fervently.

"Nor you," El-i-chi responded.

Renno made his way to the far side of the western ridge and ascended it carefully. He was in place, well concealed, when the gray of dawn came gradually. He watched the twelve mariners ride toward the south through the defile, then disappear. Those who were left in camp appeared to be in no hurry. Because of Renno's point of vantage he was the first to see the dust of de Alda's wagons in the distance.

An hour after sunup a man in the camp gathered the horses and led them behind the western ridge. Not liking the idea of having someone at his back, Renno slithered off the ridge and approached a sandy gully where the horses were tethered. The scent of pipe tobacco guided Renno to his prey. The man, a scruffy, buckskin-clad American, lay on his back on a grassy bank. When Renno suddenly appeared in front of him, tomahawk poised, the renegade yelped in surprise and sat up.

"You will answer my questions," Renno said.

The man looked around with wild eyes as if seeking aid. His hand moved slowly toward his musket. Renno bent and with a quick blow lopped off the end of two fingers. The man cried out in pain and terror and jerked the hand back.

"Othon Hugues I know," Renno said. "Who are the others, the seamen who keep themselves apart from the rest of you?"

"They be Jean Laffite's men," the man said quickly. "Crew of the ship what brung us here. Now look here, this wasn't my idee, you understand—"

"This Laffite, will he fight?"

"Hasn't yet," the frightened man said as he tried to stanch the flow of blood from his tipless fingers.

"Why did he and his men ride to the south?"

"Idee is that once them fellers with Hugues kill most of de Alda's men as they go through the pass, Laffite's men will stop the wagons at the t'other end and finish off them what's left."

Renno nodded. In the past he would have ended the conversation quickly with one blow. Uncharacteristically, though, he hesitated and took a deep breath. Was he being weakened, he wondered, by the passing years? After all, the man who cringed before him might very well have been one of those who killed Chirlo and the other vaqueros or attacked Roy and the boys.

Perhaps the doomed man saw death in Renno's eyes, for he plucked a large knife from his waist with one swift movement of his uninjured hand and was drawing back to throw it when Renno's tomahawk smashed into his forehead.

Now there were eleven men, counting Hugues, lying in wait under the cover of brush on the slopes.

El-i-chi watched impatiently as five renegades climbed the slope on the eastern side and scouted around for good positions from which to launch their ambush on the hunting expedition. He was eager to begin his day's work. He noted carefully the spots chosen by each of the five men. They tended to seek out large rocks or a mass of heavy brush to protect their backs.

"Yes, *je-yeh-suh*," El-i-chi whispered. Dogs and sons of dogs. His right hand itched with his desire to kill. He had not seen the pockmarked man, but as his steel tasted the blood of those who lay concealed below him he would remember that he was avenging Philip Woods, the good-natured young man who had outwitted Little Hawk and him the night of the now-famous snipe hunt.

When El-i-chi saw the cloud of dust being raised by the big, flat wheels of de Alda's wagons, he slid down the slope, taking advantage of any hint of cover. He had planned his way well. He moved as quietly as the white, fluffy clouds that had begun to form with the rising of the sun. His first target was Indian, by his dress a Creek, who had taken a position nearest the mouth of the defile. El-i-chi guessed that the Creek would be more alert than the others and that it would be to his advantage to silence the Indian first.

The Creek lay prone behind a boulder. His rifle was positioned in front of him, barrel propped on a stone for sure aim. El-i-chi had to crawl down a rock terrace at the Creek's back, and in doing so, just as he was ready to strike, he dislodged a single pea-sized pebble. The Creek moved with the swiftness of a coiled snake, pushing himself up to his knees and twisting around, tomahawk in hand. El-i-chi's knife flashed, meeting the Creek's throat. Blood gushed silently from the severed jugular. To quiet the struggles of the suffocating man El-i-chi used his tomahawk and then lay still beside the quivering body.

All his senses were alert. When no alarm came, he pulled himself atop the stone terrace and began to crawl toward his next victim.

*   *   *

The sachem waited until the six men, including Hugues, had made themselves comfortable in their places of ambush. He glanced over to see the outriders of de Alda's group. The party was drawing nearer. Renno moved down the slope on his belly.

The white Indian came upon a dark man dressed much like the de Alda ranch riders. He sat cross-legged behind a concealing curtain of brush and heard nothing until Renno's hand closed over his mouth and jerked his head back. Then his senses ceased functioning altogether.

The second man, no more than thirty feet away, had heard nothing, so silently had the Seneca performed. He was intent on watching the de Alda wagons as they rolled toward the defile. He died as his companion had died, silently and swiftly.

The third man was nervous, more alert. Catching a hint of movement as Renno crawled through deep grass, the renegade lifted his rifle while Renno was still ten feet away. Renno hurled his tomahawk from a prone position, sweeping his right arm backward and then forward in an arc. The weapon flew true and slammed into the man's face, blade smashing nose and upper lip.

The sound of impact was worryingly loud in Renno's ears. Apparently, however, the next nearest man heard only the crackle of a dead branch as the dead man toppled backward.

"Be quiet over there," came a hissed order.

Renno obeyed, although the advice had not been intended for him. The sachem looked across the defile but could see nothing in the dense brush. He could only presume that El-i-chi was at work. He wished that he had not instructed Roy, Adan, and de Alda to sneak up the ridges from the rear just as the leading wagons approached the defile, for he knew that his brother and he could finish off Hugues's men without assistance. When making his plans, however, Renno had no way of knowing that an even dozen of the men, Laffite and his crew, would not take part in the ambush.

With only two men left between him and Othon

Hugues, the silence was blasted by a roar of rifle fire. A few feet away a man screaming agony jumped to his feet, danced, fell, and rolled down the slope. The last man between Renno and Hugues fled. He managed to take only a few steps.

Fire erupted from across the defile as well. Renno glanced to the east and saw El-i-chi jump to his feet and wave his hands. Adan and three vaqueros were standing on top of the ridge, shooting down at the surviving ambushers.

"*Hugues!*" Renno bellowed, running toward the spot where he'd seen the Frenchman go into hiding. "Face me, Hugues. Face me now, and it will soon be finished between us."

Jean Laffite heard the burst of rifle fire. From his position atop the ridge a full half mile south of Hugues's ambush, he lifted his head and saw that the wagons were not yet into the canyon.

"Something has gone wrong," he said.

"Captain," said his first mate, "this is not our fight."

"Well, Hugues still has gold in his saddlebags," Laffite said.

"Let him keep it," the mate urged.

"Your tongue is silver with persuasion," Laffite said. "I think we need the curative vitality of good sea air."

The mate grinned. "Yes, sir!"

Now Laffite saw that men were standing atop the ridges, firing down onto Hugues's position. "Monsieur Mate, you may order that our horses be brought to us."

Laffite navigated his way to the water and reached the Gulf Coast just north of Corpus Christi. The *Julien* was a pretty sight as she swung to her anchor chain in the harbor. The crewmen left aboard her had kept her shipshape. They greeted the return of their captain with genuine pleasure and were full of questions.

The first mate presented himself to Laffite and asked, "Orders to hoist anchor and make sail, sir?"

Laffite had just come up from his cabin and a

refreshing bath. He had donned clean trousers and a shirt of silk. "I keep thinking, Monsieur Mate, of that gold in Othon Hugues's saddlebags."

"Surely he was killed with the others," the mate said.

"I think not," Laffite said, "for he has the protection of the devil himself. No, I think that one will return to us, here in the bay of Corpus Christi, with both his head and his gold intact." He laughed. "And I must admit, my friend, that I am curious about the man who met and countered every blow that Hugues could aim at him."

"If we chose not to fight Hugues's enemy on the prairie, why would it be to our advantage to risk fighting him here?"

"We will not have to fight," Laffite explained. He patted the barrel of a cannon. "And if, by some chance, we are called upon to defend ourselves, I think that we outgun yonder merchant ship, would you not agree?"

"As you say," the mate said.

Laffite had guessed rightly: Othon Hugues lived. At the first volley of rifle fire from the top of the ridge Hugues realized that he had lost again. He saw one of his men leap to his feet, do a dance of death, and tumble down the slope. He saw others die on the opposite side. But Hugues had chosen his hiding place well, having taken his cue from burrowing animals of the earth who always provided a means of retreat in the form of an escape tunnel. Hugues's route lay down an erosion ditch overgrown with brush. With his saddlebags over his shoulder he made his way to the floor of the canyon where, his movements hidden by foliage, he fled toward the south, planning to join forces with Laffite.

He found the spot where Laffite and his men had waited, only to see from the tracks that the pirate had deserted him. He cursed softly. He could hear the pounding hooves of horses coming through the canyon on the gallop. Around him the low and level grasses stretched far away. There was no place to hide. He turned to go back into the brush to make his stand, but it was as if a voice spoke . . . without words, with images only.

He formed a crude broom with tall grass and backed

toward the carcass of a large buffalo bull, wiping out any trace of his tracks with the besom. The buffalo had been skinned, but only the tongue and the tasty internal organs had been taken as meat. It stank. Vultures cried out at him and flapped into the air. Othon repressed an urge to vomit as he forced his way into the slimy, maggoty body cavity of the dead animal. He pulled his saddlebags in with him.

He could not stop the rebellion of his stomach, and his own bile spewed, adding to the stench of his refuge.

"This is my reward for doing your service?" he asked in a low, hate-filled voice. "This, my master, is what you intended for me?"

And in his head the soft, whispering voice of Melisande soothed him. "Our time will come, little love. It will come."

"Melisande!" he cried. "Where are you?"

But there was no reply as the vultures returned, ignoring Hugues inside the body cavity as they picked and tore at the rotting meat.

Renno himself passed within a hundred feet of the solitary carcass while looking for his archenemy. The bodies in the defile had been counted, the brush on either slope thoroughly searched. De Alda's men were digging shallow, sandy graves for eleven men, but there was no sign of Hugues.

"Like Hodano, who could soar, he has disappeared," El-i-chi grumbled.

"Maybe he just joined up with the sailors," Roy suggested.

"That is possible," Renno said.

The vaqueros, eager to avenge the death of their friends, had ridden swiftly to the far end of the canyon, their horses' hooves inadvertently eliminating the footprints of Othon Hugues. It was possible to locate the spot where a large group of men had mounted and ridden off to the south.

Renno and El-i-chi followed the trail of Laffite and his men until they were sure that the seamen were headed for Corpus Christi. Then the brothers rode back to join the others. The rest of the trip to the de Alda hacienda was blessedly uneventful.

There was a time of sadness as the people of the ranch mourned the dead. The vaqueros and the women began the work of curing the loads of buffalo hides.

Although Renno was restless, he agreed to stay on at the de Alda ranch until the buffalo hides were ready for shipment to the port. After all, the main reason for having come to New Spain was trade. To leave without a full cargo would cost Beth and her captain, Adan, money. Meanwhile, wagons would begin transporting cowhide leather and grain to Corpus Christi, to be stowed in the holds of the *Seneca Cloud*.

The wagons would need to be guarded. Three purposes would be accomplished by having Renno and El-i-chi accompany the first shipment: the wagons would be safe; Renno would have the opportunity to make certain that Othon Hugues had not made it safely to Corpus Christi; and lastly, with time hanging heavy, it was something for him to do.

Chapter XII

It was a time of plenty in the lands to the west of the Mountains that Smoke and east of the Tennessee River. Soft rains had come at just the right intervals to produce bumper crops in the gardens of the Cherokee and Seneca women. The hunting was good. The sun was kind. The cooking pots steamed with the delicious aromas of the fruits of the earth: beans, potatoes, squash, peas, cabbage, corn, pumpkin. Melons were ripe, much to the delight of the younger ones. In sunny spots drying racks were laden with thin strips of venison, for even during a time when everyone's belly was distended from a surplus, it was smart to look ahead to a time when the sun would be chilled by the breath of the north, when fresh vegetables would be nothing more than a memory, and the women would prepare . . . corn—parched corn, boiled corn, stewed corn, ground corn baked into bread, roasted corn.

The Cherokee Se-quo-i had enjoyed his share of the bounty of summer. At times, when he looked down at his expanding waistline, he wondered if he had taken a bit

more than his share. But that was life. Familiar as he was
with the white man's written word and the white man's
philosophies, he was still Cherokee, and a Cherokee ate
fresh, fried, stewed, and boiled squash when it was
available.

Of late the scholar had been alternating between
working in silver and painting. He enjoyed fashioning
ornate spurs in the gleaming metal, but he derived almost
as much satisfaction from painting. His favorite subjects
were horses and buffalo.

He was neither chief nor shaman, but he held a
unique place in Cherokee and Seneca society. Before his
accident had left one of his legs shorter than the other,
he had fought at the side of the chiefs Rusog and Renno.
As a result he held the honors of a warrior of a tribe that
historically had loved the clash of war.

Se-quo-i was not a proud man. When he was trying
to master the use of a white man's turning plow, he did
not take offense when men laughed at him. Nor was he
bitter about having been injured in the attempt. And he
was willing to share his vast knowledge. When anyone,
including the principal chief, wanted to know something
about the ways and the thinking of the whitefaces, it was
Se-quo-i who was asked. He knew how to use the medicines of the whitefaces, and he was an expert in the appli-
cation of the traditional curative herbs used by the
Cherokee. To the disgust of the tribal shamans, he was
often called upon to administer cures to the ailing and to
assist the midwives in birthing.

It was in the latter capacity that he was now in the
home of Rusog and Ena. Their only daughter, We-yo, was
in labor. The lodge was crowded with midwives, relatives,
and well-wishers, for Rusog and Ena were much honored
by the people of both tribes, and the impending birth was
a social occasion of note.

Of course Toshabe was there. In spite of having taken
advantage, along with everyone else, of the bounteous
produce of the gardens, she was still a bit thin from her
serious bout with the winter fever.

A chorus of happy voices could be heard: matrons
giving advice to the midwives and to We-yo, senior war-

riors of the Seneca congratulating the proud grandfather-to-be, and Ena graciously accepting gifts of food for the celebration.

Ho-ya sat anxiously in one corner. He watched a tribal shaman toss a pinch of tobacco onto the fire. Aromatic smoke swirled upward, wafted back and forth, then sought the open air through the smoke hole. When We-yo's body stiffened as a contraction came, Ho-ya's body stiffened with hers, although he felt only mental pain. He caught his twin's eye and winked with encouragement. She motioned for him to come to her.

"Sister?" he asked, leaning close.

"Please take me out of here," she whispered.

"Sister, it is night, and you're in the middle of—"

"Please, please." Her lips tightened as a contraction came.

"I will do as you ask," Ho-ya agreed. He called out to a young warrior.

When Ho-ya's intentions became clear, the midwives protested. But Ho-ya's face was stern, and in that moment he looked very much like his father. "It is my sister's wish," he said flatly.

As he and his friend gripped the deerskin on which We-yo lay and carefully lifted her, Ena rose nervously. But Rusog took her arm and indicated to her that she should take her seat. Silence fell over the crowded lodge as another pinch of tobacco was dropped into the sacred fire to send its aroma toward the sky.

"Yes," Ena admitted, "it is in her blood, the desire to be one with the earth in her time of triumph."

Outside, Ho-ya placed his sister under a large oak tree. As the midwives streamed out of the lodge to surround her, he whispered, "I will be within call."

He walked slowly away and only once looked back to see her writhing in pain. He straightened his back in pride, for not one sound escaped We-yo's lips. He entered the lodge. His father, fully recovered from the wound given him by the dead father of We-yo's child, looked at Ho-ya.

"She is well," the young man told him.

"You may go to her," Rusog told Ena.

"In a little while," Ena replied.

Now the group in the lodge consisted mostly of men and a few young boys. Rusog lit a pipe and forced himself to draw on it slowly. Time seemed to crawl. He had felt apprehensive about this birthing for months . . . ever since he had learned that his daughter was with child. Ena, on the other hand, had welcomed the news of We-yo's pregnancy with great joy. We-yo, unfortunately, showed little interest in anything save her mourning for the dead Mingo White Blanket.

"Se-quo-i," Rusog said, making a concerted effort not to bite through the pipestem and chew it to bits, "the minutes are leaden. Lighten them with a story."

"Soon I must go to We-yo," Se-quo-i said.

"As it should be, old friend," Rusog agreed.

"A short one, then," Se-quo-i said, smiling. He closed his eyes for a moment and then opened them. "In the beginning, in the old days, the animals had speech, just as we do."

The younger boys found comfortable positions and assumed an air of expectancy. Se-quo-i's tales were always interesting.

"Man was just another animal, dwelling in peace with his brothers. But as it happened, man bred more rapidly than his brothers in the forests, and soon the old friendship between man and animal was strained. The animals were being crowded out of the forest, and due to his great numbers, man was hungry and cold."

"As the whitefaces seek to crowd us out of our lands," an old man remarked.

"Man made a stone ax," Se-quo-i continued, "and with it he killed a deer for its flesh and for its skin. He made a bow and arrows, and soon he was slaying many animals. At first the animals were angry. Old White Bear, chief of the bear tribe, called his people together to condemn man for his killings. All of the bear tribe voted for war, but they had no weapons. To remedy this situation the bear tribe made a bow from an excellent piece of wood. One brave member of the tribe willingly sacrificed himself to provide gut for the bowstring. But none could use the weapon because the bear's long claws got in the way. The bears would have to cut their claws; but if they did that, they could no longer climb trees or kill game, and, thus, all would starve.

"Meanwhile, Little Deer called the deer tribe into council." Se-quo-i looked around, and his dark eyes sparkled. "Now I am not implying that the deer is wiser than the bear, for at least one of us"—he nodded at Ena—"is a member of the Seneca Bear Clan. Consider this, however. The deer in council knew that they could not fight man, so they said: 'If any man kills a deer without asking the pardon of the deer's spirit in a proper manner, let him be struck down with rheumatism and be made a helpless cripple.' Little Deer, the deer tribe chief, notified man and instructed him in the proper manner of asking pardon of the slain deer.

"Thus it is that each time a deer is killed, the spirit of the old chief, Little Deer, runs through the forest to inquire of the spirit of the slain one if the hunter has asked for pardon. If the reply is yes, Little Deer returns to the spirit world; if the answer is no, Little Deer tracks the hunter to his lodge and strikes him with rheumatism."

A young boy sighed worriedly. "Sometimes I find it hard to remember the proper words with which to ask pardon of the slain animal's spirit."

"I think, young one," Se-quo-i said, "that it is the intent, not the exact wording, that is important. However you thank the dead animal's spirit for providing food for you, he will hear; but you will find it easier to remember the proper words as you grow older."

"Is it not true, Se-quo-i," a young warrior asked, "that you can turn Little Deer aside from your track by leaving a fire burning on the trail?"

"So I have heard," Se-quo-i answered. "Wouldn't it be simpler, though, to ask for pardon? Otherwise there might be so many fires that they would burn down all the forests."

"I seem to remember," Rusog said, "that there is more to this story."

"Indeed," Se-quo-i said. "Next the fishes and the reptiles met in joint council. To punish man, who ate the fishes and slew the snakes, often without eating them, the snakes and the fish agreed to haunt man's dreams."

"It is true," confirmed a warrior. "For I have dreamed of snakes coiling around my limbs."

"And now the birds and the insects got together with all of the smaller animals," Se-quo-i continued. "With the squirrels, the rabbits, the opossums, the raccoons, and all the smaller things of the earth. Because they were little and could not face man, they invented disease. They cursed man with the winter fever, with the pox that came with the whiteface, with the disease of old age that makes the limbs weak and stops the heart, and with all the other ailments that can sap a man's strength and life force."

"*Ooooo*," a young boy quavered.

"Man had one group of friends," Se-quo-i said. "Only the plants. The plants had always been friendly to man, sharing their fruits with him. Now they said, 'This is not right, to plague man with disease.' So each tree, each shrub, and each herb, down to the mosses and the grasses, agreed to supply a cure for the ailments invented by the birds, insects, and small animals. And thus it was that medicine came into being. As the shamans know, when our treatments fail to relieve the sick one, we turn to the plant world for a remedy."

The gathering remained silent for a moment, reveling in the pleasure from his tale. Then they thanked the Cherokee for entertaining them.

Se-quo-i accepted their gratitude, then rose. "Now I must go."

Ho-ya followed Se-quo-i out of the lodge. They went to We-yo and spoke with her. Her contractions were close together now.

"Soon," Se-quo-i told her as he soothingly stroked her sweat-dampened head.

"Se-quo-i," Ho-ya said, still troubled by the fable, "it is true that as man crowded the animals and then began to kill them, the whitefaces crowd us, have killed us, and will do more killing."

"At the moment there is peace," Se-quo-i said.

"But for how long? How long will it be before the

whitefaces of Tennessee tell us that it is time to revise the last treaty?"

"I am not wise in all things," Se-quo-i said. "I know only that men whom I trust want peace. Your uncle Renno says that we must become as the white man and adapt to his way of living. That change is under way. The United States gives plows to the Cherokee." He grimaced and patted his thigh. "*I* don't want another one, but the plow makes it possible for one man to do the work of a hundred women. The Cherokee plant cotton, card it for their own clothing, and sell their surplus to the white man. Some are growing sheep for the wool that makes warm clothing for the winters."

"I do not want to be a white man," Ho-ya protested. "I do not want the women of my family to marry whites and produce mixed bloods. I am Cherokee."

"And yet your mother—"

"I am fully aware of my mother's white and Seneca blood," Ho-ya said. "But she is Cherokee. I think that if given a choice, she would not become white, as my uncle Renno advises." He was silent for a moment. "Se-quo-i, when We-yo and I traveled with White Blanket, we saw lands where there were no men. I am told that beyond the great river there are endless reaches of forests and plains teeming with buffalo."

"So it is said. So did Renno and El-i-chi report from their own travels. But if you are thinking what I think you are thinking, keep in mind that those lands are occupied by tribes, some of whom would fight any intruder."

"It would please me to go far away from here," Ho-ya said. "To take my sister and those who would not become white men with dusky skins and find a place where there is no whiteface."

"I'm not sure that would be possible," Se-quo-i said. He was going to elaborate on the explorations of French and British trappers, and on the current expedition of Lewis and Clark, but We-yo's time was upon her.

"Come," a midwife called to Se-quo-i.

We-yo was squatting, held up under her arms by two matrons. Her face was strained and pale as she bore down.

"Ah," Se-quo-i said as he caught the baby in tender

hands. "A girl, We-yo," he said, taking a quick glance even as he cleared the child's throat with a finger and turned her upside down to give her bottom a little whack.

With the first enraged wail of the newborn, Ena and Rusog came hurrying out of the lodge.

"A complete one," Se-quo-i told Ena.

"Thank the manitous," she breathed.

Ho-ya waited until the relatives and important guests had examined the child. We-yo, having given birth in close contact with Mother Earth, was resting. He knelt beside her and whispered, "She is a fine child."

"Have you thought, Brother, that my child is more Seneca than you and I?"

"We are all of one blood," he said.

"My father and mother, who are Cherokee—"

He did not bother to remind her that Ena had been Seneca, for he, too, considered his mother to be Cherokee.

"—brought about the death of my child's father, who was Seneca. I will give her a Seneca name."

"Have you decided upon such a name?"

"I have considered many," she said, "but am still undecided."

"She was born in the late summertime," Ho-ya said, "and she is fair, like the moon of the warm and pleasant nights."

"Ga-ha-neh So-a-ka-ga-gwa," she said. "Summer Moon."

"Ga-ha-neh," he said. "Summer, a good name."

"So will it be."

He brushed We-yo's lank hair, wetted by her sweat, off her forehead. "I have thought to leave this place."

She did not hesitate for a moment. "Give me time to rest and to become strong for the baby—for Summer to become strong—and we will go with you."

He nodded.

"Brother?"

"Yes?"

"My baby is Seneca, not Cherokee. She is now in the hands of the shaman, who would feed her nothing but tea for long days in order to ward off evil. Bring her to me."

"It is done," he said.

Little Summer Moon was indeed in the hands of the shaman. She was sucking tea eagerly from a leather teat. Ho-ya pushed his way past his mother and father and other paternal relatives. "Give me the child," he requested.

"She drinks," the shaman said.

"I will say it only once more, old man," Ho-ya said. "My sister wants her child. Give her to me."

The shaman looked up questioning at Rusog.

"It is customary for the shaman to care for a Cherokee child," Rusog said.

"Ga-ha-neh is not Cherokee," Ho-ya said, driving a spike into his father's heart. He took the baby from the old man. Deprived of her teat, Summer began to wail.

Rusog's face darkened.

"No," Ena said, clinging to her husband's arm. "We-yo has given her a Seneca name."

"My granddaughter is Cherokee," Rusog said.

"One-quarter of her blood is Seneca from our mother," Ho-ya said. "One-half is Seneca from the man whom my sister loved."

"Let him give the child to her mother," Ena urged.

Rusog's heart was heavy. Since his children had returned to the village, We-yo had been distant, seeking solitude, and talked at length only with her brother. He had hoped that the birth of the child would ease the grief that still burdened her. Apparently it had not. He would allow We-yo more time. It was true that the child had more Seneca than Cherokee blood. He would humor his daughter . . . for the time being. His decision was reinforced when he went outside to see the baby at We-yo's breast. And he was greatly pleased when, after We-yo had been moved back into the lodge, she presented little Summer to him and said, "Your granddaughter, Great Chief."

From that moment We-yo's withdrawal from the society of her family was no more. Rusog and Ena agreed that having their granddaughter bear a Seneca name was a small price to pay for having their daughter back. Neither of them could guess that We-yo had decided to leave them.

Ho-ya, meanwhile, began to travel among the villages to the west. There he talked to young warriors and their mates and found kindred spirits who agreed with him that leaving the land of their birth was preferable to being turned slowly into white men.

When Renno and El-i-chi arrived in Corpus Christi, a few inquiries led them to the *Julien,* Jean Laffite's ship. A gangplank was down. They were not greeted until they stepped onto the deck.

Jean Laffite, in the silks and velvets of a chevalier, offered them an elaborate bow, sweeping his plumed hat in front of him. "Gentlemen," he said in French, "I have been expecting you."

Renno was fully alert. He carried a musket in his hand. El-i-chi, at his side, held his rifle across his chest.

Laffite's crew stepped out from behind the ship's house and the windlass and the mainmast. Each man was armed with a rifle.

"I didn't expect such a greeting," Renno said, as if responding to flattery. "It was not necessary to turn out the entire crew."

"On the contrary, monsieur," Laffite said. "I have seen you in action, and although I do not consider myself a coward, neither do I think of myself as being careless or foolhardy."

"You made one miscalculation," El-i-chi said. "You failed to realize that you will be the first to die."

"Please," Laffite said, lifting both hands palms out. "Let's be reasonable. Is it possible that enough have died? You are here, the two of you, and that can only mean that my erstwhile employer, Othon Hugues, is unable to join us. Is that not true?"

Renno studied the young captain for a moment. "You did not participate in the fighting, either when the wagons were attacked at night or during the ambush," he said. "Why?"

"I had decided that it was not my battle. We talk, then?"

"Yes," Renno agreed.

Laffite gestured. The men of the crew lowered their weapons. "My ship was chartered to bring Monsieur Hugues and his ruffians to Corpus Christi, then wait for them while they made a trip inland. They offered more money through a messenger if I would join them. Several of my men and I decided to do so. Waiting can be so tedious. Do you not agree?"

Renno nodded.

"At first I was under the impression that Hugues's purpose was looting, not wholesale killings. Being in the business of acquiring loot myself . . ." He shrugged, spreading his hands wide. "And so, my friends, no apologies, just an explanation. If further violence results, it will be of your doing and, I think, short-lived."

"I am Renno, sachem of the Seneca."

"You are far from home, Sachem." He bowed again. "Jean Laffite, at your service: captain, privateer with license from the republic of Cartagena, and lately, an American. May I offer you refreshment?"

"We search for Othon Hugues," El-i-chi said.

"My brother, El-i-chi, shaman of the Seneca," Renno said.

"Well, I thought perhaps you could assure me that I had to wait no longer for Monsieur Hugues," Laffite said, clearly disappointed. "He is still alive, then?"

"Let me say only that his scalp does not hang on my lodge pole," Renno said. He quite often, in talking with Europeans, reverted to Indian expressions. He found it to be to his advantage to have people underestimate him.

"Too bad," Laffite said. "Have you by any chance seen his odd lady, the one with black teeth?"

Renno shook his head.

Laffite clucked his tongue. "It leaves me in an awkward position. Privateer I may be, but I am also a man of honor. I have accepted Monsieur Hugues's money, so I am obligated to wait here until I am certain that he, at least, is not coming."

"Would you object, Monsieur Laffite, to our searching your ship?" El-i-chi asked.

"I would object very much," Laffite said. "Such action would indicate that you think me to be a liar."

"I am sure that Monsieur Laffite's word is good," Renno said to El-i-chi. "We bid you good day, Captain."

"You won't take supper with me? I'd be pleased to know why a Seneca sachem and his brother are so far from home."

"Another time," Renno said.

Laffite followed them down the gangplank, then offered his hand. It was taken first by Renno, then by Eli-chi.

"Somehow, my friends, I have a feeling that we will meet again," Laffite said.

"It is in the hands of the manitous," Renno replied.

The cargo of the first caravan of wagons from de Alda's ranch was soon transferred to the holds of the *Seneca Cloud*. A day and a night of watching the Frenchman's ship produced no sign of Othon Hugues.

"I think it is time to go back to the ranch," El-i-chi said. "The pock-faced one ran. He won't show himself where we can find him. If there is any justice, he ran to the north to be killed by the Comanche."

Renno, too, was ready to go back to the ranch. He was eager for Adan and de Alda to finish their trading so that he could start the long journey home. His older son was in New York State; his daughter was in France. He had Ta-na and Beth by his side—and Beth filled a very important part of his life—but he missed his people.

"It's time to go home, Brother," he said with a grin. "We have a wedding to organize." He laughed. "I have to remind myself now and then that that old bear of a white man who was once my father-by-marriage is going to become my father again."

"I do my best to forget it," El-i-chi said, but his grin was a fond one.

Othon Hugues, his clothing and hair stiff with the rankness of rotted flesh, managed to catch a saddled horse that had strayed from the others after Renno killed the man watching them. He rode solely at night, for he was alone now, with only his one gun available to face his enemies. When he reached a stream he soaked himself and scrubbed his skin with sand, but the rank stench of decaying flesh clung to him for days as he rode southward. He lost his direction, came to the gulf far north of Corpus Christi, and had to follow the coastline to the town. He was bearded, ragged, and he stank when he presented himself to Laffite.

"Mon Dieu, man," Laffite said, waving one hand toward the gulf. "There is an ocean of water. Could you not take time to avail yourself of its cleansing properties?"

"You waited," Hugues said, amazed.

"When Laffite makes a contract, he keeps it." He was pleased to see that Hugues carried saddlebags over one shoulder.

"We will sail for New Orleans immediately," Hugues said.

"One item of business first," Laffite said. "You owe me gold."

"You will have it when we reach New Orleans," Hugues said.

"I think not," Laffite responded. "I think I should have it now. And not just the paltry amount you promised. The situation has changed, you see. I have been visited by two very deadly gentlemen of Seneca blood. Let us say that the increase in the cost of your contract with me is due to the increased hazard."

"You'll get only what we agreed upon," Hugues said harshly.

"Then, my friend, I think that you will have to find another way to return to New Orleans. I hereby break our contract on the grounds that you misrepresented the danger into which you led me and my crew. Please leave my ship."

Hugues started to raise his rifle. He heard half a dozen clicks as members of the crew cocked their own weapons. He lifted his head and roared at the sky, a mad sound of rage and frustration that carried away from the waterfront and caused people to halt, to turn, to stare. As if the sound had eased him, he tossed the saddlebags to Laffite. "Take them, then," he said. "Take the gold and enjoy." He did not add, "While you can."

"Thank you," Laffite said pleasantly. He turned. "Monsieur Mate, you may make sail for New Orleans, if you please."

The *Seneca Cloud* sailed out into the gulf some weeks later. She was laden with dried beef, buffalo hides, and the tanned leather of cowhides. Gao and Ta-na were rich in relics—the rattles of snakes, silver spurs given to them by Señor de Alda, cow horns carved into signaling devices, and vaquero hats and whips.

Beth was happy to be back aboard ship—one of her own—and to know that the journey to New Spain would be quite profitable. She realized that it would be the first of many to come in the years ahead. Her family and de Alda were fast friends now, and the relationship would prove profitable. Ah-wa-o was content, for she was with her husband.

Renno prepared a letter to be taken by the *Cloud* to Wilmington for forwarding to Thomas Jefferson in Washington. It would make the trip faster by water than if he waited until he was at home to report on the continued efforts by James Wilkinson to foment revolution on the frontiers of the United States. That chore finished, he spent some lazy time sitting in the sun, being rocked by the *Cloud*'s smooth passage through mild seas. Beth was at his side, her creamy skin protected from the sun by a hat and a parasol. Life was good. He was going home.

The subsquadron of American ships that Thomas Jefferson sent to go into action against the pirates of North Africa sailed from the United States in mid-June. Unexpected storms at sea delayed the Atlantic crossing so that the squadron, under the command of Commodore Samuel Barron, did not arrive at Gibraltar until late July.

Barron was eager to send the news of the squadron's arrival to the commander on the scene in North African waters, Commodore Edward Preble, so he dispatched his smallest frigate, the *John Adams*, to Tripoli, where Preble had established a tight blockade.

William Eaton, who had been in Washington to push his plan to subdue the Barbary pirates with a land force, had crossed the Atlantic as a special guest on board Barron's flagship. His time in Washington had not been wasted, although he had been unable to talk with the president himself. Mr. Jefferson had been on an extended vacation in Virginia with his daughter and his grandchildren.

From the War Department he had procured one thousand long rifles. From Robert Smith, secretary of the navy, he had wrangled an odd title, United States Naval Agent on the Barbary Coast, plus written authorization to draw artillery from the Mediterranean Squadron. From the Department of State he had forty thousand U.S. dollars.

While it was true that the United States had some reason for pride in her fleet, the tide of war was still turning slowly in favor of the bashaw of Tripoli. One of William Eaton's pet projects, to have a popular revolt displace Yusef on the throne, had failed miserably, although Eaton's choice to rule Tripoli, Hamet Karamanli, was still alive and in hiding.

The one victorious act enjoyed in the region had caused much comment in the United States. American sailors aboard a captured Tripolitanian ship rechristened *Intrepid*, under the command of Lieutenant Stephen Decatur, stormed the *Philadelphia* in Tripoli Harbor, drove her Arab crew into the sea, and burned the captive ship to the waterline without the loss of a man.

Understandably, William Eaton was not content to take pride in the destruction of an American ship, nor to wait patiently for the blockade to force sense into the bashaw. He had plans of his own and the means, now, of beginning their implementation. He left his thousand rifles and his personal gear in Gibraltar, in the holds of the *Constitution* and the *Constellation*, but carried with him now forty thousand in U.S. government money and twenty thousand of his own dollars aboard the *John Adams*.

*   *   *

The *John Adams* cleared Gibraltar Harbor just before time for the evening meal in the captain's mess. There it was that Midshipman Hawk Harper met the United States consul to the Barbary nations.

William Eaton shook his hand with a good, manly grip and smiled into his eyes. "Welcome to the Mediterranean, Midshipman," Eaton said. "I would give my right arm for a thousand like you."

Little Hawk had been dining in the officers' mess all the way across the Atlantic, so he knew the ship's officers well and the captain somewhat. He had made it his habit to be respectfully silent unless someone addressed him directly. He did not depart from that habit on the first night that Eaton was aboard. The consul was the center of attention.

"My position, gentlemen," Eaton answered in reply to an indirect question from the ship's captain, "is somewhat ambiguous, although I daresay that it will become more defined in the near future. At the moment I am on loan to the navy from the State Department—the navy's own diplomat, if you will. At the same time I have a direct assignment from the secretary of state to conclude a new treaty with Tripoli."

"I would like to use the guns of the *Adams* to write a new treaty with Yusef," the captain growled.

"And well you may, sir," Eaton said. "For I have made a vow to myself to see to it that the bashaw is driven from his perch by force of arms."

"He has threatened to torture and behead all of the prisoners from the *Philadelphia*," an officer said.

"God help him if he performs such a criminal act," Eaton said solemnly.

Lieutenant Harper was exercising on the deck after the evening meal when he saw Eaton emerge from his quarters. He gave the diplomat an informal salute and continued his walk. Eaton increased his pace and fell in alongside him.

"Well, young man," Eaton said, "I am pleased to see,

judging from your appearance, that the Marine Corps is adhering to its high standards."

"Thank you, sir," Little Hawk said.

"I understand that you are to join my marine guards in Tunis."

"Those are my orders, sir." Little Hawk was struck by the quirk of fate that had put him aboard ship with the very man he had been ordered to assess.

"I know Lieutenant P. N. O'Bannon well," Eaton said. "In fact, I've had several very rewarding conversations with him. He and I are in full agreement as to the course of action the United States should take against Yusef."

"Sir?"

"I have begged for a thousand young men like you, Harper, just one thousand marines, but my pleas have gone unanswered. With such a force I would come upon Yusef's rear. He would then be pinned between my force and the guns of the fleet, and that would be the end of one pirate with a fancy title."

"I would agree with that course of action, sir," Little Hawk said.

"I thought as much," Eaton said. He slapped Little Hawk on the back. "You'll be taking orders from a fine young man in O'Bannon. And perhaps you and I will have another opportunity to discuss the demise of the bashaw Yusef."

The *John Adams* arrived off Tripoli Harbor on the morning of August 9, 1804. Commodore Preble, in charge of the blockade, was informed that the big forty-four-gun frigates of Barron's subsquadron would be arriving soon.

Little Hawk did not see William Eaton again until the morning of August 11, when he was ordered to go by boat to the flagship, the U.S.S. *Constitution*. William Eaton was waiting for him on deck.

"Midshipman," Eaton said, "I'm going ashore under a flag of truce. If you're agreeable, I'd like you to be in charge of my official escort."

Little Hawk believed that Eaton's choice was an odd

one, and it was obviously not popular with the *Constitution*'s marines. The lieutenant in charge was glowering as he stood at attention.

"I've asked for four men, in addition to you," Eaton said.

"Yes, sir," Little Hawk said. "My pleasure to accompany you, sir."

"Fine, fine," Eaton said. Then he continued dramatically, "Well, to quote our glorious first president, the man who won the war for American independence, that glorious man, George Washington—" He paused to look with one eyebrow raised at Little Hawk. "You do remember George Washington's famous words, which he delivered just before crossing the Delaware in the dead of winter to attack the Hessians and change the course of the war?"

"No, sir, I'm afraid I don't," Little Hawk admitted. "What were his words, sir?"

Eaton lifted one hand, pointed his forefinger into the air, and in a deep voice bellowed, "Get into the boat, men!"

Chapter XIII

Two gunboats escorted the *Constitution*'s gig past Tripolitanian warships toward the harbor front. The Arabs made no attempt to dishonor the white flag that flew from the gig's stern. At the wharf Midshipman Harper and his detail of four uniformed and armed marines leaped up onto the rough planks and stood at the ready, rifles at port arms. A group of hostages from the *Philadelphia* was laboring nearby on harbor defenses in the burning sun. When they saw the five marines and William Eaton, who joined them on the wharf, they began to cheer.

"There they are, my boy," Eaton said sadly. "That's why we're here."

Little Hawk saw head-wrapped and gowned Arab overseers snapping their whips and screaming obscenities at the American prisoners in an effort to get them back to work. The cheers of the hostages rang out again and again in defiance. The American consul in place, Nicholas Nissen, came trotting down the wharf to greet Eaton. Eaton took advantage of the fact that few of the Arabs

around him understood English. He looked directly at
Nissen and spoke in a loud voice, his words intended for
the American hostages.

"My fellow countrymen," he said, "it is my pleasure
to tell you that I am here representing the United States
Navy and that I am followed closely by the strongest
armada of ships ever sent by our country to the Mediterranean. I assure you that the president and your fellow citizens have not forgotten you and that we are determined
to obtain your release. Be brave. Be of good faith. All
America stands behind you."

Eaton and Little Hawk sat in a hot, stuffy room and
waited until early afternoon before Yusef, bashaw of Tripoli, agreed to see the diplomat. Eaton greeted the bashaw
in perfect Arabic, telling him that he had no need of an
interpreter. Yusef launched immediately into a laughing
belittlement of Eaton's efforts to return his brother,
Hamet, to the throne. Little Hawk could not understand
a word that was being said. Now and then, as the bashaw
rambled on threateningly, Eaton would interpret. Then
Eaton went back to listening without comment. At last,
when the bashaw stopped talking, Eaton quickly raised
the issue of the American hostages. The bashaw responded
immediately and emotionally.

"He's offering to give us a discount on releasing the
hostages," Eaton explained as Yusef waved his hands and
ranted in his shrill, unpleasant voice. "He'll settle for a
hundred fifty thousand dollars instead of the half million
he demanded previously." He winked surreptitiously and
told Little Hawk what he planned to say. "Watch this."

In the bashaw's language he repeated, "The national
honor of my country will be redeemed by steel, not gold."

Little Hawk tensed as the bashaw screamed angry
protest. Guards rushed into the room, brandishing drawn
scimitars. Little Hawk's hand was on his sword, his only
weapon.

"Easy," Eaton whispered, and again he prepared Little Hawk for what he intended to do.

The American consul proceeded to break every rule
of diplomacy. It was unthinkable to insult an Arab ruler

in front of his subjects and even more disrespectful to do it in the ruler's own language.

"I will tell you this," Eaton said softly and evenly. "If one of the Americans in your hands dies, regardless of the cause, I will hang you from the yardarm of the American flagship."

The bashaw was so shocked that, for a moment, he was speechless. Eaton turned to face the bashaw's court. "I call upon each of you to bear witness to my solemn promise. Should one of the hostages die, I will remind you of my words when Yusef swings from a gibbet."

Now the bashaw exploded into incoherency. Four of his guards leaped to seize Eaton's arms. Little Hawk, knowing that he was about to enter a battle he could not hope to win, reached for his sword.

"No!" Eaton told him sharply. "Have patience." To the bashaw he said, "Think, Yusef, for even as I speak, four of the most powerful frigates of the American navy are approaching your harbor. I might remind you that the American fleet has not yet used its full power, but it will unleash destruction upon you if you harm me."

Yusef continued to shout for a moment. Then, perhaps fearing that the American *did* speak the truth, he ordered the guards to release the consul.

"This manhandling," Eaton said, "is, of course, a violation of a flag of truce."

"Leave me!" Yusef roared. "Leave me, or in the name of Allah I will have your head before the sun sets."

There were those among Thomas Jefferson's cabinet and supporters in the Congress who deemed it unwise for the president to take an extended vacation in an election year. After all, a war was going on in the Mediterranean, and Spain was threatening action over the loosely defined boundaries of the Louisiana Purchase. The country was remarkably intact, however, when "Long Tom" came back to Washington, feeling refreshed and rejuvenated after a visit with his daughter and his grandchildren.

Among the papers that his secretary had laid out for his attention was a letter from the Seneca sachem Renno, reporting on the success of the Ceremony of Transfer in

New Orleans. On a continent of such vast distances and unpredictable mail delivery, it was not unusual for the president to be reading of events that had occurred months before. The letter had originated in New Orleans, had come by ship to the port of New York via the Bahamas, and then by coach and rider to Washington, a time-consuming trip. Since he had a tendency to think in his secret heart that more than doubling the area of the United States would be his one great claim to immortality in the history of his country, Jefferson took great interest in Renno's literate description of events.

He could almost hear the drums rolling, could envision the flashes of red, white, and blue as the Stars and Stripes was run up a pole in a huge, public square. Around the flag were grouped soldiers, American boys neat in swallow-tailed blue tunics and white trousers bloused over high, black boots. White webbing crossed in an X on their blue backs, and they wore dark tricornered hats decorated with a feather in the manner of Mad Anthony Wayne's American Legion. He could hear in his mind the officers shouting orders and could smell the stench of cordite as a multigun volley of rifle fire saluted the unfurling of the flag.

American boys and the flag with its thirteen stripes denoting the original thirteen colonies . . . Soon that banner would fly over the major portion of a continent, from sea to glistening sea. And, thinking thus, he whispered, "Ah, Meriwether, where are you now?"

Distances . . . to the west lay a vast wilderness known only to the native Indians who hunted the plains and the forests. Parts of the west had been penetrated by Spanish and French trappers and explorers, but no man knew the full extent of the lands between the Mississippi and the Pacific. The Lewis and Clark expedition would be somewhere on the Missouri, traveling northwest into the unknown. God only knew when and if he would hear from his former secretary.

When Jefferson ended his reverie and returned to Renno's letter, he frowned as he read. Not for the first time he regretted the fact that he had been so involved in working with the Congress regarding appropriations to pay Napoleon's price for Louisiana and to strengthening the navy to fight the pirates of North Africa. During that crucial period of time, James Wilkinson's appointment as governor of a major portion of the Louisiana Territory had slipped through almost by default. And, by God, the president knew that the man had actively tried to sabotage Anthony Wayne's war efforts against the tribes of the Ohio Territory. George Washington had once told him that Wilkinson had been given a commission in the army in an attempt to keep him out of mischief, and now, if the statements in Renno's letter were true, the sachem had cause to suspect that Wilkinson was up to his old tricks, planning to split the western frontier territories away from the United States. The letter went on to say that Renno and his party had decided to travel west into Spanish lands, to check the veracity of the rumor. Once the truth had been determined, the sachem planned to send a second letter to the president to bring him up-to-date.

Jefferson's stomach churned at the mere thought of a conspiracy. He made an effort to calm down.

Kentucky and Tennessee were states now, he reminded himself. William Henry Harrison had things well under control in the lands taken from the Ohio Indians after the Battle of Fallen Timbers. He made a mental note, however, to keep an eye on General James Wilkinson.

In fact, his resolve in that regard was reinforced one evening shortly thereafter, while he was lounging comfortably, dressed in slippers and gown, in his living quarters in the executive mansion. While having a glass of after-dinner wine with his secretary of state, James Madison, a servant announced that Mr. Alexander Hamilton was at the front door, asking for a few minutes of the president's time.

"Although we will never be fully rid of the financial system he imposed upon us," Jefferson told Madison, "I did think that we were rid of Hamilton himself." Resigned to the unwelcome intrusion, he nodded to the servant. "Please show Mr. Hamilton in."

"You must remember, Tom," Madison said, "that

Hamilton went against his own party and supported you during the battle with Burr in the House of Representatives."

"Only because he hates Burr more than he hates me," Jefferson said ruefully.

"Nevertheless, he lost a lot of prestige with the Federalist party because of his support for you," Madison said.

Alexander Hamilton had a regal bearing, although his suit was not of the finest quality. He was still slender, and at forty-nine, his light hair showed no gray. "I do apologize for the intrusion, Mr. President," he said as he came into the room. "I know it's late and that I have not had the opportunity to ask for an appointment." For an instant his face revealed his disapproval of the president's informal attire.

Jefferson, the taller, smiled down at Hamilton and extended his hand. "Always happy to see you, Mr. Hamilton."

Madison shook Hamilton's hand, then Hamilton sat at Jefferson's invitation. Madison brought Hamilton a glass and poured wine. For a few minutes there was small talk. Hamilton's wife and seven children were, he said, all in good health. As for his law practice . . . he laughed. "The health of my law practice is not as vigorous, I fear, as that of my young ones."

"So, Mr. Hamilton, what can I do for you?" Jefferson asked, wondering if the man was going to request some legal work from the government to bolster his income.

"Perhaps, sir, it is what I can do for you," Hamilton said. "I assume that you are aware of the effort by certain Federalists in New England to arouse secessionist sentiments."

"We've heard rumors," Jefferson confirmed.

"I fear that they are more than mere rumors," Hamilton said. "My position in the party is not as secure as it once was, but I do have my sources of information. I can give you the names of several active secessionists. It will, however, be necessary to name only one man—Aaron Burr."

Jefferson cast a quick look at Madison as if to say,

Well, it is nothing more than that old enmity between Hamilton and Burr rearing its ugly head.

"Will Mr. Burr be elected governor of New York?" Madison asked.

"Not while there is breath in my body to resist it," Hamilton said. He turned his cool eyes back toward Jefferson. "The disunionists want Burr to be governor of New York so as to have a powerful ally in their bid to secede. Burr must be stopped."

"Somehow, Mr. Hamilton, I can't seriously believe that the New England states would follow a few malcontents into secession," James Madison said.

"Perhaps not. I myself feel that there are enough men of solid mind to prevent Burr from being elected, and without a man in the state house the disunionists will lose their battle. I am here for two reasons, to ask that you throw the power of the presidency against Aaron Burr in the June elections in New York State—"

"You're advocating the election of a Republican?" Jefferson asked, raising one eyebrow.

Hamilton laughed. "Yes, that is ironic, isn't it? But I think that history will record that it was Thomas Jefferson, not Alexander Hamilton, who caused the death of the Federalist party."

"An interesting statement," Jefferson murmured.

"How best to destroy an opposition party than by taking its goals and policies as your own?" Hamilton asked, spreading his hands. "History will record, Mr. President, that Thomas Jefferson did not republicanize the Federalist party, but that he federalized the Republican party."

Jefferson stiffened because the barb hit close to home. In the years since he'd taken office, national needs and priorities had caused him to abandon first one and then another of his most cherished political ideals. Now, to cover his chagrin, he poured more wine, leaning forward to fill Hamilton's glass.

"But on to the second purpose of my meeting," Hamilton said. "I state that Aaron Burr is a potential traitor to this country and that after he fails to lead the New England states into leaving the Union, he will turn his attentions to the west. I have no documented proof, but I am certain in my mind that Burr is plotting with certain officers of the western army—"

The name of James Wilkinson popped into Jefferson's head.

"—to use frontiersmen and mercenaries to invade the northern Spanish provinces of New Spain and there to set up a separate and independent nation with Mr. Burr as emperor."

Both Jefferson and Madison were silent. It was inconceivable to either of them, each being a man of honor, to think that a vice president of the United States would plot treason. Jefferson thought, *Wilkinson, perhaps, for he is a little man. But Burr? Never.*

"Mr. Hamilton," Jefferson said, "I thank you for coming. Your warning will not be taken lightly, I assure you. I am, of course, opposed to Mr. Burr's election to the governorship of New York and have so stated and will so state again."

Hamilton rose. "Thank you for your time," he said. "Before I leave, Thomas, I want to tell you that you did your country an immeasurably great service in your purchase of the Louisiana Territory."

"Thank you," Jefferson said, extending his hand. "I appreciate that."

"Odd man," James Madison said after Hamilton was gone. "He could have been president."

"Might very well be yet," Jefferson remarked.

"No, no," Madison said. He smiled. "I have some small ambitions along those lines myself, Thomas, when you're ready to go back to Virginia." He mused, rubbing his chin. "No, there's an air of defeat about the man— something almost tangible, something that I could feel in the very air. Perhaps he has always been too much the man of action, too eager to leap into a fray, and now that he's been forced out of the whirlwind center of politics—" He shook his head. "This feud with Burr, which began when Burr published Hamilton's attack on John Adams, is an obsession with him. And as I've already mentioned, he used up much of his political influence by supporting you against Burr for the presidency. Now he's going to bankrupt his leadership of the Federalist party by getting down in the mud to do battle with Burr over the governorship."

"Hamilton is the brightest brain in the Federalist party," Jefferson pointed out.

"Yes," Madison agreed. "He's their last chance at survival, the only man who could lead them back to prominence. I should be glad of his fall; I'd hate to have to face him in an election battle. But I find it sad to see him lower himself to Burr's level."

Jefferson was to remember Madison's musings when, on July 12, Alexander Hamilton died after having been shot the day before by Aaron Burr in a duel at Weehawken, New Jersey, on the very heights where his eldest son, Philip, had been killed in a duel three years previously. The president sent a small contribution when Hamilton's friends took up a collection for the widow and her seven children, for Hamilton had been deeply in debt, a condition with which Jefferson could easily empathize.

When the states of New York and New Jersey issued warrants for Aaron Burr's arrest—dueling was illegal—the man fled to Philadelphia.

On board the frigate *Constitution* Midshipman Hawk Harper found himself to be once again in an odd position. As a junior marine officer he was nominally under the command of the ship's senior marine, but William Eaton, it seemed, had claimed him for his own.

Little Hawk stood on the quarterdeck with the captain and Eaton as the *Constitution* led the squadron into Tripoli Harbor on August 28 to pound shore installations and anchored Tripolitanian ships of war with a deadly cannonade. The next day the naval gunfire was concentrated on the bashaw's palace. American optimism ran high.

Then, on September 4, the *Intrepid*, the captured ship that had been used by Stephen Decatur to burn the *Philadelphia*, was surprised by a Tripolitanian boarding party. Rather than suffer the same fate as the crew of the *Philadelphia* and live enslaved, the *Intrepid*'s captain, Richard Somers, blew the ship's magazine with all hands aboard.

The bashaw still refused to release American hostages without a ransom.

"We have wasted enough time," Eaton told his new marine aide. "I do not intend to let the United States lose this opportunity to win a victory and to establish a lasting peace on this barbarian coast."

In search of support, Eaton and Little Hawk sailed to Malta, then Syracuse, where the young man explored ancient Roman ruins while Eaton conducted single-party tours of the rounded assets of a young, redheaded woman called Maria.

The commodores of the naval squadrons in the Mediterranean gathered in Syracuse to discuss the futile efforts to force the bashaw to an honorable settlement. There Eaton cornered them and, invoking the name of the president and the secretaries of state and of the navy, spoke for two hours with, it was said, "great persuasion."

In the end the commodores agreed that Eaton would organize a military coup around the man who had originally held the throne of Tripoli, Hamet Karamanli, who was somewhere in the vicinity of Cairo. Eaton was to go to Egypt to persuade Hamet to take command and assure him that he would have the backing of the U.S. Navy in a heavy bombardment in April or May.

"My boy," Eaton said to Little Hawk, "the president and Secretary of State Madison will not send me ground troops, but both men have approved a land campaign in Tripoli, conducted by Tripolitanians. Do you fancy a trip to Egypt?"

"That would please me very much, sir," the aide said.

"Get in the boat, men," Eaton called out.

What William Eaton, the pudgy, soft-looking American businessman did not say—not to anyone, not even to his young marine aide—was that he had no intentions of turning command of *his* army over to Hamet Karamanli or any other Tripolitanian. So it was that when Little Hawk and he left for Alexandria, no one suspected that this man who was a civilian State Department employee on loan to the navy would promote himself in one giant step to become General William Eaton or, as he was to be called by some, Eaton of Arabia.

Celebrants in New Orleans, that new American city near the mouth of the Mississippi, were kicking up their heels in a very rowdy manner. Now that the Mississippi was open once and forever to the produce of Tennessee, Kentucky, and the Ohio Valley, it seemed that every frontier trader, intent on welcoming the city into the United States, had floated on his flatboat down the river.

Hunters, trappers, would-be explorers, potential settlers, and what appeared to be a good portion of the Indian population of the lower Mississippi valley had poured into the city. Business in the waterfront grogshops was brisk. The military forces left behind by General James Wilkinson were kept busy breaking up fights and carting off the dead and injured. Wilkinson himself had departed the city to conduct official business in the east.

"Whatever he's doing, I'd say he's up to no good," Roy Johnson remarked.

Beth Huntington felt that the influx of Americans had enlivened New Orleans society. She danced sprightly reels with young army officers and drank toasts to the United States with as much sincerity as she would once have reserved for Great Britain. Renno, El-i-chi, and Roy Johnson, all handsome and—at least in Roy's case, with his gray hair and air of maturity—dignified in formal clothing, conferred with officers who had served up and down the Mississippi, exchanged memories with veterans of the American Legion, and listened with great interest to vivid accounts of the vastness and beauty of the lands on the upper Mississippi, at the mouth of the Missouri, and west of the big river.

Adan and the *Seneca Cloud* had left New Orleans. The *Cloud*'s cargo had been sold at a great profit, and Beth seemed determined to spend most of the proceeds on hats and bolts of cloth from Paris; sets of delicate bone china from Prussia; locally made kitchen utensils to be given as gifts to the women of the two villages; books and a writing desk for her friend Se-quo-i; attractive jewelry for Ena, We-yo, and Toshabe; a set of fine pistols for Ho-ya; and such a variety of other goods that Renno rolled his eyes and estimated that it would take a whole train of wagons to move her purchases up the Natchez Trace to Huntington Castle. And the woman was still browsing for a wedding gift for Toshabe and Roy.

The morning after a military ball at which Roy Johnson drank two young whippersnapper officers under the table, he joined the others at breakfast in the hotel dining room. He looked a bit peaked. Gao and Ta-na were stuffing rich French pastries into their mouths as quickly as their teeth could handle the demand. El-i-chi, Roy saw, was feeling rebellious; the shaman came into the dining room wearing an open-front deerskin shirt and a breech-clout. Beth was radiant in blue. Ah-wa-o was pretty in a little white morning dress. Renno was the consummate white man, in dark gray and gleaming white linen. Roy sat, put his pounding head in his hands, and moaned, "Is that coffee?"

"It is," Renno said as he continued to eat.

"Well?" Roy mumbled.

"Yes, it is coffee," Renno said seriously, spearing ham and eggs with a fork.

"Mind if I have some?" Roy asked.

"Not at all," Renno replied.

There was a long silence, during which Ah-wa-o and the boys were trying to hide their amusement.

Roy sighed. "Renno, can I please have some dag-gummed coffee?"

Renno looked up. "Like some coffee, Roy?"

Roy rolled his eyes toward heaven.

"Well, why didn't you say so, Roy?" Renno asked.

"I thought I had," Roy muttered, pouring rich, thick Creole coffee, then lightening it with fresh cream.

"Did anyone hear Roy ask me to pass the coffee?" Renno asked in appeal to the entire group.

"I didn't hear him ask for coffee," El-i-chi replied, grinning.

"Trouble with you yahoos is you don't speak English," Roy growled.

"El-i-chi, Gao, Ta-na," Renno said, "if Roy had asked me to pass the coffee, would I have understood?"

"I'm not quite sure," El-i-chi answered, his mouth full of buttered roll and honey.

"I would have," Gao said.

"I, too," Ta-na agreed.

"We seem to have mixed opinions. Since it's your native language, Roy," Renno said, "perhaps you should make it a habit to try to be more concise, to speak more clearly."

Roy groaned and cradled his aching forehead in his palms. "Renno, it's time to go home."

"I understand that language," El-i-chi said.

"Why do you say that to me?" Renno asked Roy. "It is Gao and Ta-na who want to stay to eat more of the delicious pastry of the French chefs. It is they you will have to convince."

"Yay!" the boys cheered together, then Ta-na suggested that all might be appeased by starting the trip home but bringing pastries along for the journey.

"I suppose we could consider going home," Renno allowed, "if my wife can bring herself to refrain from buying any more goods to be transported."

"So," Beth said, lengthening her face and lowering her voice in what she had come to call Renno's "me-big-chief-Injun" act.

"If you are so eager to leave," Renno said to Roy, "I will delegate you to find wagons and mules and to stow my wife's purchases snugly. I should think that will take you, perhaps, two days."

"Oh, lovely," Beth said to Ah-wa-o, "we have two more days to shop."

"Not on your life," Renno said, lifting a finger.

"Just a few hours to find the wedding present," Beth said. "After that, you will have to entertain me." She turned to him and, unseen by the others, licked her lower lip in seductive suggestion.

"I suppose I can manage that," Renno said.

General James Wilkinson's intention was to meet with Aaron Burr in New York, on business of a personal nature.

He arrived in Philadelphia after a restful voyage through the Gulf of Mexico, around the southern tip of Spanish Florida, then up the Eastern Seaboard. His plan was to travel in civilian clothing on to New York by land.

When news of the duel between Burr and Hamilton finally reached his ears, he was shocked. Apprehension took hold when he learned of Hamilton's death. Now Burr was a fugitive but, conveniently, living in Philadelphia.

It was nearing midnight when Wilkinson walked the deserted streets to the house that had been leased by Aaron Burr. There was one light in the window. The general knocked and waited, almost hoping that Burr was either abed or not at home. But the door opened immediately.

"Well, General, what a pleasure," Burr said.

Aaron Burr was forty-eight years old. His hair receded from a sloping forehead. He affected side-whiskers that were narrow at the temples and spread down onto the cheekbones. His prominent nose was sharp, his chin the same.

Wilkinson entered. Burr closed the door. The single lamp lit a room of rump-sprung furniture and peeling wallpaper. "The hospitality here will not, I fear, compare favorably with that at my home, General," Burr said, referring to Richmond Hill, where they had last met. "But that will not lessen your pleasure in seeing me."

"Damn, Burr," Wilkinson said, coming right to the point, "this thing about Hamilton concerns me."

Burr pulled himself up, and his hard, cold eyes played over Wilkinson. "He called me despicable," he said in a low voice. "No man calls me despicable."

"With so much at stake could you not have borne the insult, for a little while at least?"

"Well, General, perhaps what happened was for the best, after all," Burr said. "Would you take a bit of brandy?"

Wilkinson nodded. Burr poured two servings, not into the fine crystal snifters he would have used at his New York mansion, but into two ordinary kitchen mugs.

"Had I been elected governor," Burr continued, "there would be no need for you to be here."

"But since you were not—?" Wilkinson asked.

"I am thus free to pursue what will be a far greater goal than a four-year term as governor of New York. Let us drink a toast, General, to a new nation, with New Orleans as its capital and with Aaron Burr and James Wilkinson hailed as its founding fathers."

"I'm not sure that is possible anymore."

"Of course it is!" Burr scoffed.

"You are a marked man."

"It will pass," Burr said. "Believe me, it will pass. The authorities are just going through the motions, that's all. Men may pass laws against dueling, but deep in their hearts they believe in honor, and they respect a man who is willing to fight for his. Actually, the duel might turn to our advantage. The type of men we need to invade the territory of New Spain should willingly follow a leader who's proven he'll fight for his interests and his reputation."

Wilkinson drank his brandy and remained silent.

"Or," Burr challenged, "is it simply that you doubt your own ability to turn a significant portion of the western army to our cause?"

"I can hold up my end of it," Wilkinson said with an edge to his words. "I have not seen the influential support you promise."

"Nor will you until we are ready to move," Burr told him. "I assure you that my contacts on the frontier are ready. The widespread dissatisfaction with the Indian policy of the United States will bring men flocking to our cause. Thus we will take the frontier regions with us, join them with Mexico, and rival the United States itself. Where once feeble Spain sat astride the mouth of the Mississippi and access to the Gulf of Mexico, there will sit our empire."

Wilkinson's eyes gleamed as he thought about the picture Burr had painted. Burr had not lost his old magic; he was still a very persuasive man. "I will travel to St. Louis soon," the general said.

"It would have been better had you managed to become governor of the southern portions of the territory."

Wilkinson shrugged. "For the time being I obey

orders. I will have a free hand in all the territory above the thirty-third parallel. My headquarters will be at St. Louis, but I can move downriver at any time with my army."

"Good, good," Burr said. "We will succeed, my friend. If we continue to work together, we will succeed."

"When will you come west with funds and with those who support you here in the east?"

"Soon. We must let this little escapade of mine lose its odor. That will not take long. In the meantime, we will keep in close touch with each other. I will be using my influence to turn men to our cause, as I trust you will."

Wilkinson nodded, finished his brandy. "It's quite late."

"Is it?" Burr asked, taking his watch from his pocket. "So it is. Lately I find it easy to lose track of time."

Wilkinson, deep in thought, walked back to his hotel. When he first contacted Aaron Burr about his old dream of forming a separate nation in the west, Burr was vice president of the United States and stood an excellent chance of being governor of New York. He had been a man of power and influence, a worthy partner. Now? Well, Wilkinson would just have to wait and see.

The British consul at Alexandria, Samuel Briggs, greeted his visitor warmly. Eaton presented a letter of introduction from Sir Alexander Ball, governor of Malta.

"I must warn you, Mr. Eaton," Briggs said when he learned of Eaton's intention to travel to Cairo, "that the country is in a state of near-anarchy. It's due to the war, mostly."

The sea war between Great Britain and France raged on. Without the steadying hand of a European power, Egypt had fragmented into warring factions. The Copts, Egyptian Christians, faced extermination. Major factions, remembering the centuries of Turkish rule under the guidance of Islam, were threatening to kill all Moslems.

"But I have my military escort," Eaton said, patting

Midshipman Hawk Harper on the back. "You'll protect me, won't you, Hawk?"

"I'd feel better if I had a squad or two of marines to protect *me*," Little Hawk admitted.

While in Alexandria, Eaton hired barges and rowers. He required quite a few, for he had to transport the thousand rifles he had brought to North Africa aboard the *Constitution*. The navy assigned twenty-four sailors from the United States ship *Argus* to accompany its naval agent. The barges flew both the American and British flags. Eaton put Little Hawk in charge of the sailors, whose senior man was a young officer named Blake. The first thing Little Hawk did was post sentries night and day.

So, under the fiery, impartial sun that had, across the centuries, looked down upon English armies, Napoleon, Turkish hordes, the Roman legions of Julius Caesar, Cleopatra and Mark Antony, the Greeks of Alexander the Great, the departure of the people of Moses, the Sea Peoples, the Persians, Nubian pharaohs, and the great ones of Egypt's glory, an American Indian who proudly called himself a Seneca traveled up the Rosetta branch of the Nile toward Cairo. It was a journey of one hundred thirty miles in a land where violence had become commonplace.

The barges tied up for the night twenty miles below Cairo, near a native village of mud-and-stone houses. Little Hawk made his rounds of the vessels before the evening meal. He spoke briefly to the fifteen-year-old midshipman who was officer of the guard. The boy reported that the sailors, made nervous by shouted threats from the dark-skinned Egyptians along the banks of the Nile, were alert.

Little Hawk finished his meal. Eaton was settling in to write in his journal. A wind blew from across the water, discouraging the flies—dark, disgusting clouds of flies, biblical hordes of flies that tried to crawl into a man's eyes to take moisture, or up a man's nose, or into his mouth. He dozed and was awakened by a shout, "Officer of the guard, post number two!"

Post number two was on the barge where Little Hawk and Eaton slept. Little Hawk jumped to his feet, for he heard a low and menacing sound coming from the land. He arrived at the bow of the barge along with the fifteen-year-old midshipman.

"I think I heard something, sir," the guard said.

"I believe you did," Little Hawk muttered as, from the shoreline, the forefront of a mob of Egyptians surged around a group of mud huts on the edge of the village. The low roar of voices became louder. The Egyptians were carrying sticks, stones, a few ancient muskets, and rusty swords.

"Mr. Evans," Little Hawk said to the guard, "please prepare the cannon for firing."

"Yes, sir!" the young midshipman shouted, leaping to obey.

Blazing torches arced away from the front of the mob, the barges their intended target. Luckily the primitive missiles fell short, on the riverbank. More torches were launched.

"Fire!" Little Hawk said over his shoulder.

The cannon boomed. A ball hissed across the Nile and over the heads of the mob. The leaders tried to stop but were pressed forward by those behind.

"Fire!" Little Hawk ordered again when Evans and the gun crew had reloaded.

This time the ball cut a swath through the mob. Blood poured over the ground. Women screamed shrilly. The mob dissolved in terror, leaving behind their dead and wounded.

"Mr. Evans," Little Hawk ordered, "take a detail and see if you can help the wounded."

"Oh my God," the fifteen-year-old croaked. "Oh my God, look at that."

A man whose leg had been smashed by the cannonball was trying to crawl away, trailing blood behind him.

"Mr. Evans?" Little Hawk said.

"Yes, sir," the guard said, coming back to himself.

William Eaton, alerted by the cannon, came to stand beside Little Hawk. "Spot of trouble?" he asked mildly.

"I couldn't let them get close enough to set fire to the barges, sir."

"Indeed not," Eaton said. "Not with all those weapons on board. Killed a couple of the blighters, did you?" He turned and walked away. He did not mention the incident in his journal.

Cairo was a city of walls and confining, canyonlike streets . . . a beehive city abuzz with abundant humanity. As a boy-man from the American frontier Little Hawk's first encounters with Cairo reduced him to a state of breathlessness. Often he had heard his people say that the whitefaces of the United States and Europe bred like rabbits and mice. Then what could one say about the concentrated millions of Cairo? That they reproduced like the flies that tormented them?

"I know this city," William Eaton told Little Hawk. "I have read so much about it that wherever I am in its labyrinthine mazes, I feel at home."

Indeed, Eaton had abandoned his western clothing immediately upon arrival in the old city and looked more Arab than many of the city's denizens.

The navy escort's job was completed once Eaton's arms arrived in Cairo. The sailors boarded the barges to go back down the river, leaving Eaton and his marine aide alone in a sea of Near Eastern humanity.

In an effort to determine the exact whereabouts of Hamet Karamanli, Eaton introduced himself at the court of the Turkish viceroy, where he found some of Hamet's former adherents. Each of them promised to take Eaton to Hamet in exchange for gold. Eaton, familiar with the Arab world, said that he would pay gold when he stood face-to-face with Hamet. He finally received fairly reliable information that the man he sought was living at the Minyeh oasis, over a hundred miles from the city.

While Eaton was deciding whether or not to venture to Minyeh, Lieutenant P. N. O'Bannon arrived from Tunis, with a small detail of marines, sent by a concerned navy to "protect" their diplomat.

"How in God's name, O'Bannon, do you propose to protect me against that?" Eaton asked as they stood on a balcony and watched a savage riot erupt in the streets.

"It's a lunatic house here. Men are murdered in the streets for no reason at all. The riots are a daily affair. And you're going to protect me with six marines?"

"Seven," O'Bannon corrected. "You're forgetting Midshipman Harper."

"Well, we mustn't forget him," Eaton said.

Instead of traveling to the oasis where Hamet was said to be living, Eaton sent letters. While he waited for a response, he had Little Hawk don Arab dress and, much to Lieutenant O'Bannon's disapproval, accompany him on jaunts through the dangerous city.

"You must learn the language, Hawk," Eaton said. "It's a difficult one until you begin to understand it. Then you'll find it rather primitive."

Little Hawk, who could speak Spanish, French, English, Seneca, Cherokee, and smatterings of other Indian languages, found Arabic to be just so many sounds.

"And you need a proper weapon," Eaton continued, twirling his scimitar over his head.

"That's quite a trick, sir," Little Hawk said.

"Not at all. Learned it from an ex-member of the Janissary Household Regiment of the Turkish sultan in Constantinople. The idea is that it looks so difficult and makes me seem so damned skillful that some street ruffian will think twice before he tackles me."

On one of their excursions into the streets Eaton obtained a recruit for his army. Four yelling Arabs were besetting a man in western dress. With a cry of defiance in Arabic, Eaton drew his scimitar and ran to the attack. The Arabs, seeing his skill with the curved and deadly weapon, fled.

"I am much in your debt," said the man who had been rescued from an uncertain fate. "You do speak English, I pray."

"When necessary," Eaton said.

"Good. I am Leitensdorfer. I am an American." He looked a bit seedy, and not merely from being manhandled by the Arabs. The man's thick accent caused Little Hawk doubt that the man had lived in America for very long.

Within minutes Eaton, who prided himself on being

a good judge of human character, had discovered that Leitensdorfer was a military engineer. The consul had him enlisted on the spot as a member of his brigade, with a fifty-dollar advance in silver to seal the commitment.

At last a messenger arrived from the Minyeh oasis with a letter from Hamet. Hamet would not come to Cairo. He explained that it was too dangerous.

"Well," Eaton said, "it looks as if we go to Minyeh."

Since the city of Cairo and his efforts to recruit an army were depleting his funds at a faster rate than expected, the consul decided to wait until he could obtain more money from the navy. While Eaton waited for a messenger to go to Alexandria and return with the funds, he suggested to Little Hawk and O'Bannon that they take advantage of what might be their only opportunity to see the wonders of ancient Egypt.

Chapter XIV

Lieutenant P. N. O'Bannon was a second-generation American whose Irish father had fought with the Swamp Fox, Francis Marion, in South Carolina. "You see," O'Bannon told Little Hawk as they crossed the Nile by ferry toward the awesome piles of the pyramids at Giza, "I was a by-blow of the Battle of Camden. After beating the British general Gates, the old fox had to rest his men. My father—I'm named for him, Presley Nicholas—was slightly wounded and was being tended tenderly by my mother, a Camden lass with the lovely name of Camelia Inabinet."

The voices of the Arab passengers on the crowded ferry rose and fell in a confusion of sounds. O'Bannon was speaking in a soft voice so as not to be overheard. "I assume, judging by the fact that I was three years old before my father came back to make my mother's name Camelia Inabinet O'Bannon, that she tended him all too well. But then there you are."

Presley O'Bannon and Little Hawk were following

William Eaton's advice in two ways: one, they were taking a look at some of the wonders of ancient Egypt; and two, they were dressing in the style of the natives. That last had presented a problem for O'Bannon.

"Damn me if I'll wear a ladies' gown," he grumbled. "At least not without proper trousers under it." So he had sacrificed one of the benefits of the Arab robes, coolness in the dry heat of the desert, for modesty.

Little Hawk was awed by the bulk of the great, soaring masses of stone that, incredibly, grew even more impressive as the ferry neared the Giza bank of the river.

"So you see," O'Bannon was saying, "being a military man is in my blood."

"*Look* at them," Little Hawk whispered, thunderstruck.

O'Bannon turned to face the pyramids. "Big, aren't they?" he asked. "How about you, Midshipman?"

To date Little Hawk had found O'Bannon to be a good officer and a fair one. Although he was senior he had soon caught on to Little Hawk's special relationship with the boss, William Eaton. For his part, Little Hawk treated the lieutenant with all due military respect, all the while remembering the advice given to him by a marine aboard ship—not to try to fool O'Bannon about having been trained as a marine.

"I grew up in a Seneca longhouse," Little Hawk said.

"How in the names of all the saints did you get from a Seneca longhouse to the Marine Corps?"

"I suppose you could say that I come from a rather warlike family myself." He smiled and said with deliberate understatement, "My father and my uncle have done a bit of fighting. And my father and aunt scouted for George Washington during the War."

"Your aunt? Gor!"

Little Hawk laughed. "My aunt Ena taught me how to throw a knife."

"No one like that in my family. My mother, bless her and may she rest in peace, was a gentle girl, all lilac smells and soft little kisses for her little boyo. No other women in my life, except my mother." He grinned and spat into the Nile. "Speaking of women . . ." He leaned closer.

"What do you suppose they hide under those acres of cloth and the veils?"

"I would guess standard issue female equipment," Little Hawk replied.

"You didn't say how you got to marine officer's training," O'Bannon said, gazing off upriver while brushing the persistent flies away from his eyes.

Little Hawk did not miss the quick glance of inquiry that followed the casually voiced question. "Well, sir, I didn't. I took my military training at West Point on the Hudson."

"You never!" O'Bannon said in amazement. "You were trained for the army?"

Little Hawk grinned. "A pretty sharp marine officer aboard the *John Adams* on the way over here told me that I couldn't get away with lying to you. I don't think I have to say it, sir, but it is a confidential matter that I have been seconded to the Marine Corps for temporary duty."

"Hell," O'Bannon scoffed, "you could have gotten away with it. I knew within a couple of days you hadn't gone through marine training, but I figured you were some rich bastard's kid, or the nephew of some politician who had wrangled a direct commission. So no fooling, you're a West Point man?"

"No fooling."

"And I guess I can't ask why you're in a marine uniform, huh? And so close to Eaton?"

Little Hawk, staring at the largest of the pyramids, did not reply. The ferry was nearing the bank, and the Egyptians aboard were preparing to fight for the doubtful honor of being first to disembark.

"No, I reckon not," O'Bannon said. "But I do wonder just where in hell your orders were written."

"Well, I'm not sure you'd believe me, but maybe I'll be able to tell you that before it's all over," Little Hawk said.

They used Turkish gold given to them by Eaton to rent horses—beautiful animals, Arabian stock, slim limbed, and built for speed. The tombs of Egyptian kings who had been dead for thousands of years towered over the two travelers. As they picked their way through lesser ruins, the sun reflecting up from the sand threatened to give them a permanent squint, so brilliant was it. Egyptian peddlers cried out to them, brandished items of food and merchandise. The men dismounted and gave two native boys small coins to watch the horses, then promised more money if the boys and the horses were there when they returned.

They chose the largest pyramid and began a climb that became more and more intimidating as they mounted the steplike terraces formed by huge blocks of limestone. The relentless sun burned down. Little Hawk and P.N. rested at intervals, but each of them, enticed by the expanding view as they made their way toward the sky, was eager to reach the top.

They found an Egyptian man sitting on the small platform of stone at the top. He wore the usual robes and a brightly colored silk head covering. A walking staff lay by his feet. He smiled at them and spoke in Arabic.

"I think we are about to be found out," O'Bannon said. He was breathing hard from the climb.

"Ah," the Egyptian said in English, "you are not quite what you seem, young sirs."

"I fear not," Little Hawk said. He put his hands on his hips and turned slowly, letting his eyes sweep over the desert.

"You have chosen the tallest of the monuments," the Egyptian said. "Do you know what it is called?"

"The Great Pyramid, I think," O'Bannon said.

"The Horizon of Khufu," informed the Egyptian, raising a finger. "Khufu the great king. Khufu the great god. It is his place, and it rises high toward the sun, toward the great and good god Ra."

"Just how high are we, sir?" O'Bannon asked.

"Figures are so meaningless," the Egyptian said. "We are higher than they." He pointed down toward the antlike figures of men on the ground. "But we are lower than those who have joined the gods and shine forth at night as stars in the sky."

Little Hawk shaded his eyes with his hands and gazed across the desert. Ruins dotted the sands as far as he could

see, and there, far off to the south, he saw the shape
of other pyramids. "Manitous," he whispered, "how they
worked."

"We labored for our king," the Egyptian said.

Little Hawk looked at the man more closely. There
were age wrinkles around his eyes and at his mouth.

"For he was our god," the man continued. "And we
honored him and were honored in return with bread, and
beer, and protection from the enemies who surrounded
us."

"Talks as if he was there," O'Bannon whispered to
Little Hawk.

"And so I was," the old man declared.

"Nothing wrong with your ears, sir," O'Bannon said.

"I hear many things, young one. I hear the whispers
of those who have gone, those whose retreats have been
ravaged by the greed and ignorance of man. I hear the
voices of the great kings, of Khufu, and Khafre, and Men-
kaure, those who had these monuments erected. They are
old, those voices from the past, but not as old as those
yonder, where your eyes see." He was looking at Little
Hawk. The Egyptian's eyes were milky, Little Hawk saw
with shock, and clouded over by disease.

"But how—" Little Hawk began but stopped, since
his question would have been impertinent.

"How?" the old man asked. He tapped his temple.
"I see it all here." He indicated his eyes. "With these I
see dimly, but well enough to know that your skin, young
gentlemen, is pale and that you are strangers to our land.
Not Turks, not French, not English."

"American," O'Bannon said. "From the United States
of America."

"You have come far indeed." The Egyptian took the
long staff in hand, rose, and moved toward the precipitous
brink of the stone tip of the pyramid.

"May I help you, sir?" Little Hawk asked nervously.

"That will not be necessary, thank you. It is so kind
of you to offer." He turned, smiling, showing long, yellow
teeth. "You will ride on to the north, young gentlemen
from the United States, and see the true age of Egypt."

"Perhaps," Little Hawk said.

The old man, feeling his way with his staff, was making surprising speed going down the pyramid. He halted, turned, and called up, "One more thing, young gentlemen. Do not be overconfident on the way down. More people are broken and killed in the descent than in the ascent."

"Thanks a hell of a lot," O'Bannon said. He whispered, "Odd old bird."

Little Hawk grinned. "Be careful. As you said, there's nothing wrong with his ears."

"Well, I think one pyramid is enough for me," O'Bannon said.

"He's coming back," Little Hawk said.

Indeed, the old man was laboriously heaving himself up and over the huge blocks of stone. Little Hawk clambered down to meet him.

"The step pyramid at Saqqara," he said with great feeling. "The first of the royal tombs. The step pyramid of Djoser." He turned and without another word, no explanation, descended lightly to a lower level, and then another.

After the long climb down, the two Americans sat in the shade and drank thirstily from goatskin water bags. It was past midday. The shadow of the Great Pyramid was lengthening.

"I think we need to get back to the city before dark," O'Bannon said.

Little Hawk felt almost as if he could hear the voices from the past, the voices that spoke to the old man. There had been an intensity in the old man's voice when he said, "The step pyramid of Djoser."

"I thought we might ride up north to this Saqqara place," Little Hawk suggested.

O'Bannon laughed. "You're a glutton for punishment."

"But as Eaton said, Pres, this is probably the only chance we'll ever have to see these things."

"Well, young gentleman, if you want to avail yourself of the dubious opportunity to freeze the seeds of your future offspring by spending a night in the desert, I won't pull rank and order you back to the city. By giving you your commission, the Congress of the United States has affirmed that you are an officer and a gentleman, not a kid from the backwoods who doesn't shave yet—"

"We Indians have very little facial hair," Little Hawk said, rubbing his cheek. "Besides, I think being yellow haired—"

"Don't despair. I'd reckon the half of you that's white might develop a whisker or two when you grow up," O'Bannon said. "But as I said, if you're old enough to wear the insignia of a marine officer, you're old enough to make your own decisions."

"Thanks, Pres," Little Hawk said sincerely. "I'm extremely fascinated by all this. These structures were here before Joseph came to Egypt—maybe even before the time of Abraham. Moses probably led his people through their shadows at the beginning of the Exodus."

"Didn't fancy you to be a Bible pounder."

"Never was," Little Hawk said. "Before."

"Well, if you're determined . . ."

"I'll camp in the desert tonight. I've got a blanket and the necessities in my kit."

"Well, have all sorts of fun."

Little Hawk bought water for the horse from a vendor before setting out toward the north. It had not looked to be a long ride, but distances were deceiving in the clear desert air. By the time he came within good viewing distance of the odd, misshapen step pyramid, the shadows made an eye-straining contrast to the red glow of the evening sun. He approached the huge pile of stones past lonely columns of granite protruding from a covering of sand. In growing darkness he walked to put his hand on the stones of the pyramid and remembered the old man's words.

Darkness followed brief twilight with a suddenness that caught him unprepared. He found shelter behind a crumbling stone wall, unsaddled his horse and tethered it, then gazed upward as a glory of stars sparkled with the brilliance of diamonds. The Seneca called the stars the lights in the sky. The old man atop the pyramid had indicated belief that man rose from the grave to shine forth forever as a point of light from the velvet blackness.

The desert sent him an eerie howl, a sound that William Eaton had previously identified as the call of a jackal. Perhaps it was only the fact that Little Hawk was so far from home and so alone, but the howl seemed ominous, supernatural. The howl of a wolf in the American wilderness or the melancholy keening of a coyote was sometimes a bit unnerving in the blackness of night, but at least one could be sure that the sound issued from an animal made of flesh and blood.

Little Hawk shivered involuntarily. There was, of course, no wood to make a fire, and it could get cold in the desert at night. He unrolled his blanket and wrapped it around him. He was beginning to regret his decision to follow the old man's advice. Perhaps there *were* spirits here in this place that was so old, so very old. The man had said that the pyramid built in terraces was the first of the great royal tombs.

He laughed at himself. If spirits were here, they were the ghosts of another people. He himself was far from the lands where the manitous of the Seneca spoke with his father and his uncle El-i-chi. It was said that when a man deserted his homeland he traveled alone, that the manitous did not leave their ancestral hunting grounds.

There were more sounds throughout the night. A cold wind blew past the towering, dark pyramid. A low and eerie wail came now and then as the wind blew and whistled through some oddly shaped crevice in the stones— or so Little Hawk rationalized, that supposition being preferable to others that flitted around in the dark corners of his mind. He welcomed a glorious orange moon that brought a surprising amount of light as it pushed above the eastern horizon. Never had he seen the moon so bright.

Little Hawk heard faint sounds of movement. He was sure he was in the company of small, scurrying things. In his loneliness, he felt certain that he was the only living man within miles of that pile of stepped rock built on the orders of a king called Djoser. It was the light of the full desert moon that saved his life. He saw the glint of moonlight on metal and rolled out of his blanket, narrowly avoiding a killing slash of a scimitar as a man hurled down from the top of the sheltering wall.

Little Hawk came to his feet with his sword in his hand and with cold Marine Corps steel met the charge of his attacker. His saber opened the Arab's stomach. He stepped aside from the final swing of the dying man's weapon and saw the curved blade fall to the sand.

A bellow of rage caused Little Hawk to turn to face others. He could not count them all at first. He could only back away, parrying and slashing, as they tried to surround him. He put his back to the ancient stone wall. His saber cut the legs out from under one man. The injured one fell, his blood dampening the sand, and moaned as he tried to crawl away. Three more attackers jumped over the wounded man and closed in on Little Hawk. A scimitar ripped his robe but did not make contact with his flesh as he thrust the sharp point of his weapon into the hollow of a throat and felt it grate on bone before he could withdraw it. With a backswing he left another Arab's arm hanging uselessly, muscles severed.

Four men were down, victim of his skill with the saber. But still others came. Four more faced him. Fortunately their anger and eagerness to avenge their fallen comrades caused them to interfere with one another. Steel clashed on steel. Little Hawk slipped a fatal slash past the guard of a scimitar-wielding Arab and now faced only three. He fought in silence, although his enemies shouted and taunted and threatened with words whose meanings were clear only in the inflection and volume. The Seneca laid open a scalp with a mighty, downward blow, then slipped away from a savage attempt to behead him. He leaped high over a low-swinging scimitar after whirling in midair to open a belly. He caught a quick glimpse of purple, extruding things as the man fell.

One man faced him, screaming in what could have been fear or hatred or anger. A scimitar flashed and whistled as the Arab spun it expertly over his head. Little Hawk showed his teeth in an amused grimace, for Eaton had done that trick better, and Eaton was the first to admit it was all show, something designed to intimidate rather than to kill.

Little Hawk shouted, "Ha!" as he leaped forward, one foot extended, plunging his saber into the man's solar plexus before the whirling scimitar could be lowered into position for a defensive blow.

He leaned on his weapon, breathing hard. Seven Arabs lay on the sand. Two of them were still alive. The man who had been cut deeply across both thighs lifted himself and drew back his arm. Little Hawk, seeing the glint of metal, ducked to avoid a knife. His action was purely reflexive as he ended the wounded man's pain forever.

Seven bodies . . . The man with the badly slashed arm was not to be seen. With severed arteries he would be busy trying to stanch the flow of blood, if, indeed, he had not passed out from the pain.

It wouldn't do to try to sleep with fresh corpses lying about. Fortunately it would be a simple matter to move his camp. The young Seneca bent to pick up his blanket. A large stone struck him in the small of the back as he bent, knocking the breath out of him and flattening him on the ground. Gasping, lungs spasming, he rolled out of the way of another large rock that was hurled down by the man with the injured arm from atop the crumbling wall. Little Hawk managed to get a breath, bring out his knife, and send it winging to bury itself in the man's stomach.

He ached terribly all over, although nothing seemed to be broken. He retrieved his knife from the fallen enemy, cleaned the blade by thrusting it repeatedly into the sand and wiping it on the lower portion of his robe, picked up his blanket once again, threw his saddle over his shoulder, and leading the horse, walked toward the step pyramid.

More alert now, he was choosing a place among fallen building blocks, preparing to spread his blanket, when he heard the soft sounds of men running in sand. They came bursting around the nearest corner, a larger group by far than the nine who had attacked him.

Many times Little Hawk had heard his uncle El-i-chi say that Renno had never run from a fight. In one split second Little Hawk remembered that; but in that same instant common sense told him that his father had never deliberately entered a fight from which he had no hope of emerging. Valor was one thing, idiocy another. There were at least sixteen brigands in the mob that came streaming toward him, their weapons gleaming in the moonlight. He left his blanket and saddle and ran to the horse, loosed the hobbling rope, and catapulted onto the animal's back.

A shot rang out, and he heard the impact of the ball in the horse's chest. The splendid animal screamed as his legs collapsed. Little Hawk went tumbling, rolled on the cushioning sand, but came to his feet running, having now only one option, to put his back to the stones of the pyramid.

The new group of attackers did not seem to be in a hurry. Perhaps some of them had seen from a distance the effectiveness of Little Hawk's saber. Perhaps they were sadistic and did not want to rush their enjoyment of killing him.

In that desperate moment Little Hawk found himself praying to the God of his mother, the good God of the Bible.

"The Lord is my shepherd—"

Dark faces in the moonlight . . . bared blades . . . the semicircle closing, closing . . .

"Thy rod and thy staff they comfort me—" He caught a blur of movement on the first level of stone at his right. "Yea, though I walk through the valley of the shadow of death—"

The blur was a small man who faced him, dressed in a pleated kilt, sandals, and nothing more save an ornate jeweled ornament that hung from his neck. He was just five feet tall but made taller by a towering headpiece that seemed to be formed of two parts. In his right hand was a spear, in his left an oddly shaped war ax.

Little Hawk prepared himself for attack from this new quarter. Moonlight gleamed off the gold of the small man's neck ornament. He had a sharp face with a prominent nose, and his eyes were outlined in black. He spoke. The sounds were alien, but somehow their meaning formed with absolute clarity in Little Hawk's mind.

"I saw you, warrior. Would that I had had a thousand

as valiant as you with me on the banks of the Euphrates."
He leaped to the sand to stand as a helper beside Little
Hawk.

The ring of attackers halted, exchanged glances, then
surged forward.

When Little Hawk heard an odd, sizzling sound, he
glanced to his left to see a man six feet tall, grasping a
huge war spear. He, too, wore a short kilt. The tail of a
lion hung down behind him, attached in some way to the
garment, and on his head was an object that was similar
to the head wear of the smaller stranger.

"Warrior," the bigger man said to Little Hawk, and
again the sounds were odd but their meaning clear. "I,
too, am with you."

As this strong man came to stand at the Seneca's
side, a quavering moan of fear went up from the would-be
attackers. Still another figure materialized. He was
dressed much like the others, but he wore a war helmet
shaped like a turtle shell and cut away above his dark-
outlined, almond eyes.

"Warrior," the latest arrival said, "you are no longer
alone against these many jackals."

Now, directly in front of Little Hawk's startled eyes,
there appeared one final figure, the old man from the
Great Pyramid.

"Young gentleman," he began, and time stood still as
the gang of cutthroats was frozen, "it was I who sent you
here, but not to be set upon by murderers. I sensed in
you an affinity for the glory and honor that has accrued
to the brave from the beginning of conflict. I sensed in
you a receptivity, which, I believed, would benefit from
contacts with the royal spirits who inhabit this area of
entombment." He hung his head, turned, looked with
disgust upon the brigands, still paralyzed in place, some
with weapons raised threateningly.

"I did not send you here to join these spirits in the
afterworld," the old man intoned. "And so I have appealed
to the greatest warriors of ancient Egypt to stand at your
side." He fell to his knees before the handsome, youthful
warrior in the gleaming, turtle-shell helmet. "Amenhotep,

great king live forever, son of Thutmose, grandson of Amenhotep, the son of the great Thutmose, third to bear the name."

Handsome Amenhotep inclined his head in brief acknowledgment of the old man, then the Seneca.

Next the old man crawled on his hands and knees and paid homage to the small one. "Great Thutmose, wearer of the crowns of Lower and Upper Egypt, conqueror of Megiddo and Kadesh, mighty warrior-king, may your glory outlast the stars."

Little Thutmose stared straight ahead, his eyes fire and ice, his expression arrogant.

And finally, "Narmer, wearer of the white crown of Upper Egypt, great ancestor, your name lives from the time before the pyramids."

The worthy man narrowed his kohl-lined eyes, which sparked with a dangerous light.

The old man's image rippled, then faded, leaving Little Hawk inspired and filled with wonder. The frozen lowlifes suddenly sprang back to action.

Thutmose III, the warrior-king, shrilled a battle cry and leaped toward the cringing attackers. Little Hawk roared the challenge of the bear, totem of his clan. The four moved forward together, ancient kings and the heir to a chieftain, with spears and ax, club and saber.

Moaning and crying for mercy, the attackers fell, bled, screamed in terror, and fled. And then, all about, there was silence except for that odd wailing of wind through some crevice of stone in Djoser's monument.

"Great kings," Little Hawk whispered, "may you live forever."

"Warrior," said the old one Narmer, "with you at my side, Lower Egypt would have been mine."

"May you return in safety to your far land," said Thutmose III, who, in spite of his small stature, had rescued his country from chaos, given Egypt back her empire, and restored her glory.

"You fight well, warrior," commended handsome Amenhotep III.

Then they were gone.

Little Hawk walked among the bodies. He could see the results of his own weapon—the stab wounds and slashes. But the greatest number of dead had no visible wounds, although, in the heat of battle, he had seen both club and spear bring bursts of blood.

He knelt facing the weathered pyramid. "God of my mother, God of Abraham and Moses, my mother taught me that there is but one God, and my stepmother continued my mother's teachings. Forgive me, I am confused. I equate you, Father God, to the Master of Life, and that is not too difficult. But this—"

He looked up at the silent, hard-edge stars and felt the chill of the night drying his robes, which, in the exertion of battle, had become sweat soaked. "My father fights on the side of the good, as I pray I do. Help me. Reveal to me how, since these men of Egypt worship old and odd gods, numbers of them—"

He could not go on. The handsome face of the pharaoh Amenhotep III haunted him. And the young Seneca knew he could have fought proudly at the side of the small one, the warrior-king. He also felt great respect for old Narmer, whose stern visage had inspired him.

A glimmering shone at Little Hawk's side. As it took form, it whirled, weapon at the ready. And for a moment great sadness almost bent the young man double in pain, for at first, as the manitou materialized, he thought that it was his father, that Renno had gone to the Place across the River. Then he saw that the manitou's shaved head sported only a Seneca topknot, and the skin was fairer than his father's.

"Yes, warrior," said the spirit of the first Renno, "you fought well."

"Great-great-Grandfather, explain it to me," Little Hawk implored. A part of his heart filled with joy, for he, like his father and his uncle, spoke with the manitous. "It is said that the manitous of the Seneca do not leave their hunting grounds."

"I hunted wide," the manitou said, "as you do, my little hawk. To explain the rest? You will know all in time."

The vision began to fade.

"Have you no advice for me, manitou?" Little Hawk cried.

"Fight well, Son of my sons, and fight bravely. Your fate is but a feather blowing in the wind."

The moon, at the zenith, had shrunk. The stars, souls of the past according to Egyptian belief, lanced sharp edges of light. A jackal wailed. Little Hawk moved yet again to be away from the dead. Before dawn he was trudging toward the Nile. He was exhausted both physically and emotionally, but he knew it would not be wise for an American marine in native dress to be found in the presence of so many dead Egyptians. He reached the cultivated fields before the heat of the sun was severe, breakfasted on ripe figs, then paid a boatman to take him across the river to Cairo.

He regretted greatly not being able to speak the language of the country, for he would have liked to ask the boatman about his beliefs, about his gods, his ancestors. Egypt was said to be a land of the dead, where the living endured only hardship and misery; but the farms looked prosperous, the boatman sang a merry tune as he sailed, and the teeming mobs of Cairo, not yet rioting because it was quite early in the day, hurried about their business. As they clogged the narrow streets, many of them were laughing, and all of them were talking, talking, talking.

"So, home is the hero," Presley O'Bannon said when Little Hawk entered the marine quarters. "How did it go?"

"Well," Little Hawk said vaguely. "It went well."

Perhaps one day he would tell his father and his uncle El-i-chi that he had fought throughout a starry, cold desert night with the spirits of ancient Egyptian pharaohs. He was certain that no one else would believe him.

Because of Beth's baggage train, it was necessary to travel by road (such as it was) from New Orleans to Natchez and the beginning of the trace. Renno's group rode through leafy tunnels whose overhanging branches blocked out the sky. That curious air plant called Spanish moss draped the limbs of the great, lowland trees in eerie gray shrouds.

The travelers passed great plantations and small farms, the huts of Creek, and a Choctaw village called There Are Fleas Here. The east bank of the Mississippi between New Orleans and Natchez was becoming an area where the might and power of the European races was dominant. Although Creek war parties raided from time to time, they primarily vented their wrath on their eastern borders with the state of Georgia.

Everyone was eager to reach Natchez and start the longest leg of the journey. Ta-na and Gao spoke of home and their friends. Beth longed for the comfort of Huntington Castle. Roy was thinking more and more of Toshabe. Ah-wa-o tried to keep track of the lively boys and stay close beside her husband at the same time, not always with success.

Rain turned the rutted tracks into mire that bogged the three wagons to their axles. The mule skinners—Renno, El-i-chi, and Roy, two of them having accepted the job very reluctantly—shouted and snapped their whips over the rumps of the draft animals.

"The problem is," Roy grumbled, "that with all these women and children around, a man can't talk to these long-eared varmints in a language they understand."

"If you think stronger language can succeed in doing something about this," Beth said, "we'll send the boys away, and the women will stuff something in their ears."

Roy experimented with some earthy muleteer talk and cursed so eloquently that Beth, only pretending to hold her ears, looked at him in wonder and admiration. "Roy," she said, "you're a poet. Profane, true. But quite expressive."

Thus encouraged, Roy, grinning, rose to new heights, and his team on the leading wagon struggled forward to more solid ground.

At Fort Adams just across the boundary that had once separated the Mississippi Territory from Spanish Louisiana, they learned that the American army was moving westward into the Louisiana Purchase to establish posts on the Red River and the Ouachita. There they saw newspapers for the first time since leaving New Orleans and read that Thomas Jefferson and George Clinton had defeated the Federalist ticket handily, 162 electoral votes to 14, and that the naval war between England and France raged on. They also found out that General James Wilkinson had moved his headquarters upriver to St. Louis.

"Took that ugly woman of his with him," a young captain remarked.

Renno heard and made no comment. His unspoken question was answered, however, by the next speaker, an even younger lieutenant, who put in, "Sometimes she's not so ugly, sir—not when you look at her close."

"Not ugly?" the captain asked, sneering. "With black teeth?"

"Did a Frenchman with a pocked face accompany the woman and Wilkinson to St. Louis?" Renno asked.

"I know the one you're talking about," the captain said. "Nope. He hasn't been seen in months."

So, the witch had gone to St. Louis with Wilkinson, Renno thought. And Othon Hugues had not been seen. That could mean that Hugues had not returned from New Spain. As for Wilkinson, he was governor of the Louisiana Territory north of the thirty-third parallel of latitude, a man in charge of a small army and an unknown but vast expanse of land. Either Renno's second letter of warning against the general's treason had never reached Thomas Jefferson, or the president had chosen not to take action.

The travelers accepted the hospitality of the small garrison at Fort Adams for one night. The few officers used the occasion as an excuse for a party, and although it became tiring, Beth and Ah-wa-o did their duty by dancing with each of the young men in their natty uniforms. Roy proved once more that he could outdrink and outlie any young fellow in the army.

When the wagons rolled north the next morning on the way toward Natchez, the Tennesseean was moody and hung over. The roads were marginally better than the route up to this point, and the weather was dry and balmy. The wagons made good time—for wagons. Only a few hours out of Fort Adams, the group was overtaken and passed by an enlisted man riding hard, a pouch of the type used for mail attached behind him to the saddle. He did not pause to talk; he did nothing but wave as he rode past.

"Wouldn't want to move quite that fast," Roy said, "but I'd like to move a little faster than these dag-blamed wagons."

"He'll be in Natchez before we're halfway there," El-i-chi muttered.

"The sadness of your plight breaks my heart," Beth said. "Remember that the wagon you drive is loaded with gifts for our people. That should make you feel more patient."

El-i-chi hid a grin and grumbled, "The place for a woman's tongue is behind firmly closed lips."

Beth stuck out her tongue at him, causing him to laugh. "All right, Red," he surrendered. "I stand reprimanded. I will complain no more."

It was a good time for Renno. He had with him several of the people who were most important in his life: his wife, his brother, one of his sons, his father-by-marriage and father-to-be, plus his sister-by-marriage, little Rose, and her son, Gao. He would soon kiss the cheeks of his mother and his sister and exchange greetings with his brother-by-marriage, Rusog. Only Little Hawk and Renna would be missing from his life once the party reached home.

He was content; he was on the move. He would have preferred to be on foot, traveling at the warrior's pace, but even from the seat of a wagon he enjoyed new sights. Sometimes he climbed new heights to look down and away over the tops of the forests or sometimes skirted along the floodplain of the Father of Waters to see the fat, dirty-brown water moccasins sliding lazily into muddy pools.

He estimated that they were only two to three days south of Natchez when he began to feel a vague discomfort that made him think, at first, that he was coming down with some ailment. He decided to take time to hunt alone and to run until the feeling of disease had been dissipated. He returned to the camp a few hours later with two wild turkeys. While they roasted, the sachem dozed on his blankets, only to awake with perspiration pouring down his chest. He had dreamed that Little Hawk was crying out to him for help. The dream was unclear, the scene alien and misty, but the danger to his son had felt so real that Renno's mouth was dry and his heart pounding. He prayed, directing his unspoken plea for his son's safety to both Jesus Christ and the Master of Life.

The nagging threat of the dream stayed with him. He ate little.

"You aren't feeling well, are you?" Beth asked, putting her hand on his forehead to test for fever.

"I'm fine," Renno assured her.

He went to sleep quite soon after dinner but awoke in the night to a feeling of dread. He slipped from his blankets without waking Beth to go into the forest. He could not take the time to fast, to purify himself before appealing to the manitous. There was an urgency in him now, unexplained but associated with the dream about Little Hawk.

The white Indian sat on a fallen tree and, chanting softly, remained alert to the night sounds of the forest. As if in answer, the fear for his son vanished, but it was replaced by such a feeling of impending disaster that he ran back to the camp, only to find everyone sleeping soundly.

"Renno?" Beth muttered sleepily as he came back to his bed.

"Go back to sleep," he said.

He himself lay awake, however, until the birds began to greet the dawn with their glad songs. "Today," he said, "I will take the lead wagon."

"Dag-gummed if you will," Roy said, getting up and stretching his back. "It's bad enough that you make a mule skinner out of this poor old man. I'm sure not going to eat your dust all day."

The feeling that something was wrong would not leave him. Once they were on their way, he handed Beth the reins of the wagon, leaped down, and ran ahead, moving at full speed to scout their way for well over a mile. The running helped to ease his tension for a little while, although he continued to check the road until late afternoon, when he located a good camping spot. He turned back and took his place beside Beth on the wagon seat.

She could not help but notice Renno's restlessness. In answer to her questions he denied any physical ache or pain or fever.

"Then come and rest," she said when they reached the campsite. "You're pacing like a caged bear."

"We will post a guard tonight," he told Roy and El-i-chi.

"We're no more than thirty miles from Natchez," Roy said. "I don't know about you, but I need my sleep after wrestling mules all day."

"Then my brother and I will share the duty," El-i-chi offered, knowing that if Renno was concerned—and only that explained his restlessness and the fact that he had felt it necessary to scout ahead during the day—then El-i-chi was concerned. Nothing untoward happened during the first long hours of night while the shaman sat watchfully outside the glow of the dying fire.

Renno took the duty at midnight. Nothing disturbed the peace of the forest. Renno woke everyone early, just before light, ignored Roy's protests and the sleepy mumbling of Beth. The wagons were moving a little after sunup.

The road, after crossing the little creek, went straight across a rough, uneven, brushy meadow some few hundred yards wide, then disappeared again into the tree line. Within a half mile from the campsite, Renno, having helped Beth get the wagon rolling, was preparing to leave her to drive while he scouted ahead. Roy was driving the lead wagon when a volley of rifle fire erupted in ambush from the trees. A mule screamed in agony.

Roy reached for his musket, lurched sideways on the wagon seat, clutched for support, and tumbled to the ground. The iron-rimmed wheels of the wagon narrowly missed his head as he lay still, blood staining his tunic.

Chapter XV

J ames Madison, being a family man, did not share the president's predilection for working at night. When Jefferson called, however, Madison immediately answered with his presence in the living quarters of the executive mansion, where Long Tom had made himself comfortable, as he often did, in slippers and robe.

"I sent for you, James," Jefferson explained, "because I want your appraisal of a certain communication I have received from North Africa."

The letters had been long in coming because they had made a Mediterranean and Atlantic crossing, not because Mr. Jefferson's personal agent, young Hawk Harper, had been lax in following orders. In a series of communications, all of which had arrived at one time, Little Hawk began with an account of having met William Eaton aboard the *John Adams*. There followed a number of factual reports on Eaton's activities. Jefferson skipped through most of the material by saying, "The young man whom I sent to give me an appraisal of William Eaton has seen a lot of the world. First Gibraltar, Tripoli, the islands of the Mediterranean, and now Egypt."

Madison settled himself in a wing chair with a glass of Jefferson's fine wine.

"As you remember, Mr. Eaton was given a thousand rifles," Jefferson said. "It seems that he's going to put them into the hands of Arabs. My young man seems to be very impressed with Mr. Eaton. He states that the consul is honorable and has considerable military skills. In short, Midshipman Harper seems to think that Eaton can recruit an army to fight under this Hamet Karamanli."

"Mr. President, are you going to base a major policy decision on the opinions of a twenty-year-old marine midshipman?" Madison asked.

Jefferson rubbed his chin thoughtfully, and then he smiled widely. "James, you've found me out."

Madison laughed. "I suspected as much all along, actually. You had your mind made up about Eaton from the beginning, didn't you?"

"Well, I try to be humble," Jefferson said. "I didn't want to say—not even to myself—look, Tom, you're such a splendid judge of character that intuitively you know that Eaton is the man to handle things in North Africa."

"And in the event that questions are raised in the future," Madison said, "you can state that you sent a man to report personally to you. It's purely coincidental that he happens to be a young fire-eater who would be favorably impressed by Eaton's overt patriotism and his abrupt way of dealing with the nation's enemies."

"Of course," Jefferson said. He raised one finger. "But a good man, mind you. A solid-minded young man whom I trust implicitly."

Madison nodded. "So you're going to give Eaton the commission of raising an Arab army to attempt the overthrow of Yusef."

Jefferson nodded. "I have so ordered. Meanwhile Eaton has renewed his request for American ground forces, but he has lowered his request to just one hundred marines."

Madison smiled. "If our marines are that capable, our investment in the corps is quite worthwhile."

"And Mr. Eaton wanted another ten thousand dollars, which has been delivered to him," Jefferson added, "although no marines are being sent."

"If he accomplishes half of what he promises, we will be getting a bargain," Madison said.

"The British seem impressed with him."

"Ummmm," Madison said.

Jefferson sipped wine. "James . . ."

"Sir?"

"From Harper's letters and from what material I have received from the navy, I get the impression that Eaton plans to lead this invasion force himself."

"Surely not!" Madison sputtered, sitting upright. "No sane man would try to lead a mob of Arabs across hundreds of miles of desert. It might have been a different story had we sent him the thousand marines, or even the hundred he wanted."

"He has marines," Jefferson said.

Madison became more alert and lifted his eyebrows in question. "Oh?"

"Five or six of them, or maybe one or two more."

Madison laughed. "Well, then, there we are. The battle is all but won."

Jefferson did not join Madison in his amusement. "The navy considers this scheme of Eaton's to be nothing more than a diversion. They don't really expect a ragtag expedition of Arabs to *take* Derna. After all, the place is fortified. But an attack from the land would divide the attentions of the defenders and make it easier for the navy to take the city by shell and storm. The only problem is that I get the distinct impression that both Mr. Eaton and my young midshipman have different ideas."

"Since you asked for my opinion, sir, I think that the man should be prohibited from involving himself or members of the armed forces of the United States in a land war in North Africa," Madison said. "After all, we don't want to get bogged down in desert sands and find ourselves in the position of being forced by public opinion to mount a full-scale land war there either to rescue or avenge a few Americans. As you know, public sentiment is running high against the Barbary states because of the treatment of the crew of the *Philadelphia*. If we had American marines in an Arab prison in Derna—"

"You have an excellent point," Jefferson conceded. "Would you please convey my concerns and yours to the secretary of the navy and have him take the appropriate steps to safeguard against such an eventuality?"

Madison nodded. "Of course. On another subject, I have received from Captain Amos Stoddard, in St. Louis, the names of several young men whom he recommends for appointment to the military academy at West Point."

"Good, good," Jefferson said. Before leaving on his long journey into the unknown West, Meriwether Lewis had suggested that appointing the sons of prominent residents of Upper Louisiana to become officer candidates for the army would be an excellent way to begin to bring that new territory of the United States under control. The names of the candidates, as Jefferson scanned the list handed to him by Madison, told him something about the type of men who lived in and around St. Louis—Gratiot, Chouteaus, Loramier, Valle, Bouis—French names all.

The most densely inhabited area of Louisiana, the districts around New Orleans, seemed to be adapting easily to being American.

"I can foresee a new state in Orleans," Jefferson said, "and rather quickly."

"Much to the displeasure of the Federalists in New England."

"What do you think about the future of the rest of Louisiana, James?" Jefferson asked.

"St. Louis, being the gate to the West, will cause that area to grow and prosper."

"The territory is so vast," Jefferson mused. "I have written to John Breckinridge, suggesting that the best use of the central areas of Louisiana would be to exchange them with the Indians for their lands east of the Mississippi. We would promise them that no emigrants would cross the river until we have filled up our vacant country on this side."

"There just might be some opposition to that idea from the Indians," Madison pointed out.

To that, Jefferson offered no comment.

*   *   *

Presley O'Bannon and Little Hawk, natty in the uniforms of the U.S. Marine Corps, were at dinner in their quarters in Alexandria. Their coats were blue, their pantaloons white, the facings red. The cut of the clothing was European, with a high collar. Their calf-length gaiters were highly polished black leather, and most impressive of all was the tall shako with a red plume and a large octagonal brass plate embossed with an eagle, and the word *Marines*, the motto *Fortitudine*. They had, of course, removed their shakos upon entering the interior.

The food, spicy Arab specialties for which O'Bannon had developed a taste, was being served by a comely, dark-skinned woman who was at least ten years older than Little Hawk. They were eating Arab style, dipping a firm, chewy bread into a stew of chicken seasoned with olive oil, prunes, tomatoes, onions, lemons, and exotic spices that neither of them even tried to identify.

"Have you been with the general lately?" O'Bannon asked.

Little Hawk winced. None of the marines called Eaton by that title, but the men Eaton had recruited did. They ranged from Selim the Janissary, who had been drummed out of the most elite corps in the Turkish army because of his very un-Muslim liking for alcoholic beverages; a Macedonian called Captain Luca Ulovic; Marius Metaxas, a Greek who claimed to be from Delphi but was actually a fugitive from Athenian justice; the chevalier Davis, who spoke fluent French but was Spanish; and one Lieutenant Connant, who claimed to be English when he wasn't stating that he was an American or a West Indian by birth.

"He's been a busy man," Little Hawk remarked.

"He's a madman," said the lieutenant.

"True."

"We don't have to go with him, you know," O'Bannon said. "His authorization does not include making either himself or any American a part of the expeditionary force."

"You don't. *I* do."

"Ah, that mysterious commission . . . Still, it has its appeal, doesn't it?" O'Bannon asked.

Little Hawk laughed. "If you call it appealing to hike a few hundred miles across unknown stretches of desert in the company of an Arab mob and a few wild men to attack a strongly fortified position."

"Don't you?" O'Bannon asked.

Hawk's eyes twinkled. "By God, Pres, I do."

O'Bannon laughed like a little boy. "So help me, so do I."

"Even with Eugene Leitensdorfer as the general's adjutant?" Little Hawk asked.

O'Bannon rolled his eyes. The man whom Eaton had rescued from attack by Egyptians was one of the more interesting members of Eaton's human menagerie. O'Bannon and Little Hawk had heard what they believed to be Leitensdorfer's life story, but considering the type of men Eaton had recruited for his officer corps, one could never be sure what was true and what was imagination and bravado. One night, when Leitensdorfer and O'Bannon were drinking a particularly vile alcoholic native concoction, the new adjutant had confided that he'd been born the son of a farmer near Trent and that his given name was Gervasio Santuari. He ran away from a bad marriage, attained the rank of sergeant major in the Austrian army, deserted after the battle of Mantua, and joined Napoleon's army under the name Carlo Hossondo.

"But, my friends," he said, "I knew too much about the Austrian army, you see. So the French accused me of being a spy, and I had to desert another army."

In Switzerland, he said, he was in the jewelry business, and that trade had brought him to Egypt, where he suffered hard times and made a living by running a coffeehouse and by providing girls for high-ranking Turkish officers, among the girls his own Egyptian wife.

"And then, by the gods, Napoleon came to Egypt, and I had to run again."

He went to Messina and entered a monastery under the name Father Anselmo but found the holy life to be dull. He made his way to Constantinople and became an officer in the Turkish army. He worked to make himself indispensable to a Turkish pasha who took him along to Mecca, Suez, and Jeddah, where he was hired as an interpreter for an Englishman, only to be abandoned to a hungry fate in Alexandria.

"I guess, Hawk, only two fools would voluntarily join such a mob," O'Bannon said, shaking his head.

"I'm sure you're right," Little Hawk said. "But I'm afraid I'll miss something if I don't go."

Little Hawk had picked up enough Arabic to communicate on a very rudimentary level. Being more curious than Pres O'Bannon, he spent a lot of time exploring the city. He had met and hired Fama, the woman who kept their quarters. She was a widow who cooked native specialties that smelled and tasted delicious. She made it clear from the beginning that she was willing to warm the bed of both young Americans but was not insulted when only O'Bannon accepted her generous offer.

Little Hawk learned more Arabic from her and asked her questions about Alexandria. One of his goals was to have a fine scimitar like the one that Eaton wielded so expertly, but the weapons for sale in the public markets were inferior products of metal that would shatter or bend at the first blow. Fama suggested that Little Hawk visit the quarter of the blacksmiths and gave him directions.

He made his way through narrow, crowded streets to a little alley that smelled of burning coke. He stood in an open door and watched a muscular middle-aged man pounding an iron wagon wheel into shape. The scent of the white-hot metal was acrid.

"Father," Little Hawk said in Arabic, "I would purchase a blade of the finest steel."

The man pounded with his heavy hammer until the metal had cooled to the point of needing reheating. Then he thrust the wheel back into the firebox while a young boy worked the bellows.

"Abd Al Rashid," the man said, pointing down the alley. Then he returned to his work.

The street of the metalworkers rang with the sounds of the smith's hammer on heated metal and with the lighter tappings of workers in copper and brass. Little Hawk was not able to read Arabic. Each time he asked for Abd Al Rashid he was directed farther down the street.

He passed shops with heavily barred windows and doors where goldsmiths and silver workers fashioned things of wonder and beauty. A woman, heavily veiled, her slim fingers laden with gold rings, came out of one of the shops, cast almond-shaped eyes on Little Hawk for a moment, and then entered a closed carriage.

Ahead of him, as the narrow street dwindled into nothing, he saw the desert. And there, separated from the linked shops of the street by a muddy pen where two fat, dingy sheep lay on scattered straw, was the forge of the blade maker, Abd Al Rashid, a man as evil looking as any Little Hawk had ever seen. He was reminded, in fact, of the Frenchman Othon Hugues, he of the pocked face and ice-clear eyes.

Rashid's face was deformed by angry, inflamed bumps, some of them as large as a pigeon's egg. His eyes were watery and red; his nose was long.

The working area was open to the desert on the southern side. The floor, of course, was sand, and it was studded with blackened flakes of metal. Rashid wore a leather loincloth, and his bare chest was well developed and heavily haired. The muscles of his right arm and shoulder bulged, making that limb twice as large as his left.

"I have been told," Little Hawk said as the smith looked at him in silence, his watery, red eyes squinting, "that Abd Al Rashid can work the metal that bears the name of Damascus."

"So Allah wills," Rashid said.

"If it is Abd Al Rashid's pleasure, I would have a weapon of Damascus steel, a blade curved in the style of the scimitars of the Turkish guard, a blade strong enough to hew stone."

"Perhaps, then," Rashid said, "you should see Ahmed the stone carver."

"Forgive me if I give you the wrong impression," Little Hawk said. "I do not wish to carve stone, only to have a blade that is strong enough to do so."

The weapons maker scowled. "You mentioned pleasure. Abd Al Rashid does not work for pleasure."

Little Hawk produced a Turkish gold coin.

"Come," Rashid said. He led the way through a door so low that Little Hawk had to stoop. A variety of blades were displayed on a wall, mounted against black velvet. He took down a scimitar with an ornate, bejeweled handle, held it by the blade, and offered the haft to Little Hawk. "The blade is curved in the Persian style. He after whom our city was named, the great Alexander, faced such weapons."

Little Hawk hefted the blade, swung it experimentally, and frowned. Intent on the feel, which was not quite right, he did not see Rashid take down another weapon, a blade with a more pronounced curve.

"Ha!" the swordmaker shouted, and launched an attack both skilled and forceful.

Reflexively Little Hawk countered a blow. He backed away but quickly realized that Rashid's strokes, although powerful, were not intended to maim or kill but to test the metal of the Persian scimitar in Little Hawk's hand.

Little Hawk smiled in appreciation of Rashid's expertise. He tried various feints, only to be countered.

"Enough," the swordmaker said, stepping back. He nodded respectfully. "You are not Arab, and yet you handle the weapon well."

"It is a good blade," Little Hawk said. He hesitated.

"But it is not the blade for you," Rashid completed the thought for him. "Come."

He went back into the forge room, opened a chest that was covered with the dust and soot from the fire, and took out a utilitarian sheath from which he drew a blade as long as the Persian scimitar but more strongly built. Again he offered the weapon to Little Hawk, this time with a little bow.

The blade sat in Little Hawk's hand as if it had been designed for it. He made a few strokes in the air. "Now this one . . ." he said. "Ah, this."

"Yes," Rashid agreed. "It is the weapon of a warrior. It will cost you three gold coins, not one. And you will have to wait for the final tempering."

Little Hawk gave Rashid three coins. "When?"

"You have time now?"

"Yes."

"Then I will let you watch." Rashid stirred the fire in his forge. Then he yelled to bring a young boy running to pump the bellows. The boy pumped feverishly, and the hot, acrid smell of heating metal soon filled the room.

The sun was getting low. The desert to the south was glowing with the red fire of the dying day. Rashid mumbled to himself as he turned the blade in the fire, examined it, then thrust it deeper into the white heat of the coals. In the shadows the glow of the fire lit Rashid's evil-looking face from below, making him look even more sinister.

"Now, young one," he said to the boy.

The boy stopped pumping the bellows and darted from the forge, to return shortly leading one of the sheep that Little Hawk had seen in the cote next to the building. The sheep was female. She followed the boy quietly.

Rashid, standing at the forge, heavily gloved hand on the hilt of the white-hot blade, closed his eyes and chanted in a singsong voice, the words coming too quickly for Little Hawk to understand them. And then, in a blur of motion and with a brutality that made Little Hawk's stomach turn, he removed the blade from the forge, seized the sheep by her fat tail, and with one swift lunge impaled the animal from the rear, burying the blade to its cross guard in her body. It all happened so quickly, she cried out just once. Blood sizzled on the blade as Rashid pulled it slowly from the twitching body of the dying sheep. Then the Arab plunged the blade into a vat of water to complete the cooling process.

"Now, warrior," the swordmaker said, "this blade has been tempered in blood, as the weapon of the warrior should be. After it is polished, it will serve you well. By this time tomorrow it will be ready."

Little Hawk was sorely tempted to walk out, never to return. He had killed his enemy. He had seen the blood of many men, but they had died in battle. In the case of his attackers at the step pyramid, they had lost their lives making a futile attempt to kill him, to rob him of his belongings. He was not one to faint at the sight of blood, be it that of an enemy or a food animal. And yet the method of tempering the scimitar had unnerved him.

His face was pale. His stomach roiled. He left with only a nod.

Because he had paid Rashid in gold in advance, because the weapon had felt as if it had been fashioned for his hand alone, he was back the next day just before the desert turned red with sundown. The scimitar gleamed. The edge, good Damascus steel, was deadly sharp. A golden tassel hung down from the rivet on the tip of the hilt.

"May it fight only for good in your hands," Rashid said, bowing as he handed it hilt first to Little Hawk. The Seneca tied the sheath to his sash. The weight of the weapon felt good on his thigh.

When at last a contingent of navy men arrived with two small cannon and the ordnance to make them functional at "General" Eaton's desert camp, it was time. Orders were given. The Tripolitanian Arabs, who made up the largest percentage of the force, celebrated by firing their rifles in the air.

"That seems to be an Arab failing," O'Bannon said, shaking his head in disgust. "We'll have to break them of that habit, or before we arrive at the walls of Derna they'll have used up all their ammunition."

When a marine bugler gave the signal to march, the Arabs used up more powder as one group of Bedouin did their best to bring down circling buzzards. The dust of the desert was raised by hundreds of horse and camel races.

At the end of the first week O'Bannon was out of patience. Little Hawk and he found Eaton conferring with the leaders of the Arab forces and waited until he was finished. "Sir," O'Bannon said, "we're going to have to take measures to turn this mob into an army, or we'll all leave our bones to dry in the sun before Derna."

"Patience," Eaton advised. "We have over five hundred miles of desert to cross. That will give us time."

O'Bannon wasn't satisfied. "Sir, I've had a look at the maps you've provided. I fear, sir, that they are the works of artists, not cartographers."

Eaton waved his hand. "Not to worry. We have men with us who know every inch of this desert."

"Is that why, sir, we're making a dry camp where there's supposed to be a water hole?" O'Bannon asked.

Eaton winked. "A good point, my man. A good point."

When the march resumed the next morning, Little Hawk told O'Bannon he was going to take a look ahead. He scouted the desert for a few miles around, keeping the "army" in sight by its dust cloud. There was no water hole anywhere. He passed the columns and rode ahead. He had with him a copy of the map that was supposed to show the topography of that section of the desert, but he could not orient it with any visible features of the terrain.

In midafternoon, he followed the tracks of a desert jackal into a very unpromising canyon hemmed in by heavily eroded cliffs. There, in the shelter of a towering rock face, was the water hole that the map had shown to be fifteen miles farther back.

Little Hawk rode back to find Eaton at the head of the column with his Bedouin guides. He motioned the consul aside and whispered to him. The column was heading at least fifteen degrees north of the entrance to the canyon where there was water. Little Hawk hid a grin as Eaton put on a grand show, sniffing the air, dismounting from his horse to examine the ripples of the windblown sand, and then in a grand manner, robes flowing, he began to issue orders in the name of Allah. He overcame the protests of his guides and turned the column to the southwest.

Thus, early in the march, Eaton impressed the Arab mob with his ability to consult with Allah and lead them unerringly to water. Little Hawk was made the unofficial scout. He spent most of his time riding on the flanks or well in front of the column, using his tracking skills to compensate for the inaccuracy of Eaton's maps.

The North African sun began its punishment the day the ragtag army left the Arab Tower with El Alamein as the first landmark. The marines adopted a modification

of the Arabian headdress, fashioning coverings that were
worn under their government-issue hats to hang down and
protect their necks. An ointment provided by Eaton
helped exposed areas of skin to tan rather than blister,
but there was not enough to distribute to the entire force.
Some of the thirty-eight Greek mercenaries were burned
painfully. The dry air seemed to suck every drop of moisture from a man's body, leaving his throat painfully dry.
The mucous membranes of the nose dried out. O'Bannon
was plagued with nosebleeds for the first few days.

The craving for water became almost maddening.
There were strict guidelines for consuming water on the
march, since the water holes and the infrequent oases had
not been placed by Allah for the convenience of a force
invading Tripolitanian lands from Egypt. Moreover, the
nomads of the desert held strong claim to any water and
were prepared to defend their rights to the death. Because
the nomads could move about familiar territory much
faster than Eaton's unruly mob, word of Eaton's intention
to attack Tripoli from the land was spread ahead of his
army.

The first indication of hostility from the desert people
came as Eaton led the foreguard into a canyon where
Little Hawk had located water. A volley of rifle fire burst
from the protection of rocks. Men fell. A horse screamed
in fear or pain. Little Hawk drew his scimitar, yelled out
an order to the marines nearest him, then led a charge
up the slope and into the rocks. He found the places
where Arabic tribesmen had lain in wait, but the attackers
had fled.

"Sir," Little Hawk said, "I think I'd better take a
small force and clean up around the water hole."

"No," Eaton told him. "We do not want to have to
fight our way all the way to Derna. Come with me."

They found an old sheikh in dirty, white robes standing defiantly in the sand. A half-dozen sullen, younger
men were at his back, rifles at the ready. Eaton dismounted, bowed, expressed formal greetings, and asked
permission for his men to share the water and grass for
the animals for the night.

The old man went into conference with his men.

"He doesn't like it," Eaton said in English to Little Hawk, "but Arab courtesy makes it necessary for him to say yes." In this he was right, and a pattern was set. Eaton made it a point to order every man in his force to be courteous. "Molest one girl, one woman," he told them, shouting in perfect Arabic, "and I, personally, will cut off your head. Any one of you who creates trouble with the desert people will face this." He twirled his scimitar expertly.

After a visit to any occupied oasis he left generous bribes behind him. Soon the news traveled ahead of the army that Eaton Pasha was a kind and generous man who was on intimate terms with Allah.

Still there were attacks, for not every desert wanderer was a reasonable man. Ambush came from rocky slopes, then the attackers galloped away, hiding their trail in fields of stone and gravel. During such attacks Eaton rode up and down the column, risking being a target, for he was conspicuous on a great, white horse, warning his men not to go after the ambushers. Fortunately, most Arabs were poor marksmen, so that casualties to Eaton's men were light. The strain of being targets was beginning to tell, however.

"I think, Hawk," Eaton said, "that we're going to have to put a stop to these attacks. Let's do it mainly with Tripolitanians, so that it will be perceived as Arab against Arab. I'll leave it to you to pick, oh, a dozen good men, and the next time these brigands hit us, we'll hit back."

Little Hawk had no trouble finding men eager to give the fight back to those who fired from ambush and fled. He grouped them near the front of the column.

An attack came the very next day. Rifle fire swept across the forefront of the formation from a sandy ridge. Little Hawk lifted his scimitar and yelled in Arabic, "Now we strike!" He spurred his horse. William Eaton joined him in the headlong charge across open ground and up the sandy ridge. Leaden death pocked the sand around them. Eaton was twirling his scimitar in the manner of the janissaries and screaming threats at the top of his voice. He had time to cast an approving look at Little Hawk as he, too, expertly spun his gleaming weapon over his head.

The two horsemen burst up over the crest of the ridge side by side, sand flying. The nomads had been too slow to flee. Hawk and Eaton, bright blades flashing, were on them. A man went down under Little Hawk's perfectly balanced weapon. Eaton killed one man quickly, wounded another, then drew his pistol and brought down a man who was trying to run away.

The men chosen by Little Hawk entered the fray, and one by one the nomad band went down.

It was quiet except for the moaning of the wounded. Eaton made no move to interfere as his men dispatched the living and stripped all of the bodies.

"Divide it equally among yourselves," Eaton told the men.

"The horses, too, General?" a swarthy Bedouin asked.

"The horses, too," Eaton said. He nodded in satisfaction.

"Shall I form a burial detail?" Little Hawk asked.

"That would be the humane thing to do," Eaton said, "but no. Leave them for the sun and the scavengers so that others may come upon them and spread the word, for to be appreciated, justice in the desert must be swift and final."

After three weeks on the march, the army had reached Cyrenaica. The marines, thirsty and parched from the sun, their skin as dry as leather, were also lean and mean.

"Well, at least we'll have no more water problems," O'Bannon remarked. "We're in territory known to the Tripolitanians. They say there are plenty of wells, deep and sweet."

It was true that there were wells, and the men camped at one that was deep. The water was sweet but flowed so slowly into the well from the surrounding rocks that the corps had to go on very short rations.

"Damn, sir," a marine grunted to Little Hawk as the small group of Americans had their evening meal, "once we get out of this hell I swear to God that I'm going to live on the banks of a river that never goes dry and that I will never eat goat meat again."

Twice in the next few days men from the west met the army. Each of them brought the same message: the bashaw was sending a thousand of his finest cavalry to protect Derna. Eaton's staff was made edgy by the reports; but Hamet and his followers were more than nervous—they panicked.

"We must return to Egypt," Hamet quavered, "for we cannot hope to win against such odds."

"Do you really believe that Yusef, who faces the most powerful squadron of naval force ever seen in this part of the world, would weaken his position at Tripoli to send men to Derna?" Eaton laughed. "The man will keep his troops around him, to protect his own miserable person from Commodore Rogers and the navy."

"No, we must return to Egypt," Hamet insisted, and the refrain was taken up by his followers.

"Go, then," Eaton said in disgust. "But you'll get no rations from me. Only those men who stay with the corps will eat."

Hamet decided that his brother's troops were a less immediate threat than certain starvation. The corps was camped in the ruins of an ancient Roman outpost so far from the nearest populated area that any man going off on his own was sure to die.

Early in April the corps reached the largest oasis it had yet seen. O'Bannon and Little Hawk alerted the small force of marines, for thousands of nomads had gathered at the place, which Eaton called Eu Korrah-ke-Barre. Their caution was not needed, for Eaton promptly depleted his stock of gifts, handing out knives and other trinkets in exchange for barley and melons. A Bedouin sheikh came to him and offered to fight at his side with one hundred horsemen. Eaton was delighted.

"Yusef treats us with contempt," the sheikh explained. "Now we will help you to remove him from his palace."

The corps began to grow, and the Bedouin brought

their own supplies and ammunition. They also brought women.

Presley O'Bannon was washing himself when he realized that he was being observed. He glanced up to see a Bedouin girl. She was slim and graceful in her flowing garments, and the eyes over her veil were dark, slanted, and warm. O'Bannon knew that Eaton had ordered all men not to molest the nomad women, but this girl's eyes told him that she would not consider his attentions to be molestation. Still, O'Bannon was a cautious man. He explored the possibilities in halting Arabic, and in the end he figured that he had the problem solved, for the girl and her parents were quite pleased to sell her temporarily to him for a bag of figs equal to her weight. She was a small girl. The bag of figs hardly dented O'Bannon's wallet.

Since he was a marine and, therefore, not highly paid, O'Bannon wanted to get his money's worth. After a sleepless and rather exhausting night he sent the girl back to her father and began to prepare for the day's march. He was surprised when the father appeared, rifle in hand, the girl trailing behind him, her doe eyes flirting shamelessly with any marine who looked at her.

"What's he saying, Hawk?" O'Bannon asked as the father babbled on swiftly.

"It seems that the figs you gave him were spoiled," Little Hawk said.

"He's lying," O'Bannon said.

"Want me to tell him that?" Little Hawk asked.

O'Bannon thought for a moment as he looked at the rifle in the father's hand. "Tell him I'll replace the figs."

Little Hawk made the offer, then listened to the heated reply. "He wants fifty dollars in American silver," he told O'Bannon, "for his honor has been insulted."

"My God," O'Bannon said. "I haven't got ten dollars in silver."

"He says that unless you pay him he'll go to the general," Little Hawk said.

The situation was serious, for the general had warned the entire corps that he would personally behead any man who caused trouble with the natives. Little Hawk spoke softly to the girl's father and then called all of the marines together. He was able to raise twenty-six dollars in silver; the Bedouin refused to accept paper money. Little Hawk put the silver into the man's hand and asked him to be patient.

The Seneca found Eaton in conference. He had to wait for a few minutes and was much surprised when Eaton came to him bearing a small bag of silver. Little Hawk gulped, for the general obviously already knew about O'Bannon's indiscretion. Eaton tossed the bag of silver into Little Hawk's hand.

"I only need twenty-four dollars," Little Hawk said.

"Take it, then," Eaton said icily. "And tell Lieutenant O'Bannon that it will be deducted from his pay."

Fortunately for O'Bannon, the Arabs did not consider his dispute with the businessman who sold his daughter for a bag of figs to be a serious matter, not at all like the crisis that erupted some days later as the corps marched on toward Derna. There were now thousands of Arabs in the camp each night, and there was friction among them. As Little Hawk and O'Bannon helped Eaton to settle minor disputes, he learned that the Arabs were divided into four factions, each of which would have been happy to slit the throats of everyone else.

Serious trouble was avoided until one night when a Bedouin was stabbed by a person or persons unknown. True to his own code of honor, the dying man refused to name his assailant. His relatives and tribesmen knew, however, that the assassin had to belong to one of the other three factions and began to prepare themselves to attack in three directions at once. William Eaton's expeditionary force was about to explode into fratricidal strife.

Little Hawk and O'Bannon felt helpless. Eaton, more in tune with Arab mentality, stood before the army and said in a loud, penetrating voice, "Within the next five minutes, the man or men who killed will step forward and confess to their deed. If no one steps forward, beginning in five minutes and one second, I will kill two men from each company."

Little Hawk looked with wide eyes at O'Bannon.

"Hey," O'Bannon said, shrugging, "it's a tough world."

The results of Eaton's threat were immediate. A dozen men competed with one another in naming the killers. Two culprits were dragged forth. Eaton gave the orders. Little Hawk and O'Bannon were to join the senior European officers in forming a firing squad. No Arab was included lest the relatives of the executed men feel it necessary to start a new blood feud. The killers were tied to poles stuck in the sand. They wept and begged for life.

Eaton gave the order to fire. Little Hawk lifted the muzzle of his rifle to let his ball pass over the heads of the condemned men. But enough of the others aimed true. The two Arabs slumped, dying instantly.

Chapter XVI

When rifle fire blasted out from the tree line on the other side of the brushy meadow, Renno and El-i-chi reacted instantly, but in different ways. The sachem, on the wagon seat with Beth just behind Roy's vehicle, looked up to see the smoke of several rifles drifting out of the trees. He saw Roy tumble from his wagon, and the limpness of his body was like a knife to Renno's heart. He had seen the slackness of death before. He screamed out a warning in Seneca. In the same instant he seized Beth's arm and, clutching his rifle in the other hand, hurled himself down from the wagon, pulling Beth to the ground with him.

She jerked away and, before he could stop her, ran in a crouch to catch up with the moving wagon. She clambered up onto the tailgate and disappeared for a moment, then emerged with her stout bow and quiver of arrows. She fell, then rolled behind the cover of brush as balls of ammunition were thudding into the ground all around her.

El-i-chi's reaction was to jerk his team of mules into a turn and to crack the whip not just over their rumps but onto them. The wagon heeled up onto two wheels but did not overturn. Ah-wa-o clung to him as the vehicle righted itself and the mules jerked into a lope that carried the wagon back toward the southern tree line. Gao and Ta-na, inside the wagon, yelled in protest. When Gao stuck his head out to see what was going on, El-i-chi said in a tone that brought instant obedience from the boys, "Stay as low as you can."

Renno crawled to join Beth, then guided her into a little depression where they could be protected as long as they were lying flat.

"Hold your fire until they are well within range," he said as forms emerged from the trees.

Beth readied an arrow. Renno sighted down his rifle barrel and was ready to fire when he saw the color of the targets' uniforms. Beth became aware of the dress of their attackers at the same time.

"They're American soldiers," she said in puzzlement.

Renno had never killed soldiers of the United States. He put the sights of his Kentucky long rifle on a man who was just a bit ahead of the others, but still he could not pull the trigger.

"Renno, why did they fire on us?" Beth asked.

"I don't know," he said.

But there lay Roy Johnson. He had not moved since hitting the ground. The unmanned wagons were moving toward the tree line. Soon the soldiers, eight of them, would be near enough to make their rifles a danger to Beth and himself. He put the sights on a target and fired. The man spun around by the force of the impact, then sank limply to the ground. The others paused, only briefly. Renno rammed home a new load, and another man died.

Beth came to her knees and sent an arrow winging. The range was a bit too much for her. Once again Renno reloaded, and when the third man of the eight who were advancing across the meadow fell, the others turned and ran back toward the line of trees. Just as they were about to reach it a shot rang out from the west, and a man fell. Renno said, "So, Brother." El-i-chi had made very good time circling the meadow.

The shaman cried out the hunting call of a hawk and was answered.

"We will move back slowly," he told Beth. "Stay down. Keep under cover as much as possible."

Shots rang out as Beth and Renno began to move, but soon they were out of effective range and running together into the shelter of the trees. They found El-i-chi's wagon not far into the woodlands. Ah-wa-o and the boys came out of hiding. Both Gao and Ta-na held rifles from the wagon.

After Renno secured the mules, he motioned the others to follow him. He made a circle around the meadow. The cooing of a dove told him that El-i-chi had heard their approach. The sachem answered.

The shaman joined them quietly. "Another squad just came down the trail from the north," he informed Renno.

The white Indian nodded. There were, then, around a dozen to fifteen men.

"Soldiers of the United States," El-i-chi said.

"Yes."

"Why?"

Renno shrugged.

"We can avoid this fight by abandoning the wagons," El-i-chi suggested.

"No," Renno said. He knew that if the women and children had not been at risk, his brother would never have proposed such an action, for El-i-chi, too, was fully aware that Roy Johnson lay on the field.

El-i-chi showed his teeth in a grimace of satisfaction. "Then it is two together," he said.

"Three," Beth said.

"You will stay with Ah-wa-o and the boys," Renno said. "Here in hiding."

She started to protest.

"We cannot hope to control the movements of so many," Renno said. "We would not want a party of them to stumble onto Ah-wa-o and the boys."

"We can fight them off," Ta-na said. "Don't worry."

"With this to help," Renno said, touching Beth's bow, "I will be less worried."

"Is Grandfather Roy dead?" Gao whispered.

"I think he must be," Ta-na said after neither Renno nor El-i-chi answered the question.

El-i-chi led the way, and the brothers faded into the forest with an almost eerie silence. Oddly enough, the soldiers were still in place at the northern edge of the natural meadow. They straddled the road, sitting and lying behind trees or brush for cover. Renno and El-i-chi were very close, close enough to hear why the soldiers had not moved. A heated argument was going on among men who were hidden from Renno's view by trees and brush.

"Sir, I don't want to sound impertinent," a young voice was saying, "but I'm sure I saw women and children. That doesn't sound like a group of murdering renegades to me."

"Sergeant," another voice said, "you saw that the drivers of two of the wagons were Indian."

Renno crept closer.

"You have your orders, Lieutenant," another man said, and Renno froze, for he recognized the voice of Othon Hugues. "Why do you allow insubordination from a mere sergeant? I swear that I will report you to General Wilkinson if you do not obey the orders he gave you."

"Sir," the sergeant said, "don't ask me to send my men into the sights of an expert marksman. We've already lost four men."

"Then send them around the meadow," Hugues said furiously.

"Sir, may I respectfully suggest that we wait for the cover of darkness?"

"Fool!" Hugues thundered.

There was a sound of struggle, harsh breathing, then a thud.

"Damn, Hugues, you didn't have to do that," the officer complained.

Renno crawled forward to see a young sergeant lying on the ground. El-i-chi, meanwhile, moved silently in another direction. Hugues and the lieutenant, Renno saw, were gone. He could hear orders being given to the men who lay under cover on the edge of the meadow. The sachem bent over the fallen soldier. The man's head was bloody, but he was breathing steadily. Renno heard men mumbling and getting to their feet. He left the unconscious sergeant and watched as Othon Hugues and the lieutenant led twelve men into the meadow. When he was satisfied that the force was going to go straight across, he went back to the fallen man.

Renno had seen many head wounds. It was obvious that Hugues had intended the blow to be fatal. As Renno bent over the sergeant, the young man groaned. Renno took the sergeant's bandanna and poured water from the army canteen at the man's belt over it. Quickly he washed away the blood that had run down into the young sergeant's face and patted his forehead with the cool cloth. The man stirred and opened his eyes.

"Who—"

"Easy," Renno whispered.

"Hugues?"

"He is not here."

"—kill that son—"

Renno helped the sergeant to sit up and lean against a tree. His eyes focused slowly, then widened. "You—"

"I am Renno, sachem of the Seneca, personal emissary of President Thomas Jefferson."

"My God!"

"What were your orders?"

"To intercept a gang of Creek and Spanish renegades trying to get into Natchez to do mischief."

"And the orders were from Wilkinson?"

"Himself," the sergeant verified, "before he left for St. Louis."

"And Hugues?"

"He arrived at the garrison a couple of days ago. He's Wilkinson's man, although he's a civilian. Something odd there, but the general often uses him to relay orders."

"I heard your doubts that our group was the gang of renegades you were after."

"Creek and Spaniards," the sergeant said, "trying to sneak into Natchez to set fires and do murder. Hugues told the general about them. Said he stumbled onto the plan while he was in New Orleans."

In retrospect, Renno regretted having stayed in the city on the Mississippi so long after the return from New Spain. His delay had given Hugues time to return to Natchez and set up the ambush that had left Roy lying in the meadow.

"Your officer's name?"

"Lieutenant Abe Fellows."

"I'm going to have to leave you."

"I'll be all right."

Renno nodded, but he knew that the sergeant was still in danger, for his eyes were becoming unfocused. With a head wound as severe as the sergeant's, death could come after a day or two.

The soldiers were disappearing into the woods on the far side of the meadow. Renno ran to the spot where Roy lay. He knelt. The ball had entered Roy's left ear, leaving a huge, bloody mess. Renno's heart sank, for now all faint hope was gone.

Roy opened his eyes and grunted, "Took you long enough."

"Manitous be thanked," Renno breathed. He examined the wound more closely. The ball had shot away the lobe of Roy's ear, making for a lot of blood, and had left a raw furrow at the base of the skull behind the ear.

"Can you walk?" Renno asked.

"I'm a little dizzy. Just been lying here waiting for you to come."

"Well, you looked so comfortable, I thought I'd give you a little rest."

Roy snorted and tried to get up. Renno lifted him and supported his weight, and they made their way as quickly as possible to the western end of the meadow to join El-i-chi. Beth and Ah-wa-o took charge of the wounded man. Renno motioned to his brother, and they faded into the trees.

"They will have found the wagon," Renno said.

Indeed, two men stood guard over the wagon. They died quickly, the cause of death being lack of training in the ways of the wilderness, the instruments being a razor-sharp Spanish stiletto in Renno's hand and a long, deadly skinning knife in El-i-chi's.

Renno stood, head bowed, over the fallen man.

"It bothers you?" El-i-chi asked.

"I have never killed soldiers of the United States."

"There are evil ones among the Seneca."

"These men were merely following orders," Renno explained.

"So," El-i-chi responded, "you remain here and chant the songs of sorrow over them if you wish. I'll do the killing for both of us. And I will not stay awake nights burning with guilt for killing those who would fire from ambush upon my wife and son."

"Come, bloodthirsty one," Renno said.

To Renno, there was a sameness about what followed. He was a warrior, and he did the job well. A man in the uniform of the United States, the rear guard, died with an arrow driven deeply into his spine at the base of his neck so that he fell without crying out. Another died as El-i-chi leaped down from the leafy cover of a tree, smashing a skull with a blow of his tomahawk just before his feet hit the ground.

The other soldiers were spread out, searching the woods. "This one," El-i-chi whispered, meaning the officer in the lead, "has a death wish."

The deployment of the men played into the hands of the two deadly Seneca who stalked the dark shadows within the dense trees and brush. Renno's English longbow was a silent and fearsome weapon. El-i-chi's cat-quiet movements put him within arm's reach of his victims before they became aware. More men died.

"We will kill no more," Renno said, for each death was painful to him. He would have felt the same had he been killing warriors of his brothers tribe, Rusog's Cherokee, for he had promised friendship to the United States, and his word was his honor.

He moved forward so that he could hear the movements as the soldiers searched in vain. His voice rang out into the quiet: "Lieutenant Fellows! You fight the wrong enemy. I am Renno, sachem of the Seneca, and I travel with my family, with women and children. We are not the renegades you were ordered to kill."

A shot rang out, and a ball cut leaves over his head.

"So much for sweet reason," El-i-chi mumbled.

"Hold your fire!" Fellows roared.

"It is nothing more than an attempt to deceive you," Othon Hugues cried.

"Ask the pockmarked man why he has lied to you," Renno shouted. "Ask him why he instigated the shooting of Colonel Roy Johnson of the Tennessee Militia."

There was a long silence. El-i-chi moved into a defensive position, certain that the soldiers were coming to the attack.

"You, out there," Fellows called. "We will give you a chance to prove your identity. Lay down your arms and come forward."

"Not likely!" El-i-chi shouted. "You come forward, or we will prove our identity by killing more of your men if that is your wish."

"I will come to you unarmed," the lieutenant agreed.

The brothers waited in good cover, ready to fight. True to his word Fellows came walking through the trees, his hands empty. Renno stepped out. "Where is Hugues?"

"Here," came Othon Hugues's voice as a rifle exploded.

El-i-chi's quick action saved Renno's life, for he saw the movement in the brush as Hugues readied himself to fire, and just as the Frenchman pulled the trigger El-i-chi launched himself at his brother and sent Renno tumbling to the ground. The ball from Hugues's rifle sliced leaves just above Renno's head as he fell.

Renno, hitting the ground rolling, sent his tomahawk whistling through the air toward the spot from which Hugues had fired; but the Frenchman, seeing his shot miss, had run.

Renno leaped into pursuit, scooping up his tomahawk as he passed. A soldier stepped out to block his way and cried, "Here, what's going on?"

Renno slashed the surprised man's throat with his

tomahawk without breaking stride. Shots rang out, and balls thudded and whistled around him. He had to turn aside, for he was running into the main body of the detail.

"Hold your fire! Hold your fire!" Fellows was bellowing from behind Renno.

The white Indian circled the soldiers who stood in his path. The forest was dense, the light fading. As he moved toward the soldiers, he saw that Hugues was not among them. He cast around, looking for a track, but found nothing as the day came to an end.

The lieutenant was very apologetic. He blamed the entire affair on Hugues.

"Strange . . ." El-i-chi said. "I saw no officer's insignia on Hugues. Why was he giving the orders?"

"You don't understand," Fellows said. "He speaks for the general. I had no reason to doubt him."

A man ran up. His mouth was open, his eyes wide. "Lieutenant, we've got dead back there."

The lieutenant stiffened. "How many?"

"Four, five—I don't know."

"Where are all your other men?" Fellows demanded, looking at Renno.

"You see them," El-i-chi said.

"You lie," Fellows accused.

El-i-chi's hand twitched on his tomahawk.

"Enough," Renno said. He opened his pouch and handed Fellows Thomas Jefferson's letter.

The wagons were back together. Beth had treated and bandaged Roy's wound. Now, as with the sergeant whom Othon Hugues had tried to kill, it was a matter of waiting to learn if Roy's injury was only on the surface or if the force of the ball as it cut the groove at the base of his scalp had damaged the soft, fragile gray matter inside the skull.

With the morning the wagons were ready to move northward. El-i-chi was alert, long rifle in hand, for the white soldiers had buried their dead at sunup, and there was angry muttering among them. "I do not want them at my back," he explained.

Lieutenant Fellows, standing stiff and tall, came into Renno's camp. "We will escort you to Natchez," he offered.

"That won't be necessary," El-i-chi told him.

"Lieutenant," Roy said, "your men lost some friends yesterday, and they're mighty unhappy about it. No insult intended, but you haven't impressed me with your ability to handle your men, letting them ambush an old man, women, and children."

"It was not an old man, women, or children who killed my soldiers," Fellows said stiffly.

"No," Roy agreed, "it was you and Othon Hugues who did that, wasn't it?" He touched his bandaged head. "Now I think my sons and I have had about enough of soldiers of the United States for a while, so I suggest, Lieutenant, that you ride on ahead and tell whoever's in command at the post in Natchez that a personal emissary of President Thomas Jefferson is coming to call. And if there's any more misunderstanding, you'll face three of us next time, and I'm not sure you could survive that."

Fellows's face was red with shame. He whirled and stalked away.

"Well, isn't Roy the diplomat?" Renno asked, shaking his head.

"He's so tactful that now we might have to kill them all," El-i-chi said.

"I don't take it lightly when someone shoots me in the head," Roy seethed.

In spite of the obvious ill will from the friends of the men who were left behind in graves marked only with crosses made of tree branches, the trip into Natchez was without incident. Renno and El-i-chi scouted ahead and to the side. Othon Hugues was still out there somewhere, and although he had been frustrated in several attempts to have his revenge on Renno, hatred as strong as that held by Hugues was dangerous.

The colonel in charge of the garrison at Natchez welcomed the travelers. The horses that had been left behind on the way south were found to be well fed and groomed. Roy's wound was healing nicely. The young sergeant who had been struck over the head by Othon Hugues had fallen unconscious during the return to Natchez and had died two days after his injury. No one in Natchez had seen Othon Hugues.

Beth, on behalf of the entire group, turned down an invitation to have dinner with the colonel. She was concerned about Renno. Having been forced to kill young soldiers was not sitting easy with him, and he was burning with the need to find Othon Hugues and kill him swiftly and finally. She knew her husband well, and she had already accepted the knowledge that he would be leaving her as soon as they arrived home, if not before. For the first time, she feared for him; she believed that he would not be content to go after Hugues but would also seek the death of General James Wilkinson.

Since none of them was eager to spend any more time than necessary in Natchez, the wagon train was under way the morning after their arrival in the city. The men pushed the mules hard, starting out early and traveling until late in the day. With each turn of the wheels they were nearer to home. No one was surprised when, four days north of Natchez, Renno announced one evening that he would be leaving them.

"I will go with you," El-i-chi offered.

Renno shook his head. "From the beginning it has been my fight with the Frenchman," he said. "I leave my wife and my son in your hands, Brother."

"I'll be around, too, in case you've forgotten," Roy said testily.

"And in your hands," Renno added. "I know that they will be doubly safe."

"What's your plan?" Roy asked.

"I'll travel up the river, by boat if possible."

"You're sure, then, that Hugues is heading for St. Louis?" Roy asked.

"The woman is there," Renno said. "And Wilkinson."

"Renno, I understand why you have to go after this Frenchman," Roy said. "He's been a threat to your family since he killed poor Renna's husband. I'd go for him myself, if I were you. I think, though, that you'd better leave Wilkinson alone."

"So," Renno said, but he looked as if he did not agree.

"He's an influential man," Roy said. "You and I know he's a scoundrel and a traitor, but they don't seem to know that in Washington City. Going after a general in his own headquarters might not be such a good idea."

"I hope you're listening to him," Beth said, shaking Renno's arm.

"I hear," Renno said, obviously not convinced.

Beth sighed. "And I know that tone of voice only too well." She clung to him. "Please, Renno, listen to Roy. If what you tell me is true, Wilkinson was and is probably under the influence of that witch. So he's not responsible, is he? Wouldn't it be enough just to kill Hugues?"

Renno put his hand on Beth's and smiled down at her. "I will not miss my mother's wedding to this old bear," he said. "I will travel fast, and I will be with you before the leaves begin to turn." He winked at Roy. "So, lover boy, you must keep your passions in check until I return."

"I'm not making any promises," Roy said with a grin. "Once a hot-blooded man like me gets together with a beautiful, mature woman—"

"You're speaking of my mother," El-i-chi reminded.

"I'm speaking of the woman I'm going to marry, sprout," Roy said.

Beth clung to Renno. "You have never lied to me," she whispered. "So I will be expecting you before the beginning of autumn."

The white Indian watched the last of the wagons go over the top of a rise. Behind each wagon a pair of Beth's fine horses were being led. When he could no longer see the top of the wagon, he felt something drain out of him, and he suffered an acute longing to forget his duty, to run after them, to take his wife into his arms, to ride with his son and his nephew, to exchange good-natured jibes with El-i-chi and Roy. With a concerted effort he turned his face toward the Mississippi and, using game trails and the tracks that connected scattered Choctaw villages, ran until his lungs ached, then continued to run until the pain and longing were past. Only then did he slow to the pace of a Seneca messenger on an urgent mission.

William Eaton's army had become a horde. When the corps made camp, the evening was filled with the mewling and crying of babies, the chattering of women as they did laundry, the bleatings of goats, the alien, grunting bellows of camels, the babble of voices in several languages.

Little Hawk had hired a woman to do his laundry so that he had clean shirts, underwear, and stockings. By day he scouted an ancient land for water and good campsites. One night he chose an ancient castle as a campground. O'Bannon and he pitched their tent in the shelter of a shattered wall. While driving the tent pegs Little Hawk found three silver coins. O'Bannon, who had been in Greece, said the inscriptions were in the language of that country.

There were two wells filled to the top with water, but the water was too bitter for drinking. Little Hawk sought out William Eaton and suggested that although the water was not fit for consumption, it would be excellent for bathing. So it was that Eaton and a bunch of naked marines splashed and cavorted and soaped themselves while Arabs, male and female, watched in awe, thinking that Eaton Pasha and his saber-wielding soldiers had lost their senses.

Freshened by the bath, Eaton sat with the marines and watched a fiery sunset. Little Hawk showed him the Greek coins. "These date back to the time of Alexander," Eaton said. "Very fine mementos of your time in North Africa, Hawk."

"Please take one of them as my gift," Little Hawk offered.

"Thank you," Eaton said. "My pleasure." He squinted up at the ruined turrets of the castle. "Built by crusaders," he mused. "It's an ancient land, boys. And we are not the first, by any means, to fight here. I'd imagine that Phoenician ships sailed along this coast. King Solo-

mon's navy of Tharshish sailed past, and then there were
the Greeks and the Romans. The Crusaders came and
went rather swiftly, and then the Turks."

"And now the United States Marines," O'Bannon
muttered under his breath.

That was the night that Hamet Karamanli deserted.
With the morning he was gone. Eaton sent a force com-
manded by his most trusted sheikhs to bring Hamet back.
They succeeded.

"I will stand no more from you," Eaton furiously told
him. "If you give me any more trouble, I will drag you
to Derna by your hair. I'm going to put you on the throne
of Tripoli if I have to do it with you in irons."

Hamet remained silent, but he began a subtle campaign among the Tripolitanians to undermine Eaton's
authority. A few days later, while Eaton was riding with
Little Hawk and an advance party looking for an oasis that
was supposed to be within reach, Hamet ordered the main
body to halt early in the day at a water hole that was
inadequate to supply the entire army. When Eaton and
the advance party rode back, the Arabs were taking their
ease at midafternoon.

"Eaton Pasha," a sheikh said, "we have no food."

"And you will not find it by sitting here in the Cyre-
naican desert," Eaton said.

"We are hungry," another Arab complained.

O'Bannon assembled his few marines, for it was evident that mutiny was in the air. Eaton, while listening to
the criticisms that began to come thick and fast, motioned
Little Hawk to his side and whispered, "Get the Greek
cavalry. Place them in battle formation behind me."

Little Hawk left discreetly. Soon the Greeks, led by
Selim the Janissary, moved into position behind Eaton.
The sound of their rifles being cocked quieted the Arabs.

Eaton dismounted and walked to a position between
the two opposing forces. "As of now," he said in his finest
oratorical Arabic, "I resign as commander of this army. I
will pay the wages of my staff and my Greeks and of the
Arab officers who have been loyal to me. I will take my

men, and I will ride to my rendezvous with the American
fleet, where there will be food and water in plenty. There
I will feast and wallow in sweet, fresh water while I forget
those who quailed in the face of danger. Finally, I will
return to my country. I will leave you, who no longer
trust my leadership, to the desert, and I pray to Allah
that you do not starve or fall into the hands of Yusef to
be executed."

A low moan of protest came from the Arabs. It was
not so much out of loyalty to Eaton, Little Hawk and
O'Bannon decided later, as out of fear of being left to die
of hunger or of the malice of Yusef in the desert.

The crisis, however, was not over. The food supply
was very short; water was always a problem. By the middle of April it seemed that Eaton's army would perish or
disintegrate. The only thing that would keep the force
together was to reach the sea and rendezvous with the
navy—soon. Little Hawk rode far in front of the army
through a forbidding landscape of sunbaked rocks and
burning sand. Night came, but still he rode on. He was
about to turn back when, topping a hill, he saw the
blessed Mediterranean. He galloped back with the good
news.

With the morning the army and its followers
streamed down the arid hills to the sea. In spite of maps
that were products more of imagination than knowledge,
and despite the self-styled guides who, had they been
followed, would have sent the group to their deaths in the
trackless deserts, Eaton had led his army to a point not
five miles from the appointed meeting with U.S. Navy
ships laden with food and water.

Little Hawk watched as Eaton rode away from the
main group. He followed. Between two sand dunes, with
the sea in front of him, Eaton fell to his knees and in a
soft voice thanked not Allah but the God of Moses and
Abraham for his guidance. The Seneca backed away, not
wanting to disturb Eaton's prayers.

The officer in charge of the naval forces was Lieutenant Isaac Hull. Hull confirmed that Yusef was reinforcing
the thousand-man garrison at Derna.

"Lieutenant Hull," Eaton said, "just be sure that your squadron is at Derna on April twenty-fifth, for on that day the battle for Tripoli will begin."

Then the general rode back to join his army.

The men who had spent weeks in the unforgiving desert felt as if they had found the Garden of Eden as they approached Derna from the land. Riding down the barren eastern ridge of a massif called Jebel Akhdar, Eaton's army came into the rich delta of the Wadi Derna, a dry river that filled only when the winter rains were plentiful. Before the troops stretched luxuriant palm gardens watered by perennial springs. The town itself was perched over a small harbor that was unprotected from the northwest to the southeast, rendering it unusable in bad weather.

Because the town was surrounded on the land side by rocky rises, stone was a common building material, giving the town a look of solidity and permanence. Native stone had also been used to construct a protective wall in a semicircle on the land side. Two stone forts faced the sea.

William Eaton was riding with his marine guards at the head of the horde when it came down from the Jebel Akhdar onto the plain. He halted and used his spyglass to examine the town's fortifications.

"No surprises there," he remarked, surveying the wall and checking the two forts. "By damn," he said, "it doesn't seem as if they're expecting us."

Little Hawk saw that a gate on the eastern wall was open.

"Hawk, let's you and me take a little ride," Eaton suggested.

"Sir," said O'Bannon, "we've come a long way. If anything should happen to you, we'll have made the trip for nothing."

"Bosh," Eaton said. "Nothing's going to happen to me."

"Nevertheless," O'Bannon said, "I submit, General, that you are too valuable to risk."

Eaton laughed heartily. "Come with us, then, O'Bannon."

"Corporal," O'Bannon yelled, "prepare to move out."

"No, no," Eaton said. "We don't want to attract too much attention. Four men total—that's all."

Eaton put the spur to his horse so that Little Hawk, O'Bannon, and the marine whom O'Bannon selected had to ride hard to catch up. Eaton was riding directly toward the fortification's gate. Little Hawk came up beside him and grinned back at Eaton's wide smile as they swept through the gate in a cloud of dust.

"There," Eaton said, pointing to two members of the town's garrison, two very surprised Arabs.

The startled men took flight but in one wild, glorious dash were scooped up by Eaton and Little Hawk and dragged out of the city. Outside they halted, and Eaton informed the two wretched Arabs that they were prisoners of the Army of Tripolitanian Liberation and the United States Marines. The prisoners rode behind Eaton and Little Hawk to the campsite, where the general interrogated each of the prisoners separately.

Eaton sought out the marines after he had heard the men out. "According to our prisoners, only a hundred and fifty of the reinforcements sent by Yusef have reached Derna," he reported. "The main body of Yusef's troops are at least three days from the city. On the negative side, the governor, Bey Mustafa, has about eleven hundred men behind breastworks inside the city walls. The southwest sector of the defenses seems to be the strongest." He nodded at Little Hawk. "Hawk, I'd appreciate one of your scouting trips, if you please. Find me the best way to mount an attack in force."

"Yes, sir," Little Hawk said.

"Come along, now, though," Eaton told him. "Before it gets dark we'll have a look from on high."

They climbed a rocky ridge to a height overlooking the walled town. To the west the sun was low. The rock face was pocked by caves. "Tombs of the ancient Greeks," Eaton said. He led the way into one of the dark cavities.

Little Hawk was saddened to see that the ancient carved Greek motifs had been mutilated.

"The Moors and the followers of Allah," Eaton explained. "Erasing reference to anything other than Islam."

He sat on a carved ledge while Little Hawk explored into the darkness. "Ah," Eaton said, sighing, "what destruction man has wrought in the name of his gods."

"Not only in the name of his gods," Little Hawk said, "for I have read that a Turk used the Sphinx as a practice target for his cannon."

"Both the Christians and the men of Islam destroyed ancient architectural works to steal the material for building their ugly little churches and mosques," Eaton said. "And not even the dead can rest in peace, Hawk, here no more than in Egypt. Once, these rock tombs held the remains of men and women who came here from across the sea to establish an outpost of civilization. Time and the Moorish hordes swept them away—even their ashes—and mutilated the decorations of their resting places. Now they, too, are gone." He rose and walked to stand in the red glow of the setting sun.

"Hawk," he said, "after we take Derna I'm going to build a fort on one of these high places, a fort strong enough so that no rag-headed tyrant like Yusef will ever again impose harsh rule on this place." He changed the subject abruptly. "There," he said, pointing. "You can see inside the walls. They *are* strongest in the southeast."

Chapter XVII

Little Hawk left the marine camp shortly after dark. He paused to allow his eyes to adjust to the light of stars and moon before making the last descent from the hills to the southwest of the city. He moved slowly and carefully toward the walls of Derna to find that there were several natural obstacles in the form of wadis, which would make a charge from the southwest very difficult. He circled the city and approached the wall from several angles, making evaluations. From inside the city he heard a dog barking steadily and tirelessly.

When he returned to camp just before sunrise, approaching it with more care then he had exercised in scouting the walls of Derna lest he be shot by a nervous Arab sentry, he went directly to Eaton's tent. The general was at his breakfast, his European staff officers around him.

"Ah, Hawk," Eaton said cheerily. "Good morning."

Little Hawk gave Eaton his report, illustrating with diagrams the various approaches to the wall.

"Good, good," Eaton approved. "So here we are, young Hawk. The *Nautilus* is standing off the harbor at this time. The *Argus* and the *Hornet* will arrive during the day. I will signal Lieutenant Hull that our attack will begin at dawn tomorrow."

Little Hawk went to the tent he shared with Presley O'Bannon. The lieutenant was up and around. He listened with great interest as Little Hawk described the best means of attaining the wall of Derna and made his own little sketches on a rumpled piece of paper.

"Now, my friend," O'Bannon said, "you'd better get some sleep."

The young Seneca tried to do so, but seemingly every Arab in Eaton's mob found it necessary to traipse past the tent while talking at the top of his voice. Camels bellowed. On the other side of the camp an alarm or a buzzard flying overhead triggered a wild spattering of rifle fire. Dogs barked. Little Hawk crawled out of his blankets and began a letter to his father.

"Lieutenant O'Bannon is determined that even though our numbers are few, the marines will do more than our share in the storming of Derna," he wrote. "He has indicated to me that he will request that we be placed to the southeast, where the defenses are strongest."

He put down the pen, tore up the paper, and began again. This time he wrote about the country, the people, and the heat of the days and the chill of the nights in the desert. He spoke of the contrast between the blistering wastes of rocks and sand and the cool, shady forests of home. He wrote of his desire to see his family and to splash in the swimming creek near the village. Before he finished, his eyelids were heavy. He sank back onto the blankets and this time was able to fall asleep. The letter he had begun fluttered in a little breeze that came in through the open flap of the tent.

In accordance with the rules of warfare, Eaton sent an offer of a peaceful change of leadership to the governor of Derna, who answered, "My head or yours."

The day seemed to pass all too swiftly. In the early hours of the night Little Hawk was once again in the fields before Derna, rechecking the lanes of approach that he had recommended to Eaton. The young marine was in bed shortly after midnight and slept well.

Eaton had divided his army into four groups. Lieutenant O'Bannon was in command of a strike force made up of his marines, plus half of the Greek mercenaries and dismounted Bedouin horsemen. Eaton had agreed to O'Bannon's request; the marine force would launch its assault from the southeast with the support of the army's few fieldpieces.

Selim the Janissary would advance from the hills to the south. His movements would be slow because of the difficulty of the terrain.

The Arab cavalry were in position to the southwest and had three responsibilities to fulfill: to cut off any retreat of Derna's garrison toward the west, to act as a mobile reserve, and to prevent Yusef's reinforcements from reaching the city if, by any chance, the relief force from Tripoli had moved faster than expected.

The last group, the largest, was under Eaton's personal command. He would hold back until the attack by Selim the Janissary and the marine force gave him an indication of the positioning of the men within the wall.

Little Hawk and O'Bannon were sheltering in a wadi when Derna's shore guns opened fire at 5:20 A.M. The muted roar of the town's nine-pounders was answered by the thunder of the monstrous twenty-four-pounders on the *Argus*. Soon the *Hornet* and the *Nautilus* joined in.

"Midshipman," O'Bannon said formally to Little Hawk, "you may tell your men to advance."

The Seneca grinned, remembering William Eaton's joke about the famous words of George Washington. What would be a good way to order American fighting men to attack a strongly fortified position in a land far from their homes?

"All right, Marines!" he shouted. "Let's go get 'em!"

Behind them the fieldpieces opened up. A ball landed not fifty yards in front of them as they advanced slowly, causing a stir of nervousness among the Bedouin. Little Hawk looked back toward the rise where the cannon were mounted, just in time to see one of them blow up. The explosion tumbled gunners, and then there was no more cannon fire. The second fieldpiece had been damaged by the explosion, and that marked the end for artillery support.

The Greeks, to the left and the right of the small marine force, were holding up well. Men advanced from cover to cover. There was no mad rush, no screaming charge with men falling to the left and the right. Rifle fire from the top of the wall was peppering all around them.

"In military terms, Hawk," O'Bannon said, "that would be called a brisk counterfire."

"In Greek we call it—" said one of the mercenaries, ending his comment with a stream of words that had the ring of profanity, even if only Greeks could understand it exactly.

"Take cover!" O'Bannon bellowed. "Fire at targets of opportunity."

The attack force to the south moved toward the heights directly south of the city and began to dig in. The marines and the Greeks kept up a steady fire against the wall's defenders. The sun climbed; the day grew hot. From inside the city much of the bey's firepower was moved to face the marines. Bey Mustafa probably saw that the attacking force to the south showed no indication of leaving the shelter of their trenches.

The air above Little Hawk's head seemed alive. The Bedouin hugged the ground, while the Greeks cursed and kept up their fire. O'Bannon sent a runner to Eaton with the message that it was getting pretty hot and that unless something happened soon, he'd have to pull back.

Eaton's response was not long in coming.

"Good God, look at that!" a marine yelled as Eaton's force charged across open ground, Eaton at the fore, long robes flying behind him, scimitar flashing and whirling over his head.

The fire that had pinned down O'Bannon's force shifted. Eaton's group was taking the casualties.

"Let's go, let's go!" O'Bannon yelled, leaping to his feet.

Little Hawk led the Greeks and Bedouin forward,

roaring the battle cry of the Seneca. Eaton's Arabs were
at the wall. Men left their saddles and scrambled up and
over the top. Little Hawk was aiming his charge at the
wall near the gate. A man to his left fell, another pitched
forward at his right.

. He yelled his defiance and was at the wall, dropping
his rifle to climb up in a frantic surge. He jumped down
the other side, slashed the throat of a defender with his
scimitar, and ran to open the gate.

O'Bannon and the marines awaiting outside streamed
through, their rifles blasting. The Greeks and the Bedouin
followed, screaming, firing, and creating a bedlam of
sound to which the roar of the naval bombardment served
as a thunderous background.

William Eaton was leading the charge toward the
breastworks. Defenders were fleeing. A man shrieked in
mortal agony. Other men threw down their weapons and
surrendered.

"Mr. O'Bannon," Eaton called out, "you may push
forward."

The city's defenders retreated ahead of the marines'
advance and crowded into a walled enclave in the western
end of the city. O'Bannon and Little Hawk led their force
to the harbor. A few screaming defenders rose to face
them. O'Bannon's saber and Little Hawk's scimitar cleared
the way, leaving the dead and dying behind them.

Three men sprang up in front of Little Hawk. He
trilled a Seneca war cry and swept his scimitar above his
head, causing the blade to whistle. The three men threw
down their arms, fell to their knees, and begged for quarter. They were handed back to the Bedouin for keeping.

The *Argus* was at anchor in the harbor, her guns
blasting away steadily. Little Hawk saluted the ship with
his blade and saw his greetings returned by a uniformed
officer on the deck.

"What do we do now?" O'Bannon asked.

Little Hawk pointed his blade toward the main harbor
fort, a pile of stone called Ras el Matariz. O'Bannon nodded, then yelled "Go, go, go!"

Marines and Greeks streamed toward the fort. There
was sporadic defensive fire, but casualties were light. And

then they were inside the fort, and the defenders were surrendering as fast as they could lay down their weapons.

"Hey, Lieutenant!" a marine yelled. "Have a look at these." He indicated several six-inch cannon in working order.

Taking advantage of the unexpected opportunity, O'Bannon sent a runner to Eaton and asked for artillerymen, and soon the guns of the Ras el Matariz were turned against their owners and shelling the last holdouts in the western part of the city.

Meanwhile, the American forces outside the city, seeing that Eaton and the marines were inside the walls, renewed their attacks enthusiastically.

By 4:15 the fighting had stopped. The governor, Bey Mustafa, was found hiding in a small mosque.

A very happy William Eaton came to congratulate the marines. He had taken a ball in his left wrist. A crude splint had been applied atop a bloody bandage.

Now it was time to rest, to count the dead, to add up the cost. The Greeks, who had fought well, had suffered casualties. One marine was dead, and two were wounded, one seriously. Both O'Bannon and Little Hawk were difficult to recognize, their faces streaked with powder stains, their uniforms soiled.

Presley O'Bannon sat on a parapet in the fort, looked out over the harbor where the flag of the United States flew from the masts of the ships, then gazed up to see the Stars and Stripes flying over the Ras el Matariz as well. He wiped his face on his kerchief and looked at the soil that had been transferred. And what were the famous words of the famous lieutenant O'Bannon after a famous victory? "Hawk," he said, "I'm so damned tired I can hardly move."

There was to be no rest for the victors at Derna. Eaton halted the celebration and put men to work building new breastworks, strengthening the walls, and putting damaged cannon back into working order. On the heights from which Selim had attacked, Eaton built a fort on the foundations of an ancient Roman installation, for he, like the Romans, recognized the site as being perfect for the defense of Derna from the land and the sea.

The commodores of the navy, not recognizing the importance of Eaton's victory, did not press the blockade of Tripoli. Eaton said to O'Bannon and Little Hawk, "If they had followed our taking of this city with a crushing attack on Tripoli, this war would be over."

On May 13 Yusef's forces attacked Derna. Eaton's fort on the heights poured deadly fire into the attackers, and the warships in the harbor joined in. The attack stalled and failed.

Little Hawk was finding that life in occupied Derna was rather pleasant. He had taken quarters in a house abandoned by one of the city's rich men. Two of the servants, a chubby older woman and her daughter, having no other place to go, begged Little Hawk to allow them to stay in their quarters. Of course he agreed. Food and supplies came to the marines from the American ships, and the two women worked miracles with the small amount of money that Little Hawk could give them.

He ate heartily and slept well. He could have shared his bed with the daughter—that was made clear to him by both the young woman and the mother. He was strongly tempted and once went so far as to call her to his room.

She was dressed in the usual concealing garment, her face hidden by a veil. He lifted the veil, saw her almond eyes, dark and sultry, saw smooth, dusky skin and lips of natural redness, and the blood rose in him, causing his breath to catch in his throat. His hands felt a small, shapely waist, moved to cup unfettered, youthful breasts, and then, as if something had spoken to him, he stepped back and sent her away. In his mind were the unabating memories from his sexual encounter with Melisande, the Witch of the Pyrenean Woods—visions of plush ripeness overlaid by the black-toothed smile of a repulsive, evil woman. Little Hawk realized that more time would have to pass before he was fully recovered from that bizarre encounter and could put the witch completely from his mind.

For the city of Tripoli the beginning of June was a terror. At last the American Mediterranean squadron was using its devastating power against Yusef Karamanli, bashaw of the pirate state. Yankee frigates thundered ruin down on the city.

The crew of the ill-fated *Philadelphia*, in the bashaw's dungeons, had listened to the sounds of the bombardment with an elation that overcame their dread of being killed by the gunfire of their own countrymen. Even those who were sick and weak gave a few feeble cheers each day when the shelling recommenced.

When the roar of the naval cannon ceased in the middle of the day on June 3, the prisoners dared not speculate on the meaning of the sudden silence. They had no way of knowing that Yusef had surrendered, raising the white flag over his battered citadel, or that Colonel Tobias Lear, consul general of the United States to the Barbary nations of North Africa, and Commodore John Rogers, American commander in the Mediterranean, were at that very moment signing a preliminary treaty with the bashaw.

When the portals of the prison opened late in the afternoon the emaciated, haggard Americans who had been slaves of the bashaw for so long looked with dull eyes toward the light, worried that they might see the hated, familiar faces of their overseers. Instead they saw the stern, pale face of a United States naval officer, surrounded by fleet marines.

"Gentlemen," said the officer, standing with his back straight and his eyes forward, as if to avoid looking at the abject misery of the prisoners, "I bring you greetings from your president and your country."

Joyous bedlam ensued. The officer, at attention, was saluting. The joyous crew of the *Philadelphia* swarmed around him, clapped the marines on their backs, asked questions all at once, yelled, and wept.

Stronger men helped the ailing to abandon the filthy room where they had lived for so long.

In a courtyard outside the main dungeon the men of the *Philadelphia* saw their former jailers lined up in ragged ranks. Marine carbines were pointed at them. One ragged scarecrow stepped toward the Moslems and spat into the face of a guard who had tormented him. Others jeered and offered insulting remarks about the female ancestors of the overseers.

But it was too festive a day to be spent in petty revenge. Now their thoughts turned to going home and being reunited with loved ones. The men of the *Philadelphia* were relieved to be free, in the open air, and hearing the voices of fellow Americans.

They were moved slowly toward the waterfront to be taken on board ship for medical attention. When those in the forefront of the group rounded a corner and had an open view of the harbor, they saw the American navy there, proud ships with the Stars and Stripes flying bravely from their mastheads and snapping smartly in the wind. The others crowded round. The officer in charge and the marines halted with the former prisoners, and many of them wept openly as, one by one, the newly freed Americans lifted their hands in salute to the flag of the United States.

On that same day Commodore Rogers wrote a note to Naval Agent Eaton in Derna. All Americans in Derna, along with any Christian who wanted to be evacuated, would be picked up by the frigate *Constellation*.

The *Constellation* sailed into Derna harbor on June 11, just after forces still loyal to Yusef had made another failing attack on the city. A junior naval lieutenant brought Eaton a copy of the treaty with Yusef and the letter from Commodore Rogers. Eaton's face went pale when he read that the United States had paid a ransom, after all, of sixty thousand dollars for the crew of the *Philadelphia*. But when he read the letter from Rogers, ordering him to abandon Derna, he roared in protest so loudly that it brought Little Hawk running into the room.

"Hawk!" Eaton shouted. "Can you tell me why we walked hundreds of miles through the desert?"

Little Hawk knew that Eaton did not expect an answer.

"Why did we fight and bleed"—his wrist was still stiff from his wound—"and die? Why have we worked so hard to defend this city against counterattacks, to fortify it, to bring peaceful and fair rule to the countryside here-abouts?" He threw the papers at the abashed young mid-shipman. "Why? So that those gutless blunderers could give the country back to Yusef! So that he could *save face,* by God, and so he can say, when we leave this godforsa-ken country, that he withstood the full fury of the United States of America and still collected on his ransom demands!"

Eaton was silent for several moments as he fought mightily to control his temper. "Tell your captain," he said to the junior naval lieutenant, "that Colonel Lear, Commodore Rogers, and all of their ilk can go straight to the devil."

While messages were exchanged back and forth, Eaton continued to rule Derna and the surrounding coun-tryside in the name of the hapless Hamet Karamanli. The *Constellation,* with her huge guns, was joined in Derna harbor by the *Hornet,* and there were orders from Rogers to embark all Americans by persuasion or by force. The captain of the *Constellation,* William Campbell, came ashore and ate goat-meat stew with Eaton in the gover-nor's palace. Eaton was dressed in the robes of a sheikh.

When the meal was finished, Campbell said, "Well, Mr. Eaton, odious as it is for me to do so, I must ask you your intentions."

Eaton spoke in a quiet voice. "I cannot allow a naval bombardment to be laid down by my own countrymen upon the small force of American heroes who gave our nation a great victory," he said. "We will accompany you, Captain."

Little Hawk felt his eyes sting as the Stars and Stripes flying over Derna were hauled down. He saw that Eaton was weeping as well. One of the marines who had been wounded during the taking of Derna had died. O'Bannon, Little Hawk, and the four surviving men stood at stiff attention. They were dressed in freshly washed and pressed blues and whites. Their weapons gleamed with polishing. Even as Eaton and the marines, the last men of the victorious force to leave the city, were being rowed out to the *Constellation*, Yusef's supporters were entering from the inland side.

"Well," O'Bannon said, "we're on the way home, Hawk."

Little Hawk could not speak.

By the time the *Constellation* reached Tripoli, Colonel Lear had signed the final form of the treaty with Yusef. Eaton read it in Lear's presence and turned his eyes on the colonel to say, "You have included no provision to protect Hamet Karamanli and his family. The minute we clear the harbor Yusef will have them killed, and I will not have that. Unless you amend this treaty, I will go back into the desert, reorganize my army, and personally will conduct war against Yusef until I hang his head in the public square."

The treaty was amended to guarantee the safety of Hamet and his family and to allow them to live anywhere in Tripoli if they desired.

On August 6, 1805, William Eaton and his marines sailed for home on the *Constellation*. As the frigate sailed westward, Eaton spent many hours preparing his report for the secretary of the navy, with copies for the president, the secretary of state, and selected members of the Congress.

In 1805 St. Louis was a town of just under one thousand residents, mostly of French origin. Pierre Liguest Laclede, a fur trader, had chosen the site of the town, a shelf under a river bluff, in 1764, naming it for Louis IX, the crusader king.

The Spanish takeover in 1770 did not change the essential French character of St. Louis any more than did the American flag that flew over the town, which had begun to spread to the plain above the river, when Renno arrived there in the summer of 1805. Congress had created the district of Louisiana and named St. Louis as district headquarters. St. Louis had seen all that the frontier could offer, including a full attack by the Sioux and the British during the War for American Independence.

It did not take Renno long to learn that General James Wilkinson had not yet taken up his governorship, that he was still in the east, and that St. Louis was under the command of Captain Amos Stoddard. Upon hearing that Wilkinson was not in residence, Renno had a sinking feeling that he had traveled past the mouth of the Ohio to St. Louis for nothing. He rewarded himself with a room, a bed, a bath, and some woman-cooked food before venturing out to make inquiries about a pock-faced Frenchman and an odd female named Melisande.

Although some of the homes in St. Louis had good libraries and furniture, glass, and fine china brought from France, it was still very much a frontier town. A sun-bronzed man in buckskins with a long rifle in his hand and longbow over his shoulder would not draw more than a casual glance. His ability to speak French well made him even less noticeable and infinitely more acceptable to the majority of the citizens of the town.

Men in the grogshops were willing to talk to a fellow Frenchman, by his dress a trapper. They spoke of the Americans Lewis and Clark, who had passed through St. Louis on their way to the Missouri only the year before. They talked of having lived under three flags, and most residents agreed that being a part the United States was preferable to being under the rule of the Spaniards. And, at last, one of them said, "*Oui, monsieur,* I know this one. He is *très* ugly, no?"

"His face is marked by the pox," Renno said.

"And he lives with the woman with the black teeth, *non?* What is she called?"

"Melisande," Renno said.

"*Oui, oui.*"

"Where?" Renno asked.

"This pockmarked one, he is a—something—I don't know. *Militaire, non?* He has quarters near the army post. They are calling it Jefferson Barracks, in honor of your—our president, you know."

"Thank you," Renno said.

He found a pub frequented mainly by the soldiers of the barracks and struck up a conversation with a grizzled old sergeant who wore the insignia of Anthony Wayne's American Legion on his uniform.

"Hell, I know you," the sergeant erupted after they'd talked a little while. "You and Roy Johnson scouted for the legion!"

After that there was a long time spent in exchanging reminiscences before Renno could inquire about Othon Hugues.

"That bastard," the old sergeant fumed. "We caught him molesting a young Injun girl. Right near the barracks, mind you. Captain told him to take his French wench and get out of St. Louis or be hanged."

"Do you know which way they traveled?" Renno asked. Once again he felt the onset of futility, a sense of loss touched with the sudden hope that he could go home. The feeling passed quickly, however.

"Just happen to know," the sergeant said. "Saw 'em myself. Talked to 'em. Hugues said he was going over into Illinois Territory. Said he had a hankering to meet a feller called Tecumseh."

"So," Renno said.

He penetrated into the Illinois Territory by canoe, up the Illinois River. He had never been quite so far to the northwest, although during the campaign that had ended at Fallen Timbers he had traveled north of the Ohio as far west as the Wabash, somewhere to the east. There, he knew, were Fort Harrison in the Indiana Territory and the areas governed by William Henry Harrison. White encroachment was pushing swiftly into the lands that had once been the hunting grounds of the Shawnee, Miami, and Illinois Indians.

He traveled through a wilderness that seemed far removed from the border wars and the sporadic conflict urged on by the Chief of the Beautiful River, Tecumseh.

Renno wore the paint of a Seneca messenger, a sign of peaceful intentions, and when he began to encounter those who lived and hunted along the Illinois, he gave the hand signal of peace and inquired after Hugues and the witch. For a while he thought that the sergeant had been wrong in saying that Hugues and Melisande would try to reach Tecumseh himself, for the answer to his questions was always a shake of the head.

He had to force himself to travel on. It was said that Tecumseh's home was nearby, close to the old French trading post of Creve Coeur. The white Indian traveled one more day, then two. And on the second day he had word of Othon Hugues, but not by name. No one had seen the spirit animal that had savaged a young Mingo girl of eleven years, leaving her broken both internally and externally. Renno's face set in grim lines as the father of the girl described the ravages done to his daughter.

Hugues, the sachem whispered to himself.

Men of many tribes had followed Tecumseh into the Illinois wilderness. He spoke with Seneca become Mingo, with Erie, Huron, Potawatomi, Miami, Shawnee, Illinois, and Kickapoo. As he neared the place where it was said Tecumseh judged and led his people, the concentration of population increased. The spirits of the people were high. It was as if each man, each woman, had been bewitched by the words of the chief who was not a chief. Since Renno was on a private mission and longed only to complete it and go home, he made no attempt to dispute the generally voiced opinion that *this time* the white hordes would be driven back toward the distant sea.

Upon reaching the village of Tecumseh, Renno did not identify himself. He knew that fame traveled far among those of the blood, and he was certain that Renno of the Seneca, friend of the United States, would be less than welcome.

Tecumseh was away, traveling to the east to recruit warriors from among the conquered tribes. Tenskwatawa, the Prophet, brother to the Chief of the Beautiful River, strolled the dirt streets of a sizable village and lifted his hand in blessings to the faithful, always ready to repeat his latest conversation with the Master of Life.

Renno watched from a safe distance, for he had been face-to-face with the Prophet when the young man was in the Cherokee Nation with Tecumseh. Renno followed Tenskwatawa back to a large, central lodge and saw him disappear into the house. The sachem availed himself of the hospitality of a group of Cayuga warriors who had a fresh kill of venison. He ate with his eye on the entrance to Tenskwatawa's lodge, for he had learned from the Cayuga that the Prophet had a guest, a Frenchwoman of magic, and her man, who had an ugly, pockmarked face.

He saw Othon Hugues at twilight when the Frenchman came out of the lodge and walked into the woods to relieve himself.

"It is said," a Cayuga warrior told him in an awed voice, "that the woman of magic can control a man's very thoughts."

"Does she thus control the Prophet?" Renno asked.

"We pray to the spirits that she does not," the Cayuga answered fervently. "Soon Tecumseh will return, and then we will see what we will see."

Indian women carried food and water into the Prophet's lodge. Neither Othon nor the witch emerged. Renno slept near the Cayuga, for from their spot he could watch the entrance to the lodge. He had decided that the next time Hugues came out, as he would be forced by nature to do sooner or later, he would be followed to his place of privacy in the forest. There Renno would have to kill quietly and quickly, for it was obvious that Hugues and the witch had brought Tenskwatawa under their evil influence. A single order from the Prophet would set hundreds of warriors against Renno.

Renno was awake with the sun. He freshened himself with water, then waited. Unfortunately, it was not Hugues but the Prophet who came out of the lodge. He stood in the center of the commons and chanted his morning prayers to the Master of Life. When he was finished, he looked around at the gathering who had come to pray with him.

"Brothers," he said, lifting his hands, "there is a stranger among you. Let him stand forth."

The Cayuga warriors looked speculatively at Renno.

"Brothers," Tenskwatawa said, "this stranger bears ill will. He is not one of us. If he will not stand forth himself, it is up to you to point him out."

Two of the Cayuga moved toward Renno. He put his hand on his tomahawk and told them, "I will not allow you to have the betrayal of one of the blood on your conscience." He walked to stand opposite Tenskwatawa and greet him in Seneca.

"You have come far, Renno of the Seneca," Tenskwatawa said. "We agreed that one day we would stand face-to-face again."

"I do not come to war against you," Renno said.

"Yet there is death in your heart," the Prophet said. "She who sees beyond men's eyes has told me, and now I see it for myself."

"The man I seek is not of the blood," Renno said. "His name you know, Tenskwatawa."

"The man Othon Hugues and his woman have come to us in peace," Tenskwatawa said, "and to join our cause."

"The man Othon Hugues killed the husband of my daughter," Renno said. "Follow his back trail and speak to those who also know of his evil. Only a few days ago I talked with a father who had buried his eleven-year-old daughter. He had to look closely to be able to recognize her face after the brutality of Othon Hugues."

Melisande appeared in the doorway of the Prophet's lodge and tried to catch Renno's eyes. He refused to look directly at her.

"The Seneca lies," she accused.

"When you look at this woman, Tenskwatawa, what do you see?" Renno asked. "Do you see beauty and youth, or do you see the deep marks of age, and teeth as black as night?"

Tenskwatawa was startled. "There have been times," he admitted, "when indeed the visage of the woman changed before my eyes. I had thought it to be a trick of light or the power of her magic."

A gasp of horror suddenly went up from those who had gathered to speak with the Prophet. Renno turned. Stalking him was a creature from a nightmare, half-wolf, half-man. And even as the sachem watched, others joined the creature.

Tenskwatawa took a step backward, fear plain on his face.

"They do not come against you," Renno told him.

He turned his back on the advancing spirit beasts and

courageously stared directly into Melisande's eyes as he chanted under his breath to the manitous and concentrated all of his will against the woman.

For one fleeting moment her power changed her, and he saw the smiling face of An-da, the beloved mother of his son Ta-na, and the Sweet Day who had been his wife. He turned his back on her, and the powers of the manitous caused his eyes to burn with fire. The spirit beasts sizzled and became puffs of smoke drifting away on the breeze. The witch cringed back and screamed out in frustration, while behind Renno, people cried out in amazement.

The eyes of the Prophet were wide. This was magic greater than any he could ever hope to produce, and his people had witnessed it all. His shame became anger. "You invade my home and insult me," he said to Renno. He drew his tomahawk.

Renno gave the sign of peace. "You want to fight the wrong man, Prophet."

"I fight my enemy, a friend of the white man."

"I will not raise my weapon against you," Renno told him. "I claim peace in the name of the Master of Life and in the name of the Chief of the Beautiful River, Tecumseh."

"Then let there be peace at least for the moment," a powerful voice cried out. Faces turned. Tecumseh strode into the commons. "I have heard, Seneca," he said. "And I have seen. My eyes did not believe, but they saw. Let the woman of magic and the man come forth to face us."

"Brother of my blood," Renno said to Tecumseh, "look not into the woman's eyes."

"I hear," Tecumseh said, nodding.

Melisande emerged first.

Tecumseh kept his head turned and looked at her only out of the corner of his eye. "It is true," he whispered to Renno. "Her teeth are black, and she is wrinkled."

Now Othon Hugues came into the morning sun. He had a rifle in his hand. A tomahawk and a knife were in his belt. His ice-colored eyes darted wildly back and forth, finally to center on Renno, and an animallike growl of hatred rumbled from his throat.

Melisande screamed incomprehensible words. A plague

of winged, long-toothed creatures swarmed in the air, darting and swooping toward men's eyes, slashing with long claws that dripped venom. Tenskwatawa dropped in panic to the ground. Even Tecumseh cringed down, flailing with his tomahawk at the apparitions.

"Witch," Renno called out. "Witch, look at me."

Now it was Melisande who kept her eyes averted. Renno used his tomahawk to knock down one, two, of the shrieking, darting things in the air.

"Witch," Renno said softly, "see what happens to your minions." As he chanted under his breath to the manitous, bright spots of light, brighter than the morning sun, appeared in the air. The venomous flying monsters were consumed one by one.

"Tecumseh," Renno said, "I claim the right of justice. I claim trial by combat with the man who killed my daughter's husband."

"Nooooo," Melisande wailed. "We came to you as friends. Tenskwatawa, tell him! Tell him we are friends."

The Prophet, fearfully looking up into the air, climbed slowly to his feet.

"It is not a decision for my brother to make," Tecumseh declared. He faced Renno. "You have claimed to be my enemy."

"Not so," Renno denied. "For there is as yet no battle."

"True," Tecumseh allowed. He faced his people. "It is his right, is it not?"

"Yes," came the chorus of answers, for they had seen wonders and now looked forward to more as the man of great magic faced the woman of great magic and her companion.

"So be it," Tecumseh decided. "Hugues, it is your right to choose your weapon."

"I choose this," Hugues shouted, lifting and firing his rifle in one motion.

The ball slashed through the flesh of Renno's right arm without striking bone. He felt the powerful impact, as if he had been struck by a large, blunt club held in the hands of a giant. He swayed on his feet, momentarily stunned.

Othon drew a tomahawk and sprang to the attack.

Small creatures appeared at Renno's feet, beasts with teeth that found purchase to chew on his flesh and hinder his movements as he tried to avoid Hugues's rush. In his dazed state, Renno seemed frozen in place. Othon's tomahawk was descending. Onlookers cried out with shock, for it looked as if the fight was already over.

The spirit of old Ghonka sent Othon Hugues's killing blow astray by hurling a huge, spiked war club flying toward the Frenchman's face. The spirit's weapon looked real, and Othon yelled out in surprise and pulled back. His blade whistled past Renno's head.

Renno recovered to kick the biting spirit things aside and, tomahawk in his left hand, face Hugues.

"Witch," he called to Melisande, "watch as each of your evil creations is countered by the spirits of good."

Hugues looked at Melisande and drew courage from her. "Let me win this fight," he implored.

"So will it be," the witch said. "Since he fights with only one arm, and that the arm he does not prefer, you will win this time."

The spirit of An-da spoke softly into Renno's ear. "Husband, your left arm is now your right, and as powerful."

Hugues surged to the attack, his blade flashing to crash against Renno's. The force of the Frenchman's rush carried the sachem backward. He countered blow after blow, and with each passing second he was recovering more from the shock of the wound in his right arm. He felt the very real pain of spirit fangs in his back, and his mind, reinforced by the strength of the manitous and the powers of good, sent sheets of flame into the mind of the witch.

She screamed, and the spirit pain in Renno's back was ended as Melisande devoted all her power to protecting herself.

While it was true that the manitou of An-da had given new strength to his left arm, it was still not the same as his right. The power of his blows was just a bit less than usual, his aim slightly less skilled.

Those who watched the battle realized that it was

going to be a long fight, an even fight. Some of the warriors made wagers as the combatants moved across the
commons, blades striking sparks from each other. A sigh
went up when Othon Hugues's blade sliced through
Renno's tunic and brought blood; but it was quickly evident that the wound was shallow, for the fury of Renno's
response sent Hugues reeling backward. The Frenchman
roared in pain and fury as Renno's blade glanced off his
left shoulder and blood sprang up.

Back and forth the battle surged until Renno tripped
over a spirit serpent before he could counter Melisande's
new attack. He landed on his back. Hugues sprang to
come down atop him, blade descending. Quickly Renno
rolled aside and came to his feet. But it was too late to
take advantage of the Frenchman's surprise, for Hugues
had recovered and was crouched at the ready.

"You're not the great warrior you think yourself to
be," the Frenchman said, sneering, as he cautiously edged
forward. "You're nothing more than a shell, Seneca. I toy
with you."

Renno sent a feint to Hugues's throat, then switched
to strike the belly. The Frenchman parried the blow and,
laughing, swaggered forward. "You're only slightly more
skilled than the boy I killed on the banks of the Mississippi
River. And soon you will join him in death."

"But am I not just a bit more dangerous than eleven-
year-old girls?" Renno inquired.

Hugues roared in anger at the insult and rushed forward, only to fall away with a groan as Renno went low
and laid open a great gash across the Frenchman's thigh.

"Melisande!" Hugues cried out. "Melisande."

The ground rippled and rose up in folds in front of
Renno when he moved forward to finish off the French
fiend. He had the feeling that he was going to be sucked
into the maw of the earth, to be buried alive, and he
called upon the manitous to overcome the evil. Hugues's
tomahawk was coming in slow motion at his face. Renno
felt as if he had an age to move to one side. He swung
his own weapon under the blow and tilted it upward so
that the sharp blade sliced Hugues's Adam's apple and
windpipe, his tendons and arteries. The Frenchman top-

pled like an axed tree, blood gurgling in his severed throat.

A wild scream of anguish filled Renno's ears. He whirled just in time to avoid a swing of a tomahawk in the hands of the witch.

For one moment she was vulnerable. In that moment he could have killed her; but she caught his eyes, and her beauty blossomed. She was a young and innocent girl, and Renno did not kill girls. He drew back his weapon for a blow but held it as he fought to overcome her hypnotism, and by the time he saw her distorted face and her gleaming black teeth, it was too late. She was fading before his eyes and then was gone.

He turned. Othon Hugues's legs jerked and were still. Blood dampened the ground. To make certain, Renno bent, took a close look, and saw the glaze of death in the icy-pale eyes.

All was silent. The witch had vanished. Those who had witnessed her disappearance offered different versions of what had happened to her, but only a few were willing to admit that she had faded like the mists of a cool night in the warmth of the morning sun.

"Justice has been done," Tecumseh proclaimed.

"I pray, Chief, that it will be done on a larger scale," Renno said.

"As you fought for justice, so must we," Tecumseh intoned.

"Each man must make his own trail," Renno said. "My thanks to you, and my farewell."

"My healers will treat your wounds."

"They are nothing," Renno said.

"Go, then," Tecumseh said. "Now that I have seen you fight, Sachem, I pray that we never meet on the battlefield."

"As do I," Renno said.

He paused to clean his tomahawk of blood at the nearest stream, to cleanse his wounds, cover them with a leafy poultice, and to freshen himself. Then he turned his face toward the south and began to move at the warrior's pace. He had a long way to go before reaching home.

Chapter XVIII

The *Constellation* put into Gibraltar for supplies, but because Spain had become involved in the naval war between Great Britain and Napoleon's France, food was difficult to find. Sailing was delayed. Little Hawk and O'Bannon took long walks and, like good soldiers, complained. Finally, during an unpleasant crossing, the frigate sailed through Atlantic gales.

In Baltimore, Little Hawk said good-bye to O'Bannon and the four marines who had survived the taking of Derna; then he traveled to Washington with Eaton.

Little Hawk knew that Eaton had spent a lot of time writing his report to the powers in Washington, but since leaving Derna, Eaton and he had not been close. The general was obviously dissatisfied over the outcome of the war in North Africa but had not discussed it with his personal marine aide. Upon their arrival in the capital city Eaton, preoccupied, shook Little Hawk's hand and wished him luck.

The Seneca made his way to the executive mansion.

General William Eaton would not have been the only one to be surprised had he seen how quickly the midshipman was admitted to President Thomas Jefferson's office.

Little Hawk was impressive in his marine blues and whites. He had spent hours on his uniform, and the *Constellation*'s barber had trimmed his hair just before the ship reached Baltimore. He stood at attention and saluted.

Jefferson rose, came around his desk, and with genuine enthusiasm shook Little Hawk's hand. "I have reports, of course, of the march to Derna," he said, "but I want to hear your personal account." He frowned and flicked a glance toward the door. "The problem is that there are about a dozen men waiting to see me, all who consider themselves to be much more important than a marine midshipman. Since some of them have a vote in Congress, I guess I'd better appear to agree with them. Will you please come back tonight at eight o'clock?"

"Yes, sir."

"In the meantime, perhaps you should find yourself a room nearby. Do you need money?"

"No, sir. I'm quite rich, having gotten all my back pay before leaving the *Constellation*."

Jefferson laughed, for he knew how little a midshipman earned.

"There is one thing, sir. I'm quite eager to go home to see my family."

"Understandably. We'll speak of that tonight."

Little Hawk presented himself at the executive mansion ten minutes early and was shown into Jefferson's favorite room, where the president sat with his secretary of state. After greetings, Little Hawk sat stiffly. At first he refused the offer of tea, but upon gentle insistence from Jefferson said, "Yes, thank you, sir."

"I've asked Mr. Madison here because he, too, is interested in hearing about your adventure," Jefferson explained.

"As a matter of fact," Madison said, "on my desk I have a pile of reports that is just about twelve inches high. But I'd like to hear your firsthand account before reading anything. You just may save me from a lot of boredom."

"Where shall I begin?" Little Hawk asked.

"The last letters I had from you came from Egypt," Jefferson said. "You described the rather interesting collection of ruffians that General Eaton had gathered to be his staff officers."

Little Hawk took a sip of tea to wet his dry mouth and began. Now and then one of the statesmen would interrupt to ask a question. An hour later Little Hawk finished his account, ending with the taking of the harbor fort in Derna.

Jefferson remained silent for a long time. When he spoke his voice was soft. "You were quite close to General Eaton?"

"Yes, sir," Little Hawk said. "I think he used me as a sounding board for his ideas. I suppose he knew that whatever he said to me would remain a confidence between us."

"You believe that Eaton did the right thing?" Madison asked.

Little Hawk noticed that the secretary of state did not call Eaton "general."

"Yes, sir."

"And your opinion of what happened after Derna?" Jefferson wanted to know.

Little Hawk cleared his throat uncomfortably. "I don't think, sir, that it's my place to judge the actions of my superiors, especially civilian diplomats."

"No, it isn't," Jefferson agreed with a smile. "But just among friends here in the privacy of my study, I am curious to know what a man who fought at Derna thinks of the final outcome of the war."

Little Hawk's neck turned red, for he felt that he should keep his face straight and his big mouth shut. Still, he had been asked to speak, and he did so with great feeling.

"I believe, Mr. President, that the men who wrote and signed the treaty with the bashaw Yusef were dimwitted sons of bitches—" Flushing, he paused and said in a weak voice, "Pardon me, sir. I didn't mean to be vulgar."

"We'll forgive you," Madison said, holding back a

laugh, "but I would like your promise that you'll not apply for a position as a diplomat with my department."

Little Hawk grinned ruefully.

"Please proceed with your characterization of Colonel Lear and Commodore Rogers," Jefferson encouraged. "Why do you think that they are, uh, dim-witted, uh—"

"Sir, some of the crew of the *Philadelphia* came back with us on the *Constellation*. We all had a chance to speak with them, and believe me, they were more than willing to tell us how they were treated while they were slaves of the bashaw. They were beaten and starved. Six of them died. Two of the marines in my group died at Derna, and they died bravely."

"On that subject," Jefferson said, "I am going to ask for commendations for medals from your commanding officer, Mr. O'Bannon."

"The lieutenant deserves his own medal, sir. As do a great number of Europeans and North Africans who joined with us to overthrow a tyrant, sir," Little Hawk went on. "We gave the navy the means of beating Yusef when we marched across the desert and stormed Derna, for we provided a base there from which a fair government could have been built . . . even if Hamet Karamanli wasn't the man to run it. There were, in my opinion—" He flushed again, for he realized that he, a mere marine midshipman, was, in effect, reprimanding the government of his country.

"Go on," Jefferson urged.

"In my opinion, more than one course of action could have been followed. First, by applying the strength of the navy at Tripoli immediately after the fall of Derna, it would have been possible to rid the world forever of Yusef. Failing that, since we were ordered to evacuate Derna anyhow, why didn't we offer to trade Derna for the *Philadelphia* hostages instead of paying sixty thousand dollars for them? As it was, we made a free gift of Derna to the bashaw." He paused. "Sir, I'm really shooting off my mouth."

"Do you have more that you want to say?" Jefferson asked.

"Well, we marines wondered why we fought. We

asked ourselves why two of our number had to die just to rid the bashaw Yusef of his most dangerous rival and make him more secure on his throne."

James Madison frowned. "I don't quite follow what you're saying."

"I'm afraid it's true, James," Jefferson said before Little Hawk could answer. "We beat the bashaw militarily, but we didn't press our advantage. In effect, we gave him the victory by paying ransom. We signed a treaty with him that, by putting Hamet Karamanli under Yusef's protection, virtually guarantees his throne."

"May I say just one thing more?" Little Hawk asked.

"Please do," Jefferson said.

"General Eaton is a student of the Islamic world," Little Hawk said. "Through him I learned a lot. I picked up enough Arabic to be able to talk with the Arabs who marched with us. I think the best way to put it is that they're not like us. They have a different way of thinking. Allah ordains all. And in the promise of rewards to a soldier, the Moslem paradise is, I'm afraid, superior to our Christian heaven. A follower of Allah who dies fighting for his country, his honor, his religion, will be rewarded not by being given a harp and a cloud to sit on where he spends his time singing praises to God, but by sweet, running water in plenty, by the ripest figs and dates and the most savory meats, and by as many beautiful slave girls as he can handle."

"Well, Tom," Madison said, joking, "perhaps we should give some thought to converting to Islam."

Jefferson, looking grim, did not acknowledge Madison's attempt at humor.

"So, you see, sir," Little Hawk went on, "it doesn't matter to an Arab whether he wins or loses a battle. As long as he fights honorably and bravely and is true to Allah, he will be rewarded in the next life. Therefore, he is more willing than we are to give up this earthly life. He knows that Allah will see to it that he wins in the end, be it in this life or the next. By paying Yusef ransom and by leaving him on his throne, we proved to every follower of Allah that what they have been told all of their lives by their holy men is true. Yusef lost the battles but won the war. And sooner or later, sir, American men will have to go back to some desert in the Moslem world. We may not be fighting the same enemy; we may not even be fighting a Barbary nation. But we'll have to fight because we won a couple of battles but gave up the victory to the bashaw Yusef Karamanli, and the Moslem world has a long memory. They will believe with all their hearts that Allah will, once again, give them the final victory, even though we might be the stronger militarily."

Madison cleared his throat. Jefferson, much impressed and deep in thought, rubbed his chin. "Well, Mr. Harper," he said, "I'm sure I'm going to hear something similar from the general, and there are members of Congress who are already expressing a desire to hold hearings on the whole matter." He rose. "You mentioned that you wanted to visit your home."

"Yes, sir, I do."

"There's also the matter of what we're going to do with you."

"Sir, if possible I would like to stay in the marines."

"I don't see why not. If West Point is good enough to turn out officers for the army, I don't see why it couldn't turn out at least one marine."

"Thank you, sir!"

"I'll write your orders myself," Jefferson said. "That will save time. I don't want to have to explain to half a dozen navy commodores why I gave an army cadet a commission in a branch of their service. And for the same reason I want you out of town so that some congressional committee can't get hold of you as a witness. How much time do you want before you report for duty?"

"Well, sir, it's a long way to Tennessee and the Cherokee Nation."

"I'll give you an open-ended leave," Jefferson said. "You've earned it." He laughed. "If you happen to time your return to active duty to coincide with the conclusion of any congressional hearings regarding the Tripoli affair, I will not object to the length of your leave. Please give my secretary an address where we can send your pay."

"Would it be possible for it to be held, sir, until I come back to duty?"

"Of course. Tell my secretary to arrange it. Perhaps he could open a bank account in your name and deposit your pay to it each month."

"Thank you, sir," Little Hawk said.

"You're carrying a very interesting weapon, Midshipman," Madison remarked. "May I?" He put out his hand.

Little Hawk passed his scimitar to the secretary of state. "Did you find this more effective than a regulation saber?"

"Very much so, sir. It has a better balance. It's made of Damascus steel, which holds an edge better than the navy-issue saber."

"Hmmm," Madison mused. "What is it called?"

"A scimitar. More specifically, a Mameluke scimitar, as opposed to a Persian scimitar. Most of the men in North Africa adopted it, sir, instead of the saber."

"You might bring that to the attention of your superior officers when you report back to duty," Jefferson suggested. He scribbled out brief orders for Little Hawk. "When you come back from your visit please drop by to see me," he said as Madison handed back the weapon, then walked Little Hawk to the door.

Now the Great Bear in the Sky tipped his dipper and poured out the colors of autumn over the earth. Little Hawk rode through mountain passes painted in blazes of glory.

And from the northwest Renno, his wounds healing, traveled more slowly than he wished. He saw cottonwood trees aflame, oaks displaying the deepest of wine reds, and dogwoods with their particularly brilliant yellows.

Roy and the others had been home for well over a month. At Huntington Castle, Beth supervised the slaughter and dressing of a food animal newly introduced to the Cherokee Nation. Soon salted hams were being cured in a smokehouse that had been built near the kitchen by Roy Johnson and two of Se-quo-i's nephews.

In the adjoining Seneca-Cherokee villages thin strips of venison were drying on racks in the sun, and the Indian youngsters were gathering nuts in competition with the squirrels. The last of the corn crop was in storage. Both Seneca and Cherokee women were busy preparing the family wardrobes for winter, patching up older buckskins, and chewing hides to soften them for making new deerskin garments.

It was a good time. El-i-chi took Ta-na and Gao on a hunt and came back laden down with meat. Ena was spoiling her granddaughter, Summer Moon, shamelessly. To Ena's pleasure, motherhood seemed to have mellowed We-yo somewhat. The girl had not forgotten the Mingo, White Blanket, but she no longer closed her parents out of her life. Ho-ya had taken his place among the tribe's young warriors. His outspoken opposition to further white expansion into Indian lands was earning him the reputation of a leader among many younger Cherokee.

Toshabe, to Roy's surprise, had acted rather cold toward him when he first returned. He didn't understand her aloofness. True, she had had a long time to think about her promise to marry him. He, if anything, was more interested than ever in sharing his life with this woman he so admired. He had come as close to death as he ever wanted to come before his final time. On the ride back to the villages he had thought, *Well, if that ball had been an inch to the right I would never again have had the chance to feel the warmth of a woman in bed next to me*.

He decided to get to the bottom of her apparent change in attitude.

Since his return he had taken meals in Toshabe's longhouse, but always there'd been others present. Now they were alone. The clear, dry air held a hint of the winter to come. The fire had burned down to glowing embers, and the longhouse was lit dimly by the glow of an oil lamp. The light was flattering. Roy found himself remembering Toshabe as she had looked when her son had first married his daughter. She'd been a beautiful woman. Still was, he thought.

"Now dag-gum it, Toshabe," he protested. "You made me a promise, and I know that you're not the kind to go back on your word."

She spoke in Seneca, as if to illustrate the differences in their backgrounds. "And why would you want an old woman like me?"

"I thank the Good Lord every now and then that as a man grows older, his taste in women matures with him," Roy answered in the same language. He shifted to English. "Wouldn't I be a pretty sight out chasing some young girl?"

She laughed. "It is just that I thought you might have regretted your offer," she admitted.

"Nope," he said. He went to her and sat beside her. She did not object when he put his arm around her shoulders. "Now you listen to me, Toshabe. Those two sons of yours have already threatened to scalp me if I so much as lay a hand on you before we're married, and since I'm not quite sure whether or not they're joking, I think we're going to get hitched pretty soon, or I just might lose control and do something desperate, like this."

Kissing was a white man's thing. Toshabe accepted the kiss for a long moment, and then broke away, giggling like a girl.

"No laughing matter, woman," Roy grumbled.

"It's just that—"

"What?"

"Kissing is for the young," she said, but she made no further protest when he put his hand under her chin and turned her face so that her lips touched his. After a heated few minutes Roy sighed and pulled away.

"I reckon I'd better go," he said, his voice thick with need.

"If it is my sons you're worried about, leave them to me," she said, her eyes twinkling, her face looking very, very youthful in the dim light.

"How 'bout my conscience?" he whispered.

"We're both too old to worry about *that*," she said, pulling him to her.

Roy found that it was very good to have the warmth of a woman next to him in the coolness of an autumn night. When he sneaked out of the longhouse before first light to make his way across the commons to Renno's house, where he was staying, there was a light frost on the ground.

Gao, having just entered his teens, and Ta-na, only a year younger, were feeling quite grown-up. They could draw a man-sized bow, and each of the boys had bagged his deer with that traditional weapon, since El-i-chi still delayed giving them a rifle of their own. The shaman said that a hunter should be skilled enough to stalk his game, not just depend on the range of a long rifle.

On a day of bright sun and crisp, pure air, the two boys had hunted their way northwestward along the trail leading to the Tennessee border and Tellico Bloc House. At first they'd been serious about tracking deer, but now they were so far from home that there was a tacit agreement between them to ignore fresh sign. They had no desire to carry a deer for so great a distance. They were indulging a male behavioral quirk that was not limited to young Indian boys or even to the Indian in general—the urge to see what was around the next curve in the track.

But soon it would be time to turn back. It was past midday, and they'd eaten only a couple of the delicious Cherokee honey-and-nut balls that Ah-wa-o prepared so well.

"We will go to the top of that rise ahead," Ta-na said.

"Beat you there," Gao challenged, breaking immediately into a run.

Ta-na allowed his cousin the head start, for although Gao could match his speed for a short distance, Ta-na was the stronger runner. When lungs began to labor, the heart to pound, the pain to build in one's legs, then Gao faltered slightly.

After a couple of hundred yards Ta-na drew even with Gao and slacked the pace. The trail was fairly well traveled. It followed the wanderings of a deer track, as did many developed tracks and roads, through a forest of hardwoods. Leaves rustled under their feet and gave warning of their approach, but the boys were in home territory and felt safe. Years had passed since any war party, small or large, had invaded Cherokee lands so far to the east.

The trail wound directly into the tangled limbs of a forest giant that had been toppled by age or storm. A detour had been put into use to go around the fallen tree. Gao fell in behind Ta-na to take the narrowed route, so Ta-na was the first to run into the arms of the buckskin-clad warrior. One small yelp of alarm passed his lips. Gao was not able to stop, and he slammed into his cousin's back. Now both boys were wrapped in the warrior's arms and struggling to get free.

"Had I been a Creek out for scalps," Renno said, "these boys would have no hair."

"Father!" Ta-na cried. He went limp with relief.

"By the manitous," Gao said, gasping.

Two excited young lads escorted the sachem to his home. As they neared the village they ran ahead so that when Renno came up the hill from the swimming creek everyone had turned out to say, "I thank thee that thou art well" in the age-old, formal Seneca greeting. There were a clasp of arms and an embrace with El-i-chi, a pat and a hug for the little Rose, and a solemn and fond greeting for his mother, who stood near a grinning Roy Johnson.

" 'Bout time," Roy muttered as he exchanged the warrior's clasp and then pulled Renno into his arms.

"What's this?" Renno asked, rubbing a finger over Roy's clean-shaven cheek. "Are you trying to become civilized?"

Roy winked. "Been doin' a little courting, Son. My girl doesn't like my whiskers to scratch her face."

Toshabe hid her mouth behind her hand and laughed.

"Now don't give me any trouble, Renno," Roy warned. "Just go on and get your celebratin' clothes in shape, because we're gonna have the best wedding you've ever seen."

"Mother, Mother," Renno teased, "I leave you alone with this old boar bear and look what happens." But he moved close, embraced her, and whispered, "Be happy."

He looked up to see his flame-haired Beth hurrying down from the castle. Grinning, he went to meet her. He was home at last.

*   *   *

They gathered in the council house, senior warriors, matrons, guests from Rusog's Cherokee, to hear the sachem tell of his travels. They expressed polite appreciation when he told them how St. Louis was growing and how it was destined to become a gateway for the white man to enter the West. Their real interest, however, was in how the sachem killed the Frenchman, the pockmarked one, for had the white Indian not killed the evil one, they knew he would not have come home. Renno was a good storyteller. He drew out the suspense until Ta-na, unable to stand it any longer, cried out, "But how did you kill the Frenchman?"

"He didn't," El-i-chi joked. "What sits here among us is the manitou of Renno."

When Renno finished, all was quiet.

It was Ah-wa-o who asked, "But where is the witch?"

Renno spread his hands and shrugged his shoulders. "With the wind she vanished," he said. "Like a feather on the wind."

The marine appeared just before sunset the next day.

Renno and Beth were sitting on the front porch of the castle, listening to the sighing of a wind that promised to bring colder weather. Beth had been complaining mildly because Toshabe and Roy would not let her give them a big wedding in the castle. Suddenly the white Indian and his woman heard a growing cacophony of voices from the village. Renno peered down the long lane and saw a group of people flowing out of the village. Although he thought nothing of the gathering, he did notice that the pecan trees along the lane were growing well and would produce a crop within the next one or two years. He yawned lazily and said, "Well, Roy can be as hardheaded as any man I know."

"I think it would be fun to have a wedding dress of silk made for your mother," Beth said.

Renno gave it some thought. "No, no," he said, "I would say that my mother would best be served by white deerskin cut in the ancient mode of our ancestors."

"Me hear heap big chief," Beth said. "Heap big chief full of—" She paused and looked down the lane. "Renno?" she said, her voice rising.

He saw a tall, well-built man in the uniform of the United States, the red plume of his shako dancing in the wind, white pantaloons flashing with long, hurried strides. It seemed that half the village was following the uniformed one. But Renno had eyes only for the man in white and blue with red facings. He rose slowly, walked down the steps, and stood stiffly as his son came up the lane, crossed the yard, and came to attention about five paces away.

"Thank the manitous," Renno whispered.

"Little Hawk!" Beth cried excitedly as she rushed down the steps to embrace her stepson.

"Mother, you are more beautiful than ever," Little Hawk said.

"And *you* are beautiful," she said, stepping back to get a good look. "So tall and handsome!"

"I thank thee that thou art well," Renno said, extending his arms.

"I honor thee, my father," Little Hawk said, clasping Renno's forearms before the two embraced ferociously.

And so once again they all gathered in the council house and listened as still another white Indian told of travels in far-off places, of strange men, savage battles, and blades tempered in blood, of death, the sea, and the desert's heat, of endless sand, ceaseless wind, and heart-stopping beauty.

It was late. Black clouds had moved in from the west, bringing a slashing rain that drummed on the sides of Toshabe's longhouse and came down the smoke hole to sizzle in the fire. Only the family was there. Little Hawk had changed into buckskins. Little Summer Moon, one year old, had taken a liking to her cousin and was in his lap.

"I'm thankful that Mr. Jefferson has found himself another Indian ally," Beth said, referring to Little Hawk. "Maybe now I can keep my Indian at home."

"This president of the whitefaces," said Ho-ya, "he has sent explorers beyond the Mississippi. He has set up army posts on the western bank. Once, the whiteface promised not to covet Indian land west of the mountains. Then he said he would not come beyond the Ohio. Now he goes beyond the Father of Waters itself."

Little Hawk had heard from Beth a quick overview of We-yo's marriage to the Mingo and of the events that followed.

"Doesn't that bother you, Cousin?" Ho-ya asked. "You who wear the uniform of the United States?"

"I am Seneca, Cousin," Little Hawk reminded.

"I'm afraid, Nephew," Ena said, "that my son has become the tribe's militant."

"With due respect, Mother," Ho-ya said, "I think that more than one is needed."

"Will Tecumseh gather the tribes?" Little Hawk asked.

"Many will follow him," Renno said. "I pray that my nephew Ho-ya will not."

"I have not settled upon my intentions," Ho-ya spoke. "But I have given serious thought, Uncle, to traveling across the Mississippi, with others who feel as I do."

"To do what?" Renno inquired.

"To *live*. To hunt as our ancestors hunted. To be far from the nearest whiteface."

"And how do you plan to claim these hunting grounds as your own from the people who presently live there?" Renno asked. "Or will you take a page from the white man's book and seize them?"

"I have heard you say, many times, that we are all of one blood. I feel that, those who are on the land will accept a small number of people who flee the encroachment of the United States."

"Before you take action, Nephew," Renno said gently, "let us speak further of this matter." He watched as Ho-ya cast a quick glance at We-yo. She had not met his eyes. The sachem realized that plans were already in the making, although the twins were keeping them secret.

Ho-ya nodded. "I have heard you and my uncle El-i-chi describe the great and empty spaces to the west. Are you now telling me that there would be no land for us there?"

"We will talk," Renno with finality.

The wind howled. Beth shivered. "I think, my love, that I would be much more content in the warmth of our bed."

"This is my wife," Renno said expansively, spreading his hands and smiling. "She was educated in the British manner. She makes excellent suggestions."

Beth, laughing, hit him on the arm and made a face. He helped her don her cape.

"There's one subject you keep avoiding, Sachem," Roy said.

"I don't think I deliberately avoid any subject," Renno said, his eyebrows raised.

"It's just that the old bear has a one-track mind," El-i-chi said. "And a lusty one at that."

"I'm telling you two yahoos that I'm gettin' married," Roy said. "Now if you two want to have a part in it, you had better get your feast clothes on, because my girl and I are tired of waiting."

"Mother, are you tired of waiting?" Renno asked innocently.

"Three days from now," Toshabe said, "Roy Johnson is going to get married."

"Now you're talking," Roy said, then whooped. "What have you rascals got to say to that?"

"I suppose, being a dutiful son," Renno said with a bow, "I will say, yes, Mother."

The celebration began early. Women of the two villages had been preparing good things to eat for a week, and the feast was spread on blankets around the commons. A bunch of village urchins had been detailed to keep the dogs away from the food, so there were considerable yellings, barkings, and yippings when a dog getting too close to the heaping bowls and platters was kicked or chased away.

Everyone, including the young guards, began cheering when Roy, clean shaven, freshly bathed, and stuffed into his best Sunday-go-to-meeting suit, strode across the commons and asked the sachem for permission a woman of the tribe, one Toshabe.

Renno facetiously went through the formal, traditional speech of advice to the young Seneca warrior about to be married for the first time.

Roy, playing along, listened with a serious look on his face, then winked when Renno finished.

"I'm happy for you both, Roy," Renno said earnestly.

"I'm right happy myself, Son," Roy replied.

The eating continued throughout the day. With the sun low in the west, the traditional Seneca wedding ceremony was performed by the tribe's shaman and younger son of the bride. Ena led a few of the matrons in weeping silently, then smiling through happy tears to congratulate the newlyweds.

There was more eating and some dancing. Young maidens at the nubile age looked shyly upon the handsome, fair-haired son of the sachem.

Ena, playing at matchmaking, pointed out a particularly pretty Seneca girl of about fifteen years. "She is the daughter of a Pine Tree," Ena said, "an honorable family. As your aunt, I would be proud to see a girl like that welcomed to the family."

"You're rushing me a little bit, Aunt Ena," Little Hawk said.

"You're almost twenty-one years old," Ena protested. "It is time to rush you just a little."

Then *her* face popped unbidden into his mind. Naomi Burns . . . He shook his head. Years had passed since that first kiss. Surely she would be married.

"Let's take it one wedding at a time," he said good-naturedly.

Roy and Toshabe were walking hand in hand to disappear into Toshabe's longhouse. A hush fell over the crowd before someone began to sing. It was traditional, of course, to tease the newly wedded couple about their impending nocturnal activity.

When the food was gone, the guests began to drift away. Women went about their usual business of cleaning up from the festivities and putting children to bed. Beth took Ena, We-yo, and little Summer Moon to the castle with her, leaving behind Renno, Little Hawk, El-i-chi, the two younger boys, plus Rusog and Ho-ya.

The men and Gao and Ta-na went into Renno's longhouse, where the adults smoked and made low conversation. Two hours passed. Then it was time for carrying out another tradition: to disturb the concentration of the newlyweds.

El-i-chi rose and removed padding from around the clapper of a cowbell. Little Hawk and Ho-ya grinned at each other as they, too, got out noisemakers. They crept into the night and surrounded Toshabe's longhouse. El-i-chi started it with his cowbell, and then bedlam broke loose. Others came out of their longhouses and cabins and joined in, dancing, rattling noisemakers of all sorts, and singing songs of taunting happiness as they circled the longhouse.

It was Gao who became curious as to why his grandfather Roy had not come roaring outside to chase everyone away. He opened the door a bit and peeked inside to see a vacant room. He called to Ta-na, who came and confirmed that the couple who were being serenaded were not at home.

El-i-chi went into the longhouse, then came out yelling for everyone to be quiet. "They've taken clothing and kits," he said.

"He is robbing us of our right to annoy him on his wedding night," Renno protested. "Are we going to stand for that?"

"No! No! No!" they chanted.

"But we can't track them at night," Ta-na said.

"Then we will wait for the morning," El-i-chi said.

By first light enthusiasm for tracking the newlyweds had faded in all but the brothers, their male offspring, Rusog, and Cousin Ho-ya. The trail led eastward, toward Knoxville, where Roy still owned the house in which he had lived with his first wife, Nora.

"You're not really going to go all the way to Knoxville just to indulge in a barbaric custom," Beth said in protest.

"We have been cheated of our right by an old boar bear," Renno said, defending himself. "We cannot allow that to happen. And don't act so self-righteous. You English have the same custom—shivaree."

Beth grinned. "Well, wait until I pack a few things. And I'll get Ah-wa-o. If you're going to Knoxville, we might as well go along."

Renno rolled his eyes. "And do some shopping? Please tell me that I don't need to take along a wagon train."

"Would you please saddle my horse?" Beth asked, batting her long eyelashes and avoiding his question.

Andrew Jackson was, once more, retired from public life. He'd spent a few years on the bench of the state supreme court, but financial difficulties had convinced him that it was time to quit being a public servant and make some money. Now he was in Knoxville on a lovely day, doing a bit of profitable law work. He had rented a room in a small hotel on the edge of the business district.

He enjoyed an early supper and, feeling just a bit sorry for himself and a little lonely, decided to take a walk. He had a lot of things on his mind. For one thing, he'd been mulling over a proposition he'd received from Aaron Burr. It was a damned appealing idea to Jackson, who had served on the Tennessee convention for statehood and helped write her constitution, and who had served in the U.S. House of Representatives and been openly critical of the great deity George Washington. Yes, Jackson mused, damned appealing. He could see it in his mind, Burr and he at the head of an army moving into Spanish Mexico to build the foundations of a new state of the union.

He walked toward the open countryside. Knoxville was still a small place. The street looked familiar. He remembered riding down it to the house of Colonel Roy Johnson after being elected major general of the Tennessee Militia back in '02. Yep, there was Johnson's cabin, with a light burning in the window. Might be interesting to drop in and see if it was old Johnson himself at home.

Jackson lengthened his stride, only to halt in his tracks as all hell broke loose around the colonel's house. He reached for his pistol, then reminded himself that there hadn't been an Indian attack in Knoxville for decades. He heard men and boys shouting, cowbells ringing, rattles rattling, and uproarious laughter.

Curious, Jackson walked on and in the light of a good moon saw a gang of men and boys prancing around the house. The men were in Indian deerskins.

A woman approached him from the shadows near the house.

"Don't worry, sir," she said, "it's not a massacre."

"Beth Huntington?"

Beth drew closer. "Why, General!" she said. "How nice to see you!"

"Who got married?" Jackson asked, knowing now that the hullabaloo was nothing more than a shivaree. She told him. "Well, dog my cats," he said, grinning. He moved forward, nodded a greeting to Renno, linked arms with the sachem, and began to howl like a wolf.

When Roy gave up and threw open the door, the first face he saw was that of General Andrew Jackson. "Goddamn, Andy!" he bellowed. "I thought you had better sense!"

"Well, you never know," Jackson said, his face split in a grin. "You got any liquor in there, Roy?"

"Just might have," Roy said, "if you can quiet down those wild Indians so I can hear myself think."

The group piled inside. While Roy and Andy Jackson tilted a jug, Beth and Ah-wa-o hugged Toshabe. Little Hawk and Ho-ya sneaked into the bedroom and tied Roy's long underwear and the bed sheets in knots.

"I hear, Hawk," Jackson said, "that you're an officer in the marines."

"Yes, sir."

"Goin' back, are you?"

"Yes, sir. Sooner or later," Little Hawk said.

"Shipboard duty?"

"I will apply for that, sir. I share enough of my father's blood to want to see some more of the world."

"Well, I reckon you'll have your chance," Jackson said. "Funny to think about it, sitting here a thousand miles from the sea, but this is an ocean-linked country, my boy. We've got produce to sell and ships to carry it in. So my guess is we'll be a power at sea someday." He tilted the jug, took a long drag, said, "Ah."

"Just look at your mother," Beth whispered to Renno. "Have you ever seen anyone look so *smug*?"

"But you take care of yourself, Hawk," Andy Jackson was saying. "This war 'tween France and England—sooner or later we're gonna be dragged into it."

"I pray not," Beth said fervently.

"They're losing a lot of ships," Jackson said. "Both sides. And men. First thing you know, England will realize that some of the sailors who have deserted the Royal Navy are sailing in American ships. They've stopped our vessels at sea and taken men off before. They'll do it again."

There was a heavy silence.

"But this is a happy occasion," Jackson said, quickly perceiving his faux pas. "I want to drink to the connubial happiness of my old friend, Colonel Roy Johnson. And to his lovely lady."

Toshabe smiled a very smug smile.

Author's Note

~~~~~~

The history of the early nineteenth century moves at a pace set by full-rigged sailing ships slicing through the vastness of the oceans and by the gait of a horse, a team of draft animals, or a man's own legs challenging the intimidating distances of the North American continent. Often the demands of fiction compress time and, for the purposes of good story-telling, make contemporaneous events that were in fact separated by months or even years in those more unhurried days of the past.

In the continuing saga of Renno and his family we strive to be true to the times. We do not, for example—as in some books that I remember reading in recent years—speak inaccurately of the "rockbound shores of the Cape Fear," or place Independence, Missouri, in the locale of St. Louis, or have Daniel Boone meeting Buffalo Bill Cody. The effort to be historically accurate while performing what I feel to be the writer's first duty—to tell an entertaining story—leads to some interesting discussions among those of us who are involved in producing the *White Indian* books. Perhaps we indulge in a bit of nitpicking now and then, as when we exchanged multiple telephone calls and letters in deciding whether (in *White Indian* Volume Twenty-one) to use the eighteenth-century name, St. Domingue, for a French colony in the Caribbean or the modern, more familiar name, Haiti. Both the author and the editors at Book Creations share a common goal, however, and that is to show Renno as a man of his time interacting with the great and near great of the era.

Some historical characters seem to hover in the background through book after book. The enigmatic Aaron Burr touched the life of a man who has made cameo appearances in at least three volumes and who will become a major presence in the future—Andrew Jackson. And we will hear more from Burr.

General James Wilkinson, whom we first met prior to the battle of Fallen Timbers, survived decades of official knowledge that he was in the pay of Spain. In fairness to the general—if such a rogue deserves consideration—his role in this book is almost totally fictitious, although, as stated, he was on the commission that accepted the transfer of Louisiana to the United States, and Thomas Jefferson did let Wilkinson's appointment as governor of the Louisiana Territory slip past him. Wilkinson, too, was involved with Aaron Burr. In our series he will be seen serving under his fourth president, James Madison, before, at last, being forced out of positions of power.

William H. Eaton, Eaton of Arabia, who called himself a general, enjoyed the status of hero only briefly after his return to the United States from Tripoli. He was acclaimed by the Congress, by the press, and by the public. The man who crafted the shameful treaty with the Bashaw Yusef Karamanli, Colonel Tobias Lear, was summarily dismissed from public service by Jefferson; but Eaton's triumph ended there. His penchant for drink, a choice of bad companions, and his appetite for the ladies alienated the press. With Andrew Jackson, Eaton testified at Aaron Burr's trial for treason. He wrote the story of his life, a work used as a reference for this book, while living in obscurity. On his deathbed he said to his wife, "I regret I didn't arrange to die much sooner." He passed away in his sleep on June 1, 1811.

The war against the pirates of Tripoli was primarily a naval war, and it was a small war when compared to the epic conflict that was in progress between France and England and to the War of the Revolution. The impending War of 1812 was beginning to cast an ominous shadow over the United States even while Eaton was being given his brief moment of glory in 1805-6. In most history books General Eaton's march to Derna is, at most, a footnote. In fact, the Tripolitanian War itself rates no more than a paragraph in most books.

Lieutenant Presley N. O'Bannon fades into the mists of history after Derna, although he and the seven or eight marines who stormed the southeast face of the walls of Derna are commemorated in "The Marines' Hymn," in the line that reads: "From the halls of Montezuma to the shores of Tripoli." (Some sources say that there was a marine midshipman with O'Bannon, a sergeant, and six marines.)

And, in 1826 Lieutenant O'Bannon's Mameluke scimitar—the weapon attributed to Little Hawk in this book—became the pattern for the sword that is still worn on dress occasions by Marine Corps officers.

Some of the naval officers involved in the Barbary action went on to greater glory in the Naval War of 1812, Lieutenant Stephen Decatur among them.

The hapless Hamet Karamanli, older brother of Yusef, fled Tripoli under threat from Yusef and went into permanent exile in Egypt.

Now, in 1805, the white Indian and his family stand on the verge of being involved in a sweep of intense historical actions leading up to the second war with England, and the era of Andy Jackson.

I want to thank my editors at Book Creations: Laurie Rosin, senior project editor; Marjie Weber, copyeditor; and Judy Stockmayer and Elizabeth Tinsley, who shared proofreading responsibilities.

And I want to thank you, the readers, for staying with us.

DONALD CLAYTON PORTER

THE WHITE INDIAN—BOOK XXIII
SENECA SOLDIER
by Donald Clayton Porter

Little Hawk, on leave from the Marine Corps, visits the sweet, innocent Naomi Burns, who gave him his first kiss. But she has become the dull-eyed slave to the repulsive Morgan brothers, who killed her father and stole his farm. Little Hawk is their next intended victim, but he overwhelms his attackers, saves Naomi, and brings her to his village. Disgusted by what she has become, the young Seneca returns to active duty. President Jefferson sends him by ship to the Pacific Northwest, to join the Lewis and Clark expedition.

Renno and Roy Johnson travel to Indiana Territory, where Aaron Burr is gathering an army to wrest land from Spain and declare it an independent nation. Renno must sabotage Burr's plan and face Melisande, witch of the Pyrenees, in the final, ultimate battle against evil.

During the men's absence, the Morgan brothers trace Naomi to Huntington Castle. Alone, Naomi and Beth must fight off the criminally insane murder-rapists.

Little Hawk's shipmates attack the Columbia River tribes but are murdered. His life is saved by a young Indian girl. With her help, the Seneca must locate Lewis and Clark in the vast wilderness and return east with them or be forced to build a new life, thousands of miles from his home village, never to see his loved ones again.

(*Read* SENECA SOLDIER, *on sale late in 1992 wherever Bantam books are sold.*)

A Proud People in a Harsh Land

THE SPANISH BIT SAGA

Set on the Great Plains of America in the early 16th century, Don Coldsmith's acclaimed series recreates a time, a place and a people that have been nearly lost to history. With the advent of the Spaniards, the horse culture came to the people of the Plains. Here is history in the making through the eyes of the proud Native Americans who lived it.

☐ 26397-8	**TRAIL OF THE SPANISH BIT**	$3.50
☐ 26412-5	**THE ELK-DOG HERITAGE**	$3.50
☐ 26806-6	**FOLLOW THE WIND**	$3.50
☐ 26938-0	**BUFFALO MEDICINE**	$3.50
☐ 27067-2	**MAN OF THE SHADOWS**	$3.50
☐ 27209-8	**DAUGHTER OF THE EAGLE**	$3.50
☐ 27344-2	**MOON OF THUNDER**	$3.50
☐ 27460-0	**SACRED HILLS**	$3.50
☐ 27604-2	**PALE STAR**	$3.50
☐ 27708-1	**RIVER OF SWANS**	$3.50
☐ 28163-1	**RETURN TO THE RIVER**	$3.50
☐ 28318-9	**THE MEDICINE KNIFE**	$3.50
☐ 28538-6	**THE FLOWER IN THE MOUNTAINS**	$3.50
☐ 28760-5	**TRAIL FROM TAOS**	$3.50
☐ 29123-8	**SONG OF THE ROCK**	$3.50
☐ 29419-9	**FORT DE CHASTAIGNE**	$3.99
☐ 28334-0	**THE CHANGING WIND**	$3.95
☐ 28868-7	**THE TRAVELER**	$4.50

■■■■■■■■■■■■■■■■■■■■■■■■■■■■■■

Available at your local bookstore or use this page to order.